PRAISE FOR THE
NOVELS OF THE HALF-LIGHT CITY

Iron Kin

"Strong and complex world building, emotionally layered relationships, and enough action to keep me up long past my bedtime. I want to know what's going to happen next for the DuCaines and their chosen partners, and I want to know *now*." —Vampire Book Club

"*Iron Kin* was jam-packed with action, juicy politics, and a lot of loose ends left over for the next book to resolve that it's still a good read for series fans." —All Things Urban Fantasy

"Scott's writing is rather superb." —Bookworm Blues

Blood Kin

"Not only was this book just as entertaining and immensely readable as *Shadow Kin*—it sang in harmony with it and spun its own story all the while continuing the grander symphony that is slowly, becoming the Half-Light City story. . . . Smart, funny, dangerous, addictive, and seductive in its languorous sexuality, I can think of no better book to recommend to anyone to read this summer. I loved every single page except the last one, and that's only because it meant the story was done. For now, at least." —seattlepi.com

continued . . .

Also by M. J. Scott

Shadow Kin
Blood Kin
Iron Kin

FIRE
KIN

A NOVEL OF THE HALF-LIGHT CITY

M. J. SCOTT

A ROC BOOK

ROC
Published by the Penguin Group
Penguin Group (USA) LLC, 375 Hudson Street,
New York, New York 10014

USA | Canada | UK | Ireland | Australia | New Zealand | India | South Africa | China
penguin.com
A Penguin Random House Company

First published by Roc, an imprint of New American Library,
a division of Penguin Group (USA) LLC

First Printing, May 2014

ISBN 978-0-451-46538-2

Printed in the United States of America
10 9 8 7 6 5 4 3 2 1

For my big brother, Richard.

I tagged along after him in this reading business and he led me into fantasyland.

I never came out.

ACKNOWLEDGMENTS

I started out this series thinking it was a trilogy, but it grew a little. Luckily for me, my wonderful editor didn't mind. So thank you, Jessica Wade, for liking what I do and for letting me share my stories. I look forward to our continuing adventures. Thank you, too, to the awesomely talented art department at Roc, who make my books look gorgeous every time, and to everybody else there who helps get them out into the world.

I also need to thank Miriam Kriss, my awesome agent. Without her, there may have been no Half-Light at all.

I'd also like to thank all the readers who e-mail me, tweet me, Facebook me, and let me know they love these stories, because that means more to me than anything. I hope this one works too!

Lastly, at the end of what has been another year that had some roller-coaster moments, much love to all my friends and family who got me through again. Smooches.

Fire dances
It lights the night
Warms the heart
Sparks from nowhere
To blaze a path
To clear the brush
To burn it all
Raze what stands
And leave that which remains
Ashes or something forged anew
Will you burn?

Chapter One

ASH

Fire is deceptive. From a distance, it hides its heat and fury and shows its dancing light instead. From my vantage point on the city walls, the fire looked almost beautiful, a thousand shades of twining red and orange, its smoke causing strange shadows that snaked through the moonlight.

The blaze was back under control now. It had given up the fight, calming to my will.

I despise using fire as a tool of war and hadn't planned to today. The idiot sergeant who'd set the first firepot would be dealt with now that I had the situation in hand. After all, my client wouldn't appreciate having the city he'd paid us to help him recapture burned to ashes.

Even if ashes were what he deserved.

The wind whipped smoke toward me, the gusts stinging my eyes and burning my throat with each breath. Ashes were about what I deserved too.

"Captain Pellar."

The familiar rough voice stopped my reverie. Just as well.

"Yes?" I swung around, stepped down from the half-shattered battlement. Owens, my body man, didn't like heights. He turned visibly green every time I climbed up anywhere more than six feet above the ground, and I was too tired to take any enjoyment in teasing him.

His face, devoid of the ash and grime that coated mine, looked relieved as my feet hit the stones that lined the parapet. "Captain, there's a message for you."

"Can't it wait?"

"No, sir, he says not."

"He?" Messages from the lordlings who ran this army usually came on paper. What in the hells had happened that warranted them sending someone in person? I glanced back over the walls, toward the outer perimeter of our camp where the command tents were. Behind me, the dying fire still played softly in the back of my mind, almost like the purr of a cat. But I wouldn't be rubbing its belly anytime soon. I sent another short burst of power at the hottest spots, sinking the heat back deep into the earth.

"Yes, sir." Owens looked vaguely worried. Which translated to a slight drawing together of his eyebrows. Master of the impassive face, Owens. "The Templar."

I paused outside the command tent to splash my face with the water Owens proffered and scrub away some of the salty ash sweat caking my face with a towel. The sentry stepped aside so I could make my way inside. Sure enough, there was a Templar knight standing at parade rest in front of the rough table I used as a desk on campaign. He swung around as I entered, revealing a pair of very green eyes in a dark face. His Templar tunic was travel worn, dusty and dirty, and, I noted with surprise, tailored to accommodate the fact that the knight's left arm ended at the elbow.

A crippled Templar?

"You're a long way from home," I said. I moved around him carefully. One-armed or not, a Templar was no one to be trifled with, and I had no idea if he was friend or foe. He would've had to surrender his weapons before he was allowed in the tent, but I could feel the magic rising from him. A sunmage, this one. A strong one.

"You are Asharic sa'Uriel'pellar?"

The hairs on the back of my neck prickled. That was a name that very few people called me anymore. "That's Captain Pellar to you."

"Yes, sir." The knight's voice was deep, deeper than his young face would have led me to expect. His tone was respectful but resolute. "But you are—"

I cut him off. "Yes." I wondered if he would ask me to prove it. My Family ring was attached to the chain around my neck, hidden from view by clothing and glamour. I hadn't worn it for a very long time. Likely longer than the Templar had been alive.

"In that case, sir, I have something for you." He reached into the leather pouch slung over his shoulder and withdrew a large envelope. It was wrinkled and crumpled, much like him, further evidence that he had traveled hard and fast. But the red wax seal, stamped with the Templar cross, was intact. In the light of the lamps hanging around the room, the wax shone like fresh blood.

He held out the envelope. I took it reluctantly, senses still prickling. I hadn't heard of any Templar campaigns here in the Voodoo Territories for quite some time. But then, I didn't really track their movements very carefully. I had no quarrel with them. Still, I had to wonder . . . which Brother House did this young knight belong to? And whose message was he bearing?

I squashed the thought.

"And your name?" I asked, turning the envelope in my hands, reluctant to open it. To open it would extinguish the small spark of . . . no, not hope; I'd given up on that particular emotion many years ago . . . possibility perhaps?

"Liam, sir. Liam Hollister."

"Brother Liam, then. My man will show you to a tent to rest."

"Thank you, sir. But the matter is urgent."

"If I'm any judge, you've been on the road for weeks."

"Yes, sir, several." His voice stayed calm. "But I cannot waste any time."

"You're no good to whoever sent you if you fall off your horse and break your neck on the return journey."

"I'll be fine. And I can be on my way somewhat faster if you'd read the message."

That was bordering on rude. Templars were usually respectful of authority, and this one was young. He should be following protocol. The fact that he wasn't made me wonder if he was cocky or desperate.

I pulled my dagger from the sheath at my hip and slit the heavy envelope. The note it contained slid free of its confines with a sound like the memory of a sword slicing through air.

But the words written on the paper cut deeper, making my gut tighten and the taste of ash fill my mouth again. "Is this a serious offer?"

"Yes, sir."

I shook my head. "Impossible. I'm exiled."

The knight's eyes dropped, his mouth suddenly flat. When he lifted them again, his green eyes were full of something I thought might be sympathy. "I regret to inform you, sir, that the Veil has fallen."

I groped for the chair behind me, sat down hard. "Fallen?"

"Yes."

"And who has claimed the Veiled Court?"

"The Veil stands empty, sir."

My mind swam. The Veiled Queen dead? The court without a ruler?

Fuck. I could go home.

To Half-Light. To . . . others.

Home.

If I agreed to fight a war.

We came to the City from the north. I'd forgotten how it looked, spread out across a plain in a sprawl like a tumble of children's blocks. I'd done my best to erase its image from my mind, yet the familiarity made my bones ache.

Bigger now than when I'd left. Wilder if what Brother Liam had told me was true. I still couldn't believe it. The Fae Queen dead. The treaty dissolved. A Blood lord—some upstart named Ignatius Grey and not even Lord Lucius, who was also dead—intent on overthrowing centuries of peace and taking control.

It was like the worst of dreams. The kind where you wake and can't shake the feeling that it was true and reality is the dream. I knew that feeling all too well. I'd been living it for the past thirty years. Every second of my exile.

I kept my gaze on the City, on the gleaming domes of St. Giles Hospital and the thrust of the cathedral spires and the blocky Templar Brother House . . . square and gray and solid like the men who occupied it. The men who'd brought me home.

I looked to where Brother Liam sat beside me on his long-legged bay horse, looking even more rumpled than he had looked more than three weeks ago when he came to fetch me. He'd driven us hard to get us here this fast, pushing as much as we could without injuring horses and men. We'd need those. All of us could use a few good nights' sleep in beds other than camp cots and hard earth and meals that involved more than stew and bread and cheese and whatever green things we had been able to buy or forage along the way.

Still, I was used to fast travel and my men were too.

The Templars had summoned me here. Me and the nearly two thousand soldiers I brought with me. The soldiers I'd fought with for thirty years and commanded for half that. I hoped we would be enough. My men and women were good and there were other exiled Fae like me amongst them as well as *hai-salai*, but we'd never fought an army of Blood hell-bent on domination.

Still, it was an invitation to come home.

An invitation I couldn't refuse.

I'd cursed the City and what lay to its west many times during my exile, but still it held a sway over me. A pull I couldn't resist.

I let my gaze move—finally—to the lands west of the City. To Summerdale. Fae territory. If I squinted hard, I could make out the glints of sunlight reflecting off the white marble tower that marked the Gate to the Veiled World.

My home once.

I wasn't sure if it could be again. I wasn't the same scared and bitter lordling I'd been when I'd left, and I'd left Fae politics and intrigue and protocol far behind me. I'd dealt with little but politics and intrigue and conflict since, but it was different when it didn't involve my heart.

I fought for those who could pay me best, with the rare exception for those whose cause was obviously the right one. I did my job and got results and then moved onto the next conflict.

There was always another one. Growing up in the Veiled Court had taught me that much . . . always another scheme, another shot at power.

The Veiled Queen had ruled the court with an unyielding hand on the reins of control, but she had also allowed the rest of the nobles their games of influence. Until someone fell afoul of her boundaries. Then the punishment was swift and, often, irreversible.

I was proof of that.

But now the queen was dead and my exile, under the laws of our kind, dead with her. I'd never expected it. But here it was.

The only way was forward. No matter what my reception and no matter the mix of anticipation and dread turning my guts to a tangle.

I nodded at Liam. "Shall we?" I said, and nudged my horse forward.

BRYONY

It was nearing dusk when I made my way from St. Giles Hospital to the Templar Brother House. The air was still warm, though it was starting to hint at the crisp night to come. Summer was dying, and with the autumn came both cold and dark. Shorter days were exactly what we didn't need when it came to dealing with the Blood. Their powers rose with the dark. Under moonlight no one could match them for strength and stealth and violence. But we would try.

I swung my arms wide as I walked, trying to stretch the kink from between my shoulder blades. It had been a long day and I had been looking forward to a long bath and a good night's sleep—as much as I could sleep well these days—until the invitation from the Templar's Abbott General had arrived. When Father Cho requested my attendance, I couldn't refuse. Not when, presumably, his request was related to the fact that an army had ridden down from the hills to the north of the City earlier today and camped on the northern side of the outermost human boroughs. Safely beyond the city walls but undeniably here to stay.

I was, I had to admit, curious. Simon DuCaine, sunmage, Master Healer at my hospital and brother to Guy DuCaine, one of the Templar's most feared knights, had told me that the Templars had sent for reinforcements, but I knew no more than that. Tonight it seemed I was going to find out who exactly had been summoned to our aid.

The prospect made my muscles knot more tightly. I was grateful, of course, for anything that would swell the humans' forces, but an army meant more violence. More injuries. More for the healers at my hospital and the others in the City to deal with.

We'd been preparing ourselves for weeks. Ever since the Fae had withdrawn in the wake of the Veiled Queen's assassination, leaving the humans to face the threat of the Blood and the Beast Kind. Or rather the threat of Ignatius Grey—would-be Lord of the Blood—freed from the bounds of the treaty he'd broken. He hadn't yet attacked—perhaps he too was marshaling his forces and making plans—but it could only be a matter of time until he did. Without the powers of the Fae to back up the human mages and the Templars, the humans would need the advantage of numbers.

I glanced northward. I couldn't begrudge the Templars their desire for reinforcements, but the reason for the soldiers' presence and the chaos that was about to ensue made my stomach churn with resentment and fear.

I muttered a curse on Ignatius Grey's head as I reached the gate to the Brother House and greeted the knights on guard.

"Lady Bryony," one of them said courteously as he admitted me.

He didn't offer me a blessing as he might have a human. The Templar worship a different god from those powers significant to my kind. Once upon a time, as I understood the history, the order had been a lot more hardheaded when it came to religious tolerance. But that was before the Blood had made their first attempt to take over the City.

Before the treaty and the alliance between the Fae and the humans in particular. Four centuries of that had made the Templars no less steadfast in their belief that their God was the true one, but they were no longer interested in removing the heads of those who refused to believe as they did.

The smell of men, leather, and steel hit me as I walked through the main gates. My years in the City had strengthened my tolerance to the presence of iron, but it was still uncomfortable to move amongst so many men wearing mail and carrying weapons containing the wretched metal.

I would need more than just a bath to restore myself after this. Would need to spend the time to refresh my connection to the earth and rebalance my powers.

Ah well. I was used to that.

The knights all saluted as I passed, a fact that made me want to smile. In the Fae Court the only one who was ever saluted was the queen. Or the king. Not that we had one or the other right now.

No, our queen had been murdered by parties unknown—or unproven rather, given the near certainty that Ignatius had been behind the assassination—at the treaty negotiations, bringing us to our current point of mayhem.

The Fae Court was still in turmoil, not that I had returned to the Veiled World to find out for myself firsthand what was happening. Our queen had ruled us for a thousand years, and the transfer of power wasn't simple. The strongest Fae would rule eventually, but until the backlash of magic gone wild in the Veiled World was tamed, no one knew who that person might be. There were those who already stood strong amongst the court, but the power had its own whims and fancies and it had, in our histories, chosen its bearers with no regard to their standing in the court or the rank of their Family.

My plan was to stay out of it as far as possible. I had enough trouble to deal with here in the City.

Brother Liam—I smiled to see he had returned safely— found me just outside Father Cho's office.

"Liam," I said. "It's good to see you."

He smiled back at me, eyes startlingly green in his dark face. "And you, Lady Bryony."

I studied him a moment. He looked tired but, underneath the fatigue, somehow changed by his travels. He'd been bowed down with grief at the death of a girl he couldn't protect when he was sent on his mission. Apparently that hurt had receded a little. Also, he met my gaze without a blush. Which was another welcome improvement. He was growing up, this young knight.

"How is your arm after your journey?" I let my gaze fall to the shortened left sleeve of his tunic, which bared the stump of his arm. Simon and I had been unable to save his forearm—torn to shreds by the teeth of a Beast, and it was a failing that pained me.

"It's fine, my lady," he said firmly, shifting his stance so his right side was nearer to me.

I accepted his explanation, for now. He had never admitted to pain, not even in the earliest days after his amputation. I made a note to send one of the healers to check him later.

"They sent me to escort you," Liam continued.

"Are we to meet in Father Cho's office?" I asked, respecting his change of subject.

"In the conference room. I'll take you there."

He led the way, though I knew the route all too well. There had been too many conferences with the Templars and the human council these last few months. I probably could have found my way to the conference room in my sleep.

A babble of noise as we approached the room told me that I wasn't the only one who'd been summoned.

But as I stepped through the door and saw the man who stood beside Guy DuCaine, tall and sleekly muscled with night-dark hair and dark gray eyes set in a face I had tried my best to forget, I only wanted to turn around and run.

Chapter Two

BRYONY

But running wasn't an option. Particularly not with a very solid Templar knight standing behind me and blocking any possible retreat.

I turned to Liam. "What is he doing here?"

He looked puzzled. "Who? Captain Pellar?"

Captain Pellar. Not the name I knew him by. But then again, the man I had known had left a long time ago. "Yes."

"Father Cho sent for him. The reinforcements are his army. They're good. At least, they'd better be, the amount of gold we're paying." He muttered the last part almost under his breath.

Shal e'tan mei. Mercenaries. I had tried very hard not to think about what Asharic sa'Uriel'pellar might be doing to occupy himself during the long years of his exile, and I had mostly succeeded. But in the moments when I failed, I hadn't imagined that he would have taken up fighting for gold.

What had Father Cho been thinking? Weren't there other Templar Brother Houses he could have appealed to? Or, for that matter, mercenaries not led by Asharic? I turned back to watch the group of men. They hadn't looked in my direction yet, intent on whatever they were discussing. Which gave me a few more seconds before I had to face him. And, despite my better instincts, I couldn't look away. I just stood and watched. Studied the man I didn't want to study, unable to stop myself cataloguing the changes in his appearance.

His skin had always been olive, but now it was a deeper, richer color, speaking of time in harsher, hotter climes. His dark hair was shorter than the last time I'd seen it, though it wasn't cropped human short. It fell around his face unevenly, hiding half of it from view. Just as well.

Ash.

Guy nodded at something Ash said, looking satisfied. I suddenly knew whose bright idea this had been. Not Father Cho's. Guy's. Veil protect me from DuCaines. They came up with harebrained and ridiculous schemes at the drop of a hat. Though, to give them their due, they usually managed to pull them off with aplomb. After all, Guy's brother, Simon, had managed to kill Lord Lucius, and Guy himself had braved the Veiled Courts and won a duel against a rogue Fae lord to help the woman he'd fallen for. And then there was their sister, Saskia, a metalmage who'd bonded with a *haisalai* seer who was one of the wild-card powers of the City.

DuCaines.

And now they'd done the worst thing of all. Brought back Asharic sa'Uriel'pellar.

"My lady, is something wrong?" Liam asked.

"That's—" I cut myself off abruptly. Liam was young . . . he probably hadn't been born when Ash had entered his exile and left the City. Come to think of it, thirty years ago Guy himself would've been barely five and Simon just a baby. Maybe none of them—other than Father Cho perhaps— knew his—*our*—history.

If I had my way they never would.

Ash. Veil take the man.

Take him far, far away.

It was a futile hope. If he was here, if he'd accepted a commission from the Templars, then he wouldn't turn away.

He was unstoppable once he'd decided on a course. Stupid, pigheaded, stubborn—

The chain at my neck sparked with an irritated burst of power and then, from across the room, I felt an answering pulse of magic—bright and fierce as the flames he summoned with such ease. Ash pivoted like a weather vane spun by an ill wind, and his eyes found mine.

I stayed where I was with an effort of will. Met that startled storm-cloud gaze with what I hoped was perfect calm, calling on my power to wrap myself away from any insight his power might grant him into my state of mind.

Let him look. I would show him nothing.

His expression cycled through startled to shocked to a smile of pure delight that made my desire to run stronger than ever.

A dangerous weapon, that smile. More dangerous than his magic and wit combined. Women crumpled at that smile. Men too, come to think of it.

I thought I'd forgotten it—banished it from memory over the long years he'd been gone—but now I realized I still knew it like my own face. There was a faint scar now, above his upper lip—which was careless of him—but it didn't dim the smile's impact.

"Bryony," he breathed, my name clear on his lips, though I couldn't hear his voice. Beside him, Guy swung around, eyebrows lifting.

"You two know each other, my lady?" Liam asked at my side.

"We did once," I said. "A long time ago."

"Before he was exiled?"

So he knew that much. "Yes." Thirty years ago. A lifetime for Liam. But just a fraction of mine.

Ash said something to Guy. Guy shook his head.

"Did you know him well?" Liam asked.

"He's High Family. We knew each other," I said, which was the most noncommittal answer I could come up with.

"Do you know why he was exiled?" Liam sounded uncharacteristically curious. Usually he was painfully polite and restrained. Maybe some of Ash had rubbed off on him in the weeks they'd spent traveling together. Though obviously Ash had not seen fit to share his history with him.

"That is not my tale to tell," I replied. I made myself look away from Asharic and focused on Liam, who made an apologetic face.

"Of course, my lady. I shouldn't pry."

"Don't apologize," I said. "Just don't ask me about Asharic Pellar. If you want to know about him, ask the man himself. Though I would advise you not to take everything he says as gospel." We Fae might not lie directly, but we can spin a tale if we choose to do so, and Ash was a master weaver.

Across the room, I heard Asharic's laugh and wondered if he'd heard me. The man always did have ears like an owl.

I ignored him and made myself walk into the room as though there was nothing remotely of interest about his presence.

"I see," Liam said. He opened his mouth to say more, but at that moment, Father Cho lifted his hand and the assembled Templars fell into obedient silence. It took a few seconds for the others gathered in the room to follow suit.

"Please be seated," Father Cho said. We took our seats around the huge wooden table. I took care to sit on the same side as Ash and as far away from him as possible. Liam took the chair opposite me.

"Some of you may know that we have, these past weeks, been holding our ground, waiting for additional forces," Father Cho said. "Tonight, I am happy to announce that that wait is over. I would like to introduce you to Captain Asharic Pellar, who some of you may know by reputation. Captain Pellar and his forces will be assisting us."

A ripple of low-voiced comments ran through the room, anticipation buzzing under the words. The Templars had been, as Father Cho had said, holding their ground. But against the Blood and the Beast Kind, there were not enough of them to win a victory if it came to outright conflict. Now that the problem of strength had been solved, it was time to decide what exactly happened next.

But as Ash stood to speak and I made sure to keep my

eyes on Father Cho—I wasn't ready to study Ash too closely just yet—there was a commotion outside the door.

A female voice, demanding entry. Mail clinked as the two Templars guarding the room protested. I knew who the woman was. . . . The feel of her—or rather the strange space in the earth song her presence made—was as unique as the feel of Asharic's magic. I wondered how he would take her presence. He'd been traditional once . . . nearly a proper young Fae lord.

There was another rumble of voices and then the cool female voice came again. "I can always just walk through, you know."

I hid a smile. Lily wasn't my favorite person in the world—I was still Fae enough to be uncomfortable around a wraith—but I respected her determination.

Hopefully the Templars were sensible enough not to try to bar her from the room or she might just carry out her threat, turn incorporeal as only a wraith can and walk through solid wood and metal. I hoped she would, if only to see Ash's face when she did so. But no, the dead spot she left in my senses stayed right where it was. That dead spot was, of course, the reason that my kind didn't like hers, even if wraiths were technically *hai-salai*, half-breeds. Born of Fae women. Our lore said they were soulless, based on the fact that we couldn't sense their connection to the earth as we could every other living thing. Even the Blood showed themselves to our senses, though they felt faded and tenuous and could almost disappear completely if they were using their powers of deception and camouflage.

But the guards outside apparently didn't want to risk the wrath of a wraith. The door creaked open and Lily stepped through, a scowl drawing her red eyebrows down over pale gray eyes. She scanned the room, hands resting on the daggers she wore at each hip. When she spotted Simon sitting near Guy, her face relaxed a little. Only a little. She still directed a glare at Guy as she walked around the table.

"I take it my invitation was lost?" she said as she joined Simon. He smiled at her—his eyes a brighter blue than

Guy's icy ones—looking suddenly relaxed. Summer and Winter, some of the Fae called the DuCaine brothers. Simon's hair was a more golden blond than his brother's and his eyes were warmer, yes, but he was just as fierce as Guy when he needed to be. Like now, when he was being glared at by a wraith, which was enough to make most men—human or not—quail.

I couldn't blame Lily for feeling irritated. She had earned the right to sit in our councils. Earned it with blood and heartache.

"I take it mine was too," another female voice came from the open door, and all of us not facing it turned again.

Adeline Louis, leader of those of the Blood who had broken from Ignatius and sought Haven amongst the humans, stood framed in the doorway, her pale skin gleaming against the black satin dress that clung to her body like a glove. She had taken to dressing somewhat provocatively since she came to the Brother House—Veil knew where she was getting the dresses—as though she wanted to make the knights—and everyone else—uncomfortable. Maybe she did. The Blood play at intrigue almost as relentlessly as the Veiled Court do.

"Lady Adeline." Father Cho rose courteously. "I did not think you would be abroad so early."

That was somewhat disingenuous of him. The older Blood do not have to sleep the sunlight hours away, and Adeline, while not as old as Lucius had been, had definitely seen a century or two.

"Well, I am here now," she said. Nice of her. She could've made a scene if she'd chosen but instead was behaving. Given the tenuous nature of her position and the alliance she had barely forged with the Templars, it was a sensible approach. Though, from the little I'd gleaned of her in the time I'd known her, I doubted she would remain sensible and accommodating if she was truly annoyed or truly determined to get something she wanted.

As she moved into the room, Adeline's gaze fell on Ash and she smiled, one eyebrow arching. "I seem to have missed out on the introductions."

"Captain Asharic Pellar, ma'am," Ash said with a slight bow. I had to give him credit; he hadn't yet let any startlement he might be feeling at the presence of both a wraith and a Blood lord at the Brother House show.

Adeline's expression turned both amused and speculative. She slanted a glance at me and I stared back without letting my expression alter. *Veil's bloody eyes.* Adeline was definitely old enough to know Ash's history.

"Asharic sa'Uriel'pellar?" she asked.

Ash nodded, his expression turning faintly wary.

"Well, well, well. How . . . interesting. Welcome home . . . Captain." Her eyes slid back toward me for a moment, but then, to my relief, she turned her attention back to Father Cho. "Where shall I sit, Abbott General?"

Father Cho jerked his chin at one of the younger Templars seated a few chairs down from me, and the knight rose rapidly, vacating his seat then holding the chair politely for Adeline.

"Will anyone else of your party be joining us?" Father Cho inquired.

Adeline shook her head. "Digby is outside, but I will fill him in later. Do continue."

Father Cho nodded and turned back to Ash. "As I was saying, Captain Pellar has brought his men to strengthen our forces."

Adeline leaned forward in her seat and stared at Ash. "And are you intending to use your men, Captain Pellar, or perhaps just burn out the warrens on your own?"

Damn. She did know Ash's history. Including, it seemed, his vaunted ability with fire. He could tame fire or call it. But I didn't think even he could control a fire the size it would take to burn the warrens—the underground realm of the Blood that stretched for miles and miles beneath the City streets—and the mansions that stood above them. And without control, such a fire could consume the whole City, and it wouldn't discriminate between Blood and Beast and human while it did.

Besides which, unless he had changed greatly from the man I knew, I didn't think Ash would agree to do such a thing, kill so many indiscriminately. I hoped the wince that had flitted across his face at Adeline's questions meant I was right. If I wasn't, I couldn't imagine that the Templars would sanction such an approach. They killed when they had to, but they didn't slaughter without reason.

I held my breath, hoping I was right, as Father Cho regarded Adeline steadily for a moment before he said, "For now the plan is to hold the boundaries while we see what develops in the Veiled Court."

"And if Ignatius presses the point?" Adeline asked.

Father Cho shrugged. "We will deal with that eventuality when we have to."

Thin eyebrows, painted stark black to stand out against white skin, drew together. "There are innocents in the warrens. Humans."

"We are well aware of that," Lily said, her voice edged with impatience.

She knew the warrens better than any of us, having grown up there. Which reminded me, I needed to speak to her, to see if she'd had any time for one of her covert night missions into the warrens lately. We still hadn't found any trace of any of the Fae women who'd disappeared in the months before Ignatius broke the treaty.

"Good." Adeline's expression was fierce. "I hope you remember it, in the days to come."

"Are you asking us to show mercy to Ignatius Grey?" Guy asked.

"I'm asking you to think about the consequences of the decisions we make here."

"We always do," Father Cho said. "And we have no desire to cause any harm to innocent bystanders."

I pressed my lips together. I wasn't so sure I agreed with that statement right at this moment. After all, no one had thought through the consequences of bringing Asharic back to the City. At least, not the consequences to me.

"It seems to me that the only way to another lasting peace, in addition to defeating Ignatius, is to convince the Fae to form the treaty again," Adeline said.

"The Fae remain in Summerdale," Guy said.

And seemingly not inclined to help the humans.

The Veiled Queen was dead. She had been the one to forge the treaty and to hold the peace for four centuries, and look what it had gotten her. I doubted that our next ruler—and Veil only knew who that might be—would be so quick to put themselves in danger to protect the City. The Veiled Queen had spread her protection over the City and around the surrounding land until it reached the borders of the adjoining human territories. The Veiled World—Summerdale—shared some edges with the City and the human lands, but they were not quite of the same world. Another realm, really.

One where the Fae could live in safety without ever having to interact with the outer lands if they chose not to. Our future ruler might choose to withdraw and not expose themselves to the risks the queen had taken. Judging by the current lack of communication with Summerdale, that option seemed more than likely.

True, it wasn't the humans who had killed the queen. But it was to save the humans that the queen had made the treaty and enforced it all these years. Since then, the humans had grown stronger and the City had flourished but at the same time become more inimical to my kind as the use of iron, even rationed as it was, spread. There weren't many places in the City—in the human boroughs at least— where there was no iron.

There had been those in the Veiled Court who had wanted to break the treaty before this, to leave the humans to their fate and retreat to the safety of Summerdale. My father was amongst that faction. No doubt he would be doing what he did best and busying himself politicking at the court, trying to influence who might next assume the Veil. Much good that might do.

The court could scheme all they wanted, but the power would fall as it would. To the strongest of us. Whoever that might be. The High Families were powerful, yes, and their magics ran deep, but there were others who were strong. Those who stayed apart from the court and the games of power.

I couldn't help looking at Ash. Why had he returned?

Was it really so simple as being asked now that the queen was dead? Did he have another agenda? He was powerful. More powerful even than he'd been when he was exiled. I could feel his magic from where I sat, like a fire banked within him. When last I had seen him, it had been wild and headstrong. Bright with anger and rebellion, barely controlled. Frightening. It was that power that had gotten him into the trouble that led to his exile. Had drawn the attention of others in the Veiled Court. Others who chose to view Ash as a threat.

Now it curled to his will, quiescent, so that only a whisper of its song caught my ear. But beneath the calm, I could feel its depth like an ocean beneath my feet, making my skin tingle. He had mastered his gifts during his exile. Grown into them perhaps. Who knew what he could do now?

Most of the Fae healers I worked with at St. Giles were powerful and skilled, but their magic didn't feel like this. At least not here in the City, where iron tamped all of us down. It was almost as though Ash carried a piece of the Veiled World with him, letting his power run free. Or maybe he had learned a trick or two whilst he was away.

Either way, I would not care, I told myself firmly. What lay between us was an old, old story and I had no intention of cracking open its dusty pages.

There was quite enough chaos in my life already.

I realized I had missed the last few sentences of the conversation as Guy rose to his feet and leaned over the map spread across the center of the table. We all leaned in, waiting to see what he wanted to show us.

Or show Ash and his men, more to the point.

The rest of us were all too aware of the situation in the City, of the boundary lines that had been drawn between the human boroughs and the ones belonging wholly to the Night World now. Of ground lost and won. Of loyalties stretched and strained and nerves fraying along with them.

Guy's finger traced the line of the humans' territory slowly, as if he was marking off each of the boundary points where sunlamps and Templar forces kept the Blood from crossing each night.

There had only been minor skirmishes up until now, but we had all felt the weight of anticipation building, the roiling anxiety and pressure in the air. Ignatius had to make his move at some point.

Had to try to take control.

Otherwise the Blood would eventually be cut off from the supply of blood that the human Nightseekers surrendered to them. They could drain their Trusted—the humans who served them—dry, of course, but then they would be defenseless during the day. And they would have no hope of a future without Trusted to turn into the next generation of Blood.

Ignatius wanted power, not to preside over ruin. He needed humans. Wanted them to be his to do with as he pleased. Which meant sooner or later he would start his push into our territories. Unless we could stop him.

Guy spoke calmly, setting out the situation for Ash, giving him both the background and the latest intelligence we had.

Lily spent half her nights roaming the Night World, walking the shadow where only she could go, but so far that was all she did.

Personally, in Father Cho's place, I probably would have sent her to kill Ignatius by now, but the Abbott General had not been taught the art of ruthless politics by my father. He was still seeking a lasting resolution for the conflict. One that would restore the peace in the City and let the humans walk the nights in relative safety once more.

"This is all very well," Adeline said when Guy paused in his monologue. "And I'm sure Captain Pellar appreciates the information, but we still don't have a plan as to how we're to solve this problem once and for all."

It concerned me, sometimes, that Adeline and I seemed to think alike. The Blood were only a few steps away from abomination to my kind, their undying life after death unnatural in our eyes. I shouldn't think like one of them. War, it seemed, made for strange bedfellows.

And that thought sent my gaze skittering back to Ash, like a compass seeking north. I pulled it away again and, in need of a distraction, said, "I assume what Lady Adeline is trying to ask is, what we are going to do about the Fae?"

Guy nodded. "We had agreed to wait and see what overtures might come from Summerdale, Lady Bryony."

"That's true," I agreed. "But a month has passed since the Fae withdrew. A month with no news at all and no one has left Summerdale that we can tell."

The humans had watchers in the villages outside the Gate to the Veiled World, and it had stayed stubbornly shut since the Fae had retreated after the queen's murder. Some of the Fae in the City had fled home, but no one had emerged.

"Are you saying we should send a delegation?"

"I'm saying we're nearing that point." I'd led the last human delegation into Summerdale. That time, thanks to the sacrifice of Fen and others, we had convinced the queen to return to the negotiations.

Which had led to her death.

Guilt and regret still turned my stomach to acid every time I thought of it. I could not claim to have ever been close to the Veiled Queen. I had decided the healer's path was for me early on and had stayed out of court politics as far as that was possible for anyone raised by my father. And I'd left Summerdale altogether when Ash was exiled, not wanting to be forced to either play the games of court or become another of their unwitting victims. But close or not, she had been my queen, and I, like all the Fae, had felt the whiplash shock of her passing and the aching void in the threads of power that should have linked us all.

Like reaching for something that had always been there and feeling nothing. Worse than nothing.

I looked at Liam, at the space beneath his neatly shortened sleeve where his forearm was missing. I wondered if that was how it felt for him when he tried to use his arm. I still regretted that I hadn't been able to save his arm, but it had been nearly severed, hanging by skin alone, too grave a wound for me to heal fully here in the City. And he would have died from the blood loss if we'd tried to take him to

Summerdale—even if we'd been able to convince the Fae healers there to heal a Templar.

"Lady Bryony?" Father Cho prompted. "Do you think it's time?"

"Yes. We need to discuss how we approach the Fae, unless we are abandoning the hope of a renewed treaty for all-out war with the Blood."

My words caused more than a few muttered responses. I knew that some of the Templars would welcome a chance to wipe the enemy from the City completely. But there were Blood in other lands and sooner or later they would try to return. Better to reforge the peace and the balance between the races.

Though I doubted that could be done with Ignatius Grey still alive. His death, I was prepared to accept.

Father Cho shook his head. "No. No, I do not think we are ready to abandon hope." He sighed then, ran a hand over his cropped head, and rubbed at the back of his neck. "But that is a longer conversation, and the night is growing darker. Captain Pellar, do you have the information you need for now?"

Ash nodded. "Yes. My men will be able to relieve yours tomorrow, if you can hold for another night. They will do better if they have one good night's rest."

"I think that is a request we can accommodate," Father Cho replied. "Things are not so dire that we need you immediately."

This caused another, slightly more annoyed-sounding murmur to roll through the room. The Templars were stretched thin and all of them were tired. But I had to agree with Father Cho. Mixing one tired force with another who hadn't even been properly briefed on the situation wasn't a good solution.

"Thank you, sir," Ash said, and then leaned back in his seat. For a moment I thought I saw fatigue on his face, but then it returned to his set expression of earlier.

"Good." Father Cho turned to Guy. "You can continue to brief Captain Pellar tomorrow morning."

"And the Fae?" Adeline asked.

"Lady Bryony and I will also discuss that in the morning. She is best placed to advise us how to make the approach."

I breathed a sigh of relief. I had been expecting Father Cho to ask for a meeting tonight. Perhaps I had some hope of seeing my bed at a reasonable hour after all.

Though, after the sudden reappearance of Asharic in the city, I wasn't at all certain that I would sleep.

Chapter Three

ASH

I rose as Father Cho called an end to the formal part of the proceedings. My mind was working through all the information that the Templars had provided—and the implications of a wraith and a Blood lord being present at this meeting—but I couldn't give either my full attention. Not when Bryony was in the same room.

But I kept my attention to my end of the table as I stood. My legs had stiffened slightly now that I'd actually spent more than a few minutes unmoving, and I stretched to my toes to ease the ache, then leaned forward to study the map of the City again, trying to banish my distraction.

Sir Guy stood beside me, eyebrows the same pale blond as his hair drawn together as he stared down at the map too.

"Are you patrolling tonight?" I asked, wondering if the tension riding the massive Templar was from that or something deeper.

He nodded. "Late patrol. After midnight."

I grunted sympathetically. Midnight in most battles was the dead watch, unlikely to see much action, though staring into the darkness, trying to tell simple shadow from actual foe, was never easy on the nerves. But here, where the enemy were Blood and Beast Kin—creatures who dwelled easily in the darkness of the City nights—midnight to dawn must be the most dangerous time. Which, no doubt, was why Guy was taking that patrol himself.

"I'll look for you in the afternoon, then?"

Guy frowned as he nodded but then his expression eased. He beckoned across the table to Liam. Liam rose obediently and made his way through the milling Templars and around the table to join us.

"Liam, perhaps you can keep briefing Captain Pellar in the morning."

Liam's frown was an echo of Guy's. "I'm not exactly up to date," he said. "I was playing courier, remember?"

Guy brushed his objection aside. "I can bring him up to date on the current status, but you know our arrangements and schedules and logistics better than anyone else. You can see to getting his men settled and the supply situation settled."

I almost groaned. Logistics. I hated dealing with logistics. Give me nice clean tactics and strategy. Even battle itself. But then, I knew just the solution to this particular problem. I touched the metal insignia I wore in my collar, sent a pulse of power in the direction of the person I wanted.

"I can do that much," Liam agreed, and Guy nodded approval and then made his excuses and left us to it.

"What time would you like to meet, sir?" Liam asked.

"As to that," I said. "If it's logistics you want to discuss, then I'll hand you over to one of my lieutenants. They will know best what we need."

I caught sight of the person I intended to dump this task on as I spoke. Rhian stalked into the room and scanned it smoothly, looking for me. She grinned when she spotted me and waded her way through the crowd, who parted to let her through. Possibly not used to women wearing mail and a sword nearly as long as they were, these Templars. Or maybe it was the bright streaks of blue and red dye that flared amongst the darker brown braids that flattened her hair against her head that caused the surprise on their faces.

"Rhian," I said, as she joined us. I watched Liam take her in with amusement. Obviously he hadn't come across her during our trek to the City. Easy enough. She tended to keep to herself and join the scouts on their daily rangings when she wasn't occupied with fighting, organizing the entirety of my forces to her satisfaction, or either of her other two favorite hobbies. "This is Brother Liam. He's going to be liaising with us on logistics, so maybe you can put your heads together and get us squared away."

Rhian shrugged, which was as close as I was going to get to "yes, sir" from her. She looked Liam over once, then took a second longer look before she grinned and stretched out one of her hands to gesture at the tattoo on his. The red cross was dark against his skin, the color of blood under bright moonlight. "Nice work," she said. "Who did it?"

Her sleeve fell back, revealing the intricate tangle of tattoos adorning her arm. Liam blinked as he saw them, then seemed to recall his manners. "Brother Edward is our sigiler."

"Got others?" Rhian asked, leaning in to examine the tattoo more closely.

Professional curiosity, I assumed. Rhian was responsible for the tattoos that graced any of my band who'd acquired one since she'd joined us five years ago. Curiosity and, judging by the spark in her eyes, a spot of let's tease the Templar and see what he's up for. Well, Liam was a grown man. He could fend off Rhian if he wished. She was determined when she set her sights on something she wanted, but Liam was also stubborn. Rhian might do him good. There was a sadness at the heart of him. A pain I assumed was mixed up with the tale behind his missing arm. He was far too serious for a man his age. Rhian was just about the opposite of serious made flesh. If nothing else, watching the two of them would be entertaining.

"No," Liam replied, pulling his hand back as Rhian leaned even closer. Then he cocked his head. "Have you?" He nodded at her arm.

"That's my business, knight. But if you're nice and listen to what I have to teach you and turn out not to be useless, I might show you."

I held back a laugh and left them to it. Walking back to the map on the table, I stared down at the City laid flat before me. But the lines delineating streets and boroughs were merely lines, as my mind wandered. Mostly I wanted sleep and a bed. But only mostly. The Templars had allowed me a bath and a hot meal and a change of clothing before they summoned their council. And it didn't matter what they'd given me now. I wasn't likely to sleep anytime soon.

Not when I could feel *her* across the room like a still pool of water in the middle of the energies swirling around me. The clear high notes of her power, unchanged from my memories, sang around me, making it near impossible to pay attention to what I was ostensibly here for.

I had thought my heart had stopped for a moment when she first walked into the room. I'd wondered if I might see her. Allowed myself to hope for that much. Wondered how she had changed in the past thirty years since I had been gone. Told myself I was a fool to wonder. We had not parted well, Bryony and I, and she had never been quick to forgive.

But still, I had felt her step into the room, the sense of her like lightning from a clear sky, and then I had seen her. Better than my memories. Beautiful, as all Fae were. But she had something more. Always had. Her dark hair was braided and coiled around her head, setting off the milk-pale skin and indigo eyes. She wore a long dress of dark blue, simple in cut, hardly the fashion of the Fae, and her Family ring—that gave me pause—sparkled on the index finger of her left hand.

Only her Family ring, though. No other colors graced her hands. I smothered the spike of curiosity and hope. She had hardly acknowledged my existence so far, which didn't bode well for my eventual reception when we did speak.

Still, stupid or not, I found myself lifting my gaze from the map again and seeking for her dark head amongst the crowd. I spotted her eventually. Heading for the door.

Which, if I was brave enough to take it, meant I might just get the chance to speak to her alone.

Bryony

I was halfway back down the corridor that led to the tunnels between the Brother House and St. Giles when rapid, light footsteps behind me made me pause. Then I felt the wash of power reach me and was tempted to break into a run myself. But no. That wasn't sensible. There was no need to run from Ash like a heartbroken child.

I wasn't heartbroken. Nor was I a child. He was merely an old acquaintance, nothing more.

I slowed completely and turned to watch him approaching, his stride eating up the distance too rapidly for my comfort. Clad in leather the colors of wood and shadows, gray eyes intent, he looked out of place against the pale walls and marble tile. Too fierce. Too unsettling. Perhaps I should've listened to my first instinct.

Ash halted a few feet away, opened his mouth, then closed it again. Took another half step, then stopped. Smiled a lopsided smile. "Hello," he said eventually.

"Lord Asharic," I said coolly.

His smile faded. He straightened, bowed to the correct degree of greeting between our Families. "Lady Bryony. I am gladdened to see you well."

Was he? "I'm sure your Family must be made joyful at your restoration."

"I'm fairly certain they have no idea where I am," he said. "Nor do I think they will be overly joyful when I appear on their doorstep."

"Do you intend to return to the court, then?" I asked carefully.

"I have a task to perform here in the City," he replied just as carefully. "After that, well, who knows what might happen?"

Who indeed? "I am sorry for the loss of your *in'lai'shen*," I said. The Veiled Queen had been from Ash's mother's Family. Many generations ago, but honored grandmother was close enough a term.

"As am I for the loss of your queen," he replied, keeping to the forms.

Then that smile came again. "Though given the old lady banished me, I can't say I'm truly that upset."

"Don't let anyone in the court hear you say that."

"Are you going to tell your father on me?"

"I don't often talk to my father."

"Oh?" His smiled widened a little. "Not one for court life?"

"I'm head healer at St. Giles," I said, determined not to let him gouge a reaction from me. "That doesn't leave much time for court."

"I see." He stared at me a moment. His eyes were a wicked dancing gray, a thread of humor always riding them at the most inappropriate moments.

"What?"

"It's an unexpected choice for a sa'Eleniel. For you."

"I'm not just a sa'Eleniel. Nor am I anybody you know." I snapped the words, then clenched my teeth. That was hardly a lack of reaction. Damn the man. But I wasn't going to explain my life and my choices to him. Particularly not when I'd made the choice to come to St. Giles in the early days after Ash was exiled. I didn't want to talk about that time. Particularly not with him.

I made myself turn away. "I have to get back." It was a half-truth. I was returning to my quarters at the hospital but not to work.

"Is it safe at this time of night?"

"If the Beasts and Blood have made it into the grounds of the Brother House, then it's too late for any of us." I tried not to think of the night, not so long ago, when they had done just that. The Beasts had staged an attack, and managed to burn down half a wing of the hospital, leaving dead and injured in their wake. Including Regina Foss, who had been best friend to Guy's lover, Holly, and Fen, the seer Saskia DuCaine was involved with. It was Regina's death that had put the shadows in Liam's eyes too. The Beasts had struck a deeper blow than they'd realized that night. But they hadn't tried anything so bold since the treaty was broken.

"Still, you should have someone to escort you."

"There's a tunnel that runs between the hospital and the Brother House. It's perfectly safe."

"A tunnel?" His eyes brightened with curiosity. "I never knew that. Sounds like something I should see."

Veil's eyes. I didn't want Ash in the tunnels. The tunnel that led from St. Giles to the Templar stronghold also met the branches that led deeper under the hospital. Where the hidden ward lay. Where Simon DuCaine and Atherton Carstairs—the first of the Blood to join our cause—were working to find a cure for blood-locking. The hidden ward was bound by many tons of iron and many more layers of enchantment. There was no chance that Ash wouldn't sense it.

Nor much chance that he would be satisfied with any explanation of what lay behind so much protection that I might give him. He'd always been like a dog with a bone when he got curious about things.

"I think that's up to the Templars to show you what they want to show you," I said primly. "Now, if you'll excuse me." I started off again. I only heard my own footsteps at first, and I thought I'd managed to dissuade him from following, but then I caught the sound of his steps behind me. Abruptly I changed my course and headed for the nearest door to the outside. I wouldn't lead Ash into the tunnels just because I was too flustered by him to think straight.

I was tempted to blast the door shut with magic behind me, but there was little point. First, because the Templar wards would set up a fuss if I tried to magically influence what they protected and second, because, unless my instincts were failing me, Ash was strong enough to undo any door I bound.

His powers and mine—though tending in different directions—had always had a strange sort of sympathy. We had worked well together and had little trouble unraveling the magical pranks each laid for the other. It was a sort of challenge between us.

I'd only had a chance to take three quick breaths of the cool night air when Ash opened the door and stepped out to join me. I didn't look at him. Instead I stared up at the sky, watching the moon half-hiding behind the drifting clouds. We would have rain tonight. Which would make the job of the Templars, patrolling the darkness, even less pleasant.

"You know," he said softly, almost as though he was speaking to himself, "you're ruining my plan."

I didn't take the bait. He wanted me to ask what plan.

"What plan might that be, Ash?" he said after another moment, his voice high pitched and squeaky in the way it always was when he wanted to annoy me with a bad imitation of my own.

"I'm not in the mood for you, Asharic," I said sharply. "I have things to do."

"After thirty years, that's all I get?"

"Did you expect more?" Now I did look at him, hoping my face would stay calmer than the angry memories rising inside me. Hoping he would take the hint and leave.

"Yes," he said simply. "Like I said, I had a plan."

"If I let you tell me what it was, will you go away?"

He stilled. And I could tell my words had stung him. Well, good. Better to hurt him a little now and make sure he knew where he stood. Save us both a lot of hurt later from breaking open old wounds that should be left alone.

"If that's what you want," he said.

"It is," I replied firmly. "So tell me."

"You've changed," he said.

"You've been gone thirty years. Everything's changed."

"Is that so?"

"You've changed too," I countered.

"But not for the better, judging by your welcome."

"I don't have time for catching up with ancient history. I have work to do. In case you haven't noticed, there's a lot happening here."

"Ah, and Lady Bryony has to hold it all together, as usual."

"Not all of us can cut and run at the least sign of trouble," I snapped.

Ash flinched, and the expression bit at me against my will.

"It's late," I said more gently. I didn't want to hurt him. I just didn't want him here. Didn't want to have to think anything about him. Wanted to return him back to the tightly walled up caves of memory where I'd consigned him all this time. "I have to go."

"I was going to tell you my plan," he said.

His voice was soft, almost sad, and I felt myself waver. I'd always been a fool for that tone. "What plan?" I asked against my will.

"The plan where the first thing I'd do if I ever saw you again would be to kiss you," he said.

I nearly choked. Then managed to find my voice. "Well, I hope you're a wiser military strategist than you are a romantic one."

"You don't like my plan?"

"It's not a plan. It's a fantasy."

"I liked it."

Part of me liked it too. The foolish part of me that held the remnants of the woman I'd been thirty years ago. But we were about to go to war and I had no time for fantasy. "Good night, Asharic. Please don't follow me."

"Good night," he said. I walked a few steps and no footsteps came after me. Instead all that I heard was the soft "I missed you" that floated toward me like a gossamer dagger.

Chapter Four

BRYONY

In the end my night bore no resemblance to good at all. I lay awake and stared at the ceiling, only to fall into a sleep haunted by the sense of something wrong that made my heart pound even in dreams.

Sometime near three, I came awake in a flash when someone knocked on my door, my response honed by years of hospital duty. I slipped out of bed, into a robe, and reached the door to my rooms before I'd barely finished tightening the belt around my waist.

The face that greeted me outside my room was pale and drawn. Sam, one of the youngest of the sunmages—barely out of the academy six months—jerked his head down in a hurried nod of greeting. "Lady Bryony. You have to come."

His sandy eyebrows—match to his always rumpled sandy hair—nearly met in the middle of his forehead, the frown emphasizing the worry in his blue eyes.

"What's wrong?" I asked, hoping it was just something straightforward like a birth come too early or a person taken by sickness in the night.

"Burns, my lady. Lots of them. Please come."

My stomach twisted. Burns. *Veil's eyes*. What had happened? But demanding that Sam tell me the whole story would only delay me getting to the patients who needed me. "Of course. You go. I'll come when I've dressed."

Sam nodded and sped off with no further pleasantries, which said something about his state of mind. He, like a lot of the younger healers, was always almost painfully polite when addressing me. That was the problem with cultivating a reputation as one not to be crossed. Eventually no one wanted to even approach crossing you. There were the odd exceptions, of course, senior healers and everyone that Simon DuCaine seemed to drag into his orbit. And my fellow Fae didn't exactly tug their forelocks, though they did maintain the proper courtesies.

I went back to my bedchamber to change, snatching a dress at random from my armoire and pulling it and undergarments on with no care for how they looked.

Burns. I hated burns. They caused so much pain to those who suffered them. That was the hardest part. The human healers didn't, as far as I could tell, feel the physical sensations of their patients, but we Fae did. Not full strength but we caught echoes of the sensations flooding the nerves of those we treated. And when the pain was very bad, even an echo could be hard to take.

Perhaps I should have grilled Sam after all. Then I could prepare myself. Plan ahead. Different kinds of burns required different treatment, but no doubt my staff would have that part under control. I trained them well and St. Giles ran like the finest clockwork money could buy most of the time. Tonight wouldn't be one of the exceptions if I could help it.

The babble of voices and the spiking flows of human and Fae healing powers at work reached me well before I got to the top of the massive staircase that descended to the ground floor of the hospital from the third floor where my rooms were.

Too many voices. It sounded as if every healer who worked at St. Giles had been pressed into duty. I hurried my step, pushing away the worry winding its way around my spine with cold tentacled fingers. Exactly how many people had been hurt? And what in seven hells had happened?

The tentacles turned to claws as I reached the second-floor landing, where I could actually peer over the railing to see into the foyer. I hadn't seen this many people crowded into the entrance of the hospital since the night that Treaty Hall had exploded a month or more ago.

I spotted Lily's red head in the middle of the swirl, helping to direct patients and families. Which meant that Simon couldn't be far away. I hurried down the remaining flights.

Simon met me at the foot of the stairs.

"What happened?" I demanded.

"Bunch of idiots decided to go Beast baiting. They were in one of the taverns right on the edge of Gillygate, celebrating the fact that they'd managed to corner a few and inflict some damage, when the Beasts decided to bait back. Apparently an oil lamp got knocked into a couple of bottles of whiskey and the whole place went up." He started walking back toward the throng of people.

I followed. "How many are hurt?"

"We have about thirty with burns, a few more with minor injuries. And five dead," he said grimly. "The worst of the burns are in here."

We'd reached the biggest of the ground-floor wards, which was reserved for times like this. It held twenty beds, and ten of them were occupied with men surrounded by healers. The stink of burned flesh hit my nose and I sucked in a breath, determined not to let it bother me.

Mercifully nine of the patients were unconscious, whether from their injuries or the work of my healers, I couldn't tell. One, however, was screaming as one of the Fae healers tried to lay a dressing on the red raw ruin of his arm.

"Why is he conscious?" I asked, approaching the bed.

"I tried to send him to sleep," Bard said with a frown. "It didn't work. And I can't get a sedative into him while he's screaming like that."

I looked at the man. Black hair, brown eyes that were half-closed as he screamed. He looked as though he might be just twenty or so. There was another angry burn on his left cheek, spilling down onto his neck and upper chest. Not as deep as the burn on his arm but nasty enough.

"Let me try."

I stepped up to the man and reached for the nearest body part I could get hold of—his foot in this case—and sent an urgent surge of power through him, willing him to sleep. It rolled over him and then bounced back at me. Damn. Bard was right. Which meant the patient was either warded or not entirely human.

"Fetch some nightleaf." It was the concoction we used to knock out Beasts on the rare occasions we had to, one of our strongest sedatives. Bard nodded and the orderly who was helping him hold the man down bolted off. I sent a more subtle thread of power toward the man, trying to sense a ward or indeed if he had more than human blood in his veins. I felt no echo of power, so that was a relief. A human under a ward strong enough to resist my magic would be a concern on more than one level. It would have to be set by another Fae, and I was the strongest Fae in the City that I knew of other than Asharic. Who was unlikely to have been warding random humans since his arrival.

That much settled, I turned my attention deeper, trying to decipher the different flows of energy in his body. Finally I caught it, a faint thread like the silver gleam of moonlight on dark water. A familiar sensation that I associated with Beast Kind. Someone in this man's ancestry had definitely had some Beast Kind blood. It wasn't strong, likely a few generations back, but it was enough, as with many of the mixed-blood humans in the City, to give him an odd reaction to our normal treatments.

The orderly returned with the potion. I took it from him, made a quick calculation of the man's weight, and diluted it a little with water. He wasn't a full Beast after all. Then I summoned my most commanding tone, the one I used to put the fear of seven hells into my staff, and leaned close to him. "Stop. Screaming."

He blinked and looked at me for a moment. I held the vial of potion in front of his face. "This will take the pain away. But you have to stop screaming long enough to drink it. Do you understand me?"

He nodded. His skin was an unpleasant grayish shade beneath its olive tones, and sweat beaded on his forehead. He pressed his lips together, so hard the edges of them turned white. The echoes of his pain battered at me, making my nerves twinge in sympathy. I pushed the sensation away before it could distract me, using my training to close my mind to the pain as much as possible.

"Good." I held the vial to his lips. "I know it hurts. But drink."

He nodded again and his hand came up around mine, painfully tight. He tilted his head back and tipped the contents of the vial into his mouth, swallowing desperately. Then his lips clamped shut again.

"Well done. Now lie back. Carefully. We'll support your arm." The orderly was, thankfully, several steps ahead of me and was busily placing pillows so that the man didn't have far to slump backward. I put a cushion of power around his arm, shielding it from the contact of the mattress and the rest of his body, counting silently in my head. By the time I reached fifteen, the man's face relaxed into slack insensibility.

With the patient now rendered unable to resist, I set to work. Heat fairly radiated from his arm, and the protesting nerves and dying flesh called out to me. I drew on my power and sent it into him again, hoping like hell that his blood wouldn't resist my healing in this as it did the command to sleep. If it did, and if it resisted the human mages as well, then he was likely to lose part of the use of his arm. The burn was deep and the muscle would warp beneath the scar tissue. His Beast Kind heritage would, if he was lucky, defend him from infection and prevent him from losing the arm entirely. But it wouldn't save him from being partly crippled if my magic didn't work.

Several seconds passed as I poured power into him, trying to push past the hints of resistance I felt. I was beginning to think that it wasn't going to work, that I should ask the orderly to bring Simon over, when something gave inside him and his body began to respond. Heat receded. Tiny vessels began to mend, flesh to heal. I breathed relief and focused again, lessening the flow of power to a steady stream rather than a torrent. No point draining myself when there were many more patients to come after this.

I nodded to Bard and told him to move on to another patient and settled myself for a long night's work.

It was a long night—or a very early morning—I was never sure which to call it. In the Veiled Court and the Veiled World, time is more flexible than it is in the City. Night and day do not necessarily follow strict rules, depending on who holds sway in any given realm. The Veiled Queen, seemingly fond as she was of humans, had let the Fae mostly have free rein in that respect. And in the court itself, more than just time bent to her will. It was hard to keep track of time when the mere mood of the queen could change the land from night to day.

As the sky outside the windows began to show the first hints of light, we had tended to almost all our patients. I left the other healers working on the last few—those with the most minor injuries who'd been able to wait for treatment—and made my way around the wards and the waiting areas, soothing anxious relatives and friends.

By the time the cathedral bell tolled eight, I was ensconced in my office, occupied with the records and logistics the frantic night had left in its wake. I filled in forms and gave directions to the staff to ensure we were restocked and to adjust the schedules to accommodate the new patients during the sleepless night. We needed to be ready for whatever this new day would bring.

I took comfort from the familiar surroundings of my office and from the feel of the hospital around me. St. Giles was part of me now, sunk deep in my bones. I don't know if I'd been thinking straight when I left Summerdale thirty years ago and come here, seeking a place where things were different. Different from the self-absorbed, self-willed, restricted world of Summerdale. The world that used people's lives as pawns.

I'd wanted to use my healing abilities for good, to make a difference rather than tending to minor hurts incurred by pampered Fae in pointless challenges. I'd wanted meaning. And I'd found it, much to my surprise. The humans had welcomed me, taught me as much as I taught them, taught me more perhaps. They'd changed me for the better. They too were part of me now.

And I would do my best to help keep them safe and to mend their hurts if safety became impossible.

I was just giving instructions to the hospital's head house-keeper, a short, wiry woman who'd worked at St. Giles as long as I had and had the all-too-human gray hairs to show for it, when someone knocked on the door. This time there was no urgency to the sound and I finished speaking to Agatha before I acknowledged the knock. She bobbed her head to let me know she had all my instructions clear—she never wrote anything down—and Liam stepped through the door to replace her when she left.

"Good morning, Lady Bryony." He bowed courteously.

"Good morning." I picked up the pile of papers in front of me. The patient names and details of what had happened during the fire that we'd gleaned from those we'd treated. I assumed the Templars would want to talk to some of them, particularly the three survivors of the group who'd started the trouble. "These are the notes on last night." I offered them to him.

Liam held up a hand. "That's not what I came for, my lady."

"Is something wrong?" I asked, coming to my feet. I'd thought I'd managed to dispel all the tension of the night before, but his words sent it winding around my muscles again, which, strangely, made the fatigue I'd been ignoring even more apparent. I hadn't been getting more than a few hours of sleep a night for weeks now and I was starting to feel it. Maybe that was why I had been so rattled by Ashar-ic's unanticipated reappearance last night.

Liam tilted his head. "Not wrong exactly."

He looked tired too. He didn't patrol anymore. Even though he was still a fierce swordsman—I had seen him in training—and a sunmage of no little power, his missing arm was a liability when facing opponents as fast as Blood and Beast Kind. But when his brother knights were out patrolling I knew that he busied himself making sure they had everything they needed. And then I recalled that Guy had set him the potentially frustrating task of trying to wrangle Asharic's forces into some semblance of order.

"What is it?" Were Ash's soldiers causing trouble already? I had no doubt he was a skilled commander and that his men were formidable fighters—the Templars would never have sent for them were that not true—but I couldn't imagine that he ran his little army with the sort of fierce discipline the Templars instilled in their knights.

"It's the Fae, my lady. There's a group of them at the Brother House. They say that Captain Pellar has to come with them to Summerdale. He sent me to fetch you."

I stared at him for a moment. *Shal e'tan mei and double that.* I hadn't seen that one coming. Where was Fen when I needed him? But obviously our resident seer hadn't seen it either or he would have warned me. What did the Fae want with Ash so urgently? And who had sent word so swiftly to Summerdale to let them know that he had returned?

I could think of a number of possibilities. He'd been exiled—unable to set foot over the borders of the lands the queen had claimed—but the queen had died and it was tradition that exiles could return when the ruler who'd sentenced them was no longer ruler. In practical terms that meant that most exiles lasted the equivalent of several human lifetimes at least. Usually more. The Fae did not change rulers very often.

And then there was the simple fact that Ash was Ash. Drawing trouble. He'd certainly not been popular with certain Families and factions at court. Unpopular enough, in fact, that I was certain his enemies had engineered the duel that had led to his banishment. Even though those who I suspected were behind it had been related to Stellan sa'Oriel, whom Ash had killed during the fight.

Ash had only been gone thirty years. A long time for a human to be banished, but for one of us, barely time for tempers to cool, let alone for sentiments to change.

Were there those in the court who still wished him ill? Undoubtedly. There was hardly a Fae amongst the High Families who didn't have enemies. I had a few myself, though I didn't think any of them wanted me dead. They were satisfied with—and probably considerably cheered by—the fact that I spent almost all my time far away from court in this crazy iron-bound city. Ash, on the other hand, had been good at making enemies of the serious kind. He'd been too strong, too brash, and too full of his own sense of how he was going to live his life not to.

Not to mention that his Family was related to the queen herself. But now the queen was dead and that connection wouldn't protect him when he did return to the court. Damn. Why had he come back? Couldn't he have seen that this was going to happen?

Or, even worse, was he looking for trouble?

"My lady? Will you come?" Liam's words interrupted my reverie.

I straightened my shoulders. I couldn't stay out of it, as much as my instincts warned me that that was the smart thing to do. The Templars needed Asharic's army, which meant they needed Asharic. So I couldn't let him be dragged off to Summerdale and become the subject of some obscure Fae machinations. We didn't have time for that right now. Time enough to settle old scores once the city was safe again.

"Of course," I said.

Chapter Five

ASH

I spent the night on a flat piece of roof atop one of the square towers of the Brother House. I'd been tired before the Templars' meeting, but seeing Bryony had taken care of that. Nothing like a good adrenaline surge of nerves, nostalgia, and regret to burn away fatigue.

So instead of resting, I alternatively tried to clear my mind with the disciplines I'd been taught as a youngster and stared out over the darkened City, trying to convince myself that I was actually home again.

Or close enough to home. As close as I was going to get for now. The lights of the City seemed subdued; not as many lanterns and gas lamps breaking the night into the pools of light and darkness as I remembered. Except, that is, for the long clear line of sunlamps and guard fires that edged the winding borders between the human world and the Night World.

Those were not as I remembered them either. They had shifted with the ending of the treaty. There was no longer the no-man's-land of the border boroughs standing between the humans and the Night World. No. From what I'd been told, all the border boroughs had chosen their allegiance now. Some had joined the humans—Gillygate, Brighttown, Westerbray, and Oldberry—while Seven Harbors, Mickleskin, and Larks Fall were now under the sway of the Night World. Which meant the line of guardian lights swooped and curved and made strange detours along its path.

I wondered how the new borders had affected the railway. The main rail line of the City bisected it neatly along its north and south accesses, a path that used to take it mainly through human and border boroughs with only a few of the offshoot branch lines heading into Night World territory and then, mostly, into the Beast Kind boroughs rather than the Bloods' domain. Now the Great Northern Line would cut through at least three Night World boroughs.

Had the railway come to a halt? That would be a strain on the City. The railway, which had just been nearing completion when I left, was one of the City's main supply lines to the markets and farms and smaller towns that provided the bulk of the raw materials for the food its inhabitants ate and the clothes they wore.

Guy hadn't mentioned the trains to me, so I was assuming they were still running. The Templars had stockpiles of food and ammunition and weapons, but he would surely have told me about something as vital as the City's supplies being cut off. If that had happened, restoring them would need to be a priority.

I was still on the roof when Rhian came to find me an hour or so past dawn to discuss the arrangements she'd made with Liam. She brought Charles Simpson, the most senior of my lieutenants, with her.

Both of them looked more rested than the previous day. From my vantage point, the night had been relatively quiet. There'd been a fire in one of the former border boroughs that had caused a flurry of activity and I'd sent a thread of power to help the fire die as fast as possible. From such distance, with all the iron in the City affecting my powers, it was as much as I could do. I watched the distant movement of men and horses and carriages ferrying the injured back to the hospital. I'd been tempted to go and offer my assistance, but Bryony would be there and I doubted she'd welcome my help.

Apparently the Templars hadn't sought assistance from any of my soldiers and Rhian and Charles had both slept through the commotion. Charles was his usual quiet, solid self, his reddish hair cropped close to his head, clothes neat, face clean shaven. Rhian, in contrast, still looked rumpled, but her braids were tamed against her head, the blue and red strands bright in the early light.

They'd earned their sleep. They'd spent the rest of the previous day and evening working hard to get our men bedded down and liaising with the Templars on the mundane but vital details of housing, food, supplies, and command structures here in the City. They filled me in as we breakfasted with the Templars and then, after I dismissed them both to get on with settling the men in, Guy came to brief me on the night's activities before he went to bed.

After Guy left, I got Liam to take me back to the map of the City in the Templar's vast conference room and made him drill me on the streets and lanes that had grown less clear in my memory than they had been before I went away.

And it was there that Father Cho came to find me to tell me that there was a delegation of Fae at the Brother House gates, requesting that I accompany them to Summerdale.

Fuck. "Get Bryony," I hissed at Liam, and he wheeled and set off with speed.

Father Cho tapped his chin as he watched him go. "Problem?"

"I don't know," I admitted. "Do you have to let them in?"

He shook his head. "No. The Brother House is a Haven, so if they request sanctuary I would have to grant it, but otherwise they don't have a right to enter. Do you have reason to believe they mean you ill?"

I shrugged. "That largely depends on who they are. Did they give any names?"

"The man who made the request said he was Tomar sa'Uriel. Does that mean anything to you?"

Tomar? "He's one of my cousins," I said. More like a

brother than a cousin. My parents hadn't been blessed with any children other than me. Though after having me, they might have thought it a blessing that there were no others to trouble them as I did. Tomar and I had grown up together, along with his sisters, Roslyn and Rowan. Our Families had shared a territory, and the houses were close together by Fae standards.

But Tomar had not sided with me in the trouble that had led to my exile, and I had no idea where I might stand with him now. "Was there anyone else with him?"

"Four other men. No women. Three of the men have Family rings that are red and orange and yellow. The other's is black and dark blue. He's older than the rest of them."

Older? Bearing black and blue Family colors. That sounded disturbingly like someone from Bryony's Family. They definitely hadn't been on my side. Lord sa'Eleniel had not approved of Bryony associating with a troublemaker like me. And I doubted I'd done anything to improve his opinion of me when I'd been exiled and broken his daughter's heart.

But it seemed unlikely that Lord sa'Eleniel himself would come for me. The other three, red and orange and yellow, were sa'Peniel'istar, a minor Family related to the sa'Uriels. My own Family ring was ruby and topaz and diamond. Theirs would be ruby, topaz, and citrine.

But whether or not they would support me would depend largely on the current state of affairs between the various branches of the Family, and that was something I knew nothing about.

Regardless of whether they were friends or foe, I had no desire to return to Summerdale now. I had a job to do here in the City and was more than willing to put off facing my past.

"I'd better go down and talk to them," I said finally. "If Liam gets back with Bryony, send her to me."

"Do you want me to ask the gate guards to let them in?"

"No." I would feel safer with iron between me and them. For a start, it would put a crimp in their style if they tried to use any form of magical compulsion on me. As would a couple of Templar knights at my back.

I walked out of the Brother House with nerves prickling my skin and twisting my guts. I was used to fear. It's a given in battle, no matter how many times you experience fighting. I knew how to master it in the moment. But to tell the truth, it was a long time since I'd felt a weight of dread like the one I did now. There were Fae amongst my men. Exiles like me or a few who chose to leave the Veiled World of their own accord. But while they were friends in some cases, none of them were High Family. Not from the world I had grown up in or from any of the clans that made up the Veiled Court.

Not my blood and my memories. Not like what Tomar was. Or had been.

Bryony hadn't exactly welcomed me home with open arms, and I was beginning to wonder if anyone would.

Hadn't anyone missed me in the time that I was gone? I had been young and foolish, yes, and caused my share of trouble, but I had thought I had true friends.

None of them followed me into exile, nor had I expected them to. But I didn't like to think that they had forgotten me. Or worse, that they felt ill will toward me for what had happened. I knew that there would be those of Stellan's Family who did, of course. Though he was the one who'd challenged me to the duel, I had been the victor and he had paid the ultimate price.

Amongst a race so long-lived as ours, it is rare to lose one so young other than in battle, and killing him had been nothing I relished doing. But I had not been willing to sacrifice my own life to appease those who had plotted against me.

I stepped out into the early-morning sunshine and squinted toward the gate. Just as Father Cho had said, five Fae men were arrayed outside the iron barrier. Four of them sat on horses, while Tomar had dismounted from his—a massive bay of the kind he always favored—and stood by its side a few feet from the gate itself. Distancing himself from the iron, I presumed. He would not be used to it, unless he had changed his ways and started to venture farther from Summerdale than he used to.

Even I, who was used to weapons and armor, could feel the pull of those solid bars, like a silent pulse, that made the connection to the earth and all that surrounded me feel discordant and faded.

Tomar stood quietly in the sunlight, not talking to the Templars who faced him or the Fae behind him. The light bounced off his dark brown hair and threw a shadow on his face so that I couldn't see his eyes or read their expression.

I could see his mouth, though, and it wasn't smiling.

I slowed my walk, hoping Liam would return soon with Bryony. Her Family was nearly as high in the court as you could get without being of the queen's line. Equal to mine. Besides which, she, from what I could gather, was well loved in the City and respected for her skill at healing and the way she managed St. Giles. Which meant the Templars wouldn't let anything happen to her. And no sensible Fae would cross Lord sa'Eleniel by offering offense to his daughter. Or so I hoped.

I studied the men behind Tomar as I walked the last few paces. The one with darker hair than Tomar's—near black like Bryony's—would be the one wearing sa'Eleniel colors. I didn't recognize him. Definitely not Bryony's father, which was a relief. Perhaps one of her myriad uncles, whom I had never been able to keep straight. Her father's father had had several wives so far and had sired nothing but dark-haired, blue-eyed men who tended toward severity and politics.

Bryony was a rare female in that line. Which made them overly protective of her. A fact that she didn't like but that she had lived with until she had escaped their oversight and become a healer in the City. Which wouldn't have improved their disposition toward me any.

Bryony was supposed to be making astute liaisons and swelling the Family ranks and influence. As far as I knew, based on the fact that she still only wore one Family ring, she hadn't yet made any sort of partnership and her ring lacked the deep blue topaz that the sa'Eleniels gave to the mothers of their line, so I had to assume she hadn't borne any children while I was away.

The other three, who had darker skins and bronzy hair, would be the Istars. They looked young to me, but then, I was somewhat out of the habit of judging the ages of Fae, which was an art of reading the experience in the small signs of the body and the eyes, not just the ageless faces.

I knew that I looked older than when I had left. Injury and strife had taken a toll, as had the things that I had seen. The Fae in my company likewise looked older than their years, which ranged from younger than me to several hundred years older.

So the five men before me now, including Tomar, looked strange to my eyes. Too perfect. Inhumanly so.

But I couldn't put it off any longer. I had to deal with them.

"Cousin," I said as I came to a stop at a distance from the gate that matched his. Possibly I could have offered him a more formal greeting, but that would be setting a tone for the encounter that I was trying to avoid.

"Asharic," Tomar said.

We stared at each other for a few seconds. Then Tomar took a deep breath. "I have been sent to bring you home."

I nodded. "Then I will have to ask you to send my regrets. I have an engagement here in the City that will be occupying me for some time."

He looked surprised. "The court requests you to attend."

"That's flattering, but my understanding is that the Veil currently stands empty. Which means that the court can request all it wishes but I don't have to answer. The court has survived without me for many years now. I'm sure it will continue to do so."

That made one edge of his mouth flicker upward. Nearly a smile. The tension in my stomach eased a little. Perhaps the cousin I remembered wasn't quite so far away after all.

"As you are aware, the court is currently disrupted."

"Well, they can't blame me for that, at least. I was nowhere near the City when the Veil fell. *Shai'el el'aria demain.*" The last meant something close to "blessed be her memory." The queen might have exiled me, but I had always liked her, as much as you could like someone who was closer to a force of nature than a person. And she was of my blood, and Tomar's. My Family would be feeling a double loss.

Tomar inclined his head, granting me the point. "No. But still, the court must fill the Veil. Which means all the High Families are summoning their kin home."

That much I could believe. But there were those who wouldn't be summoned. Bryony was still here for one—though right now her "here" was still elsewhere . . . where the hell was she?—and there were other Fae still at St. Giles. Some of them had to be High Family as well. The healing magics ran strongest in the blood of the court for some reason. Maybe because the High Families were far more prone to damaging one another in the course of their jockeying for position. Perhaps the magic had developed in those directions in self-defense. The thought amused me, but I kept the smile from reaching my face. It might be misinterpreted by Tomar's friends.

"If my Family wishes to summon me home, then why didn't they send just you?" I asked Tomar. I jerked my chin at the other four men. "Who are they?"

"These are uncertain times. No one is venturing from Summerdale alone."

I quirked an eyebrow at him. Our kind cannot lie, but we are very, very good at dissembling. We can avoid saying what we do not want to say. Tomar could be speaking the truth and the four men with him were friends who had volunteered to accompany him safely to the City and back, or they could have a different agenda altogether. One that he was failing to mention. Like dragging me back to Summerdale for a purpose far less pleasant than seeing my Family and taking my part in the court shenanigans that would accompany the seeking of a new ruler. And the latter was guaranteed to be quite unpleasant enough as it was.

I shook my head. "I'm sorry but I can't. Please convey my apologies."

Tomar, I realized, wasn't listening to me. Instead he was staring past my shoulder. I hadn't been paying attention. Bryony had arrived.

"Can't what?" she asked, coming to stand beside me. Today she didn't feel still. No, today her mood crackled around her, sparking the air to life. I hid my smile. No one sensible crossed Lord sa'Eleniel, nor should anyone annoy his daughter too much when she was in this temper. I wondered if Tomar remembered that.

"Tomar here has come to invite me home."

Bryony flicked me a rapid sidelong glance. Then she straightened her shoulders and aimed her disapproving gaze at the Fae men. "Is that so?"

"Apparently. He seems quite insistent."

Bryony glanced backward. I followed the line of her gaze and saw Liam and Guy DuCaine standing a few feet behind us. More reinforcements. Excellent.

Bryony turned back to Tomar and inclined her head toward him a little. The chain around her neck glimmered purple for a moment. "Tomar sa'Uriel'aven. I have not seen you in the City before." Her gaze moved past him and onto the men on their horses. "Nor you, Uncle. Did you feel like an outing? I understood the Gate to Summerdale stood closed."

So I had, at least, correctly identified one of the men. The dark haired man stared down at Bryony with an expression that was part amusement, part exasperation. "Your father thought that if Tomar was coming to fetch the young Pellar here, then it was worth me coming to talk to you again. Ask you to come home too."

She shrugged. "Has the court convened for a coronation?"

Her uncle shook his head. "No. The Veil still stands empty."

"Then there is no need for me to return, is there?" She tipped her head toward me. "And the City needs Asharic for now. Hard as it may be to believe, he apparently has his uses."

"Bryony." Her uncle's eyes didn't even flicker in my direction. From which I was to understand, or so I gathered, that I was not even worthy of a moment of his attention. It didn't impress me. "Won't you see sense?" he continued. "It's dangerous here."

"It's no less dangerous in the court right now, I would imagine. At least here, the enemies are clearly identifiable." She smiled, the expression carrying a dangerous edge.

He pursed his lips, disapproval clear in his face. "No one will offer you harm while your father is alive."

"Depends on your definition of harm," she muttered in a voice so soft that only I could hear. She flicked a hand toward her uncle, the sunlight catching her ring, the dark stones flaring to match the temper in her eyes.

"I'm afraid you'll have to go back empty-handed," she said. "Unless Asharic wants to go with you." She turned to me.

"I have already explained to Tomar that I'm needed here in the City," I said.

"Good, then that's—" Behind her, Guy coughed and Bryony paused. Then turned to the Templar and beckoned him forward. The big blond man strode to her side and bent to murmur something in her ear, his head so close to hers that I had to fight back a pang of envy that cut more fiercely than Tomar's lack of any sign of happiness at my return.

Bryony nodded at something Guy had said and then the Templar stepped back again. They exchanged a long look and eventually Guy shrugged as if to say "It's up to you."

The twist in my stomach tightened a turn or two. What were the two of them contemplating?

Bryony turned back to her uncle. "Although," she said, "perhaps not quite empty-handed."

"Oh?"

"You can take my father a message from me. Tell him that if he will allow me and a delegation from the humans to come to Summerdale to discuss the treaty, then he will see me return for a time."

"Summerdale is closed to any non-Fae," her uncle said bluntly.

"Perhaps he would like to reconsider that policy."

"It is the court's decision."

"Then perhaps my father can turn his thoughts to changing their mind."

"The court is not inclined to help the humans."

"Then the court needs to start thinking clearly," Bryony

snapped. "The queen held this peace for so long because it was beneficial to all of us. If the Blood reign here they will bring more than disaster for the humans.

"The court is occupied with finding the new holder of the Veil."

"The court, in my experience, is more than capable of doing more than one thing at a time. In fact, they delight in doing so. But there is little point to you and me standing here arguing, Uncle. The quicker you return to Summerdale, the quicker you can tell my father what I have asked."

"Oh, joyful fortune," her uncle muttered. But then he nodded. "I will ask. But do not hold your breath for a response that will please you."

Chapter Six

BRYONY

Uncle Mikel stepped back and I could tell that he was happy that he could at least tell Father that he had spoken to me and delivered the message. He was less happy about the request that I'd made in return, but he was fond enough of me that I believed he would do as I had asked.

Of all my father's myriad brothers and half brothers, Mikel came the closest to having an actual sense of humor. Not that he was allowed to use it all that often within the court. The sa'Eleniels did dignity and pomp. Frivolity wasn't to be indulged. I'd always thought that that was the reason that my father had disapproved of Asharic so vehemently. Ash, when I knew him, had been the very definition of frivolity.

I'd often wondered whether Fen's father had been from one of the Families in Ash's lineage. That same sense of wickedness and charm that burned bright and enticed all who came into its boundaries burned strong in him. But Fen had never shown any inclination to discussing his Fae heritage with me—not that I could blame him—and since the queen had taught him control of the visions that had plagued him so badly, he no longer had any need to seek out any help from his Fae relatives.

Indeed he was wise to avoid them. The Sight is a highly valued gift, and depending on the attitudes of the Family that Fen's father came from, a *hai-salai* with such powers would be an extraordinarily valuable tool, to be caged and cossetted like a favored lapdog but also strictly controlled. He definitely wouldn't be allowed to run free in the City to consort with humans and do whatever he willed. He would be kept safely in Summerdale to do his Family's bidding.

Maybe that was the solution to Ash as well. Send him home to Summerdale and let them deal with him. Let me continue the life I'd forged for myself in the City. It had taken me some time to find my balance in this place. I had no desire for Asharic to upset it. Though Ash clearly had his own ideas about that.

But, tempting as it was, it would be asking for trouble to allow the Fae to sweep him off now. The Templars needed his forces and Veil only knew what they would do if their leader was taken from them. There was enough strife in the City without adding several thousand angry mercenaries to the equation.

Tomar was staring at his cousin, studying him in a way I recognized. As though he wasn't entirely sure that he wasn't seeing a mirage or a cruel joke conjured with glamour. The same way I'd felt when Ash first appeared.

When Ash first left I'd spent months thinking that I saw him in a crowd or across the street. I would wake with the scent of him in my nose and the sensation of his body next to mine strong in the shivers of my nerves. But that had faded, as heartbreak does. I had locked away those memories. There had been little choice. Exiles rarely returned. And to go with him would have been to choose exile myself. And giving up the healing path and the training I was undertaking.

I hadn't been able to take that path with him. I wondered how much of it had been the sheer fury that had burned through me at the time. Anger at Asharic for being so stupid. Anger at the court. Anger that he couldn't understand why I wouldn't come with him.

There had been anger enough between us to set the City on fire.

As there had been desire.

But that was before. And this was now. Ash and I were a story that would remain untold.

Tomar, however, looked as though he wasn't entirely sure how he wanted the rest of the tale to go.

Ash, standing still beside me, did not seem inclined to make the choice any easier. That much, it seemed, had not changed.

"Asharic, you should come with me," Tomar said. "The court is—"

Ash cut him off with a sharp gesture that showed no inclination to accede to his cousin's request. He had grown used to being obeyed in his time away from us. And, I guessed, far less used to having to submit to anybody's authority. A mercenary took instruction from whoever hired him, I supposed, but the bond was one of money, not honor or loyalty. You could walk away if you were willing to forgo the payment and face the consequences. And Ash had never been one to be easily swayed from his path by the threat of consequences

"I said no. Let them come to me."

"I'm here," Tomar said. "Is that not enough? You have been away from us for many years. Are you not eager to rejoin your Family?"

Ash shrugged. I suspected that it cost him, that air of casual disinterest that he donned so readily. "I have a job to do. The court—and my Family—have waited this long for me. They can wait a little longer. And they can send me a warmer welcome than five armed men."

"Ash . . . ," Tomar said with a hint of pleading in the word.

"Good day, cousin. I have business to be about. And you have a journey back to Summerdale to undertake. You would not want to be caught here after sundown."

There was time enough and more for a journey back to

Summerdale. It only took a few hours—three at most— to reach the Gate.

"I will return," Tomar said.

"I will be glad to see you, cousin," Ash said with a bow. And then he turned and walked back into the Brother House. I watched Tomar carefully, waiting to see if he would do anything foolish like try to challenge the Templar guards for access to the order's grounds and pursue his cousin within the walls. But Tomar had never been as foolhardy as Ash and he stayed where he was.

The three men behind him looked somewhat annoyed by the turn of events, but they didn't dismount. And Uncle Mikel had merely watched the whole exchange with a kind of benign disinterest. But inevitably, his gaze returned to me.

"You will take my message, Uncle?"

"I will."

"Then I too have business to be about." I nodded at Tomar. "I wish safe journey to you all." Then I turned and followed the path Ash had taken back into the Brother House. It was bordering on rude for him to leave as he had done, but I didn't blame him for the retreat. It was sensible to put himself beyond the reach of the five Fae if they did decide to change his mind more forcibly, and in any case, he had probably grown out of the habit of court manners living the life of a mercenary, traveling to whatever provinces might need his services.

I could see how that part of the life he'd chosen would have been inviting. Being free to set one's own destiny was vastly appealing after the strictures of court life. It was the same reason I'd chosen to work at St. Giles rather than be a healer in the Veiled World. Escape.

But at the same time, Ash had been loyal to the queen's edicts and had never tried to return, never—as far as I knew—tried to contact any of his Family in all the years he had been away.

The question now was whether it would be possible for him to connect with them again. If they wanted him to. If he wanted to.

A thousand questions. Though it seemed so far that he

was willing to let those questions go unanswered and fulfill the promises he had made to the Templars.

Which I couldn't be displeased about even though I didn't want him around. I was hoping that he would have disappeared into the bowels of the Brother House and that I would be able to make my way back to St. Giles without having to speak to him again. But no, he waited for me just inside the door to the main entrance, staring up at the giant carved cross that hung on the wall, all his attention seemingly focused on it. But I wasn't fooled and he, at least, didn't try to keep up the pretense once I crossed the threshold.

"Have they left?" he asked.

I shook my head. "I don't know. They haven't tried to enter, so it doesn't matter, does it?"

"I'd rather they left. I have things to do and I'd rather not dodge my cousin and his friends around the City."

"Why don't you want to go back with them?" I asked.

His gaze sharpened. "Why didn't you want to go with your uncle?" he countered.

"I don't have time for court politics right now," I said.

"Nor do I," he said. "And I can't be sure that there aren't those in the court who wouldn't wish my head to be separated from my shoulders. I'm fond of my head." He smiled then, suddenly hitting me with some of that fatal charm. "You were fond of it once too."

"I'm sure you have plenty of people to admire your head," I said tartly. "And I've outgrown many foolish things I liked when you knew me."

He feigned a pained expression. "She wounds," he said dramatically.

I shook my head. "I don't have time for your games, Asharic. I've been up all night."

The playfulness in his face evaporated. "Patients from the fire?"

"What do you know of the fire?"

"I sensed it."

It was my turn to look askance at him. "From so far a distance? Here in the City?" Exactly how strong had he become?

"I saw it," he said before I could ask a further question.

"I couldn't sleep. I was up on the roof of the Brother House and I saw the commotion. And before you ask, yes, I did what I could to help, but from the distance, as you say, that wasn't much."

"You still work with fire, then?"

"Amongst other things. But, yes, I still have a little skill with fire. Were there many wounded?"

I figured he had a right to know when he was going to be joining the City's defenses. Last night's encounter had to be factored into any strategy he and the Templars were formulating. So I reeled off the facts and figures about the victims of the fire for him.

"Idiots," he said softly as I finished.

"Young men often are," I shot back, and then wished I had bitten my tongue as I heard the bitter undertone to my words. I didn't want him to think that I still harbored any hurt over his leaving. That would only encourage him in whatever ridiculous fantasies he had been spinning for himself about there being a chance for anything to ever grow between us again.

"Sometimes they learn," he said softly. "Sometimes they regret." His eyes seemed very gray in the shadowed hallway, the color of deep water.

Or deep trouble. I took a breath. He was beautiful. He'd always been beautiful. And he'd always been trouble. I doubted that that had changed. And I'd learned too.

"Sometimes it's too late," I said. "I have to go."

He drew back then, bowed crisply. "As you like. Keep running. It works. For a time. But, Bryony?"

I turned back. I couldn't help it. "Yes?"

"Eventually you have to stop and face what you're running from."

"I'm not running from anything," I snapped. Technically true. If I chose to misunderstand what we were discussing. Which I did. I turned again and this time he didn't call me back. I ignored the little pang in my heart that found this troubling.

ASH

I watched Bryony walk away. I wanted to follow, but this clearly wasn't the moment. I had thirty years of distance to overcome. That was going to take some time. But first there was work to be done. So I went in search of Rhian.

I found her, somewhat unsurprisingly, in the stables, tending to her horse, an unassuming-looking gray gelding whom she doted on. With good reason. He would win no prizes for his beauty, but he moved like lightning when he wanted to. And I'd seen him kill a man with a well-timed kick on the battlefield.

Rhian's kind of horse.

I clucked my tongue at him over the stable door, digging into my pockets for sugar cubes.

Rhian looked up from her brushing. "Morning. You look tired."

"I'm fine."

She started to work on the horse again, brushing his neck with long, sure strokes. "Did you spend your night howling at the moon and mooning over that Fae lady?"

She didn't miss much. Damn it. "There was no howling. Or mooning."

Rhian snorted. So did the horse, which made Rhian laugh. "I saw you going after her last night. Haven't seen you look at another woman like that. Is she the one you left behind?"

"It's complicated."

She pointed the brush at me. "It always is. Best approach is to grovel. If you were thinking of mooning, that is. Groveling always works well."

I was sure Rhian had had many, many men groveling at her boots in her day. She should be an expert on the subject. I wasn't sure there was enough abasement in the world to get me back into Bryony's good graces, however. "Thanks for the advice. How did you get along with Brother Liam last night?"

She grinned at my change of subject and set back to work, the muscles in her tanned arms rippling under her tattoos. "Too pretty to be a knight, that one."

"Well, he is a knight. Bound to his God. So try not to break his heart."

"Templars aren't celibate."

I couldn't deny that. "No, but he's very young."

"Not that young. Not after whatever did that to his arm."

"He didn't tell you?"

She hitched a shoulder, ran a hand down the gelding's neck as though testing if his hide was smooth enough for her satisfaction. "Didn't ask. He'll tell me if he wants to."

I'd seen Liam with his shirt off just once while we'd traveled to the City. There was a jagged scar made up of four parallel lines across his torso, angling down from his missing arm. If I were any judge, it was a Beast who'd torn him up, but I'd let Rhian discover that for herself.

"Is there anything you need me to decide right now?" I cast my mind back over the stream of details she and Charles had spouted at me earlier. "We need to get the billeting worked out today."

Rhian ducked around the gray and started work on his other side. "You need to think about where you want them. There are some empty buildings nearer to the border we can take over for lodgings and supplies if we need them." She twisted her head toward me. "Not sure how close you want to be to the front line, so to speak. There are other options. The Brother House has room to house a few patrols we could rotate through. And Liam was going to show me through their storerooms today, see what room there is for our supplies and figure out what extras need to be laid in."

If it came down to outright war, then being camped right near the edge of human territory wasn't the smartest move. Then again, the Templars were paying us for a show of force. And inside the City was safer than camped on the outskirts. We hadn't had any trouble yet, but if the Night World chose to go on the offensive, then sleeping in open space at night would just make my men sitting ducks.

"Put half the men near the border," I said. "Enough not

to make them an easy target. We'll rotate through the patrols there and at the Brother House and wherever else they can put us."

Bryony had mentioned tunnels to the hospital. If the humans were smart, they would've built extra rooms and storage when they laid the tunnels. "There may be room at St. Giles," I added.

"Near your pretty friend?" She smirked at me. "Convenient."

I rolled my eyes at her. "Don't let Lady Bryony hear you say that. She might turn you into a frog."

Rhian's eyebrows shot up. "Can she do that?"

I grinned. "She's a healer. They can make bodies do all sorts of interesting things." Wait—that sounded wrong.

Rhian obviously agreed, her smirk returning. "Well, now, I'm sure I wouldn't know about that. But apparently you do."

"Remind me again why I keep you on?"

"Because I'm better at my job than any of the others," she said. "Plus, I'm more decorative than Charles." She held out a hand, squinted down at the pattern spiraling across the back of it with a considering eye. "This needs more work."

"There are sigilers in the City."

"Good ones?"

"Ask around. You'll find out. When I was here last, there were definitely some sigilers from the Silk Provinces working here."

Her eyes lit up. "They do good work."

"That's your department. Just don't do anything that's going to put you out of action. The situation around here is chancy. It's going to go up in flames at some point, despite what the humans want. We need to be ready."

"Liam said the Blood lord gaining power is bad news."

"Blood lords often are." I'd never led a campaign against the Blood before. The odd rogue Beast Kind, and definitely some other strange beasts, including a truly unnerving battle against a cadre of mad bokors down in the Voodoo Territories, but not vampires. When I left the City, the Blood had been firmly under Lord Lucius' control and I'd had no desire to cross paths with him. In truth, I hadn't often left Summerdale back then. I'd been too busy having a good time in the court and, once I'd met Bryony, with her to venture too far from home.

But now, from what Guy had told me and from what I could read of the mood of the City—and, yes, a city in trouble has a distinct atmosphere; I'd learned that well in thirty years of war—whoever this Ignatius Grey was who was leading the Blood now, he was at least as bad as Lucius. Perhaps worse. He was younger, for one thing, and that meant inexperienced. He was obviously ruthless to have won control over the Blood at such a young age. But whether he was clever and strong enough to keep it was something yet to be proved. Certainly he was reckless to break the treaty that had kept the Blood somewhat protected over the years despite their preying on humans.

Obviously he thought he could succeed.

I was here to see that he failed.

That meant our paths were bound to cross.

I felt my power stir at the thought. The Blood were easily killed by fire. One word from the Templars and I could send an inferno raging through the Blood territories that would solve the problem once and for all.

But not without a terrible cost.

A price the Templars and the humans weren't willing to pay. Not yet.

I hoped it wouldn't come to that. I wasn't sure I could bear to pay that price either. I'd used fire a few times early on in my mercenary career and caused things that still sometimes haunted my dreams. As I'd grown more skilled in war, I turned to other tactics where I could avoid using my powers. Safer all round.

I was skilled with fire, true, but the fire, once it reached a certain point, inevitably grew too large for even my control. In a city as big as this one, that point would come sooner rather than later. And an out-of-control inferno would kill more than just vampires.

"Was there something else you actually wanted, boss?" Rhian said, amusement dancing in her eyes. The gray snorted again, turning to nudge her pocket, and she gave him sugar while she grinned at me.

"Just keep your eyes and ears open." The Templars were being open with their information, but nothing was better than intelligence gathered by people I knew.

"We're going to go look at the buildings near the border. Do you want to join us?" She turned to stow the brush in the leather saddlebag hanging on the wall with several bridles.

"Yes," I said. I needed to get the lay of the land.

I wondered whether Tomar and his companions had left the City limits yet. I didn't want to cross paths with him again so soon, but I couldn't hide in the Brother House forever. There were things to do, and, as always, the stone walls were starting to feel restrictive. Or maybe that was all the iron. Whatever the reason, the Brother House felt heavy around me. Its walls were old and went deep, whispering of time and duty and stability.

All the things I wasn't good at.

Growing up in Summerdale—where nothing stays the same for very long and where, if you're bored and strong enough, you can change the land to suit yourself—wasn't a good training ground for the type of settling in one spot that the humans went for. Nor was the life of a mercenary.

Rhian nodded as she came back to the stall door. "I need to talk to the stable master about how many horses he has space for as well. And how many other liveries there are in the City."

"There are parks too."

"Liveries are easier to guard at night," Rhian said.

True. But whether the humans had enough spare stable space for all our horses was doubtful. We might just have to use the parks and take our chances. We could ward them and set guards. The parks I knew of were well within the human boroughs. If the Blood and Beasts got far enough in to attack our horses without being challenged or stopped, then we had bigger problems than worrying about our mounts.

"I'll get Aric saddled," I said. We had pushed the horses to get here fast but not enough that they needed days of rest. Extra rations, yes, and a few days of not doing too much, but they were used to traveling, so some gentle exercise wouldn't hurt.

"Liam should be here soon."

I nodded and went down a few stalls to saddle Aric. His name meant "light" in the Fae tongue, which was a misnomer, given that he was so dark a brown as to be nearly black and mean-tempered with it. But he'd had the name before I'd acquired him and I wasn't about to change it.

It wasn't long at all before Liam arrived, Guy DuCaine with him as well as another of the Templar brothers called Patrick whom I'd met briefly the night before.

Shortly after the Templars appeared, three of Rhian's squad turned up as well.

Seven—eight counting me—seemed like an excessive number for a daylight trip to a destination within the human boroughs but apparently the Templars didn't believe in taking chances. They were the ones who best understood the situation, so I didn't say anything.

Plus, a few more bodies around wouldn't hurt if we did come across any more Fae looking to an extend an invitation for me to return to Summerdale.

Rhian hadn't been joking about how close to the front line the buildings were. From where I sat on Aric's back, I could see down the unusually quiet street—deserted apart from us—a few hundred yards to a crossroads marked by a tall metal lamppost on one corner. From it swung one of the sunlamps that marked the border between the humans' world and the Night World.

It swayed gently in the breeze, looking innocuous at this time of day. But it was a symbol of why we were here. And how much effort the humans were putting into maintaining their safety.

Sunlamps were fueled by the power of the sunmages, and only the strongest of them could call sunlight at night. The City had a fair cadre of sunmages, but powering the sunlamps left them weakened for other tasks. Like healing. Or fighting.

Most sunmages chose one of those two paths. Most to

the former, true, like Simon DuCaine, but some chose the Templars. Liam was one of those. Or had been, given his injury. Which, at least, did leave him free to power some of the lamps. But both skills were ones that would be sorely needed if we did have to fight the Blood directly. If it came to that, we might have to choose between safe borders and survival.

It hadn't yet come to that. I frowned and turned my attention back to the buildings.

Rhian and Guy and the others were climbing down from their horses and leading them toward a narrow metal gate between two of the tall brick structures. I followed their lead, still scanning the surrounds as I passed through the gate. Both the buildings were four stories high, solid looking, judging by the depth of the openings in the walls that had both bars and glass for windows. Not as thick as the granite blocks that the Brother House was constructed from, but they were strong. A point in their favor to make up for their location.

The bricks fairly buzzed with wards too. I extended a tendril of my power and let it slide into the human magic, studying the protections, looking for weaknesses. Whoever had set the wards had done a good job, but there were a few more layers that I and some of my Fae could add.

Wards took strength to renew too, though they could be anchored down into the earth and stone, which would take the brunt of them. Still, we would all have to spare a little power to check and strengthen them each day.

Nothing like what the sunmages would be giving up for the signal lamps.

The gateway opened into a narrow lane that divided the two buildings and ended in a doubled courtyard between them. There was stabling of a sort, enough for a few horses but not a full patrol's worth.

Liam opened the thick wooden door into the building, showed us down to the storage cellars, and then through the kitchens and up to the floors above where long, empty rooms smelled faintly of the wool and spices that must have been stored here once—easy to convert to sleeping quarters with the use of our cots and tents made into screens to give the men some illusion of privacy.

"It'll do," I said, leaning to look out of one of the windows. We'd reached the top floor and it gave an interesting perspective across the City, being one of the taller buildings in the immediate area. I looked down and across to the crossroads and the lamp.

The street where the lamp stood, previously deserted, now had an occupant. A man standing on the Night World side, staring back at the very building we occupied.

I frowned and narrowed my eyes to bring him better into focus. Very tall, well muscled, longish dirty blond hair. Probably Beast Kind.

"Anyone got a spyglass?" I asked.

"What's up?" Guy said, joining me. Rhian came up to my other side, pulling a small telescope out of the pouch at her waist and handing it to me.

I passed it to Guy. "Someone's paying us some attention. Anyone you know?"

Guy studied the man for a few minutes. "By the hair, I'd guess a Delacroix."

Delacroix. One of the Beast Kind packs. "From where he's standing, I'm guessing they're one of the packs who are fully behind Ignatius."

"Yes," Guy said shortly. "Paul Delacroix was cozy with Lord Lucius and didn't take long to consolidate his position with Ignatius."

"So I guess Ignatius will know that we're moving in."

"Nothing we didn't expect," Guy said. "This close to the border, both sides are keeping an eye on things."

I nodded. It was, as Guy had said, to be expected, but that didn't mean that I had to like it. "Well, we'll just have to do our best to keep things moving around, keep them on their toes so they can't get the full picture of how many of us there are here at any one time."

"We can always glamour a few more men into existence," Rhian said.

"Not a bad idea," Guy said with a nod. "The Blood can see through glamour, but not all the Beasts can. I'm sure they've been outside the City snooping around your forces already, but the more men they think we've got, the better."

"Did all the Beast Kind packs side with the Night World?" I asked.

"Adeline says yes. Though she also says that some of them wouldn't have been very happy about it. But none of them were smart enough to lay any groundwork with us and give themselves a chance of forming an alliance so quickly once Ignatius declared himself. Any Beast Kind approaching us after that wouldn't have been trusted. So they didn't have a lot of choice."

"Unlike the Blood?"

"Adeline and her people turned up seeking Haven. Under Haven law, they can be killed if they turn on us. And they were pretty beaten up when they got here."

"Easy enough for the Blood to fake some injuries. It's not like it's going to do them any lasting harm."

"Bryony says they're not lying. Lily too. And Holly had worked for Adeline before."

And there was the holy trinity of women that Guy wouldn't doubt. That much had become clear in the short time I'd known the man. There were a few more women on that list. His sisters and his mother, primarily, probably some of the other healers. But if Holly, Bryony, and Lily were united in a viewpoint, I couldn't see him going against them without very good reason.

Which made him an eminently sensible man. A Fae, a wraith, and a former spy *hai-salai* were a formidable trio. Gods help me if they took Rhian under their wing.

Maybe we could just send the women out to solve the problem.

Or maybe not. Knowing Bryony's temper, there might be a certain amount of scorched earth to deal with in the aftermath. Women could be far more ruthless than men, given the right motivation. I'd learned that lesson well enough.

After all, a queen had banished me and I was fairly sure another woman had orchestrated my fall from grace. I had no proof, but perhaps, after all this was done, I would spend some time in Summerdale and see what I could find.

"We should get back," Rhian said, "start getting the men assigned and settled."

Guy snapped the glass shut and handed it to me. I took another long look at the man standing in the crossroads, committing his face to memory. Blood ran true amongst the Beasts. They tended to strong family resemblances. I would have to get the Templars to give us a full update on the packs and who was who.

I shook my head. Perhaps, after this, if we all survived, I would find some deserted patch of land and never get involved in anything more complicated than deciding what I might like for dinner for a decade or two. Thirty years of strategy and tactics and war were making me cynical and weary.

I had seen too many men come and go in that time. Some cashed out and retired, but more had died. A lower percentage than other mercenary troops perhaps, but still I had seen a lot of death. More than most Fae would see in their lifetimes. It was hard to watch my human friends age so quickly and pass by.

I wondered if Bryony had learned the same lesson as me. Time moved fast, no matter how much of it you were allotted. One should make the most of it.

I turned back from the window and nodded at Rhian. "All right, let's get this started."

Chapter Seven

BRYONY

It was two days before I heard back from my uncle. My father, really. Two days spent dealing with the aftermath of the fire and planning for the hospital and how we could continue to operate if any of a dozen different scenarios took place.

Two days spent doing my best to avoid Ash. I didn't manage to succeed entirely. He was working for the Templars, and the Templars were consulting with me. He managed to worm his way into the meetings more often than not. I knew he had a good reason for being there, but it was still irritating.

He was circumspect in public, but he watched me. Watched me with those deep gray eyes until my skin itched in response. Itched and tingled with awareness until I wanted to scream.

Even when he wasn't there, I was aware of him. I could feel the echo of his power, that deep hot stillness, moving throughout the City, more powerful than any of the other Fae residents. My equal. Maybe more.

And that was irritating too.

Of course, he wasn't used to the iron, so whether or not he could actually call on his full power if he needed to was a question as yet unanswered. Not that I'd ever had to try to call on mine to its full extent either. Healing was part of me, but it wasn't the whole. I had other magics that I didn't use for that skill. Magics that I barely touched here. I hoped I'd never have to.

The other thing that made me itch was waiting for my father's response. Every second that ticked away was one second longer for Ignatius to consolidate his position, for him to decide that he'd had enough time waiting and that it was time to act.

Time to start the killing.

The whole City strained with that knowledge, tension and worry scenting the air like woodsmoke.

I didn't know if the humans could sense it, but my Fae healers could. They moved a little too quickly, let frowns wrinkle usually calm faces. I had told them time and again that they were free to return to Summerdale, but the ones still here were the ones who, like me, had decided that this was where they were supposed to be, no matter what. I only hoped they would all live not to regret that choice.

At least, with so few of us left here now, we were able to keep tabs on one another, stay close to the hospital and away from the Night World. There had been no more disappearances, and for that I was thankful.

I was less thankful for Ash. And for the crumbling control I had over my memories. They kept sneaking out to catch me unawares, striking like daggers when I let my focus wander. The first time Ash had smiled at me and my heart had skipped. The first time he'd spoken my name.

The first time we'd kissed. That one kept returning. A deadly snare. Pulling me back to a night when, if only I'd made a different choice, I wouldn't even care that Ash had returned.

One night. One little choice . . .

There were flowers on my stairs again. Small unassuming flowers, delicately green and white. Glowing in the moonlight that streamed down on the garden outside my rooms.

I knew what they were, of course. Bryony flowers.

From the plant I was named for. They weren't usually beautiful, though bryony had useful healing properties.

These ones, though, were beautiful, softly shining and filled with a perfume that no bryony plant had ever issued.

I'd been finding bryony flowers in odd places for weeks now.

I thought I knew who was leaving them.

I hoped I knew who was leaving them.

But surely even he wasn't crazy enough to sneak onto my father's lands to leave flowers at my doorstep.

Asharic sa'Uriel'pellar had a wild streak a mile wide and fire that burned deep within him, but I didn't think he was insane. But maybe I was.

Because I bent to retrieve the flowers and then stepped out into the moonlight. "Ash?"

One heartbeat. Two. And a third.

Then he appeared, stepping out of the darkness beneath one of the vast oaks that grew here in our gardens to walk toward me. "You knew it was me."

Hoped. Not knew. I didn't correct him, just watched him come closer, my heartbeat speeding. He wore a white shirt, one sleeve torn, dark trousers, soft boots. But my focus was on the night-lit-water shade of his eyes. On the heat warming that color to something fierce. Something undeniable. The fire that lived in the depths of his power called to me, as did the man himself.

He stopped maybe a foot away and sketched a bow. "My lady. Do you like my flowers?"

I looked down at the shimmering blooms. "They're beautiful."

He smiled at that and I knew at that moment that the rest was inevitable.

"My lady, do you perhaps like me?"

The flowers fell from my hands, the words catching in my throat, seemingly too big to utter. Instead I moved closer and pulled him to me. Brought his mouth down on mine.

And learned what fire truly was.

Finally, near midday on the fourth day after Asharic's return, a messenger arrived. Not my uncle this time, but Hennin, one of the guards who had served my Family for longer than I had been alive, was the courier. I had never seen him set foot outside Summerdale, and I caught myself before I could express my startlement in a way that would only embarrass him.

The envelope he carried was sealed with both my father's seal and his magic, the night-dark blue sheen of it floating around the paper like fog. My father's magic always felt heavy to me, like the air on a hot summer's night. Weighty. Hard to move. Prone to storms.

I took the envelope and smiled my thanks at Hennin. "Did you come alone?"

He nodded.

Interesting. Then again, my father's logic would be that either Hennin, skilled warrior that he was, would manage the journey with ease or, if he didn't, then, well, he was only a servitor after all.

I sometimes loathed my father more than I could express.

"Can I get you some refreshment? Tea?"

Hennin, predictably, refused. Maybe I could send him down to the hospital kitchens before he returned. He might not accept food from me here in my office, where he would feel as though he was on duty with one of the Family he served, but perhaps he would bend enough to eat down there.

Or maybe he just wanted to be gone. I studied him for a moment. There was a faint sheen of sweat on his forehead, more than just the warmth of the day and his ride from Summerdale would explain.

"Is the iron paining you?" I asked.

Hennin set his teeth. "I'm fine, my lady."

I shook my head. "I'm a Master Healer. You're not fine. Please sit. Take that as an order, if it makes it easier."

He glared at me but sank into a chair. I nodded approval. "Good." I came around to him and rested a hand on his shoulder. He twitched under the touch but didn't pull away completely. I extended my powers and scanned him quickly. Sure enough, the sense of his own magic was subdued. Drained by the unfamiliar presence of so much iron.

"I can do something to help with that," I said. "It's only temporary but it will last until you're back in Summerdale."

I closed my eyes and wove the ward with the speed of familiarity. It wasn't something I used regularly but often enough. It provided respite for new Fae healers when they first came to St. Giles, let them do their jobs while they adjusted to the City enough to be able to bear the iron with a certain degree of ease. My own tolerance to iron had strengthened over time, but there were parts of the City and the hospital that were harder to be in than others. The hidden wards below the hospital, for instance.

Hennin's shoulder relaxed beneath my hand and I drew away, taking a moment to breathe and steady myself. Then I rang for tea. I needed it, even if Hennin was going to refuse to drink with me. That done, I seated myself before reaching for my father's letter once more.

The wards yielded to the touch of my hand, recognizing my power and the presence of the Family ring on my finger, the combination working to unlock the protection my father had set.

I unfolded the paper and steeled myself for the refusal I expected.

Instead, to my shock and relief, it was an acceptance. Or a summons perhaps. I was to present myself with five companions suitable to represent the humans at the Gate in a day's time.

I looked up at Hennin. "Do you know what this says?" I asked, curious as to whether the invitation came from my father or the court. If it was the court, then gossip should have spread by now and Hennin would know about it.

He shook his head. "No, my lady."

That was direct enough. So he didn't know. Which meant my father was inviting me and the humans on his own recognizance. It made me uneasy as to exactly what he was planning and what good it might do if we got to Summerdale and the court still would not hear us. With the Veiled Queen dead, no one could actually bar us from entering the Veiled World. It was what happened once we were there that was the worrying thing to contemplate.

"I'm coming with you." Asharic loomed up beside me as I left the Templar conference room, the humans inside still discussing my news and trying to decide who they would send to accompany me.

"Two days ago you were doing your best to avoid returning to Summerdale," I said. "Why do you want to go now?"

"Safety in numbers," he said with a grin.

"You're expecting my father to protect you?" I asked. "Trust me, he's not a great believer in absence making the heart grow fonder."

"I was thinking more of Guy and you," he said.

"What makes you think that I'll protect you?" I said.

"Right now you need me," he said. "So you can't let them bury me under a hill for half a century or turn me into a weasel. No me, no army."

He had a point.

"Sounds to me like it would be more sensible for you to stay here. Why take the risk?"

"Well, for one thing, I'd like to know what your father is up to," he said. "And I don't think it's wise for you to go with only human company either."

"I'm sure Holly or Fen will be coming with us," I said.

"They're both *hai-salai*," he said. "Powerful or not, they can't stand against a Fae for you."

True. And I didn't think either of them would be keen to go back to Summerdale. They had both suffered there. Gained something too, but they'd both paid a price.

I wondered if I would have to pay too, to get what I wanted. The Fae without a ruler would be fractious and fractured and capricious. Getting them to pull in one direction would be harder than herding the City's entire population of cats. Perhaps they'd already found a candidate for the Veil. Perhaps that was why Father had relented: he wanted me to be home for that.

I doubted things would be that simple, but I couldn't argue with Ash's logic. Two of us were better than one when it came to standing against the will of the court, sundered though it might be.

I shivered suddenly, wondering if it was crazy to go anywhere near Summerdale.

But there was no other choice if we wanted to have any chance at averting a war. And that was worth whatever price Summerdale might exact.

The Gate to the Veiled World was a tall marble tower that seemingly went up and up and up for hundreds of feet. I'd never been sure exactly how tall it was. It was entirely possible that it was only a few stories high and the rest of it was carefully shielded glamour to make it appear more imposing than it actually was. Glamour and misdirection are the lifeblood of the court, used to scheme and fool and gain advantage. The tower was a timely reminder of that.

I'd lived with human politics for thirty years and had followed, as much as possible, the goings-on in the Veiled World and, from time to time, returned for short periods, but it wasn't the same as living there full-time. I hoped my old instincts would rise again, honed to sharpness by a childhood spent at my father's knee, being drilled and inculcated with the ins and outs of court survival. Fae politics were ruthless and at times deadly.

And without a queen at the head of the Court to curb the worst of the excesses and impose suitable punishments on those who overstepped, it was going to be worse than usual.

I had spent much of the hours we'd had to prepare for the journey trying to impress that fact on my companions. Guy and Liam were here, representing the Templars and the sunmages. Simon was needed at St. Giles and to help power the sunlamps at the borders. The Guild had wanted to send another of their senior mages, but Liam had been to Summerdale before with me and I thought it would be easier to take someone the Fae were familiar with.

For that reason, I had also brought Robert Abernathy from the human council, Fen, and, still mostly against my will, Ash.

Fen had protested bitterly, claiming that he was persona non grata amongst the court. And that was true, but he was also the sole person from the City who'd recently spent time in the court prior to the queen dying.

Plus, he could see the future.

Both his knowledge of current court politics and his power might make the difference to us succeeding or failing. When he'd finally agreed to come, he'd tried to shoehorn Saskia DuCaine into our delegation as well, but he didn't need her to control his power any longer, and with limited numbers I'd put my foot down, backed up by Guy, who was more than happy to have his little sister excluded from the trip.

In her stead, the metalmages had sent Master Columbine, who had spent time with the Fae smiths in the past and was therefore another human well qualified to negotiate some of the perils of our world. She hadn't said much during our journey, spending the time perched sedately on the carriage seats observing everything around her with bright blue eyes that missed nothing.

The others hung back and let me be the one to approach the door to the Gate. I had expected as much. I was to take the lead. I only hoped they would all remember that once we were inside. Especially Ash.

I lifted my hand and the door swung inward before I could even knock, leaving me face-to-face with the Seneschal. Or the woman who had held that rank when the queen was alive. It was a role appointed by the queen. Technically, it ended when the reign of the queen ended, just like Ash's exile. But it seemed that no one had gotten around to replacing her, or perhaps, in these uncertain times, was willing to challenge the Seneschal's long experience and mastery of the Gate's defensive magics.

"Bryony sa'Eleniel," she said, looking down at me with eyes like smoked ice. Her white hair was bound back from her face with bands of black pearls. They matched the black silk robe draped over her usual white dress. Mourning garb. I glanced down at my own dark gray dress. Hopefully it would pass muster. Black wasn't required for anything other than the funeral of the queen and official court functions.

Attending the door was an official court function for the

Seneschal, so I guess she had no choice. I nodded and bowed politely. The Seneschal wasn't my favorite person in the court, but she had served the queen faithfully and well, and deserved my respect now in her time of grief.

"My father has extended an invitation to the people who accompany me. I trust you were informed."

Her lips thinned slightly but she nodded. Apparently my father had been his usual autocratic self when he'd issued the instructions that I, and whoever I brought with me, should be admitted.

The Seneschal stepped back from the door and I turned and beckoned the others forward. As Guy stepped across the threshold, he bowed respectfully and got a slight nod in return. So she liked him at least. She didn't pay much attention to Liam, Robert, or Master Columbine. Then Fen entered the room and her face turned thunderous.

I held up a hand to cut her off. "Fen had nothing to do with the queen's death."

"He failed to protect her," she snapped.

"So did every other Fae on that field," I replied. "He is part of my party. Unless the court has banned him." That would require unanimous agreement amongst the High Families. I hadn't heard that any such edict had been issued; besides which, they were surely too busy squabbling amongst themselves to actually stop and agree on anything right now.

"No," she said tightly. She narrowed her eyes at Fen. "Do you bear iron?"

He bowed and then shook his head when he straightened. "No," he said gently. "The queen—*asai'hara nea ai*—well, her grace holds and I have no further need of iron. My heart shares your sorrow."

May the starlight sing her memory. It was nicely said of Fen—I wondered who had taught him that particular phrase—but it didn't seem to improve the Seneschal's attitude toward him any. Still, I gave Fen points for behaving and not doing anything to make the situation worse. He looked around the round room with something close to dislike on his face, carefully keeping his gaze, I noticed, from landing on the doors that would let us through to the Veiled World.

Asharic had stayed outside while this little exchange had taken place, but now he too stepped over the threshold. This time, the Seneschal's mouth dropped open, though she recovered quickly. "Asharic sa'Uriel'pellar," she managed after staring a moment longer. "You have returned."

"My exile has ended," he said. "Though the reason for it brings me no happiness. *Asai'hara nea ai*."

This earned him a small smile. So it seemed the Seneschal was not one of those who had been arrayed against Ash back then. In truth, I didn't remember the details of his banishment overly clearly. Only, the grief and rage that had burned within me from the moment he'd decided to accept Stellan's challenge. I remembered the queen's veils swirling gray around her as she pronounced the exile and the unyielding stone of her voice but little about anyone else at the court that day. I'd barely managed to stay upright and then I'd left with Ash, desperate to spend what little time we had left together.

Only to fight with him when he begged me to go with him and I refused.

The memory shone suddenly too bright in my mind, and my hand strayed to my chest, rubbing absently above my heart, as though to ease the remembered pain.

Fen shot me a sudden look, eyebrows arched above bright green eyes, and I dropped my hand back to my side.

Asharic moved to stand near Guy rather than me, which I appreciated. It was strange enough seeing him back here, looking so different in some ways and unchanged in others.

"Will you let us pass, Seneschal?" I asked formally.

She tilted her head at me, eyes unreadable. "May your time prove . . . fruitful."

I blinked. It wasn't the traditional response, but I didn't really have time to try to interpret what she meant. Hopefully that she was on our side.

Maybe my father would know. I bowed thanks and the Seneschal opened the door to the Veiled World.

I went through first again, followed by Fen and the three humans. For a moment I stood still, glorying in the sudden rush of power that surged through me here where there was no iron to bar me and the source of our magic ran strong. Then Ash came through the door, and as his foot hit the ground, I felt the land shudder as though a vast bell had tolled beneath us. My power shivered in response. I quelled the reaction.

"What was that?" Fen asked, looking disturbed.

Ash shrugged. "Sorry. It's been a long time since I was last here. I'd forgotten the difference in our powers here. It startled me."

I eyed him warily. That wasn't what had caused that reaction in the land. It hadn't come from Ash at all. Even though there had been something in the rolling surge that had felt vaguely like him. Which meant, I assumed, that every Fae with half an ounce of sense might just have figured out who had crossed the threshold and returned.

"Welcome home," I murmured, and then steeled myself for the next part of our journey.

Chapter Eight

Ash

I didn't have long to enjoy the rush of power welling through me, circling and dazzling me like a pyrotechnical display seen too close.

Summerdale.

The feeling of it was both strange and as familiar as air flowing through my lungs. A sense of unfettered possibility. No iron to interfere with the pure song of the magic and the satisfying hum of the land beneath my feet.

I hadn't spent too much time in human cities, where iron pulsed as strongly as it did in the City we'd just left behind, but I'd spent plenty of time with armies. And a well-equipped army could have far more iron per square yard than the average city.

My own weapons and armor were, of necessity, Fae-wrought things. Alloys humans couldn't match that held the strength and sharpness of steel without the blinding bite of iron. But my men and my opponents most often carried steel weapons and as much steel mail as they could afford, to bolster the protection offered by hardened leather and lesser metals. I'd known the bite of steel a time or two. The first time—a dagger thrust to my side—had laid me low for days, my sense of connection to the earth and my power faded to nothingness as I fought off the burn of the metal. But over time, I'd become inured to some extent to its presence, though I still avoided direct contact wherever I could.

I guessed that Bryony and the Fae who worked at St. Giles had done much the same, extending their tolerance so that they could live and work in the City, surrounded by the metal that dulled their powers.

It had been almost thirty years since I had been in a place with no iron whatsoever for any length of time. There had been moments here and there, of course, an hour spent roaming far from my men on scouting missions or stolen away when we'd been between jobs to find a deserted stretch of land and just let the earthsong soak into me for a while. But even that wasn't the same as being home.

Here in the Veiled World. Where the earthsong wasn't a whisper, it was a symphony that whispered seduction in my ear and promised to do whatever I willed. Between that and the sudden pure clear access to every last inch of my power, my pulse pounded and my head spun as though I'd had too much good wine.

The last time I'd felt this good was probably the last time I'd buried myself in Bryony, our power mingling with our bodies until we were both swept away.

Veil's eyes.

I shouldn't let myself remember it. The sweetness and fire of her.

Not now.

Not when she clearly was of no mind to indulge in reminiscing, let alone let me back into her bed.

Memories were only needless torture.

But I remembered all the same.

Remembered the hunger and the pleasure of her.

Wanted it again.

Down, boy, I said sternly to myself—not addressing merely that part of me that was standing to attention.

Thankfully, my sudden lust was somewhat quelled by

the arrival of Bryony's father in a huge black carriage drawn by four of his elegant black horses.

Garrett sa'Eleniel was no friend of mine; I knew that for certain. He would be even less so if he thought I was already sniffing around his daughter again.

Though I was no longer the same young man I'd been when I left Summerdale. I'd learned a thing or two since then.

Not least of which was how not to give two fucks how my enemies felt about me.

Still, it wasn't going to make Bryony's life any easier if I went to war with her father here and now when she was trying to make peace. So I curbed my tongue and tried to rein in the desire heating my blood and turn my thoughts to the task at hand.

I wasn't entirely successful, but at least Lord sa'Eleniel didn't try to strangle me on the spot, though the look he sent my way would have vaporized me where I stood, were such things actually possible.

I bowed to him and stayed silent as Bryony drew him aside for an urgent whispered conversation. Apparently she won for the moment, because, apart from another basilisk-chilling stare, her father chose to ignore my existence for the moment and busied himself with greeting the other guests and then ordering us all into the coach he'd arrived in.

I held back so that I could sit nearest the window. I wanted to see the land as it passed, to see what had changed and what was the same. I wasn't expecting too much of the latter. The Fae shift and alter the appearance of their territories to suit their whims, and what is a deep and ancient forest one day can be a sun-drenched beach the next.

Still, the sa'Eleniels tended to be conservative and I recognized the blue, black, and purple banners topping the boundary stones when we passed into their territory.

I looked at Bryony, but she shook her head slightly and didn't speak. In fact, none of us spoke during the journey. Fen looked as if he wanted to be anywhere but where he was and Guy, Liam, and Master Columbine merely wore inscrutable expressions so alike that I wondered if they taught them in human schools.

Lord sa'Eleniel was apparently fascinated by the scenery passing by the window—he was in the seat farthest diagonally from me, thank the Veil—and Bryony, sitting next to her father, eventually closed her eyes and avoided the situation entirely by pretending to sleep.

She wasn't fooling anyone, but no one else dared to break the silence with her father perched like a giant black crow in the corner, seemingly willing to gut any of us if we annoyed him.

Mercifully, the horses ate up the miles as though they had wings and it didn't take long to reach the gates to the sa'Eleniel estate where Bryony had grown up. I recognized the gates all too well. The first time I'd snuck in to see Bryony at night, I'd climbed it in a fit of foolishness and ruined one of my favorite shirts when I fell off the other side—not to mention crushing the flowers that I'd brought for her. Not that she ever knew, unless she felt the magical repair I'd worked on them before I'd handed them over with a bow and she had kissed me for the very first time.

Her father hadn't been at home then. I wished he wasn't now. Then I might try sneaking through the gardens to her chambers once again, just to see what happened.

Bryony's eyes opened as we rumbled through the gates. I felt the wards bend and soften to let us through, snapping back as soon as the carriage was through with a ferocity and speed that spoke of a level of security that I wasn't used to in Summerdale.

So things were definitely uneasy here for one as high in the court as Lord sa'Eleniel to be taking extra precautions on his home territory.

The queen had been assassinated, but that had been beyond the Veiled World. What was there to fear in the court, unless the schisms and enmities had truly reached a tipping point?

I set my teeth, resisting the urge to demand information. Surely Bryony had the same questions and would extract what we needed to know from her father as soon as she could.

The coach drew to a halt by Bryony's house, which, other than being possibly even larger than I remembered, hadn't changed much either. The gardens had morphed a little, I thought ... more color and a hint less formality. Perhaps Lord sa'Eleniel had a new gardener. Or a new wife. Bryony's mother had died a long time ago and her father had taken only court wives since. Temporary alliances of pleasure or politics. Not another formal marriage in the way for our kind. The ones that are supposed to last until death.

Those are rarer amongst us. Given the kind of love that is required to survive hundreds or thousands of years together, that isn't really surprising. What was more surprising to me was the fact that Bryony's mother had loved Lord sa'Eleniel enough to agree to one in the first place.

I climbed out of the carriage first and came face-to-face with a dark-blue-clad servant who blinked at me, then clamped his mouth shut.

I searched my memory for his name and couldn't find it. Perhaps he'd been too young back then for me to notice. He didn't look terribly old, but he obviously recognized me.

I wondered if I needed to check my room—if I was to be given one for booby traps. The sa'Eleniel servants were fiercely protective of Bryony, or at least they had been and most of them had regarded me with much the same suspicion as Lord sa'Eleniel had, only tolerating me because Bryony loved me and their need to please her was stronger than their urge to do away with the young idiot who was seducing their lady.

As I'd expected might happen, we were shown to one of the guest suites, rooms designed to give those who stayed within them no good reason to go roaming through the rest of the house unless they were invited to do so.

Fen looked resigned as we settled ourselves on the couches. Or rather, Fen, Robert, Guy, Master Columbine, and I did. Bryony disappeared to go talk with her father.

"Same damned rooms as last time," Fen muttered as the door shut behind her. He looked up to where, instead of a ceiling, there was a blue sky with drifting white clouds and shook his head. "Gives me the creeps."

I grinned at him. "I've seen creepier things than that on a ceiling." And not just one glamoured by Fae.

"Lucky you."

I remembered that he'd spent time with the queen just before she died, so he'd spent time not here at the sa'Eleniel estates but in the court itself and even, perhaps, the queen's private quarters. I'd never seen those. Only her, the women who served her, and most trusted advisers did—or had—and I'd never been one of those. Nor did I have any desire to be. The thought of being alone in a vast palace surrounded by a handful of people I could trust and servants unnerved me more than the sight of the false sky above our heads disturbed Fen. I was used to the company of soldiers and scenery that changed because you moved through it, not because you willed it to alter.

But there above, even though there was freedom, there wasn't the magic freely stealing through my bones. I laid my head back on the sofa and let myself listen to its siren call for a few minutes, attention drifting as I just enjoyed the sensation.

"Not exactly the time for a nap," Guy said, eventually.

"He's not napping—he's power-drunk," Fen said. "All the Fae get weird when they've been away from Summerdale for a time and then come back here."

"It doesn't seem to bother Lady Bryony," Liam said.

"She's more used to it. And better at hiding it, it seems," Fen said. "Trust me, the power here is . . . considerable."

"Do you feel it too?" Guy asked.

I opened my eyes at that, curious to hear the response. I'd never thought about how a *hai-salai* might react to Summerdale. My Family wasn't prone to liaisons with humans, so I hadn't spent time with many *hai-salai* when I was younger. Don't get me wrong—I was sure there were a few sa'Uriel half-breeds around, but my Family left them alone rather than exploiting them as some of the other Families did.

Fen shrugged. "It's annoying more than anything. I can feel it, but it doesn't seem to boost my power much." His eyes turned a flat moss shade as he spoke, rather than the deeper vivid green that signaled his mixed blood clearly to any who knew what they were looking for. I wondered if he was telling the truth. Fen had more than Fae blood mixed with human in his case. He was, according to Guy, one-eighth Beast Kind, thanks to his grandmother, who'd been a seer like him. Or an *immuable* rather. One of the unchanging Beasts who tend toward sight and other unusual powers.

Not the same as a Fae seer.

Fen, who apparently saw the future, was another thing altogether with the mixed magics in his blood. Something the queen had found intriguing, I reminded myself, which meant he was powerful, whatever he might say about how Summerdale affected him. I should find time to talk to him, to learn more about exactly how his powers worked and how we might turn them to our advantage.

"How long will Lady Bryony be?" Abernathy asked, changing the topic. It was the first time he'd spoken voluntarily since we arrived at the gate. He looked somewhat wild around the eyes. I guessed he had never been to a private Fae residence before and wasn't exactly relishing the experience so far. Which was understandable. Lord sa'Eleniel wasn't an effusive or welcoming host, and it was clear that we were effectively stuck in these rooms until somebody came to tell us it was all right to leave.

The wards on the doors were almost as extreme as those on the outer gates, though I wasn't sure that Bryony had actually triggered them to keep us in.

Fen stretched back farther in his seat. "Hard to say. Her father likes to talk—or lecture. Could be hours."

"I thought we were going to the court today," Abernathy protested.

"We will. But the concept of a day is somewhat flexible here. Time can be manipulated," I said.

"Indeed," Master Columbine said. "So we should try to relax." She rose from her seat and crossed to the table where a silver tea service sat, steam curling gently from the spout.

She stopped for a moment, staring down at the pot and the simple silver cups that accompanied it, as though admiring the work. Then she turned back to us. "Tea, anybody?"

Guy shook his head. Fen also declined. But I nodded. It

was a long time since I'd had Fae tea brewed in Summerdale. And I didn't think Lord sa'Eleniel would be trying to poison his guests. Me, maybe, but the rest of them hadn't done anything to annoy him as far as I knew—barring Fen perhaps—and he couldn't know which of us would drink the tea. Or that his daughter wouldn't, for that matter. So it was probably safe.

Master Columbine poured four cups and carried them over on a tray, passing them out to Liam and Abernathy and me in a manner that told me she was familiar with Fae customs. She didn't quite have the grace—or all the precise gestures—that went with a Fae performing a true tea sharing, but her movements were pretty all the same.

I wondered how old she was. Older than Guy or Abernathy, that was for certain. Her dark hair, pulled back neatly against her head, had some silver threads but her face was mostly smooth.

"Thank you," I said when she had picked up her own cup. "This smells delicious."

The metalmage shrugged, holding her own cup forward to examine it again. "I didn't have much to do with the tea itself." She sipped, then smiled.

"Bryony said you worked with the Fae smiths for a time."

Her smile grew somewhat wistful. "Yes." She sighed. "Not long enough."

Across from her Fen frowned. "Saskia wants to learn from them too."

"They are the best at our crafts," Master Columbine replied. "They can help us make the most of our powers. Let us hope there is a return to peace so that she gets the chance to return to her studies." Her expression darkened a little, her gaze somewhat accusing as she watched Guy and Fen.

Fen held up his hands. "Don't blame me. She was determined to be part of the delegation before I even met her."

Master Columbine nodded. "I know. But you could have discouraged her."

"If you know how to discourage my sister," Guy said with a grin, "then the rest of my family will pay good money to learn the trick of it."

Master Columbine shook her head at him. "You DuCaines are too headstrong."

"We know what we want."

"That doesn't mean you know what's best."

Guy sat up a little straighter. "We've done all right so far."

Master Columbine sipped her tea again, declining an answer.

I finished my tea, savoring the last of the spicy green taste of it, and put the silver cup on the table. Sitting here drinking tea and discussing the DuCaine family wasn't exactly what I'd come for. I wanted to get to the point. Then we could return to the City and get on with the job we had to do there.

The sooner I got out of Summerdale, the better. The power was seductive, but that power also came with a cost in terms of politics and restrictions and obligations. I didn't want to get drawn back into the court if I could help it.

I wanted to see my parents and my sisters, if they would see me, but that was all the connection I desired.

I didn't know if it would even be possible, though I had no doubt the Seneschal would have shared the news of my arrival at the gate with little delay.

Which was another reason to get to the court and then get away from here. If my Family knew I had returned, so would my enemies. Thirty years ago they'd tried to kill me. No doubt they would try again. Thirty years was not long to wait for a Fae, not one bent on some scheme or other.

I'd never been entirely sure who'd pulled the ultimate strings that had led to my duel with Stellan, but I had no doubt that his mother, at least, hated me as she had back then.

I sighed and got to my feet. Sitting here doing nothing was chafing at me like an ill-fitting collar on a dog, and I had no inclination to play the obedient puppy to Lord sa'Eleniel's hand on the leash.

I extended my powers toward the wards again. They didn't immediately repel me. Perhaps Bryony hadn't sealed us in after all. "I'm going to find Bryony," I announced, and headed for the door before any of them could stop me. The wards yielded to my hand and I sealed them behind me. I knew enough about this house to avoid getting lost and getting into trouble, but the others didn't. Hopefully they were all wary enough of the idea of being here in the Veiled World to be discouraged from wandering around unescorted. Maybe Fen could undo the wards again, but I didn't think he'd try.

Once out in the corridor, I searched for the feel of Bryony amongst the multiple lines of power that sang through the air around me. It took a few seconds, but I found her, clear and cool, halfway across the house. In fact, I realized, as I got my bearings, I knew exactly where she was.

Chapter Nine

BRYONY

I'd been half expecting the knock at my door. Here in the Veiled World, I could feel Ash more clearly than ever. I'd felt him leave the suite where I'd left him with the others and move through the house like a signal fire in the night.

Damn the man.

Couldn't he even behave for an hour and wait for me to return?

The answer to that was, as always, a resounding no.

"You're not meant to be wandering the halls," I said, opening the door.

"No, but I did anyway," he replied. He spread his hands in a gesture that may have been meant to be placatory. "Can I come in?"

I hesitated. The last time Ash had been in my rooms here was the night before his duel. A night of memories I didn't want to revisit. Memories that had no power over me if I didn't let them, I reminded myself. I stepped back. "You might as well."

He stepped inside, looked around with an odd expression. "It's just the same."

I pressed the door closed, set the wards so we wouldn't be interrupted. The last thing I wanted was my father storming in to continue his lecture about my failures as a daughter and finding Asharic here. "I don't spend much time here. There's no need for me to change it." I looked at the room. The furniture in the receiving room where we stood was the same as it had been all that time ago. Low couches, a table and chairs, and a writing desk by the window. The upholstery was myriad shades of dark blue and green. Ash looked past me toward the silk curtains—in the same midnight shades—that covered the entry to my bedchamber and his eyes darkened.

"What do you want, Asharic?" I said, not wanting to let him travel too far down that particular path of remembering.

"What happened with your father?"

"If you'd stayed with the others, you would have found that out."

"How? You're hiding here in your room instead of coming back to us."

"I'm not hiding. I stopped here to get something suitable to wear to court. I would have been with you in a few more minutes. You need to learn patience, Ash. This is the Veiled World, not wherever you've been off roaming. There's a certain way of doing things here."

"You didn't like that way of doing things any more than I did," he retorted.

"Maybe I've grown up since then."

"Given in, you mean."

Temper flared. "You have no right to judge anything I've done or not done."

He held up his hands, this time definitely placating. "All right, sorry." He cocked his head, smiled one of those smiles at me. "Did you say something about choosing a dress? Want me to help you?"

"I'm perfectly capable of dressing myself."

"I know. But it's more fun to do it with someone else."

I scowled at him. "Don't."

"Don't what?"

"Don't flirt with me."

"Who says I was flirting?"

"Offering to undress me isn't flirting?"

"Flirting is playing," he said. "When it comes to undressing you, I'm deadly serious." His voice had gone low and rough and I felt the pull of it in the pit of my stomach.

"Please don't."

"Why not?"

"Because it's a bad idea."

He shook his head. "Don't you want to know?"

"Know what?"

"What it would be like between us now? Aren't you curious?"

I opened my mouth to deny it, but no words came. It was a lie. Plain and simple. And I couldn't speak it. No matter how much I wanted to. Nor could I think of any way to speak around it. It was too big. The desire coiling within me. The wanting.

I thought I'd tamed it. Buried it. Done my best to burn him from my heart and the memories of his touch from my skin. Thirty years. Half a lifetime for a human. But not for us. Not long enough for me to be successful, it seemed. Because for thirty years I had worked and slept and eaten. I'd made friends and run a hospital and tended the sick and, yes, from time to time, taken men to my bed. But it wasn't enough.

Apparently I had no sense at all.

Because I still wanted Ash. The cause of so much pain. Why?

Because he's mine, whispered a tiny, fierce voice in the far reaches of my mind.

I closed my eyes, did my best to silence it. And to silence the shiver in my skin his nearness caused. I failed. I opened my eyes again and he was still smiling.

"Don't," I said for the third time.

"Don't what?"

"Take us back there."

"Why not?"

I'm not sure I'll survive you a second time. I bit my lip, forcing the words back. "It's not a good idea."

"If it wasn't a good idea, neither of us would feel this way. We'd be able to resist."

"People fail to resist bad ideas all the time. I know. I see the results every day."

Ash moved closer. One more small—oh so small—step and he'd be touching me. I should've stopped him. But I couldn't.

"Do you really think it's a bad idea?" he asked.

"Don't you?"

"No. Like I said, I've been thinking about you for a long time."

"You want me to believe that you've been true all this time? Did you sleep alone, pining for me?"

His eyes darkened. "Did you?"

"No." *Not always* was the second part of that sentence. That much I could stop myself from saying. "After all, you weren't coming back."

"I'm back now. Things are different."

"It's still a bad idea."

"I disagree."

"You would. You never did have any sense."

"Not when it came to you."

"Ash—"

"Bryony—" he said softly, teasingly. "Are you going to stop running now and let me kiss you? Because if you're not, then I need to go set something on fire."

Say no. Say no. Say no.

"Yes," I said.

"V'lai'e'tan."

Thank the Veil. I had to agree with his sentiment. If not with his delay. "Stop talking," I said, and kissed him.

It wasn't like in a story. When the long-lost lover returns home and the kiss that seals him and his beloved back together is sweet and pretty.

This wasn't sweet. We'd never had time for sweet. No, what lay between Ash and me was wild and hungry and fierce. Consuming. He tasted like I remembered. Of fire and passion. Of dark nights and lost days and pleasure that was almost too much to bear. Almost. But I could bear it. I had borne it, and the memory of it, for too long now.

I drank him down and he drank me and I could no longer tell where I was or who I was or anything beyond the feel of him. Before I knew it, we were tumbled on the floor and his hand skimmed over my breast and I arched into him, wanting more.

I was pulling his shirt up toward his shoulders when there was a knock at the door.

We froze and reality crashed back like a cold wave. "Yes," I called, hoping I didn't sound as breathless and dazed as I felt.

"Lady Bryony, you have been summoned to court."

Fuck the Veil. A thousand curses ran through my head, but I was already pushing Ash off me. This was why we'd come here, and regardless of what I'd rather be doing, I had to take the chance now that it had come.

Ash rolled off me, his face a mix of frustration and wry acceptance. "Duty calls."

I hid my surprise. Once upon a time, he would have tried to keep me there, not willing to let me go until we were both satisfied.

Maybe he had changed.

I pushed that particular notion away too. He was being sensible because right now he was being paid to be sensible. He was still the one who had started this while we'd been waiting to be called to court. Knowing full well that this could happen. Of course, I was the one who'd let him do it, so maybe I had to absolve him of that particular infraction at least.

I could control myself. I'd been doing it for thirty years. I would continue to do it.

Asharic or no Asharic. I got to my feet, straightened my clothes with a few quick tugs and a tweak or two of glamour, and waited for Ash to do the same.

Then I crossed the room and opened the door.

·Ash

I had forgotten the size of the court . . . the way the marble that formed the floor beneath our feet seemed to stretch for miles in every direction. It wasn't quite that far, of course, but it was at least a mile square. Supposedly it was meant to be able to house all the Fae if they were summoned. I'd never seen that happen. What was more usual was that the High Families gathered here and the lesser Fae went about their business as much as possible, trying to avoid being drawn into the whims of the court if they could.

And now it seemed we weren't even to face all the High Families. The ten men and women who greeted our party, arrayed in a line in front of the empty throne, didn't represent all the High Families. Just the most influential of them.

Sa'Eleniel, sa'Inviel, sa'Uriel, sa'Namiel, sa'Liniel, sa'Seviel, sa'Kariel, sa'Anamiel, and lastly, sa'Oriel. Stellan's Family. And it was his mother, dressed in robes of the orange and brown and black of their house, who faced me now.

Salvia sa'Ambriel'imbril, who had wed Isak sa'Oriel several centuries ago and borne him a succession of sons and daughters. The youngest, and most beloved of whom, had been Stellan. Stellan of the copper hair and bronze eyes, who resembled his mother more than his father. Stellan, who'd been a complete spoiled pain in my ass but who was the light of Salvia's eyes. Those cool, cruel amber eyes that regarded me now as if I was a noxious thing crawling across her carpet.

Fair enough. I'd killed her son. Though that was as much blame as I would accept. She'd been the one in the background goading him on in his foolishness, and she was the one who had to live with that just as I had to live with what I'd done. What I'd never had time to find out was why she'd pushed him into the duel or who else might have been involved in whatever game she'd been playing at the time.

What was clear from the anger in her face, and, indeed, her very presence here, was that the game wasn't done.

I ignored her, shifting my attention to Lord sa'Eleniel and Maxim sa'Uriel. My father. Whose face was stony, as though he was determined to give no clue as to how he felt about seeing me, his wayward son, restored to the court.

I inclined my head to him, as was required, but didn't speak. No point making a move until I knew what he was thinking.

Besides which, it was Bryony who was meant to take the lead here. Bryony and the others who were here to try to get these ten to see reason and return to the negotiations. To try to stop a war. A war that I would have to fight if they failed. That had to be more important to me now.

No matter how much I wanted my father to show me that he was glad to see me.

Bryony wore court robes that matched her father's sleek black and sapphire. Heavy layers of velvet and silk and satin and looping ropes of jewels that meant she had to be more uncomfortable than I was in the robes that the sa'Eleniel servants had presented to me. They were in my Family colors but not half as elaborate as the ones worn by the Fae standing before us. For which I was thankful.

I was used to being unhampered by finery. Free to move. Free to fight.

Which I might yet need to do.

But for now I had to stay silent and let Bryony do what she had come here to do. She stepped forward, beautiful in the colors that echoed her hair and eyes, looking just as regal as the lords and ladies who waited to hear her petition.

She'd always been beautiful, but here in the court, she shone somehow. Or maybe that was just my alarming degree of sensitivity to her presence. I could still taste her kisses. Still wished to no little degree that we were back in her room and that no one had interrupted us.

Wished that that dark hair was loose and flowing over my skin so the scent of her surrounded me as we moved together.

Pay attention.

I wrenched my thoughts back. The court was no place to

lose concentration. Such a lapse could be deadly if things turned ugly.

Bryony curtseyed gracefully, straightened, and began to speak. Out of deference for those who'd come with us, she didn't speak Fae. The long, flowery phrases of greeting sounded slightly odd to my ear in the human tongue, but she made them sound weighty and respectful nonetheless.

Not that it appeared to make any difference to those listening to her. Most of them, like my father, held their faces to a bland court default of polite attention, not a flicker of emotion showing in their eyes or postures. It was almost as though she were addressing a row of finely dressed statues. Or it would have been if it wasn't for the three who were not quite so controlled.

Salvia was watching Bryony now, rather than me, but that didn't abate the anger in her eyes. Two down from her, Beran sa'Liniel looked curious. And tired. He was of the queen's Family—the sa'Liniels were the most closely linked with my own Family—and must be bearing quite a weight now that she'd gone. The queen, of course, had no allegiance to any Family once she assumed the throne, but that didn't mean that she cut ties completely, and even remote as she had been, obviously her Family—those members who were old enough to have known her before she'd come to power— had loved her. Beran had been the queen's cousin, the closest thing she'd had to a sibling, given that her parents, who had both died when she was younger than I was now, had only borne one child.

Maybe just as well. Given the power that had sprung to life in their only offspring, it was best that they hadn't had any more who might have been equally strong. That would have only caused strife in the court, where strength was the ultimate decider of authority.

If the rulers are not the strongest of the Fae, then they cannot control the court and the Veiled World.

And that can only spell disaster.

Beran's green gaze met mine as I studied him, and I made sure my face was calm. He raised one eyebrow slightly but then turned his attention back to Bryony. There were a thousand possible interpretations for that gesture, so I didn't bother trying to parse it just then. As far as I knew, he was no enemy of mine. My exile hadn't been personal; it had been the queen's only option under our law.

Fighting to the death is only allowed in challenges to decide a question of truth. Otherwise you are meant to fight to wound and stop at first blood or when one of the combatants yielded. If Stellan and I had fought at court as we were supposed to, our duel maybe would have followed those rules. But he'd insisted on the challenge being fought elsewhere and had made it clear from the first blow that he intended that I wouldn't leave alive.

Pity that he wasn't quite as good a swordsman as he'd been led to believe.

Not as good as me, at the last.

I took no pleasure in it. I hadn't wanted to kill him, but neither was I going to let him kill me. And in the heat of defending my life I hadn't thought of the consequences.

Not until I was standing over Stellan's body, staring at Tomar's horrified face, and realizing what the punishment was likely to be.

Consequences that would be more far reaching than I could have imagined.

Consequences that had taken me far away from this place and shown me strange things I might never have known.

Consequences that had cut me off from the people I loved. And now they'd brought me back again.

And it was as though no time had passed at all.

I was the one who left. I'd gotten away from the Veiled World and all that came with it, but everyone else had stayed. And had to deal with what I'd left behind.

Perhaps I'd gotten the better end of that bargain after all.

Bryony was still talking, spelling out the situation in the City, facts I'm sure the Fae were well aware of. She spoke of numbers and the humans and the increasing violence of the Blood. She spoke eloquently and made her case with determination. She was, after all, her father's daughter. And no child of Garrett sa'Eleniel would quail at speaking before the court. Particularly not under his eagle eye.

I let the words wash over me. I knew what she was saying. What was more important was to understand how those words were being received. To see if she could reach beyond those Fae facades and get to the people below. I didn't think she had much chance of swaying Salvia.

Not if giving assistance to the humans meant doing something that would provide even one ounce of assistance to me.

Beran's attention was on Bryony, no more eye contact to be had. Which left me with the other member of the court who was showing some hint of emotion.

Not anger. Not curiosity. Something closer, perhaps to alarm. Or worry. I didn't quite know how to read the emotion on Alar sa'Inviel's face. He had studied Guy for a long time when we first arrived. Guy, who'd killed Holly's father, Cormen sa'Inviel'astar. Who was an offshoot from a lower branch of the Family but still part of the house nonetheless.

Though, given that Holly and Guy had accused Cormen of treason against the queen and Cormen had chosen to fight to defend his honor rather than speak a word to deny it, perhaps Alar wasn't going to show what he thought of Guy's actions. With the queen so clearly betrayed now, it wouldn't do to demonstrate any sign that he had favored whatever plot Cormen had been involved in.

Which made me wonder what exactly he was concerned about now. Being found out if he was involved, or something else entirely? I couldn't know. Not without knowing much more about what had been going on in the court.

I glanced at Fen. He was watching Bryony and the Fae, much as I was, his eyes looking faintly unfocused. I wondered if he was using his powers, searching the future to see what might be the outcome of what was happening here.

If only he was able to let me see it too.

Bryony finished talking and her father stepped forward. "Thank you, daughter," he said. "Do you have anything further to add?"

He was clearly addressing the rest of us.

Guy looked at Master Columbine and Abernathy and then nodded. "If I could clarify a few things—"

Alar spoke up at that. "I think Lady Bryony has provided us with enough information."

Lord sa'Eleniel turned slowly and fixed him with a look that would have made a wiser man fall silent. But Alar had enough experience not to be intimidated by his fellow courtiers. Or at least not to show it if he was.

"We know the situation, Lord sa'Eleniel," he said, his use of the title rather than Bryony's father's personal name, a sign that he was, for now, keeping to protocol. "We've known it since the queen was killed. I don't see what's changed. We have more important things to do here in Summerdale."

"I disagree," Aster sa'Namiel said. "We seek a new ruler, true, but what happens outside the Veiled World also affects us. Our queen thought it important enough to hold the peace for four hundred years. Should we deny her wisdom and throw that away?" She sounded slightly exasperated, as if this wasn't the first time she'd made this argument. Which was pleasing. It meant that at least some of the Fae didn't want to retreat into the Veiled World and abandon the other lands to their fate. The question was, how many more were there who shared those views?

Lord sa'Eleniel held up a hand. "We shall not debate that here."

Which meant not in front of the humans. I was beginning to remember the things that frustrated me about my kind.

"I will ask again, do any of the others of this party wish to speak?" Lord sa'Eleniel said.

Master Columbine stepped forward. "I do, my lord." She curtseyed. Not quite as elegantly as Bryony had but skillfully enough. "Lady Bryony has told you of how things are in the City. And, yes, you can withdraw and leave us to our fate, but you need to consider all the ramifications. Trust me. If Ignatius Grey wins this conflict, he will take no chance of a return to the old days. If the Blood control the City they will also control the iron mines. What will you do if he removes the controls over iron? If the City becomes a metal fortress? That will affect you, even here. If he extends the iron far enough, it could block your gate to our world. Maybe trap you here forever."

This started a babble of voices as four or five of the Fae interjected at once. The arguments went nowhere.

Finally, after several minutes of furious debate, Lord sa'Eleniel thumped his cane again. "Thank you, Master Columbine. If there is nothing else, we shall consider your words and return to give you our verdict in due course."

"Wait."

The words were like a whip crack, my father's voice—strange to my ears after all this time. I moved forward, then stopped myself.

Lord sa'Inviel turned, his head cocked. "Lord sa'Uriel?"

"I would like to hear what Asharic has to say."

Asharic. Not my son. Was there a message in that choice of words?

I watched him, silent. His eyes, pale blue unlike mine, which came from my mother, were unreadable, leaving me with no clue of how my return affected him. Or how my exile had. Things had changed in the time I'd been gone. He was now Maxim sa'Uriel, head of the Family, thanks to the death of his uncle who had previously fulfilled that role. No longer just head of the Pellar line. Which meant that I could be too, one day.

And that technically I should no longer be Captain Pellar, but I'd grown too used to that name in the last thirty years to contemplate the change. Nor did I want to be head of a High Family one day and spend my days mired in Fae politics and the administration of a Family.

The silence stretched. Apparently my father had said all he was going to say for now. I wasn't entirely sure how I felt about that. There was an ache in my stomach, the manifestation of my wanting him to give me any sort of indication that he was happy that I was back. But he just stood and watched me steadily.

Eventually Lord sa'Eleniel nodded. "That is your right." He turned back to me. "Asharic sa'Uriel'pellar, speak."

It was clear that he had little enthusiasm for the idea, but even if he had been appointed to run things at this meeting, he didn't control the court and he had to do as my father had requested and let me speak.

I took a breath. I'd imagined coming home. Imagined speaking to my parents again. I'd not envisioned it this way, giving a performance in front of the High Families, not being able to speak of anything that had happened or even how they were.

But if I did this well, perhaps there would still be a chance for that later. I'd wanted to delay, to not see my parents until after I'd fulfilled my contract with the Templars, but now, with my father before me, I didn't want to leave without being able to speak to him.

I made my bow, the courtesies of the court too deeply ingrained in me to forget, and then straightened. "I cannot add to the facts that have been presented to you," I said. "But I will say this. I have seen war. I have seen more of it than perhaps most of you in the time . . ." I hesitated, unsure how to say what I had to say.

"In the time I have been away from the court. War and the death and pain it brings. I have seen those who have failed to defend themselves or held off too long, thinking they did not need to be involved. And I have learned this." I paused again, taking time to make sure they were all paying attention to what I had to say. Even Salvia. "I have learned that you can't always go back and change a mistake. That you have to act when you have the chance. Because war brings change. And many things that can't be undone."

Chapter Ten

BRYONY

"Do you think they'll agree?" Guy asked when we were back in the carriage and on our way back to my father's house.

I'd thought that we'd be asked to wait at court, but instead my father had sent for the carriage. I didn't know if he expected the deliberations to take a long time or whether he was being cautious and making sure that I was somewhere protected while we waited, but either way, it was frustrating to be sent away like a child.

I shook my head at Guy. "I don't know. Fen, did you see anything?"

Fen frowned. "Nothing useful. When the queen was alive . . . my visions here were strong. They're still strong but they're confused."

"Too many variables to see clearly," I suggested. "With no one in control of the Veiled World, there have to be a thousand possibilities of what can happen here, let alone in the City."

Fen growled. "Maybe. Either way, I'm no help. I saw your father in a lot of it," he added.

My stomach tightened. "Doing what?"

"Nothing in particular. But he was in almost every scene I saw."

Damn. I hoped that didn't mean that my father was going to somehow wind up in control. He was strong, yes, but I didn't think he was strong enough to rule the court. Not unless he'd been hiding his skills for a long time. Or was going to take out all his rivals.

It was a foolish system really, this reliance on sheer strength to choose a ruler. Why couldn't we have a more sensible type of government?

I knew the answer. None of the human territories had a land brimming with magic as we did. Our ruler needed to be able to contain and control that energy for us all to survive. The queen had been a good ruler. She had brought peace and relative stability to our kind and the City. I only hoped that we'd be as lucky again.

"Well, if Salvia sa'Ambriel has anything to do with it," Ash said, "we'll all rot in hell before the Fae lift a finger to help us."

"She didn't seem overly pleased to see you," I agreed. "But the sa'Oriels are not as strong as some of the other Families, and the sa'Ambriels even less so. Salvia has done more than her share of scheming and made herself a number of enemies over the years. And she's nowhere near strong enough to become queen, so her influence isn't going to be all that great in the future."

"I hope not. She'd let the City burn in the hopes of frying me," Ash said.

Guy frowned. "Which one was Salvia?"

"The redhead with the yellow eyes," Fen said. He grinned at Ash. "Don't worry—she never seemed to like me much either when I was at court. So it's not just you."

"Does this woman have something personal against you?" Guy asked.

Ash turned to me, looking surprised. "Didn't you tell them?"

I shook my head. "It's not my story to tell."

"Tell us what?" Guy asked.

The carriage jolted a little as the road took a bend, and Ash swayed with the motion. "You know that I was exiled. Well, Salvia's son is the reason for that."

"You killed him?" Fen asked, sounding startled.

"He challenged me to a duel. In the end, he wasn't as good a fighter as me."

Liam's brows drew down. "I thought Fae duels were to first blood?"

"They are if you follow the rules," Ash said. "Stellan didn't want to follow the rules. And in my defense, he was doing his best to kill me." He rubbed his side absently and I wondered if there was a scar there from one of the wounds he'd received in the duel. The Fae healers had done a perfunctory job on him at the time and I'd been forbidden to interfere. The Fae don't usually let scars form. If Ash had really been sent away with wounds partially healed, it was a measure of the disgrace he'd been in.

My hand curled in my lap. Scars marring the smooth skin I remembered seemed like a sacrilege. But no doubt he had a few. He had healers in his troop but none of them full Fae as far as I knew. And no one else had quite our skills with healing. The sunmages were strong and skilled, but the strongest of them were unlikely to be the kind of men and women who take up life with a mercenary army.

And I was suddenly, horribly, curious to see exactly where those scars might be. To learn a new map of his body.

Which was madness and I pushed away the sudden heat that threatened to fog my good sense into nothingness. I'd let him kiss me earlier. Maybe I would've let him do more than that if we hadn't been interrupted, but that had been a temporary lapse of reason.

I knew better now than to let him get his hands on me again.

The carriage jolted again, a small bump and then a larger one. I started to lean toward the window to see exactly what path the driver was taking us on for the ride to be so rough, but then Fen yelled and dragged me back and the road in front of us exploded, sending the carriage tumbling like a child's toy.

I saw stars as my head hit the edge of the seat, but somehow Fen's grip kept me from falling too hard against anything else as the carriage flipped once, twice, and then crashed to a stop.

I lay stunned, staring up at the sky, which showed clearly through what remained of one of the windows. I blinked, trying to make sense of it. Why was the window above me? I couldn't seem to quite make my brain work.

Ash's face leaned into view, his face bloodied. He peered at me, then touched my shoulder. "Bryony, we have to get out of the carriage."

Around me, I heard a variety of groans and Guy's voice asking if everyone was all right. I blinked again, aware of a pain in my arm, and then there was a bright burst of power and the side of the carriage vanished in a flash of heat.

"Everybody out," Ash ordered. His hand closed around mine and he pulled me forward toward the exit he'd made. Guy appeared in front of me, already outside, and his hands were gentle as he helped me out. The shock of air on my face seemed to jolt my brain into functioning. I pivoted and stared back at the carriage and past it to the road. Where there was a gaping hole and where the horses lay dead, half tumbled into the pit.

"Someone tried to kill us," I said, somewhat stupidly.

"Yes," Guy agreed grimly as he helped Master Columbine out of the carriage. "And they might not be finished. Can you do something about that?"

I blinked again and sent my powers seeking down into the land. It answered my call obediently. Good. We had reached sa'Eleniel territory at least. I sent a call for assistance toward the house and at the same time threw up a ward to shield the remains of the carriage and us, anchoring it to two tall oak trees and a pile of rocks to form a triangle of shelter around us.

It wouldn't hold off a sustained series of attacks, but another strike would have to be very strong to burn through wards I'd set when standing on my Family's land.

Satisfied, I turned my attention to the others. "Is everyone all right?"

Asharic had a pad of some material pressed to his head, and Guy's face was blossoming into a bruise from just below his right eye to his jaw. Robert Abernathy had a hand pressed to his side, and Liam limped as he helped the other man to walk a few steps away from the carriage. Of all of us, Master Columbine seemed to have come off best. She was rumpled, her hair falling down around her face and the sleeve of her dress torn, but she didn't move as though she was hurt seriously.

So I would start with Abernathy and work my way through the others.

I took a step toward Liam and Robert, and Guy moved to block me, his expression strange.

"What?" I asked.

"Don't you think you should do something about that?" Guy pointed at my arm and for the first time, I saw the weird angle of my hand.

As soon as I noticed it, there was a surge of pain and my knees buckled. I reached for the power around me, but it didn't help.

"Asharic," Guy snapped as he caught me. "Do something. She can't heal herself."

Ash had been studying the carriage as though it held the secret to who had attacked us, but he whirled back at Guy's words.

Pain seared again and the sky spun around me for a moment.

"Shal e'tan mei," Ash swore. "Lay her down," he said to Guy, the words half a snarl.

"You're not a healer," I managed to protest as Guy knelt and laid me on the grass.

"I've learned a thing or two while I was away," Ash said. "Now be quiet."

I didn't argue. I was too busy trying not to scream. My arm felt as though the bones had been replaced by molten iron. Burning like fire. I'd never been seriously hurt before.

Ash laid his hand gently on my arm and I made a whimpering noise before I bit my lip to cut it off. "Sorry," he said. "Just a little longer."

Power surged up my arm. I'd asked my patients sometimes what healing felt like. Most of them described a cool
sensation ... the flowing away of pain and damage. This
didn't feel like that. No. Ash's power was fire, and for a moment, I felt as if he had set my skin alight as the pain blos-
somed into something even fiercer. But only for a second
and then the pain vanished with a suddenness that made my
head spin.

When I caught my breath again, my wrist was straight and
my arm was numb. I stared down at it in surprise.

"It's rough," Ash said. "You need a proper healer."

"When did you learn how to do that?"

"I'm a soldier for hire. Knowing how to do a bit of rough-
and-ready healing comes in handy. I'm not that good at it,
but it does in a pinch."

"You need more control," I said absently. "Too much
power."

"Did I hurt you?" he asked. His hand drifted toward my
arm, but he pulled it back before he touched me.

I shook my head. "It's fine."

"You should keep it still until another healer can look at
it," Ash said. "I don't know exactly what I did."

I could look and see, but better to do as he suggested and
wait for a healer to finish what he'd started. After all, there
was nothing I could do until then. "I need a sling. Cut a
piece off my robe. About three feet by three feet." He did
as I asked and fashioned the square into a useful enough
sling without further prompting from me. My arm supported, I let him help me up.

"Now we need to get back to your father's house," Ash
said.

I walked closer to the carriage. "They'll be coming for us.
From the house. We're safe enough. If there hasn't already
been a second attack, I doubt there will be."

"How do you know?"

"We're well inside the borders of my father's land."

"That didn't stop someone doing that." Ash gestured at
the carriage.

"True. But I'd know if there were still strangers around. If they had something set to let them know when their little surprise was triggered, then they'll have something that lets them know we survived. Which means we've called for help. They'd be foolhardy to try something now." I approached the carriage cautiously, stretching out my senses to see if I could pick up anything from the traces of magic. But mostly what I got was the echoes of whatever Ash had done to blow out the side so we could get out.

"Bryony, I think Abernathy has a broken rib," Guy called from behind me.

I shot a look at Ash. "I can't get anything from the carriage, thanks to you. Why don't you go see if you can feel anything closer to the horses?"

He frowned. "What if there's another charge?"

"Try not to trigger it," I suggested. "Surely a soldier for hire can do that much."

His smile was lopsided. "I'll try."

"Good." I reached up and put my hand on the gash near his temple. It had mostly stopped bleeding, but I could finish the job. I kept my touch light and sealed the wound, encouraging the flesh and vessels to knit back to their original form and drawing the swelling and pain away.

Ash closed his eyes and leaned into the touch. "Thanks. My head felt like a mule kicked it."

"It's just a little head wound. Go look at the horses. I need to deal with the others." I drew my hand back before I could be tempted into lingering, enjoying the feel of him against my palm a little too much.

"Yes, my lady," he said, and I rolled my eyes at him and went to see to Abernathy.

By the time a band of guards arrived from my father's house, together with half a dozen horses and another carriage, Abernathy's ribs were mended and I'd done what I could for the bruises and cuts the others had sustained in the blast.

Dario, the captain of the guard, bowed as he jogged toward us, worry clear on his face. "My lady. Are you hurt?" He stopped short as he took in the sling on my arm and bellowed back toward the troop of guards to send up the healer.

"Nothing too serious," I said as he approached me, consternation clear in his face. He was the one who was going to have to explain this to my father. I was glad that I wasn't in his shoes. "We were lucky." I nodded toward the horses and the crater. "Someone didn't time their trap as well as they could."

"We will find out who did this, my lady." His voice was savage. "No one can bring harm to one of the Family on our lands and not pay."

I nodded. "I'll be interested to hear what you discover. Don't let my father kill them outright."

Not until I had a chance to question them at least. For one thing, I was very interested in who the target might have been. Me? My father? Or Ash perhaps? As far as I knew, there hadn't been an attack on our lands for a very long time. And yet here we were, not yet a day after Ash had set foot back in the Veiled World, and I'd almost been blown to smithereens. Wonderful. Yet another benefit of his return. Though maybe that was unfair of me.

"Your father has been notified. He will meet you back at the house."

"In that case, perhaps I can get the healer to give something to knock me out," I said wryly. I wasn't looking forward to discussing these events with my father. He was likely to be in one of his rages. Even harder to deal with than usual. Not to mention that pulling him away from the discussions with the other Families wasn't going to do much for our appeal for assistance.

Dario nodded and then beckoned the healer forward. He was a young man I didn't know, but if he was in my father's guards, then he had to be skilled at his job. So I put my father out of my mind for a moment and let the healer do his work.

Ash

I had seen Bryony's father angry before. But I'd never seen him quite this angry. The ground, quite literally, shook beneath his feet the first time he slammed the point of his cane down and demanded to know what was going on as he appeared in the garden, having apparently taken one of the strange Fae ways back from the Court.

Each of the Families has a connection to the court that it can draw on for near-instantaneous transport if needs be. Most only use it in emergencies because the experience isn't exactly pleasant and it uses a hell of a lot of power.

But apparently Lord sa'Eleniel was in no mood to be delayed. I couldn't blame him for that. I was feeling somewhat enraged myself. Someone had tried to blow us up. It didn't matter who their target had been—though I had a strong suspicion it had been me—they'd been willing to take out Bryony and the others to get to me. And that, in my book, had earned them a one-way ticket to whatever hell they believe in and oblivion if they didn't.

Guy and Fen and I had waited for Lord sa'Eleniel, insisting that Bryony let the healers at the house look at her, and she'd taken Abernathy and Master Columbine with her. Guy had sent Liam as well. He was a sunmage after all and another layer of protection if someone had enough of a death wish to try something here in the sa'Eleniel's stronghold.

I didn't think they would—not unless the treachery had come from within the household itself. And that was enough of an unpleasant thought that I didn't want to even try to deal with it right now.

I'd seen Bryony in a rage before and it was akin to standing in the middle of a thunderstorm. Her father was doing a close impression of that now. If he struck the ground with his cane again, there was a good chance of lightning boiling down from the clear sky and frying something.

I hoped it wouldn't be me.

"You," he snarled as he got close to us. "What caused this?"

"Someone laid some sort of ward on the road," I said. I had puzzled out that much when I investigated the bodies of the horses and the crater the explosion had left. "It was designed to react to a horse, I think." Though whoever had laid it had been careless and not figured in the time it might take for a carriage drawn by more than a single pair of horses to cross the ward after the first horse had.

Either that or the hastily flung ward I'd felt Fen send up when he'd yelled in the carriage had been the only thing that had stopped us from all being in pieces right now.

"Did you recognize the magic?"

"No, sir," I said carefully. "There was no obvious trace of power. Nothing that felt strongly of any particular Family." Which only meant that more than one person had worked on whatever they'd used to set the ward or that the working had been done by someone from a more obscure Family—a very minor house or a servant even. It wasn't a complicated spell after all.

Lord sa'Eleniel swore, then fixed his dark blue gaze back on me. "You almost got my daughter killed."

"It may have been Bryony they were after," I countered.

"No one," Lord sa'Eleniel said, dangerously soft, "would try to harm my daughter on my lands."

"I've only been back a few hours," I protested. "How could anyone even know where I was?"

He cocked his head at me, then shook it disgustedly. "Anyone with half a brain felt you as soon as you stepped through the Gate. You need to do something about that. Or don't you know your own strength?"

"I—" I realized he was right. I'd been careless. I could've shielded my presence somewhat. But I'd never had to worry about such things in Summerdale. I knew the Veiled World carried the echoes of each Fae's power. The stronger the Fae, the stronger the echo. I'd felt the jolt of the queen returning after treaty negotiations or one of the rare other times when she left Summerdale. And I'd felt the comings and goings of other powerful Fae.

"Tchah," Lord sa'Eleniel snorted, and waved his hand at me. "You always were trouble. You need to watch your back, boy. And I'll thank you to keep my daughter out of your idiocies."

"Anyone who wants to hurt Bryony will have to get through me first," I said.

His fingers tightened around the tip of his cane. "I'd prefer that it wasn't an issue. But that can wait. Just now I have to see to the security of my house."

BRYONY

My father spent little time on niceties like knocking. He came charging into my room like a tornado, demanding to know if I was all right.

Saffron, the healer treating me, twisted to face him. "Be quiet, my lord. I need to concentrate."

I hid a smile. Saffron sa'Namiel wasn't my favorite person, but she brooked no argument from anyone when she was performing her duties, and I respected that. I also respected anyone who stood up to my father.

Behind her my father looked as if he wanted to blow something up. I knew how he felt. Now that I was home and the immediate shock of the attack was wearing off and Saffron had nearly finished her work on my arm, what I was mostly left with was anger. How dare someone attack me on my own land? Attack me *and* my guests. If my father wanted to take his revenge on those who had planned the attack, then he was going to have to form an orderly line behind me. And Asharic, I suspected.

I had felt Ash's rage like a banked fire all through the short journey back to the house. I wasn't the only one. So far Saffron had refrained from trying to extract information about exactly what Ash was doing back in the Veiled World from me, but the curiosity practically rose from her like steam.

I ignored it. Saffron didn't need to know my business and

anyway, she would learn soon enough as word spread of what had happened at court today. I saw no reason to speed that process just to indulge her taste for gossip.

She'd never cared for Ash anyway.

When Saffron finally released my arm, I flexed my fingers cautiously. No pain marred the movement. "I thank you," I said.

"So you should," she said tartly. "Whoever did that rushed job needs to go back to beginner classes."

"I'll be sure to let them know," I said, hoping Saffron would think that I was referring to someone within my father's household rather than figuring out that it was Ash who had healed me.

"Is anyone else hurt?"

"Only minor bumps and bruises. I took care of them." I looked at her steadily, waiting for her to suggest that she should examine them too. She was older than me and fancied herself a better healer. And perhaps, when it came to healing Fae, she might be. But I was the one who'd spent thirty years working with the humans and I knew better than her how to heal them rapidly and well.

Saffron, perhaps with a weather eye to my father's mood and likely tolerance level, merely nodded. "Let me know if you have any further pain. It's unlikely," she added as my father started to say something. "But still, send word if you need me again."

She gathered up her supplies and then curtseyed. "My lord, I'll leave you alone with your daughter."

Father didn't acknowledge the courtesy; he came straight for me. I waved him off. "I'm fine."

"Your arm was broken."

"Well, it's mended now."

"I will find whoever did this," he growled.

"Good," I replied. "Just don't kill them until you find out what they were up to. Actually I'd like to help with that part."

He smiled at that, as he always did when he thought I was being appropriately ruthless. "They were after the sa'Uriel boy, I'd imagine."

"Ash? Why?" I'd reached the same conclusion, but I was

interested in hearing my father's thoughts on the subject. He had a much better grasp of how exactly things lay in the court.

"He's a threat," Father said bluntly.

I hadn't expected that. "Ash? A threat to what?"

"You must have felt it when he stepped across the Gate," Father said darkly. "He's grown strong, that one. And there's a power struggle going on here at the moment. None of those who are jockeying for position will welcome any extra competition."

"Do you include yourself in that category?" I asked.

He laughed, though there was an edge to the sound that I didn't entirely trust. "I doubt I'm likely to be the next ruler of the Veiled World." He looked at me for a moment. "There are better candidates amongst our blood."

"Oh no, you don't," I said, standing to face him. "I have no interest in that particular prize. Besides which, I'm not powerful enough. So leave me out of your games, Father."

"You don't know what you're capable of. You've never tested the limits of your power."

"Nor do I want to. And anyway, the land didn't ring its bell for me like it did for Ash, so that should tell you something."

"It tells me he's forgotten anything he might once have known about containing his power," Father said. "He always was a fool."

"Don't—"

He thumped his cane. "You cannot be defending him to me. He almost got you killed today. Not for the first time."

"Ash didn't put me in danger. Your stupid politics did that."

"That may be an explanation for today but not for what happened before."

"What happened before is history. And Ash never knowingly put me in danger then either."

"No, he just encouraged you to be as headstrong and foolish as he was," my father snapped. He stared down at me. "Do not tell me you still harbor any of that childish sentiment for him. You cannot be that foolish. Not twice."

"What I felt for Ash before is also history," I said. It wasn't an outright denial. I couldn't speak an outright denial. But I could prevaricate with the best of them, thanks to the lessons I'd learned from the man before me.

"Good," my father said. "See that it stays that way."

I set my teeth. Answering any further would just worsen the argument. My father didn't like Ash. He likely never would. And in his current temper he would just do something we'd likely both regret if I kept the subject alive.

"Did the court reach a decision?" I asked, reaching for the only topic that I could think of that was likely to distract him from Ash. "Before you were called home?"

Father straightened suddenly, looking weary. "Yes, they did." Something in his tone made my heart sink.

"And?"

"I'm sorry, daughter," he said. "But they decided against you."

Chapter Eleven

BRYONY

Decided against you. My father's words were still ring-ing in my ears when our carriage halted in front of the Brother House. The journey home had been even more silent than our outward one. The dull, heavy silence of failure.

The Fae had said no.

They would not help.

They would leave the City to her fate.

Which left the question of what exactly we were going to do next. Take the fight to Ignatius or continue to play our waiting game?

I had a feeling that the Templars wouldn't want to wait. Which meant war. With all the death, injury, and destruction that would accompany it. Buildings would be ruined, fami-lies torn apart, and lives lost.

All in the name of peace.

It was a strange concept. Without the Fae, I wasn't even sure that there could be a lasting peace between the hu-mans and the Blood. Adeline was more reasonable than Ignatius, and perhaps she could hold the peace awhile if we succeeded, but there would always be another Ignatius waiting in the wings.

What we really needed was the cure that Simon was working on. A cure for blood-locking. Because if blood-locked humans could be rescued, the humans would be far more ready to take the fight to the Blood. And the Blood would be more reliant on human goodwill for their food supply.

The trouble was that, so far, the cure was imperfect. Simon had roused some who'd been locked from their stupor, but none of them had returned to what you would consider normality. They were still damaged, still reliant on at least a small supply of vampire blood to function and the care of others to make sure they ate and bathed.

It was a start, but it wasn't the breakthrough we required.

I would have to press him—and Atherton—into working harder. See if they could find the missing piece of the puzzle.

Ash handed me down from the carriage after the others had descended. Guy, Liam, and Robert Abernathy were going to carry the unwelcome news to the Templars and the human council. Master Columbine would inform the mages.

Which left me to tell the Fae in the hospital.

I'd agreed not to take it further than them just now. Not that that was difficult. There were very few Fae left in the City who didn't work at St. Giles. Most of those were long reconciled to being away from Summerdale, choosing to remain here for their own reasons and generally keeping themselves to themselves. If they hadn't fled by now, they were apparently going to stay no matter what the situation might be.

The humans needed time to form a strategy before the news got out. Handled wrongly, it would just cause fear and panic. It could even trigger the conflict before we were ready. I could bind the Fae to silence if I had to, but I trusted my people. They would give me their word to maintain secrecy and they would keep it.

I watched the others head into the building, Asharic standing beside me. "Aren't you going with them?"

Ash shook his head. "No. I'll tell my men once we have a plan, same as the Templars will. Guy and Father Cho will need some time to consider their strategy."

"You think they'll fight?"

"It's what I would do in their place. Ignatius isn't going to give up, and once he hears the Fae are out of the equation, then, if what I've heard of him is true, he won't waste time trying to press his advantage."

"War," I said softly. I hadn't been born when the last war with the Blood took place, but I'd heard the tales and those were bad enough.

"Yes." He looked down at my arm. "You need to rest. Let me take you home."

"I can make it back to the hospital on my own."

"I know you can. But I'd like to see you safe. Indulge me."

Bad idea. But I was tired and heartsick at the thought of what was to come and I couldn't find the strength to keep up my protest and send him away. "All right."

The sun was nearly down, and the gardens around St. Giles were full of the sounds of birds finding their nighttime roosts and the wind speaking through the leaves. I was glad of the green darkness around me, the feel of the earth around my feet, strengthening me.

Leaving Summerdale was always odd, to feel the contraction of my powers as the miles between the Veiled World and the City shortened and the iron started to close in around me. I could feel it settling over me now, like a familiar cloak. One that I barely noticed, except at times like these when I'd been able to shed its weight for a time.

I stretched my arms to ease the ache in my back from too long in the carriage. First above my head and then out toward the setting sun. Westward. Toward Summerdale.

"Do you miss it?" Ash asked as I sighed and lowered my arms, pleased to note that the one that had been broken didn't hurt.

"Miss what?"

He gestured westward. "The Veiled World. The court."

"Do you?"

"I asked first."

I walked on and he kept pace with me.

"Well?" he persisted.

I didn't have an easy answer to the question. Missing Summerdale was the same as the weight of iron surrounding me. A familiar constant that I didn't think about often. "I miss the land sometimes. My home. But not the court."

"You don't hunger for power? Your father must be disappointed."

"He is," I said tartly. "But I stopped worrying about what my father wants me to do a long time ago. What about you?"

"I won't say that it didn't feel good to be back there. To be . . . unconstrained. I'd forgotten what it was like."

"There is that," I admitted. "But this place has its good points too." We passed a bank of Lily's flowers, scenting the twilight with a faint sweet perfume.

"Still, there's too much iron here," he said.

"You should be used to it. You ride with an army."

"It's different. Armies don't have buildings."

"You must have been in other cities."

"Yes. But they're not like this one." He frowned. Turned back toward the Brother House. "It must be the Templars," he said. "The iron feels even stronger here than elsewhere in the City."

I thought of the hidden ward below the hospital and made an agreeing noise. Damn. Could Ash sense the iron doors that guarded the ward despite all the layers of magic that Simon and I had laid over it? None of the other Fae in the hospital had ever mentioned it to me.

"Is it the Templars?" Ash asked.

I kept walking. "It's almost dark. We should hurry."

He stopped. "That wasn't an answer."

"Well, it's all the answer you're going to get for now."

"A mystery." He smiled, his teeth a white gleam in the shadowed face. "I like mysteries."

"Don't you have enough to do without going looking for trouble?"

"I especially like mysteries that involve trouble."

"Veil's eyes, Father is right. You are impossible."

"Yes, but you like me anyway." He stepped closer. Too close. Too near in the falling dark and the soft air, with the first hints of starlight above us. This night was the stuff of lovers' trysts. Nothing that I wanted any part of when it came to Ash. Even if his nearness made the hairs on my arms lift and set butterflies floating idly through my stomach.

"Don't flatter yourself."

"Deny it," he challenged.

I stared up at him for a moment, then turned and headed for the hospital once more. There was safety there. Other people. Bright lights.

Ash caught up to me in a few steps, his expression shuttered, but he didn't press the topic.

Wise man. We reached the door of the wing that held my quarters and I set my hand to the warded lock.

The door yielded obediently and I pulled it open. Ash caught it and held it for me, making it clear that he wasn't going to stop at the doorway.

I blinked as I stepped into the hospital. The gaslights were burning and it was, after the garden, surprisingly bright. I hesitated, knowing that I really should head for my office, to receive the reports of what had happened during the day and what needed my attention in the morning.

And yet . . . nobody knew I was back. No one was at my heels demanding my attention. It was a rarity in my life and I was suddenly exhausted, having pushed myself past the tolerance for no sleep in the last few days.

Surely they wouldn't miss me for a few more hours if I just went upstairs and slept? Simon was here and the hospital seemed quiet enough. Just the usual gentle hum of activity echoed through the halls, not the sharper, more urgent sounds that would mean there had been another disaster or attack to deal with.

"You need to rest," Ash said, as though he could read my thoughts.

I hoped devoutly that he couldn't. "This is my hospital. It's my responsibility."

"And it won't fall down around your ears if you take a little time for yourself," he said. "You sa'Eleniels are too damned stubborn for your own good. You were hurt today and I know that Saffron healed you, but you still need to rest. Isn't that what you'd tell one of your patients?"

I glared. "Yes."

"Then why don't you take your own advice? Or do I have to carry you up to your rooms?"

"You don't know where my rooms are."

"Is that a challenge?"

"No," I said hastily. Suspicion bloomed. Had he been asking about me? "Do you know where my rooms are?"

"I could take a pretty good guess."

"How?"

"Do you think I don't know the feel of your magic?" He pointed upward and to the right, pretty much directly at my chambers.

"This whole place has my magic running through it," I objected.

"Maybe. But that's where it feels strongest."

I studied him, perturbed by this revelation. Just how strong had he become? The land had reacted to him as it would to one of the strongest Fae. My father had said that his return would bring trouble. I was beginning to believe it. If Ash was as powerful as I suspected, then the other Fae who sought the throne wouldn't leave him alone.

And the likely outcome of that was him leaving again. I couldn't see him wanting to be king, any more than I wanted to be a queen. If he stayed, he might just be too much of a threat to be left alive.

My heart squeezed. He would leave. When he'd just come back. I bit my lip, telling myself that I didn't care. But once again I couldn't believe the lie.

"Is something wrong?" he asked.

"Nothing that time won't fix," I said. Which wasn't a lie. If he left again, then I would survive. Mostly. "You're right. I'm tired. I'm going to go to bed."

"And I said I'd see you to your door," he said. He offered me an arm. "So let me do my gentlemanly duty."

"And then you'll leave?" I said hopefully.

He didn't answer and the butterflies quivered again. Stupid, foolish body. Why couldn't it see sense and realize that Ash was nothing but heartbreak waiting to happen all over again?

I sighed and tucked my hand through his arm. He wasn't going to leave until he'd seen me to my chambers, so I might as well just climb the stairs and then make a second attempt at getting rid of him when I reached the safety of my room. My wards were strong, and power or no power, I knew Ash wouldn't actually force his way through them if I turned him away. Not if he knew what was good for him.

The only question was, did I know what was good for me and could I actually close the door in his face?

The answer, it seemed, was no. We climbed the stairs and I unlocked my rooms and then Ash leaned against the doorframe, saying nothing but speaking volumes with his failure to leave.

"Tea?" I asked eventually. Tea was safe. I could still throw him out after tea. Feign—or rather not feign—fatigue and he would leave me alone. He was concerned with what had happened today. If I said I needed to rest, he would acquiesce and leave me.

And then I'd be alone.

The tea didn't take long. I didn't have the patience for a drawn-out ceremony, so I merely poured the water over the herbs with a basic blessing and left it to steep while I fussed with selecting cups. China, I decided, not silver. Make him think I had picked up bad human habits.

On the other hand, he might be perfectly at home with china. He'd traveled with humans for years, after all. I doubted many mercenaries carted silver tea services around to battles.

Maybe he would think I was trying to make him feel comfortable.

Veil's eyes. I gave myself a mental slap and reached out for the first two cups that came to hand. Which were, in the end, a pair that Saskia had given me. Pretty silver and bronze holders with glass bodies. She had made them in her first year at the Guild of Metalmages. And the life in the odd angles and twists of their shape spoke clearly of her.

I poured the tea and then carried the cups across to Ash. He was standing near one of my bookshelves studying the rows of books. Mostly treatises on healing, though there was the odd story amongst them. Some of my favorites from the Veiled World and some of the silly entertaining tales the humans wrote. He ran his finger along the spine of one of them.

"You like mysteries too, it seems," he said.

"In books, they're easily solved. And everything works out well in the end."

"Some things work out well in life too."

"Perhaps. But some things don't." I sipped my tea and sighed with pleasure as the chamomile and mint soothed my nerves.

I settled into one of the big chairs by the fireplace and drank some more, leaving Ash to wander around the room and do what he would.

"If you're going to roam about like that, make yourself useful and bring the pot over here," I said when I had finished the first cup.

"Nice rooms," Ash said, obeying. He leaned in, refilled my tea, and then nodded toward the silk hangings in the doorway to the next room. "Is that your bedroom?"

"That isn't information you need to know," I said with a shake of my head. "Sit and drink your tea. You should be worn out after today as well."

"No." But he sat and drank a little before he leaned over, put the cup down, and stood again.

I frowned up at him. "You should be. Why aren't you?"

He shrugged and crossed to the mantel, where candlesticks and pictures and a few other trinkets lined the surface in a messy jumble. "Maybe being back in the Veiled World after so long."

"Fen calls it power-drunk," I said. "When Fae get a boost from being back in Summerdale. It wears off quickly enough."

At least I hoped it would in his case. Ash was reckless enough without the added boost of excess magic running through his veins and making him think he was invincible. Or irresistible.

"Maybe," he said with a grin. "Maybe I need to work it off." He quirked an eyebrow, a challenge in his eyes.

"The Templars have a training ground," I said reprovingly. "You could go whack something with your sword."

"I do not 'whack things' with my sword," he said. "Whacking at things with your sword is a good way to end up dead. Sword fighting takes skill."

"You can go and skillfully wield a sword to your heart's content, then."

"Ah, but that's not the type of exercise that appeals to me right this minute."

I ignored the curl of excitement in my stomach. He was flirting. I would be immune. Stone. Not flesh and blood. Not—

"Cat got your tongue?" he said softly.

"If you want a cat, go see Simon and Lily. She has a kitten."

"I'm not interested in sunmages or wraiths right now either," Ash said. "Though one day you'll have to explain the wraith to me."

"Her name is Lily."

"Lily," he amended. "But you're trying to change the subject again."

"That's because the topic you wanted to discuss is of little interest to me."

"Really?" He came over to my chair, plucked the teacup from my hand, and then, in one swift movement, grasped my wrists and tugged. I came to my feet without meaning to.

Close to him.

Too close.

I could smell him. Still slightly smoky from the explosion, but mostly he smelled like man. Of leather and horses and fresh air and the subtle elusive scent of Ash himself. A Fae scent but something all his own.

A scent that seemed to bypass every last ounce of common sense I possessed and appeal to the primitive part of me that was hungry and demanding and starved for the things he was offering.

The fire that lay beyond the flirting and the charm.

The raw power of him and the pleasure I knew his hands and body could coax from me as easily as lighting a match.

He wasn't the only man I'd taken to my bed and he definitely wasn't the most recent, but he was the one I remembered. The one who floated through the dreams that left me wet and gasping when I awoke, teasing me with wicked kisses and clever fingers before he melted away.

He would melt away again now if I pressed him to go. I knew that. But right here and right now, there was a chance to finally have more than the memory.

To perhaps even drive away forever the ability of that memory to haunt me, with one last taste of the man.

A chance to finish things.

With clear sight and a wiser heart.

Or a chance to make it all worse.

I stared up at him, seeking something in his face that would let me choose one way or the other.

"Whatever you want," he said, "you can have."

The simple honesty in those words caught my heart. "And if I want you to leave?"

"I'll go. Or I'll stay. You decide."

"You and I—"

"Yes?"

"It caused a lot of trouble the last time."

"It doesn't have to. Things can be simple. It's just you and me, after all. Just us."

His smile was crooked. I'd never had much resistance to his smile.

"My way. Whatever I want?"

"Your way," he agreed.

It couldn't be a lie. He couldn't speak a lie. Which meant he at least believed that he would walk away if I asked him to. Maybe he was better at self-deception than I was.

But here he was. After all this time. And I knew I couldn't send him away. Not just yet. "Stay," I said.

The candles flared to life behind me.

"Show-off," I said softly.

"I always liked you in candlelight." Ash studied me for a long, slow moment, heat deepening his eyes to a nameless shade of gray. "I still do."

"You liked me in any light."

"True. I still do."

I drew in a breath, not liking the small happy pang in my heart that leapt to life with his words. "This isn't that," I said. "You agreed."

"I did," he said. "But that would be easier if I could lie."

"You can't. So don't say anything. Or we'll both regret it."

"A little regret seems like a small price to pay right now," Ash said. He stepped closer, touched a finger to my lips.

I closed my eyes, wishing that I could believe that the regret—and the rest of the price—would be small. But I doubted it. I couldn't lie, not even to myself when it came right down to it. I would do this thing and I would take Ash to my bed and let him ease the ache inside me and I would pretend that it meant nothing more.

And I'd hope that the Veil might offer me grace and let me survive him a second time.

I'd almost lost him back in Summerdale. A second or two longer and he might be dead. I might be too. And even though I knew this was a terrible idea, I also knew that I didn't want to go to my grave without knowing his touch again.

I'd denied the memories of him for thirty years. And now I wanted to store up some more against the years to come.

I opened my eyes, met the dark gray gaze watching me with a mix of tenderness and hope and fire that burned me to the ash he was named for.

"Kiss me," I said simply.

He took his time. Back at my father's house there had been urgency and fire and desperate, dazed chance taking. But now we had time and no particular risk of discovery and there was no need to rush through the moment.

Ash's mouth sank over mine like the brush of velvet

wings, tasting me gently, tracing my lips with his as his hands settled around my waist and drew me close with a pressure that asked more than demanded.

I sighed into him and did as he wanted. Did as I wanted. Moved into him until we were thigh to thigh, chest to chest, mouth to mouth. He was taller than me but not by much. I'd always liked that about him, the fit of us when we moved together.

He felt familiar, like an extension of my body. I remembered this. Remembered the hard lines of his muscles and bones and the harder line of his cock standing to greet me as my hips settled into him. Just at the right point to send the heat flaring a little faster through my veins.

But I ignored that pull of wanting, determined, as he was, to enjoy the moment. There had been nights I'd lain awake when he first left, jolted from sleep by the phantom taste of him in my mouth, the ghost of his hands on my body, and the whispered echo of his voice in my ears. I'd cursed him then, cursed my memory and the treachery of a heart and body that couldn't forget, but now, now I remembered as he kissed me. Remembered precisely how it was between us. The reality was so much more than my memories.

"Bryony," he said softly as he pulled me closer still. His kiss went deeper then, his tongue stroking mine, dragging me deeper into him.

I curled my hands into his hair and let him kiss me, though it was harder now to just stay still and not move against him. His hands grew restless at my waist, fingers tightening, then loosening, his grip moving softly as one hand began to stroke my back, fingers walking up the line of buttons that fastened my dress, as if memorizing their position for later reference.

I hoped he was paying attention.

Lazy as our kisses were, I knew we were approaching the point when they would turn more serious. Where we would catch fire and burn.

I'd always burned for him. From the first time I'd seen him at court, so bright with confidence and power that he drew the eye like a diamond.

I'd never met a man like him before. Not that he was the first man who'd shared my bed, but he was the first one who caught my heart along with my desire and turned it into something more than a shared pleasure.

He made me laugh, my Ash, and laughter was something not in ready supply in my father's house.

Disapproved of.

Much as the way that Ash's hand was stealing to my breast would be disapproved of.

I, however, approved heartily and let him do what he wanted. His lips drifted down my neck, finding every secret nerve along the way and setting them to tingling life.

Fingers over velvet brushed against my breast, against the nipples turned sensitive and wanting.

His hands were warm, hot even. His skin always felt hot against mine, as if he carried the fire he commanded within him. I pulled away, suddenly too warm in my dress.

"Take off your clothes," I said when he murmured a protest and reached for me.

That earned me a grin and an answering murmur of "whatever my lady desires," before he stripped off with a speed that made me blink. Maybe living in tents and on horseback had taught him the need for disrobing rapidly, but before I knew it he was naked before me and the sight of him stilled the hands I had reached to the neck of my dress to start on my own buttons.

"Oh," I said stupidly, drinking in the sight of him.

His body was different now. Harder. Stronger. The lean lines that I remembered were more ruggedly curved, though still sleeker than a human man's. His skin was the same golden brown shade, though, seeming to almost glow in the candlelight, the flickering light lining him in shadows and highlights that painted him into a living statue. A testament to the beauty of our kind.

And then there were the scars. A long curve of silver down his right thigh. Another arc along his ribs and a less elegant ragged circle on his left biceps.

The sight of them angered me.

Someone had hurt him. Could have killed him.

But at the same time, they made him seem even more tantalizing.

He was different now. He knew things I didn't know, had seen things I hadn't seen.

Once upon a time we'd spent every minute possible together and had few secrets. Now we had been apart.

What might he have learned in that time?

What secrets was he hiding?

One of them was the story of the tattoo that splashed across his chest, an elaborate spiraling design that covered the left side of his chest and spiked down and across to curl around the scar on his arms. Bold and black with accents of red and golden brown.

The colors of his house.

The ink matched the jewels glimmering in the ring that hung from the golden chain around his neck. I'd wondered where he'd been hiding his Family ring. He hadn't even worn it to court and I'd seen the quickly hidden flash of uncertainty in his father's eyes when he'd seen his son's naked hands.

For a Fae to hide his Family colors was to proclaim he belonged to no one. But despite Ash's not wearing his ring, here he was with the colors of his house inked into his very skin.

What had he been thinking when he chose that?

Was he defying or trying to remember who he was despite being sent away to fend for himself?

I stepped closer, hand reaching for him. I wanted to touch him, to see if he was changed beneath the outer differences. And if he was, what did that mean?

But Ash caught my wrist before I could reach him.

"Not fair," he said. "You're still wearing clothes."

I paused then, drawn back from the startlement of what his nakedness revealed to the reality of what we were doing as just the folding of his palm around my wrist made me want again.

I let my gaze drift lower than it had before. To the part of him that was very much as I remembered. Hard and hungry.

I smiled up at him. "You said my rules, remember?"

"So I did. But there's a lot less fun to be had if I can't get to you." He leaned in and ran his tongue against the curve where neck met shoulder. My skin quivered.

"Don't you want my hands on you?" he said softly. "I want to touch you. Want to feel you writhe against me. Want your heat. Want to taste you."

The heat spiraled up and through me then and seemed to dissolve every thought in my head. My head tipped back and he feasted on my neck, raining kisses over my skin that burned like warm honey, then sank into my skin, the heat blooming out and through me from each point his lips touched.

His fingers made short work of the buttons of my dress, and the heavy fabric sank to the floor with little urging from either of us.

Ash swung me up then, lifting me with as little trouble as he wielded a sword, and he carried me over to the bed. I still wore my underwear, but the silk was flimsy and transparent and the next best thing to being naked to his gaze. The heat of his eyes and the look on his face were nearly as potent as the touch of his lips.

I felt my objections melting away, my good sense melting away. Gone like ice met with fire. Vanished into steam and heat and the overwhelming desire to know more of the same.

I held out my arms and he set to work, removing the rest of my clothes. There was nothing teasing about him undressing me. There was no time for more tantalizing now.

No, just as I'd known we would, we'd reached the point where it was too much for games.

It had been like this from the start for us. A conflagration of two bodies meeting. Ash touched me and I burned and he answered the fire.

It was like a drug.

An addiction.

If this was what the Nightseekers gained when they drank vampire blood, then I could understand why they chose to give themselves over to it.

Pleasure. His fingers slipped between my legs, slipped inside me, began to move, and I saw stars.

"Ash."

His hand stilled. I reached for his wrist. "Don't stop."

He smiled then and his fingers set to work again.

Veil's sacred eyes.

"I've missed that look," he said, and he bent to set his mouth to work, helping those long, knowing fingers drive me insane.

He could keep such things up for hours—and he had done so—keeping me on the brink and begging while he played. And while we had the whole night, I was suddenly out of patience for long, drawn-out beginnings. I pushed his head away.

"Problem?"

"Not if you come join me up here."

"I thought you liked that."

"I do. But right now I want you. We can play later."

"Promises, promises." He was trying to keep his voice light, but I could hear the roughness that had crept into it and the darkness flaring in his eyes. I wasn't the only one who burned. Oh no.

I eased myself back up the bed, until I rested against the pillows, and then I let my legs fall open. Time enough for acrobatics and permutations later. For now I wanted basic. I wanted him inside me, the weight of him bearing me down into the bed so I could feel every inch of him as he moved with me.

It seemed he needed no second invitation.

He came up the bed and over me, pausing only to kiss me fiercely before he set himself against me, and I had one perfect second to glory in the feel of him right there, where I wanted him, before he drove home with a thrust that left no mistake as to where he wanted to be.

He groaned as I arched to meet him, wrapping my legs around his hips and my arms around his neck.

The fire took us then, burned through any last scraps of control. We moved together in a passion more like a battle than anything else. Desperate to get closer, deeper, harder.

Trying, it seemed, to crawl inside each other's skin. I felt his power flare around me, felt mine rise to meet it, and then felt the dizzying burst as they melded around us and suddenly it was almost as though I felt what he felt.

Almost.

It was never quite true.

Never quite enough, and that made us even more frantic. As though, if we only tried harder, we might somehow get to that point where we were truly one.

But the only prize to be had was pleasure, it seemed, and it was pleasure that boiled and spiked and drove as we gasped and moved and touched. Pleasure that built and built and built until it was nearly unbearable. And then pleasure that I surrendered to as it crested through me and exploded and left me boneless and separate once more.

Chapter Twelve

ASH

The rumbling roar shook me awake. I sprang out of bed on instinct, reaching for the gun that wasn't in its usual spot beside my bed. Because it wasn't my bed. It was Bryony's.

Bryony, who had snapped awake as quickly as I.

"What was that?" she said.

"I don't know. Stay there." I reached the spot where my trousers—and my pistol and belt—lay, grabbed the gun from its holster, and sprinted for the window. Gouts of bright light shot up around the gates of the Brother House. Flames.

Fuck.

"What?" Bryony said as she joined me. I noticed she had a gun too. Good.

"I think Ignatius isn't waiting for us to decide what to do." I pointed toward the flames.

"He attacked the Brother House? Is he crazy?"

"I don't know. But I need to go." I felt the fire licking at the edge of my senses, felt the burgeoning heat of it. If I could feel it, I might just be able to control it. It wasn't that far to the Brother House gates. I pushed a burst of power toward the Brother House, feeling the resistance of the iron close around me like taffy, but it didn't stop me. Across the way, the flames sputtered and died.

My hand tightened around the grip of the pistol. It felt strange in my hand. I still wasn't used to the silver alloy bullets the Templars had provided. They changed the weight of the gun. But I would adjust. I'd hoped to have more time to practice before actually fighting one of the Beasts the bullets were designed for. But I might have just run out of time.

Speaking of fights, I was doing no good standing where I was. "I have to go," I said. "You should look to the wards here."

She nodded, put her gun down, and started to snatch pieces of clothing up from the floor, shoving the ones that belonged to me in my direction. The chain at her neck sparked red and purple in the dark room. Angry. Good. Angry was better than scared.

I pulled on my clothes and boots, wishing desperately that we had more time. Time to talk about what had happened here tonight between us, time to see if it would happen again, but it seemed the few hours we'd stolen were all that we would get for now.

"I have to go," I said again, and left after stealing one more quick kiss.

I bolted back down the stairs, taking the route Bryony had brought me. It was stupid, perhaps, to go outside rather than look for the tunnels that connected the Brother House and the hospital, but there was no time to waste. Shouts and cries and the snap of flames—apparently I hadn't completely doused the fire—carried through the night air. The cathedral bell started to toll an urgent warning. What I couldn't hear was anything that sounded like a fight. No clashing metal. Definitely no gunfire. Was this just a diversion, the real action happening elsewhere? Or was this a first strike . . . a declaration of intent by the Blood?

Pistol in hand, I ran on and almost had my head taken off by the Templar guarding the gate in the wall separating the hospital and the Brother House. My reflexes saved me, sending me ducking just low enough to dodge the sweeping blow of his sword.

"Stand down, idiot," I yelled, with no time for politeness. "It's Captain Pellar."

The Templar, to his credit, stopped himself almost instantaneously mid–second thrust. "Sorry, sir."

"What happened?" I demanded as I passed through the gate.

"Someone set a fire at the main gate."

"Any sign of an attack to follow that up?"

"Not yet," he said grimly. So I wasn't the only one wondering what this meant.

"Don't let anyone else through this gate you don't know personally," I said. "If the healers come, send them back. Tell them we don't need them. Better yet, if there's a way to get word to them without using any of your men, do that now." If there'd been no attack, there were no patients and the healers were safer at St. Giles, behind its wards.

"A patrol is already on its way to St. Giles to guard the front entrance," the man said.

"Good."

I continued on my way, running toward the remnants of the fire. It was trying to regain a hold, sparking as the heat sought for fuel. I funneled more power to it, sending the heat deep into the earth where it was safely kept away from anything flammable.

Or usually. Once I had accidentally directed a spike of heat straight down into an underground armory. Which had been half-full of barrels of gunpowder. Luckily, I had done it from a distance and it hadn't cost me anything other than considerable embarrassment and reparations to the man who'd hired us.

I'd been fortunate enough not to kill anyone. So I'd learned to scan ahead of my power now. And I didn't blow things up unless I intended to.

Tonight, the urge to do just that burned in my gut.

I wasn't one of the Templars, but I was feeling distinctly territorial about the City right at this moment.

If Ignatius Grey wanted it, he was going to be sorely disappointed.

Another group of Templars loomed up in my path, but they recognized me before they drew their weapons.

"Is anyone hurt?" I asked. Quickly followed by "Where's Sir Guy?"

One of the men pointed toward the gate.

Sure enough, I could see Guy's blond head in the crowd of Templars near the gate, his face set as he barked a series of orders.

The gate itself was twisted on its hinges, hanging open. Which was an effective nullification of the protection its iron and other metals offered from the Night World. But it wasn't on fire, so that was something.

When Guy's stream of orders finished, he stood, hands on hips, and glared at the gate. One hand swiped smoky sweat from his face as he turned back to look at the nearest Templar.

"Send for a metalmage," he said sharply. "This needs to be repaired tonight. And where are the damned horses?"

Horses? "Going somewhere?" I asked as I reached his side.

He looked at me. "Lily says she can smell Beast Kind. We're going to see if we can catch a wolf or two. Find out what they were hoping to achieve with this—" He gestured at the gate in frustration. "She went scouting ahead."

"What if that's exactly what they want? To draw you out?"

"Then they'll be happy until they find out that Templars don't play nicely with people who break their things," Guy said.

I shrugged, accepting this logic. "Can I come?"

He grinned then, the expression somewhat feral in his smoke-smeared face. "Of course. I assume you had something to do with the fire dying out so quickly."

I shrugged again.

"They wouldn't have been expecting that. Let's hope they think the spell or whatever they used to set it off was a bit of a misfire. It would be handy to keep your ability quiet a bit longer."

"Any Fae who was around before I was sent away will know that I'm good with fire," I said.

"I'm hoping there aren't too many Fae talking to Ignatius," Guy said.

"Me too." I studied the gate. "But two attacks using explosions in one day is a nasty coincidence."

The cross on the back of Guy's hand flexed as he rubbed his jaw. "I thought so too." He didn't seem to like the idea much, but there was a clatter of hooves on the cobblestones before we could say anything further and a few of the novice knights arrived, leading strings of horses.

"You mind riding a different horse?" Guy said. "We can send for yours. . . ."

I shook my head. "Let's not waste time. As long as these beasts of yours will carry someone not covered in chain mail."

Guy grinned. "It will be a nice change for them." He jerked his chin at a big rangy bay. "Take Alfie over there. He's well behaved. The novice will tell you some of the signals we use." He turned and walked over to another of the novices who was wrestling to keep an enormous gray stallion—or so I assumed from his size—from tap-dancing on the cobbles. He settled when Guy reached for the reins, ears twitching as he let Guy mount. The huge horse and the massive knight were an intimidating sight.

The Beast Kind might be in for a bad time.

I smiled at the thought, listened to the novice's quick explanation of how to make my horse rear or kick, and then swung into the saddle and took up position on Guy's right-hand side.

We didn't wait long. A charm tied to Guy's collar—one I hadn't noticed before—flared into bright life.

"Lily," he said. "She's found something."

He sent the gray forward and I followed his lead. We cantered through the deserted streets, which really shouldn't have been so deserted. The City I remembered had bustled at all hours of the night, even in the quieter human boroughs. But now, it seemed, the sensible folks stayed home after sunset.

And what exactly did that make me?

Definitely not sensible.

The horses ran easily, obviously used to the slippery cobblestones and the twisting streets. Alfie wasn't quite so
smooth and responsive to my hand as Aric, but he had
power and speed and that was all I could ask for.

Guy led the way down another narrow street—we were
closing in on the border to the Night World now—and the
tiny light at his collar flared brighter.

Ahead, I thought I saw figures disappearing around a
corner.

I hoped they were our quarry.

We picked up the pace. Guy sent half the patrol on an
alternative route, to try to cut off their path. I wondered if
we would cross the border if we reached it before we caught
up with them, but it didn't come to that. We turned another
corner and suddenly found ourselves face-to-face with four
giant, snarling wolves.

Guy's horse reared and struck with a shriek of equine
fury, which was closely followed by the sound of a sword
slicing through the air.

I tightened my grip on the reins and drew the sword that
the novice had hastily stuck in the sheath on the saddle.
Guy was closing with one of the wolves, and the other three
were snarling and twisting amongst us. I spotted the nearest
one and swung as it bolted past.

Missed.

Fuck.

The wolf snarled over its shoulder and I kicked Alfie
into action and gave chase. The wolf flattened its ears and
sped up, heading away from its pack mates toward the far
end of the alley. Unfortunately for it, the rest of the patrol
were blocking the exit.

It turned so fast I would have sworn it had twisted in its
own skin and headed back the way it had come. Straight for
me.

Shit.

The wolf was half the size of my horse and its teeth were
huge in the gaping mouth as it closed the distance between

us. Two could play at that game, I decided, and spurred Alfie
forward.

A true Templar horse, he obeyed, and the wolf, realizing
what was happening, suddenly crouched and sprang. I reined
Alfie to the side and swung my sword.

This time there was a satisfying meaty thunk as it connected and a yelping shrill snarl from the wolf. But it hit the
ground and bounced back up, turning to face me, crouching
to spring again.

Hard to kill, Beast Kind. The sword in my hand was Templar steel, the ache of the iron making my arm feel heavy
even though my hand was well protected by the leather
wrapped around the hilt. It was a good weapon, but in this
particular situation, my own sword, with its silver and Fae
alloys, would be a lot more effective.

The Beast sprang again and we did another round of
twist and slash and parry, but this time the blow I landed
was only a glancing one.

The wolf had better aim. Alfie squealed as the claws
raked his withers and I cursed the lack of my sword again.
And then I remembered my pistol.

Silver bullets and all. Maybe there was more skill and
glory in sword fighting, but sometimes guns were better.

I dropped the reins, praying that Alfie's training was sim-
ilar to Aric's, tossed my sword into my left hand, and yanked
the pistol out of its holster with my right. As the wolf turned
for its next pass, I took aim and shot it through the back leg.
It collapsed with a howl of agony, writhing on the cobbles
as the silver, now lodged somewhere deep within its flesh,
burned.

After a glance around to see where the other wolves
were—and they all seemed well occupied by the Templars—I climbed down off Alfie and clubbed the wolf over
the head with the pommel of my sword. It went limp and I
added a ward around it that would hopefully keep it still if
it did regain consciousness sooner than was convenient. I
assumed Guy wanted the Beasts alive for questioning
rather than dead.

The bullet wouldn't kill the wolf, though he would have

a hell of a limp for life if it wasn't removed soon. It would take a larger wound or a hit to a more vital part of its anatomy for one bullet to kill, and I'd been trying to avoid doing just that.

Lacking anything to tie it up with and aware that the others were still fighting behind me, I sprang back into the saddle and headed back toward the fray.

One wolf lay on the cobbles with a sizable hole in its chest. There would be no questioning him. The huge furred chest was still, the yellowish eyes gone blank.

The other two Beasts were surrounded by nine Templars. They paced a tight circle, snarling at the knights, but made no moves to try to break free.

"This will be easier if you change," Guy said. "Don't make us hurt you."

The Beasts snarled again and exchanged glances that were far too intelligent for the beasts they resembled.

I pushed my way into the circle of mounted knights surrounding the Beasts, pistol still in hand.

"Silver bullets," I said loudly. "Hurt like hell, I'm told. Want to find out?"

One of the wolves looked up at me and howled.

"I don't think your friends are coming to help you," Guy said. "Not on this side of the border now that the alarm has been raised. So it's up to you. You can give in or you can do it the hard way."

"Of course," said Patrick, one of the other Templars, "the hard way is sometimes fatal."

The wolf howled again but then he sat back on his haunches, sides heaving. His companion paced for a minute or so, then, with a final snarl, came to sit by his pack mate.

"Change," Guy ordered shortly.

They did. It was a disturbing sight. I'd never actually seen a Beast Kind change form before, and the melting shifting shimmer of flesh and bone was unpleasant to say the least. For a moment I thought one of them was going to press his luck and stay in the hybrid man-wolf form that comes between human and beast and can be the most dangerous of all three, but he seemed to decide that discretion, if not the better part of valor, might at least equal keeping his head attached to his shoulders and completed the change.

Naked in the moonlight, both covered with cuts and bruises, they were less defiant. They were both taller and broader than most human men. The taller of them would've had a good few inches in height on Guy, which was impressive. In human form, they had dark brown hair falling to their shoulders and dark eyes—brown, I thought, though it was hard to tell in the shifting yellow gaslight.

"Hands on your heads," Guy said, and as the Beasts obeyed, three of the Templars dismounted and approached with cuffs for ankles and wrists.

"These aren't silver," Guy said as the Beasts watched warily. "But we have silver. You wouldn't enjoy those, so be sensible lads."

They obeyed sullenly, submitting to the restraints. And then, brooking no chance, the knights knocked both of them out neatly with a well-practiced move.

Well, sore heads would be better than no heads.

"Take them back to the Brother House," Guy said.

"What about the dead one?" Patrick asked.

"Him too. They don't like not having the bodies to bury. It's a bargaining chip if it comes to that."

Guy's voice was flat. All business. This was the warrior, not the Templar wading through politics. He played the civilized man well, from what I had seen of him over the last few days, but apparently he had decided that it was time for the gloves to come off.

"Should dump it at the border as a warning," Patrick said.

"It may come to that," Guy said. "But let's not rush into things. We want these three to cooperate. Tell us something useful."

"Get one of the Fae to make them talk, if they won't," Patrick retorted. He looked over at me. "You can do that, can't you?"

"A geas, you mean?" I nodded, hiding my distaste. "If I have to. There are other ways. Bryony would have something to loosen their tongues, I'm sure."

"She does," Guy agreed. "So let's not waste any more time."

"How do we get the wolf back to the Brother House?" I asked. The two in human form were easy enough; the knights were already hoisting them across saddles and lashing them into place.

In answer, another of the knights patted his saddlebag, then flipped it open and drew out a massive net made out of something dark that didn't resemble normal rope.

He tied one end to the horn of his saddle and then walked his horse toward the unconscious wolf. He spread the net and then, with a grunt of effort, he and one of the other knights rolled the wolf into the net. The second knight fastened the free end to his own saddle and the horses moved obediently sideways until the wolf lifted off the ground.

"Neat," I said.

Guy grinned. "Useful at times."

"Good horses."

"Yes. And yours needs attention."

I looked down at the gash on Alfie's neck. The blood had slowed to a trickle, but the muscles around the wound quivered. I could heal it roughly, as I had done with Bryony's arm, but I didn't know much about working on animals and I didn't want to risk doing something that might render him unfit for use in the future.

I swung out of the saddle instead. "I'll walk him back."

Guy shook his head, reached a hand down. "Not safe. You can ride behind me and we'll lead Alfie. He's a tough old thing."

I hoped he was right. I'd lost horses in my time, and each time it was a wrench. Fae-bred horses had longer lives than ordinary breeds but still only another ten years or so. Which made their lives fleeting compared to ours. Some Fae hardened their hearts and saw animals as merely useful tools . . . like plants or stone. Nothing to get attached to. But I'd never managed the trick of that and I grieved for each horse that was killed or grew too old for battle. I found good homes for them to live out their years when I could but it wasn't what I wanted. So I hoped Alfie would be fine and that I hadn't shortened his career with the Templars. Though really, maybe it would be better for him in the long run if I had. He could have a nice life in a field somewhere.

As long as the Blood didn't control all the fields.

We reached the Brother House without further incident despite the prickling of the hairs on the back of my neck as we turned our back on the border and headed back toward the cathedral and the hospital.

We moved at a steady pace, Guy and me bringing up the rear leading Alfie.

I was still trying to work out what the point of tonight's attempt was when we reached the gate.

There were several Templars standing in the street, guarding the space left by the ruined gate. And there were several metalmages standing by the gate, studying it by the light of half a dozen torches and several more sunlamps. One of them was a young woman with dark hair that gleamed reddish under the sunlamps.

At the sight of her, Guy swore and picked up the pace.

"What are you doing here?" he demanded as we stopped beside the gate.

The woman smiled up at him. "My job."

"Has Master Aquinas lost his senses?"

"Have you?" she snapped back. There was something about the set of her jaw as she spoke, the angle of the head, and the set of her shoulders as she stared up at Guy that made me think that this must be his sister, Saskia. The metalmage. The one involved with Fen.

Apparently she was no one to be messed with.

"It's dangerous out."

She snorted and gestured toward Alfie. "And you've been out for a nice gentle ride around the neighborhood? We've had this conversation before, Guy. You do your job and I'll do mine. Stop worrying." She turned back to the gate and frowned. Then she reached toward one of the twisted bars and suddenly the metal began to glow and straighten.

Impressive.

Not many women had an affinity for iron, from what I knew of the metalmages. In Guy's place, I wouldn't be happy that my sister was one of them, but nor would I waste time arguing with someone clearly cut from the same cloth as he was.

Still, I was no one to counsel anybody about family disagreements, so I contented myself with climbing down from Guy's horse and leading Alfie off toward the stables, leaving the DuCaine siblings arguing in the background.

"Almost home," I muttered to the horse soothingly as he snorted a little whilst we walked.

At the stable door, several of the novices and an older knight I hadn't met suddenly appeared.

The older knight looked at Alfie, then clucked his tongue. "Beast?" he said to me.

I nodded. "I didn't want to mess around with it after it stopped bleeding."

"Good," he said. Then he took the reins from me and led Alfie toward the stables, crooning under his breath as they walked.

A man of few words, it seemed.

And one who'd just left me with not much to do. I turned on my heel and almost stumbled over Rhian.

"Boss," she said. "Back in one piece, I see."

"For now. What's been happening here?"

"A lot of sound and fury." She looked half-amused.

"No follow-up attacks."

Her amused expression vanished. "No."

"I don't like it."

"Me neither. You don't do something like that unless you want to draw folks out or test their defenses. You're all back in one piece, so I'm assuming they were testing the defenses."

"Bold move, attacking the Brother House directly."

"Yes. But if they could pull it off at a time when most of the knights were here, they would put a big hole in the humans' defenses in one stroke. And if the knights weren't here, then they'd get access to the hospital. And those other Blood. You think those are prizes they might want?"

"I can see that Ignatius might be keen to kill the Blood who've taken the humans' side," I said. "I'm not sure about the hospital. It would be a loss, but there are other hospitals and the healers can work anywhere." Healers used herbs and various potions, but they could do a lot of their healing without any of them. Particularly the Fae. I'd have to ask Bryony if there was anything I should know about the hospital or the people within its walls.

Rhian nodded. "That's what I thought. But still. I don't like it either, boss."

"I know. So let's keep sharp, eh? Are the men all settled?"

"Yes. And the patrols and rosters have been sorted with the Templars before you ask. Charles has briefed the men who will take first patrol tomorrow."

I nodded, satisfied. I'd speak to the men myself as well, but the point of having lieutenants was to have other people you trusted to get things done. "Good. Then get some sleep, if you've got nothing else to do. The metalmages are repairing the gate, and the Templars have doubled their patrols." It was also getting close to dawn, which meant the Blood weren't likely to suddenly coalesce out of the darkness and mount a second attack tonight. Sunlight was lethal to them, and they'd be heading for their warrens, ready to sleep and do whatever else it was that the older ones who didn't need to sleep through the day did when it was daylight.

"Did you catch the Beasts?"

I nodded. "Caught three, killed one. The Templars will be questioning them soon, I'd imagine." And I was going to be there when they did. Which meant I had something more to do after all.

Chapter Thirteen

BRYONY

At first the summons to the Brother House was a welcome distraction. Until I realized what the likely reason for them wanting me at this hour of night was. We'd already dealt with the minor wounds resulting from the explosion at the gate earlier. I'd been filling in time, walking the floors of the hospital, making sure that all was in order and my charges were safe while I worried about Guy and his Templars and . . . Ash. Mostly Ash, if I was honest.

I didn't want to be honest.

Didn't want to admit that perhaps letting him into my bed wasn't the simple proposition that I'd convinced myself it could be. Because with his touch came the connection we'd once had. As though his skin against mine sent fine invisible hooks sinking through my flesh to catch in my heart.

Every time I passed a window, I looked out at the darkness, turned toward the borders, and worried whether he was coming back.

Whether all of them—including Lily—who Simon had informed me with worry to equal mine clear in his eyes— had gone scouting for Guy that night.

She, at least, was safe in the darkness.

No one could reach her in the shadow. No one could slash her with claws or rend her flesh with teeth or break her bones by knocking her down.

Still, Simon worried about the woman he loved and I worried about the man I—no. Not loved. That wasn't the word.

Not one that I was going to think about, anyway.

But now it seemed they had returned and they had brought someone or several someones back with them.

And they wanted me to help question them.

I didn't like doing such things. I was meant to heal, not harm. I tried to tell myself that really it was preventing harm. If I didn't use my powers to make the captives speak, then the Templars would be forced to use other methods of persuasion that would be far less considerate.

I hurried through the fading darkness, hearing the earliest sounds of the City waking around me as I kept pace with Liam, sent to fetch me.

He looked strained as he always did these days when the Templars saw action. The frustration of being kept out of it scented the air around him, and I wished, for the thousandth time, that there had been something more I could have done for his arm.

We reached the Brother House just as the sun started to peck over the horizon, which made the feeling of descending into the depths to the cells belowground feel even more unpleasant.

A small circle of Templars waited for us outside the cells. Father Cho. Guy. Patrick and Brother Bartholomew, one of the other patrol leaders. And Ash. I almost went to him but managed to stop myself, studying him covertly to see if he was injured.

Half-dried blood stained his leather vest, and a matching splotch of dull red brown smeared across one cheek, but he stood straight and easy and showed no signs of pain, so I had to assume the blood belonged to someone else. One of the prisoners perhaps.

Fen stood with the group of soldiers, his face remote and set the way it got when he wished he was elsewhere.

It seemed I wasn't the only one with no stomach for co-ercion.

But it had to be done. One of us had to find out what had been the purpose behind tonight's attack so that we could try to figure out what was coming next.

We were all alone now, no Fae queen to come to our rescue, so if we were to survive, we had to be more ruthless. Try to think like Ignatius.

Which was a particularly unpleasant thought.

"How many?" I asked as Father Cho greeted me.

"Three," he replied. "Beasts. Theissens and a Krueger, we think."

Ah. That explained some of Fen's expression. His *grand-mere* had been a Krueger before she was cast out from her pack for the sin of loving a human. Fen didn't seem to like the Beasts, but he had little family and it couldn't be easy to see someone from the pack he had ties to captured in a plot against the side he'd chosen.

I put down the bag of supplies I'd brought with me. "Are they conscious?"

"One is. He's not terribly happy with things right now."

"Oh?" I turned toward the cell. I couldn't hear anything from its depths.

"I put an aural ward on the door," Ash said. "He was making quite a racket, and the men need their sleep."

As if to prove the truth of his words, there was a sudden shudder in the wooden door. It was made of planks several inches thick and reinforced with metal bars and nails. There should have been an accompanying crash to go with the force necessary to make it move even slightly, but there was nothing. Ash knew what he was about, apparently.

"Aren't they restrained?" I asked.

"They're shackled. And chained to the wall. Apparently we should have used a shorter chain," Ash said. He didn't look particularly concerned.

"What do you want to try first?"

"Have you got something that will calm him down?" Guy asked.

"If you can get him to drink it, yes." I had sedatives and

calmatives enough to drug several squads of knights. Beast Kind could be tricky to treat, given their rapid healing abilities, but I'd learned a trick or two over the years. I would be able to render the prisoners less excitable easily enough.

"Well, let's do that," Guy said. "Then Fen can get close enough to try seeing what there is to see before we try anything else."

Fen's jaw clenched, but he didn't offer an objection, so I nodded.

Ash dissolved his ward with a wave of his hand, and a sudden snarling crash echoed through the room.

Guy walked over to the door and flipped open the little wooden shutter that covered a barred grille. "Shut up and stand back from the door."

"Fuck off, Templar."

Ash joined Guy. "We have plenty more silver bullets here," he said, cocking his gun casually at the level of the bars. "Care to reconsider?"

The Beast said something indecipherable. I spoke a little of their language, but I didn't know that particular phrase. Probably just as well judging by the wince that crossed Fen's face.

"I'm going to give you some water," Guy said. "You must have worked up a thirst with all that yelling." He looked back at me. I took the cup Father Cho handed to me and then poured in a few drops of the mixture I thought would work best.

Guy passed it through and the Beast drank noisily, then thrust it back. "More."

Guy obliged, this time without stopping for me to doctor the liquid.

He looked back at me with a question clear on his face.

"A few minutes," I mouthed back, and we settled to wait.

Sure enough, after a few more minutes, there was a sigh and the sound of someone sliding down the wall.

"How much did you give him?"

"Enough," I replied. "Open the door and bring him out."

"Out?" Ash questioned.

"You don't want the other two to wake up and join in, do you?"

"I can put a binding on them."

"Let's not do that unless we have to." Bindings were nasty things. Guy's frown of distaste showed he agreed with me. Well, he would. He'd been on the receiving end of one once and also had had to deal with Holly being placed under a geas.

Two of the knights brought out the Beast, who was now limp and smiling drunkenly. He had dark hair and olive skin, like Fen's. And, like Fen's, his eyes flashed green under the lamps as he gazed around at us. The Krueger, then. They chained him to a chair, anchored the chains to bolts set deep in the stone floor, and stepped to stand behind him. I moved closer, studying him, trying to judge how deeply the drug had affected him.

He seemed quiet enough. And young. Too young to be here in what was really a dungeon, about to argue for his life.

Too young to be setting explosions in the night and working for a Blood lord. Though in some ways that was how it was in the Night World, the Beasts doing the Bloods' dirty work, so maybe for him it was all completely normal.

I moved closer and, when he didn't react, pressed fingers to his neck. His pulse was a little faster than I liked but within the range of what he could tolerate. The tincture I'd used did that sometimes.

I stepped back and nodded to Guy. "Ask away."

It wasn't Guy who spoke, though; it was Father Cho. "Son, we want you to tell us who sent you tonight." His voice wasn't loud, but it held a crack of command despite the pleasant phrasing of his request.

The Beast smiled and for a moment I thought everything was going well as he opened his mouth to answer, but then he threw back his head and howled and launched himself forward. The chains anchored to the floor held him in place and he jerked to a stop with a snap that made me fear he'd broken something.

Father Cho still had good reflexes, it seemed, and he'd

moved smoothly out of the way, having not been too close to start with.

I took a deep breath, trying to get my heart back out of my throat.

"He doesn't seem that calm," Ash said dryly.

I shot him a look. "Beasts are tricky. Hold him down," I ordered the knights, and they obliged, even though the Beast struggled.

I walked closer again. The Beast snarled but I ignored him, relying on the Templars to do their job and keep me safe.

The man's pupils were wide and dark. My stomach twisted. Damn. I knew what the problem was now. We weren't going to be doing this the easy way. And I didn't like the hard way one little bit.

"*Lune de sang,*" I said. The Beast jerked and snarled and I smelled the strange peppery green scent on his breath that confirmed my suspicions. "He's taken moon's blood."

"What's that?" Ash asked as the Templars muttered

"It's a drug. I don't know what it's made of—the Beasts guard that information very closely. It's used for some of their religious ceremonies."

"It makes them feel invincible," Fen said. He came closer, one hand rubbing his right wrist, and peered at the Beast. "Makes them feel like they can't be hurt." He looked at me. "Like that stuff you gave me once times about twenty if what I've heard is true."

The potion I'd given Fen to combat the pain of his iron-induced headaches during a trip to a Blood warren had enough kick to fell Guy's horse. And several others. "It also makes them resistant to other drugs," I said. "It's one of the few things that take a long time to leave their systems. I'd imagine the other two will have been dosed as well."

"What does that mean?" Guy asked.

"It means that nothing I can give him is going to make him talk if he doesn't want to. The only thing that's going to get through to him is pain."

Guy's mouth went flat. "That can be arranged."

I held up a hand, knowing what I had to do. The thought

made me want to retch—being against everything I was trained to do—but I could do it without the Beast actually being physically harmed, unlike the Templars. "No," I said, with another deep breath. "I'll do it."

The men all stared at me.

"You can't beat up a Beast," Fen said.

"I don't need to. I can make him hurt without touching him. Or without hitting him, at least." I needed contact with his skin just as I would to work a healing.

"Bryony," Ash objected. "That will hurt you too."

I shrugged. "Not much." No more than I could bear at least.

"Let me do it," he said.

"No." I wagged my fingers at him. "You don't have a delicate enough touch. You proved that yesterday. You could damage him."

"I—"

"I could ask Simon," Guy said at the same time.

I held up a hand. "No. I'll do it. I'm not going to shatter into a thousand pieces from a bit of dirty work." I shook my head at them. "Don't forget who I am."

I had no doubt Simon would do it if Guy asked. He was almost as skilled a fighter as his brother and could be deadly when he was roused to anger, but he had fought hard to conquer his darker side and valued his healing powers deeply. I didn't want to make him do something that would sully that for him. He was one of the humans I was closest to in the City, almost like a younger brother. And, like any big sister, I would protect him if I could. I would protect all of them, these men who fought so hard, but forgot sometimes that I was older and more powerful than any of them besides Ash.

"You can use that binding now," I said to Ash. I didn't like bindings, which were one step away from the truly revolting magic of a geas, but they did sometimes have their use in medicine to restrain a patient. Or for times like these. I didn't want to split my attention to hold a binding and do what I had to do. One tiny spill of power in the wrong direction and I would do more than hurt the Beast.

Ash nodded and held out a hand toward the Beast. "Step back," he ordered the knights. They did so with speed.

Ash said several quick phrases in Fae, the words familiar to me, and the Beast froze in place, only his chest still rising and falling and his gaze darting around the room, sudden panic darkening his eyes further.

"Stop," he snarled.

I looked at Ash.

He shrugged regretfully. "I can't take his voice if we need him to talk."

I'd forgotten that part for a moment. A bead of sweat rolled down my back as distaste for what I was about to do made my stomach turn uneasily.

But I wasn't going to let them see how much this disturbed me. Because then they really would try to stop me, and that would be bad for the Beast before me and the other two in the cells. I couldn't save them from pain perhaps, but I could shield them from damage and that was what I, as a healer, would do.

One last breath and I moved back to the Beast. He stared up at me and howled defiance again. But I merely reached out and pressed my hand to his forehead.

"Tell us who sent you to set the explosion tonight," I commanded, hoping that he might see reason. Hoping that there was some small part of him not drugged to the gills on *lune de sang* that might be able to decide that self-preservation was the sensible path to take.

No such luck, though. He just snarled up at me, sending hot acrid breath into my face.

"Have it your way," I sighed. Then I set his nerves on fire. Just for twenty seconds to start with.

When his scream died down. I asked him again. And again he refused to answer.

I set my teeth and sent the power down into him again, sending the message to all those delicate pathways that something was wrong. That they hurt. That they burned. Burns hurt more than most injuries, so the sensation of them was most useful in this situation. I hadn't done this before except once, when they'd shown us how to do it as part of our studies. That time, I'd thrown up afterward. I hoped to every inch of grace that any gods might wish to show me that I wouldn't do it again now. The Beast's screams rang in my ears and the echoes of his pain surged through me. Sweat slicked my back and I fought to remember to breathe as I counted down the seconds, letting him burn for longer this time.

When I took my hand away and the Beast stopped screaming as though someone had thrown a switch, I wasn't sure whether it was him or if Ash had added something to his binding to stop the noise. I twisted back toward the men behind me. Ash shook his head at me, his face set and grim. The others wore expressions that ranged from stoic to horrified to vaguely impressed. Fen's face was grimly blank, his arms crossed in front of him. His eyes had gone flat and dark. I wondered what he could see around us at this moment. What effect were my actions here having on our possible futures?

I turned back to the Beast. "Who sent you? I promise you, I can keep this up a very long time. And once the moon's blood wears off, it will hurt even more."

I saw him swallow, saw fear and struggle swim up through his wide green eyes. I waited. One heartbeat. Two. Three.

Nothing.

I reached my hand toward his head and saw in his eyes how much his body was screaming at him to flinch away. But he was held there, chained by Ash's magic and being tortured—I had no illusions about what I was doing—by mine. "Who sent you?" I asked. I tried to keep my voice strong, not pleading.

He blinked up at me. "No one, Fae bitch."

I heard Ash mutter behind me, echoed by a deep rumble from Guy. "That was stupid," I said. I didn't care what he called me. In his position, I'd call me a bitch too. But he was just delaying the inevitable and making the men behind me angry. I put my hand back down and started the process over.

He talked after two more bursts. It was impressive really, how much he could bear, but I would've preferred that he had given in much sooner. Then I might not have felt so near to fainting by the time I finished.

I stayed upright through force of will as the man first named Pierre Rousselline as the alpha giving orders, then said he'd been sent to bring down the gate and didn't know more than that.

It was a name at least. But it wasn't enough. It might be all they knew, of course, but we had to be sure. I knew it as Guy moved to my side and stared down at me for a moment, as if trying to decide what to say.

I held up a hand, forestalling anything he wanted to bring up.

"I know," I said. "Bring out the next one."

The second Beast knew no more than the first. Pierre Rousselline had sent them. They were to bring down the gate and then return. But the third, who was the oldest of the three, was a more fruitful source. Maybe the *lune de sang* had had time to work its way out of his system a little or maybe the sounds of the screams of his companions had been enough to scare some sense into him, but he came out of the cell without resisting and let the Templars bind him into the chair.

The room reeked of fear and sweat and Beast now. It stung my nose and it had to smell worse to him. He would be able to decipher the pain in the scents too. He looked up at me as I approached.

"You've heard what came before," I said. "Do you want the same or do you want to talk?"

His pupils flared and his throat worked. "Ask me what you want to know."

Guy started to run though the questions again. "Who sent you?"

"Pierre Rousselline."

"What was your target?"

"The gate."

"Why the gate?"

The Beast hesitated. "Testing defenses," he said. "I'm only a second-tier *guerrier* in my pack. I didn't hear all the plans. But they were talking about the tunnels. They want to get into the tunnels."

"Who are 'they'?"

"Pierre and the new Blood Lord. Lord Ignatius."

"You heard them say that?" Guy demanded.

"Not them. But my alpha, Luka. He was muttering about tunnels and madness when he came to pick two of us for the job. Alain and I, and then tonight we were told we were working with the young Krueger in there." He glared at me. "He's a brave one."

I met his stare coolly. "None of you are brave. If you were brave you'd stop this madness with Ignatius and want the peace restored."

"We do as our alphas command."

"That only proves my point. Your alphas are leading you to destruction. Time to choose more wisely."

Something swam in his eyes. Regret? Fear? Anger? "That's not our way."

"In that case, I hope you don't have a family. War brings death. And not just to soldiers. The humans won't let Ignatius bring this City down."

He stared at me for a few more seconds, then looked back at Guy. "Anything else you want to know?"

"Is there anything else we should know?"

"Like I said, I'm not high in the ranks. I don't know much more. The Blood are moving toward something. They're running things in the Night World now. The alphas have agreed to that." He looked disgusted. "But I don't know what Lord Ignatius wants in your tunnels. Then again, you probably do." He stopped then and hung his head.

Guy looked at Father Cho, who made a little gesture as though to say "enough." The knights put the Beasts back into cells—the three of them separated now, in case they decided to turn on one another—and then we were left standing there.

There wasn't much more I could do. Father Cho and Guy knew what was in the tunnels below the hospital as well as I did. And I wanted more than anything to take a bath and sleep for a time. Maybe I would forget what I had done. Maybe I would be able to wash the slimy feeling off my skin.

Maybe.

Ash

Bryony turned away from the cell door, moving slowly.

"I'll go back to St. Giles now," she said to Father Cho.

He nodded, patted her shoulder. "Rest, my lady."

Rest? He'd just watched her torture two men and thought she'd be going home to sleep easily? My gut twisted.

Bryony nodded and headed for the stairs. I followed her up out of the dungeons, trailing a little behind her. I would do her the courtesy of not pressing her while we still had an audience.

She walked more slowly than usual, her shoulders almost painfully straight. Trying too hard. She wasn't all right. I could feel the ripples of discord in the usual deep calm of her power. When she stepped outside the Brother House she sighed, then stood a moment, sucking in lungfuls of air as though she could purge something from her body with each breath.

"Is there anything I can do?" I asked, moving to block her path. She looked too pale and the chain at her neck gleamed a bruised pale green that didn't ease my concern any.

She waved me away. "I'm fine. Let me go."

"No."

"Don't push me, Ash. I'm not in the mood."

"And I'm not in the mood to be pushed away either. Either you're upset by what happened down in those cells or you're upset about the attack."

"Those are my only two options, are they? I'm glad you know every detail of my life."

Anger glimmered in the depths of her eyes. Which was good. Anger was better than her looking washed out and pale. Anger meant she was alive and fighting.

"I don't. That's true. But those are the main things that have happened since I climbed out of your bed," I pointed out. I tried to figure out how long ago that was. I'd heard the cathedral bell toll nine while we were down in the cells. It must have been near four when the explosion had happened. Had it really only been five hours? It felt like days.

I was starting to feel desperately tired. Adrenaline wearing off compounded by little sleep. "Unless you're telling me that something else momentous happened in the last six hours."

She rolled her eyes. "You consider yourself momentous, do you?"

"I consider you letting me into your bed momentous." I risked a smile. "I'll let you decide the rest."

Her mouth twitched, but then she shook her head. "Don't try and charm me."

"So it is last night? You don't have to worry. If you tell me to go, then I'll go."

A brief flash of vivid red ran the length of her chain, disappearing so quickly I was half afraid that I'd imagined it.

"Says the man who's standing in my path."

"I'm concerned about you. That was difficult, down there."

"I've done it before."

"That doesn't mean you like it. I've killed plenty of men on the battlefield. Doesn't make it any easier."

She straightened her shoulders. "Nor does discussing it."

"What you did or what he said?" I asked. "Do you know why Ignatius is so curious about the tunnels?"

"He wants to be able to attack the Brother House and the hospital."

It was a part truth. Bryony was good at dissembling, like all Fae, but I could also tell she wasn't telling me the whole truth.

"Perhaps I need to go take a look. If there are weaknesses down there, I need to know about them."

She bit her lip.

"Problem?"

"Why can't you just leave things alone?"

"Because the Templars are paying me a nice pile of money to help them out. And I can't do what they're expecting for all that gold if there are cracks in their security that I don't know about."

"The security in the tunnels is nothing to concern yourself with."

"You know that for a fact?"

"I set the wards myself. And I'm not the only one who worked on the defenses."

"Seems like a lot of trouble for some disused space."

"The tunnels are a strategic target."

"Yes, but you've only been fighting the Blood for a short time. You're not even officially fighting them yet. Are you telling me all those wards are new?"

"No. The Blood have always been a danger."

"They're not likely to get in through the Brother House, and to get through St. Giles would take a major offensive. So either the humans who built the hospital were particularly paranoid or there's something else down there that you're not telling me about. Is there?"

It was a direct question. She had to answer or say nothing.

Or so I hoped.

She stayed silent. Which meant she didn't want to answer.

I folded my arms, prepared to wait her out. The silence stretched past a minute. Stubborn woman. "Perhaps I'll ask Guy."

Her fingers stole up to clasp the chain around her neck. Worried. Or annoyed. "Just leave it alone. For now. Can't you do that much?"

"I wouldn't ask if it wasn't important. You wouldn't want to keep it a secret if it wasn't important."

"I can't tell you. Not just now."

"Is that the truth? Or a shade of it?"

"I'm asking you to wait a little while. The sun is up. The Blood can't try anything just now."

"Beast Kind don't need moonlight to attack."

"No, but they're a hell of a lot more obvious during the day. And they wouldn't have the Blood to back them up if they did try anything."

"Maybe we should just go over there now and take them out, then." I was only half joking.

"There are children amongst them."

"Some would say they're children who would grow up to be our enemies."

Her mouth flattened. "And you? What would you say?"

"I don't kill children," I said. "Do you think I would?"

"I don't know. I don't know you anymore."

"Yes, you do. I'm the one who was inside you last night."

"Sex isn't knowledge."

"Maybe. But that wasn't just sex."

She paled and I cursed myself beneath my breath. I'd only come after her to make sure she was all right, and here I was, making things worse.

I held up my hands. "Look, forget I said that. But I swear, you know me. I'm still me. Still the one you used to . . . care for."

Her eyes glimmered for a moment with something that, in anybody else, I would've said were unshed tears. But Bryony didn't cry. "Maybe you haven't changed. But I have."

She turned and I couldn't help it, I caught her wrist before I thought. "Don't go."

"Why not?"

"Because you're upset and I want to help."

"Why?"

"Because I haven't changed."

"That's what scares me." The words came too quietly. And while I was still trying to work out what she meant, she slipped her hand free, turned, and vanished.

Chapter Fourteen

BRYONY

Maybe it was childish, using an invisibility charm. And maybe it was futile and Ash would follow me anyway, tracing my path by the feel of my magic, the same way I would be able to trace him.

But I couldn't face him anymore.

I couldn't afford to believe that his words were truth and that he still cared for me. That this time perhaps we had a chance. Because I wanted too much for those words to be true and I feared too much that they weren't.

And, after so short a time, both of those things scared me.

I walked cautiously at first, turning to see if he followed. But he hadn't moved. He was looking in the direction I was taking, but I couldn't tell whether he could sense my direction or whether he was just guessing my path. But by the time I reached the gate in the wall that stood between the Brother House and the hospital grounds, he still stood there, just watching, his face troubled.

I lingered for a moment, there at the junction between his world and mine, watching him too.

He was rumpled, dressed in his brown leathers and shirt, dirt on his breeches and on his long boots. The bloodstains had faded to brown too now. All those browns echoed the shades of his hair and made his skin look even more tanned than usual. Long fingers drummed on the hilt of his sword hanging on his hip.

Fingers bare of his ring.

I remembered the feel of those fingers against me last night and I almost gave in and went back. The urge to take him by the hand and see if I could drive that troubled look away and if he could ease the regret in my heart for what I had just done burned fiercely.

But I didn't. I just took a few more seconds, drinking in the sight of him, part of me still not convinced, it seemed, that he really was back and needing the proof of sight. And touch. But no. Last night was done and it was a new day. I had to be strong.

Ash could've been killed last night by one of those Beasts. He could be killed any moment. And if he survived it all, then most likely he would ride back out the City gates and disappear from my life for a second time.

Last night I had been weak. It had been pleasurable, yes. Beyond pleasurable, but that was exactly why I couldn't let it happen again.

Right now I had just enough strength to resist him. If I let him snare me in that web of pleasure that he wove so easily, then those threads of strength would snap one by one until the last of them gave way and I fell into a place that there would be no returning from.

Once I passed through the gate, I sped up, almost running. Across the grounds, through the nearest door. Down the stairs, into the tunnels, and down the familiar twists and turns of the way to the hidden ward. Normally I didn't seek the place out. I visited daily to see how Simon and Atherton were progressing, but the iron doors that guarded the ward made it uncomfortable to be in for any serious length of time.

I had a high tolerance to iron, but so much in one place, so close, was past my limit.

As I approached the door, my stomach started to roll in protest and I wondered if I'd made a mistake.

But then, maybe Simon would be able to do something to ease my nausea. It might have been caused by the mental stress of what I'd done, but that didn't mean he couldn't remove the physical symptoms at least. My mind, I would have to deal with myself.

And I would.

I stopped before the door, to reach into the well-warded niche where I kept a stash of leather gloves, and pulled a pair on. They let me press my hand against the doors to work the wards, even though the iron made them ache down to the bone, as though I'd drenched them in freezing acid.

But the sensation was only temporary, or so I reminded myself every time I did this.

I closed the second door behind me gratefully and stepped into the outer room of the ward.

Atherton wasn't at his desk. No doubt I'd find him inside, tending to his patients.

Sure enough, I heard voices from the room beyond. Atherton's tenor voice and Simon's slightly lower rumble. Female voices too. Three of them. Holly and Lily, I thought. And maybe Adeline, given that I couldn't feel any hint of Saskia's magic.

We'd sworn Adeline to secrecy when we showed her this place, making it a condition of her and her group of refugee Blood being granted Haven here at St. Giles. Along with her agreement to help Simon and Atherton with their quest for a cure.

So far she'd seemed to have kept her promise.

I opened the door to let myself through into the inner room. The hidden ward had six rows of beds, most of them occupied. Almost fifty patients. Once upon a time, before Lucius had died, all the occupants had been silent and unmoving, comatose for all practical purposes, blood-locked and senseless. Now some of them were awake, though they still need encouragement to talk and walk and do anything near normal activity. It was progress, but it was, in some ways, harder to take than their former state had been. Like being able to see the light at the end of a tunnel but having the path to that light blocked by an impassable barrier.

Nothing we'd tried so far had enabled us to progress past rousing them to this point. Right now returning them to their families would just mean a life sentence of having to be cared for day and night. A stopgap, not a cure.

When Simon and the others saw me, the conversation died. Not the effect I wanted to have on people right at this moment, but I understood. They wanted to know what news I brought. What new twist to our situation might have occurred.

Lily spoke first. There were shadows under her clear gray eyes, something I'd rarely seen. She had been pushing herself too. Maybe we all needed to give one another a talking-to and convince ourselves that sleeping occasionally was acceptable.

"What happened?" she asked.

She was involved in what had happened last night, I knew. She'd found the Beasts for the Templars. Which explained the exhaustion on her face and the worry on Simon's.

"Yes, do tell," Adeline added. Her voice was light, as it often was, but she too looked nervous, though in a vampire, it can be hard to distinguish. Her pale hair was impeccably dressed as always and her skin was the clear white of moonlight or milk, gleaming against the startling red slash of paint on her lips. Her stark black dress set it all off. Of the six of us, she was the only one who didn't look as though she'd been awake for days and possibly sleeping in her clothes before that.

"One of the Beasts they captured talked," I said shortly. "He confirmed that Ignatius was trying our defenses. He mentioned the tunnels as a target."

That hardly lightened the mood. It wasn't as though anyone here could have been expecting anything other than Ignatius being curious about what was down here. Adeline had been unable to tell us if he had any inkling of what Simon was up to. Lord Lucius had suspected, but Simon and Lily had killed him. And he wasn't exactly the type to share information with his underlings until he had to. Back then Ignatius had only been on the fringes of Lucius' inner circle. But we couldn't discount the fact that he might know something.

Even if he didn't know about Simon, he knew that Adeline and her party were hiding in St. Giles. Had probably heard that we were housing them underground in some of the disused wards. That on its own was a big enough draw.

If Ignatius could kill Adeline, then he would have killed the last of the Blood who openly stood against him.

Plus, getting to her down here in the heart of the humans' stronghold would send a fairly clear message of his degree of power.

Which was why we couldn't let that happen.

"Did he say anything more specific?" Simon asked eventually after they had all taken a moment's silence to digest the information.

"No. Sorry. From what he claims, he's a lower-ranking *guerrier* in the Theissen pack. Not privy to any high level plans. One of the three is Krueger, though, so Martin was involved. And they all said it was Pierre calling the shots." Pierre Rousselline was the alpha who had been closest to Lucius and he'd worked hard to keep that position throughout the Blood Court's power struggles. Whatever he was doing, the orders were coming straight from Ignatius; of that much we could be certain.

"I see," Simon said.

"What about Fen?" Holly asked. "Did he see anything?" Of all of us, she looked the most tired. Almost as pale as Adeline and she'd lost weight again. I made a note to spend a little time with her as soon as possible. She had taken Reggie's death very hard, and though she seemed to be improving, I didn't like the strain I still sensed in her.

"They'd taken moon's blood. Not making much sense. They need time for it to clear their systems. So he's going to wait until later to try to see more."

"Fen could see even if they were unconscious, couldn't he?" Lily said, frowning.

"He wanted to wait." I didn't want to explain that he'd

seemed to be the worst affected by what I had done. Almost as though he could sense the mental trauma I was inflicting with the pain.

He'd left almost as soon as the last of the three Beasts were locked in the cell, looking almost as ill as I felt.

"So nothing has changed, really," Adeline said.

"No. But afterward, Captain Pellar was asking about the tunnels. About what's down here."

"Did you put him off?" Simon asked.

"For now. But he's right to ask. If he's to help defend the city, then he needs to know what he's defending."

"Do you think we should tell him?" Holly asked.

"Yes." If only to stop him driving me insane whilst trying to find out on his own what was down here.

"Do you trust him?" Atherton said suddenly.

I hesitated. I didn't want to answer too quickly. That would reveal too much about the feelings I was trying to deny. "Yes," I said. "I've never known him not to keep his word when he's given it."

"People change," Atherton said.

"Guy trusts him too," Simon said. "We need to trust Guy and Bryony's judgment."

Holly nodded, her expression frustrated. It was hard on her these days. Before Ignatius had drawn his battle lines, she had been able to find information for us. But now she was cut off from her networks and the opportunities afforded in the border boroughs' taverns and theater halls for the gathering of intelligence. Now she had to wait, unable to go roaming freely through the night like Lily. And Holly wasn't the sort of woman who took waiting on the sidelines well.

"So, do we agree? That Bryony should tell the captain what's going on down here?" Lily asked.

Adeline pursed her lips. "I think we should take care. You may trust Captain Pellar, but he's not just one man. He brings an entire army with him."

"An army loyal to him," I said. And how had I worked myself into the position of now defending Ash to them? "An army who are mostly human and have no reason whatsoever to want to help the Blood. Some of them might even be from here." I realized I had little idea about Ash's men. I'd been too busy with my own issues to take the time to ask him about them yet. Or ask him anything much about his time away from the City. Did I truly not want to know? Or was asking admitting to myself that I was curious?

"A mercenary," Adeline said. When I shot her a look she twisted a hand in an elegant palm-up gesture. "I am merely pointing out the reality. I have nothing against your Captain Pellar."

"Not my Captain Pellar," I said automatically. Adeline merely smiled at that. Whereas Holly and Lily looked too interested, sharing a curious look at our exchange. Damn. Did they know about last night? Had someone seen Ash come to my rooms? Or seen him leave? I didn't remember passing anyone as we'd arrived there, but I hadn't been with him when he left so precipitously.

Anyone could have seen him. And put two and two together. As Holly and Lily were apparently beginning to do, I wondered if they would come right out and ask me. Lily might. She didn't care much for social niceties.

"I doubt any man would remain long under his command if he wasn't loyal," Simon said. "That's a quick way for a mercenary troop to implode."

And Ash wasn't the sort to take disregard to his authority lightly. He acted casual and free-spirited when it suited him, but underneath the frivolity he'd always taken any responsibilities he accepted seriously. It was that damned attitude that had led to him taking part in the duel in the first place. He had decided that he needed to face Stellan's challenge, and there was no way he would back down from that decision once he'd made it.

I was sure that he ran his army with suitable discipline and would weed out any true malcontents. From what I'd seen of his men so far, they were well presented and competent. Plus, they hadn't caused any trouble in the City— none of them had turned up at St. Giles after a drunken brawl or such—which spoke well of their training.

"So we will show him the tunnels and this ward. When?"

I asked. Part of me rankled at the thought. Ash would take this as a sign that he had been right all along.

He would tease me about it. And bantering, witty Ash was when he was always at his most charming and most appealing. I wanted surly, cranky Ash. Far easier to resist.

Simon looked down at the notebook he carried. "It makes little difference. Perhaps later today? Both of you have been up all night and from what Lily tells us, it was eventful up there. Take some time to rest, then bring him later."

"Any progress?" It was my daily question and today, as usual, I got a shake of the head.

"We're still at an impasse," Atherton said. "We can rouse them from the stupor mostly—but not all of them. And there's still no one close to full recovery."

Across from him, pain flickered over Holly's face. She had lost a friend to blood-locking and Ignatius' machinations. Just as Simon had lost a sister, years before. It did Holly credit that she still spent time down here every day helping Atherton and Simon when every moment must remind her of Regina.

But she insisted. With most of her links into the Night World and the border boroughs cut off by the curfews and current events—not to mention Guy doing his best impression of a man about to explode when Holly had suggested that she could try to reopen some avenues of communication and putting his foot down so thoroughly I was still surprised there wasn't a dent in the granite floor of the Templar conference room where she'd made the suggestion—her abilities as a spy were not much use to her now. And she'd closed her modiste salon in Gillygate—which had been the cover to explain away the money she'd made spying—after Reggie's death, so she didn't even have that to occupy her.

Reggie had been her partner, and the genius seamstress who'd translated Holly's dress designs in the business. Holly had said she didn't have the heart to look for another seamstress even though her customers amongst the humans were still anxious to secure her services.

I had one dress that Reggie had made for me, a gift in the early days when Holly and Guy had first gotten together. It was beautiful. Made of glorious silk a shade or two darker than my eyes and fitting like a glove, even though Reggie hadn't taken my measurements. I'd not yet had an occasion to wear it. There had been no more treaty balls after what had happened at the negotiations, and it was a distinctly human gown, not really suitable for Summerdale even if I'd been inclined to spend time there.

"I'll bring Ash this afternoon, then," I said, then kicked myself again for the slip of the tongue that I had let myself call him Ash in front of them rather than Captain Pellar. Adeline's mouth quirked and Holly's expression turned speculative.

I turned to go before they could interrogate me and Simon followed me into the outer room.

"Are you well?" he asked as I started to pull on my gloves again. "You look . . ."

"The interrogation wasn't pleasant. But I will be all right with some sleep and tea." And a long, hot bath to wash the memories of pain off my skin.

He came closer. "May I?"

I nodded. The truth was I was still feeling queasy and if Simon could take that away, then all the better I would be able to get more done today if I was feeling well.

Simon put his hand on my wrist, about the edge of the glove, and closed his eyes. After a moment I felt the warmth of his power flow through me, making me feel as though I were temporarily bathed in sunlight. Tension ran out of my back and shoulders and I heard myself sigh as the knots in my stomach eased as well, the sour taste retreating from my mouth.

"Thank you," I said when he let go of me.

He smiled. "You should have asked. And if there are any more interrogations, you should let me help."

I smiled back. "No. You have enough to do down here. Don't worry about me. I'm tougher than I look."

"I'm well aware of that," he said. "But you can run yourself ragged just like anybody else. So make sure you take time to rest. Let yourself find some comfort occasionally . . . whatever form that may take."

Damn. So the women weren't the only ones who were curious about Ash. Simon's face was earnest, but his eyes showed amusement.

"Taking comfort isn't always simple."

"I know," Simon agreed. "And he's been gone a long time."

I made a frustrated gesture. "A long time by human standards. But not by mine."

"Is that a problem?"

"Maybe. I wish I knew. Sometimes it feels like I'd forgotten him and that it was the right thing to do. And sometimes it feels like barely yesterday and everything is . . ."

"Unresolved?"

"That's close enough."

"Sometimes you just have to accept the unexpected." He smiled suddenly. "Sometimes the unexpected can be better than anything we could have dreamed of."

"We can't all be you and Lily," I said. I fussed with a wrinkle in my sleeve, uncomfortable with the direction of this conversation.

"Really?" Simon said. "Why not?"

ASH

When Bryony vanished, it felt as if she had punched me in the stomach. There could be no clearer sign that she didn't want my company or whatever comfort I hoped to offer her. In fact, she wanted it so little she was determined to make sure I couldn't follow her.

I could sense the charm she was using and sense her magic as it retreated from me. But if she wanted to be alone badly enough to use an invisibility charm, then I was going to let her be, no matter how much I chafed at my inability to make her feel better. She lingered for a moment at the wall between the hospital and the Brother House, and hope flared, though I set my jaw and clenched my teeth in my determination not to let it show. But then she continued on her way.

I followed the fading sense of her for a while and then decided that it was pointless to drive myself insane and that perhaps it was time to seek my own bed and try again when we were both more rested.

But it wasn't to be. As I made way back into the main Templar building, Fen found me.

He had been uncomfortable down in the cells, that had been plain, but he'd stood his ground, which impressed me. The first time I'd witnessed a battlefield interrogation, it was under the tutelage of an employer who wasn't as compassionate as Bryony. He'd had no compunction slicing bits off his chosen victim until the man had shrieked and sobbed and begged for release while spilling everything he'd ever known about anything.

I'd left that tent and found the nearest private spot and thrown up for about an hour.

I'd tried to limit such practices amongst my own men. As Bryony had demonstrated, there are other ways to extract information, and although she'd had to resort to pain in the end, she had avoided damaging the Beasts, for which I and I imagined Fen—had been grateful.

"Captain Pellar," Fen said as he stepped into my path. "Can we talk?"

I studied him for a moment. The haze of power that surrounded him was unlike any I'd felt before. Fae seers trail power like mist, tiny tendrils that drift through the room and entwine with the threads that others leave behind.

But Fen was nothing like mist. His power was more like a cloud—or an atmosphere. Something close to the thundercloud sense that I got from Bryony when she was angry, a presence that pushed outward from him and made the air crackle. Almost luminous. It didn't feel strictly like Fae power, which made sense, given that he was only partly Fae. But it was obvious that he was someone to be reckoned with. I didn't know what other skills he might have, but his powers of foretelling—if that was what fueled the signals I was picking up—were clearly formidable.

"About the interrogation?" I asked, slightly wary. Seers are uncanny at the best of times. Knowing the future is a chancy business and one that wise men avoid.

"About several things," Fen said. He nodded his head toward the outer doors. "Perhaps we can walk? I, for one, could use some fresh air."

I had no argument with that. Some earth beneath my feet would do me good. "Can we go toward the hospital?"

One side of his mouth quirked, the green jewel in his ear glinting in the light as his head tilted.

"There's less iron there," I explained. "It's more comfortable. And the gardens should be empty, so there's privacy as well."

He nodded. "As you wish."

We took a different path from the one that Bryony had used. We came out near the east side of the hospital where one of the buildings stood surrounded by scaffolding and several bands of workmen swarming over its walls, repairing what looked like damage from a fire.

Fen glanced up at it, and his mouth flattened. Then he turned his head away and led me farther still into a side garden shaded by tall oaks at either end.

I'd been right about needing to be outside. Under the trees, some of my fatigue disappeared.

Fen stayed silent as we walked the length of the garden, but as we neared the wall that surrounded the hospital, stepping into the shade of the oaks there, he began to mutter something under his breath.

I halted. "Problem?"

He stopped beside a tree, pressed a hand to its bark. I wondered if he drew strength from the earth like a Fae. Or whether he was just pausing while he decided what he wanted to say.

"I wanted to tell you something about what I saw," he said. "Back there in the cells."

"I thought you hadn't really seen anything," I said, somewhat confused. "That you were going to try again."

"Not about the Beasts. About you."

I froze. "Don't you need to touch someone to see his future?"

Fen shook his head. "No. It helps if I want to see something very specific to that person, but I get glimpses around most people all the time."

I pulled a face. "That sounds unpleasant."

"It used to be. I used to drink a lot of brandy to avoid exactly that."

"And now?"

"Now I have control. I can choose when I want to see. Most of the time. Your queen granted me that gift when she . . . healed me."

The queen had healed him? That, I needed to hear more about. She'd never been one for going out of her way to help out the *hai-salai*. For her to step in for Fen meant what he could do was valuable indeed, but right now I was more interested in what he'd actually seen. "What does most of the time mean?"

"Sometimes I still see things involuntarily. When there's someone with an especially strong destiny or if he's in the middle of important events."

"That could be anyone in the cells last night. What's happening right now meets the very definition of important events."

"Yes," Fen agreed. "Which makes it even more interesting that it was only you that I saw."

I didn't think that "interesting" was the word. "Appalling" might be closer. "What exactly did you see?"

"Several things. You with Ignatius Grey. You with a bunch of Fae who didn't look overly happy. A dagger. Fire. Lots of fire. And arrows." He frowned. "And a feeling of . . . danger. There are people who want you dead, I think."

"That's nothing new."

"This felt . . . immediate," Fen said.

"And do the things you see always come true?"

His expression turned unhappy. "No. But when I see something often enough, then the likelihood seems to rise.

I saw arrows and fire around you the day you arrived, but I assumed that was just because you're a soldier."

"Maybe it is. I've been in plenty of battles in my time."

"That doesn't explain Ignatius or the Fae."

"There are those in the Fae Court who aren't keen on my return. Those who still want vengeance for the things that happened a long time ago."

"Guy hasn't told me what did happen. But I think I got a glimpse of that too. You killed someone? In a duel?"

A cool chill quivered down my spine. Strong indeed, this one. "Yes," I said shortly. "He tried to kill me. He failed."

"Or you succeeded."

"I was defending myself. I'd rather I hadn't killed him, but he left me no choice. My life would have been very different if I hadn't." Or much shorter.

"Maybe it was meant to be."

"Do you believe in fate? That the Lady sets a path for you and that you can't step off?" I asked, curious to hear what a *hai-salai* thought about it. It was a subject that I had thought about a lot when I'd been first exiled. Whether my banishment was meant to be. But then I'd decided that I didn't care what the Lady thought and that if I was going to make a life for myself, it would be one that I enjoyed. And was profitable. Soon after that I'd joined a mercenary troop and the rest was a story already written.

Fen shrugged. "I believe that sometimes certain people are meant to do certain things. Otherwise what I see wouldn't come true. I also believe that most of the time you can move away from a destiny, if you want to. Some would say that Saskia was destined to marry a rich human and bear a bunch of children to carry on his name, and yet here she is, with me. And no one would have predicted that Lily would break free of Lucius and find a new life for herself. I believe in both fate and free will, I guess."

"Then it matters what we choose to do?"

"Yes. For some, those choices will be the right ones to lead them to where they are supposed to be. For others, well, choosing to do good is always better than the alternative, isn't it?"

"So we should try to do what we think is right and let the Lady take care of herself?" I liked that philosophy. It was pretty much what I believed as well. Fen was somewhat spooky in his abilities, but I thought that maybe I would enjoy sitting down with him and some good brandy and whiling away a few hours doing nothing more than drinking and spinning tales at some point.

If the Lady was going to grant us a chance to do that.

"I'll stay on the lookout for people trying to kill me," I said. "I can manage that much."

"I hope so," Fen said. "Lady Bryony seems to be—" He cut the words off.

"Did you see Bryony?" I asked, suddenly unbearably curious. "In what you saw around me, was she there?"

"Should she be?" Fen's expression was faintly challenging. "If you are trying to do the right thing, should she be?"

Was that his way of asking me whether I had honorable intentions toward her? Bryony definitely had a lot of friends here in the City, whether she knew it or not. "Bryony and I have a long and complicated story," I said. "I care about her, if that's what you mean, and I have no intention of hurting her. But if you saw her, that may mean she's in danger too, so tell me."

"No intention doesn't mean you won't," Fen said.

"No. But I'll try not to," I said. "If that's what you're concerned about. I'm not toying with her and I don't take her lightly. I don't know what the future holds, but I do know that much. So, please, tell me what you saw."

Fen sighed. "I saw her. With you. In the Veiled Court. And elsewhere." His eyes went distant for a moment and I decided I didn't want to know exactly what elsewhere entailed. It was odd enough to be speaking to him about my possible fate without getting confirmation that he'd seen Bryony and me doing anything potentially embarrassing for both of us.

"I see. Thank you." I pushed away from the tree. "For telling me. I will keep her safe if it's in my power to do so."

"I would say see to your own safety and the Lady will take care of the rest, but Lady Bryony is special to us here in the City, so I will say thank you for considering her." His mouth twisted. "I know it's not easy to be ... tangled ... with someone complicated. But it can also be worth it."

"Perhaps you could tell her that," I said.

He grinned. "I have no desire to be turned into a frog."

"I'm not sure she can actually turn anyone into a frog," I said. I paused, considering. "She might be able to glamour you so you thought you were a frog, I guess."

Fen pursed his lips. "I'd rather not find out. Safer to just stay away from the subject of you when I'm speaking to her."

"Coward."

"Pragmatist," he replied, and then he laughed. "Not that that helps either."

"You know, you're not being terribly comforting," I said.

"It's not my job to be comforting," he said. "Or yours for that matter. And I've kept you from your business for long enough for one day." He straightened, then bowed a shallow bow, oddly formal after our strangely intimate conversation. And then he strode off through the trees, leaving me with a sense that things had just taken a turn for the peculiar.

Chapter Fifteen

BRYONY

The clash of two autocabs—precipitated by a startled horse and an overturned hackney—resulted in an afternoon that was busier than I'd anticipated. The hackney driver had several smashed ribs, meaning several hours of painstaking work to convince all the pieces to knit back together, and the two cabdrivers had enough gashes, bumps, and broken bones between them to keep several other healers fully occupied. Of course, I could have let them do all the work, but the chance to throw myself into something that required as much concentration as coaxing shattered bone back into place did was welcome.

By the time the hackney driver was safely transferred to a ward for rest and observation and another round or two of healing in the morning, the sun was starting to lower in the sky.

Damn. I should have kept better track of the time.

I was supposed to have taken Ash to the hidden ward, but it was getting close to too late now. The Templars, and Ash, I assumed, would be settling down to an early meal in preparation for the first patrols going out before sunset.

Of course, Ash could be on a later patrol.

Did I want to actually tell him?

No. But there was part of me that wanted to see him all the same, despite our earlier disagreement.

So, despite my better judgment, I set off for the Brother House, lingering a little on my path through the garden to soak up some of the warm green light shining through the trees and feel my aches eased by the earth beneath my feet.

As I'd expected, when I asked after Captain Pellar when I reached the Brother House, the knights at the now fully repaired gate directed me toward the dining hall.

Ash sat at a table with the tattooed girl—Rhian, I'd heard him call her—Liam, and seven other men that I didn't know. Some of his mercenaries, judging by their lack of Templar accoutrements.

They were laughing uproariously at something one of them had said when I stepped into the dining hall. The laughter continued in a second wave as I approached until one of them looked up, saw me, elbowed his right-hand companion with a somewhat awed expression, and jerked his chin toward me.

Ash, spotting this little exchange, turned in his seat. When he saw me, the angle of his head increased to a questioning one.

"Don't let me interrupt," I said.

"Isn't that what you came for?"

"You're obviously eating. It can wait."

"I'm done." He pushed back his chair and came over to me as though to demonstrate the point. He gestured toward the door and we walked out together.

"What did you want?" he said courteously once we were alone. Courteous yet cool, I noted. Still wary after this morning's exchange perhaps? "Did you rest?" he added, eyes narrowing suddenly as he took in my dress—the same one I'd been wearing earlier.

"Don't worry about me," I said. "I came to see you about what you wanted before. About the . . . tunnels." I glanced around and then threw up a ward around us, just in case of prying ears. Better safe than sorry.

Ash looked suddenly more interested. "What about them?"

"I can show you, if you want. I'm sorry. I meant to come earlier but there was an accident in Silverstown and they needed me."

He looked back toward the dining hall. "I'm on first patrol. It will be late by the time we return and I have more work to do. Tomorrow perhaps?"

I didn't know if I was relieved or irritated by the delay. "All right," I said. I knew I should go back to the hospital, but once I left I knew that Ash would ride out. Toward danger. Which made my stomach knot with worry, but there was nothing I could do that would stop him short of knocking him senseless or using a binding. Neither of which he'd thank me for. I made myself smile at him, trying to project airy confidence. "Tomorrow, then. Good hunting."

ASH

The patrol was nervous; I could feel it. Not just in the extra jingling from the horses' tack as they tossed heads and flicked ears as though straining to hear things that were beyond the reach of both our hearing and theirs. That was one sign—the horses were trained well, but they couldn't help picking up the nerves of their riders—but the men were nervous too. Our orders were straightforward. Ride the boundaries along our assigned section of the border, make sure that no one was sneaking across in either direction to cause trouble, and enforce the curfew on the human side.

Normally that sort of detail would be carried out with a certain degree of relaxation. But there were no jokes or casual conversation tonight. I didn't know whether my men had picked up the grim mood from the Templars who accompanied us or they were just nervous about facing Beasts and Blood.

Most of the wars and disputes we'd fought in were human matters. We had from time to time, of course, been involved in skirmishes that involved nonhumans, but that was different from knowing that half the City—the half that contained your enemy—was full of creatures who were faster and stronger than you.

The humans who made up my troop had come from places spread across the earth. All of them knew about Fae—obviously—and Beasts and Blood and various other creatures, but not many of them were from places like the City, where there was such a concentration of all the races.

Mostly because in other places, territories belonged firmly to one race or the other and the consequences for humans trying to press into Blood or Beast territories were dire.

The early hours of the night passed slowly. Nothing happened, which only made the mood more tense. It was normal to have nerves early in a patrol, but then the men usually settled into the rhythm of it and boredom and familiarity conquered the worst of the uneasiness. But tonight it didn't. I felt it myself. A phantom tingle on the back of my neck. Faint noises catching my ears that were happening no place but in my head.

I set my teeth against the distractions, running through the exercises that I'd been taught to calm my mind and soothe anxiety. But at the same time, I sent my senses roaming as far as they could, using little bursts of power to try to see if there was anything actually lurking in the dark that could account for the unease we all felt.

For a long time the answer was no. We rode the assigned section of the City, a long stretch along the street that ran down one side of the Great Northern Line railway and then a slightly more jagged path that traced the new borders between former border boroughs that now belonged to the humans or the Night World.

There were few humans out and about and those that were had papers to show they had business to be conducted at night. They were only too happy to produce them when the Templars asked. We were nowhere near Brighttown, where some of the theater halls and taverns still operated, in a pretense at normality that I found strange but that the humans seemed to find comforting.

Denial. I was no one to point fingers at anyone for spending some time wrapped deep in its depths. Though if Ignatius did start things soon, those businesses would have to be closed—if they weren't destroyed in the opening skirmishes. The last thing we needed were places where large groups of humans gathered at night.

That would be taking the concept of being a sitting duck to a whole new level of stupidity.

We turned off the street we'd been working our way up and back onto the one that ran parallel to it for yet another loop. We made it down one block before I felt a tingle on the back of my neck. One I was sure was real this time. Watching eyes.

I twisted in the saddle, scanning the rooftops and buildings on the other side of the railway, seeing if I could spot anything.

"Trouble?" Patrick asked, riding up beside me.

I shrugged. "Not sure. Just a feeling."

"Someone watching?"

I nodded.

"Not unexpected." He gestured across the railway line. "But you won't spot a vampire watching you unless you have some Fae trick up your sleeve that I don't know about."

"Nothing in particular. But I do see better than you do."

He looked the length of the street and back, peering into the dimness, and then shrugged. "Look away."

I did. Scanning the buildings for a patch of extra darkness that might tell me that a vampire stood there, drawing the shadows around himself. The Blood couldn't do as wraiths did and turn incorporeal, but they could—and did—make themselves near enough to invisible when they had darkness to cloak them. It was their particular form of glamour, really, blending in with their surroundings so well that you could walk past right them and never suspect they were there until it was too late.

Unfortunately, unlike with a glamour, they were able to do it with no telltale trace of magic to give them away.

I looked for heat too. The Beasts ran hot, and the difference in the temperature of their bodies was enough for me to be able to feel the difference between them and a human. But the night air was cool as I ran my mind across it, which made me think that there were no wolves lurking on the rooftops.

But I couldn't shake the skitter of nerves at my back, the sense of being under surveillance. We moved down the street, the horses' shoes making their familiar soothing clopping noise against the cobbles. They, at least, had calmed down now that we'd made several passes, which meant that the men were starting to relax too, I supposed.

When we turned down the side street that formed part of the border, heading down toward where the warehouse/barracks we'd set up was, the tingling on my neck vanished and I twisted in my saddle once more.

Rhian had made her way up next to me and she turned too. "Something out there, boss?"

I shrugged. "Maybe."

"Feels edgy to me," she said.

"Me too." I peered into the darkness, then made myself look away.

"I hate border watch," Rhian muttered.

"Bored?" I said with a grin.

"Yes. Isn't it better to just take the fight to them if we know we're going to have to eventually?"

I nodded up toward Patrick's broad back, where his Templar cross was a dull red against his white tunic in the strange light shed by the gas lamps. "That's for them to decide."

"Hope they make up their minds soon. Waiting just puts everyone in a bad mood."

"There are bigger considerations than people's moods," I said gently.

Her face twisted. "I know. Lots of people in this City. Lots of families." She said the last word with the faintest wistful hint to it. She was an orphan, as far as I knew, but she'd never volunteered the story of how that had come about or how she'd become a soldier. I assumed the former had something to do with the latter and that therefore it wasn't a memory she wanted to relive. So I respected her right to keep it to herself.

Ask no questions.

I hadn't wanted to share much of my own story with my men, so the policy seemed to work for the troop as a whole. People who become mercenaries often have secrets. As long as my men were loyal and obeyed the rules I set, I wasn't looking to pry their histories out of them.

I scanned the way behind us one more time, then shook my head and sent Aric walking forward once more. There might be watchers in the night, but we still had a job to do.

The street back to the warehouses where half my men were garrisoned seemed much longer on foot. But the horses were more tired than we were—Rhian and Charles and I had ridden a second short patrol today after the previous night's nervous yet ultimately uneventful one, and I wanted them well rested for the night to come. The streets were quiet in daylight and I didn't think dismounting to spare them was any great risk.

I'd sent Charles back to the Brother House to join the Templar briefing but had decided to accompany Rhian back to the barracks. I hadn't had time for a proper inspection of them yet, and it was best to do it while the situation was still quiet.

The late-afternoon sun was pleasantly warm as we walked, and the men and women going about their business in the streets gave us cautious smiles of greeting. Rhian kept up a running commentary on the night's adventures and the state of our supplies and the myriad logistic details of integrating the men with the City and the Templar forces. I listened with half an ear, the rest of me distracted by thoughts of sleep and food and coming up with a better plan for the next night's patrols.

I needed to talk to Simon about the sunmages and how we might be able to better use their resources. I understood the need to protect the border to the Night World and I understood the value of the symbol that the sunlamps provided and how that symbol assisted in keeping the human population from panicking, but the truth was that sooner or later the Blood were going to figure out a way to breach the border en masse and cross over.

When that day came we didn't want one of the best forms of defense we had—the sunlight the mages could call and store—concentrated on the border where it would be useless once the Blood had crossed.

We had turned the last corner toward the warehouses when I caught a sudden hint of magic from above me, and then there was a shattering *crack* as a bullet hit the cobblestones by my foot, showering my boot with shards of rock.

"Holy mother of—" Rhian swore beside me, and shoved me toward the nearest building. Her shrill whistle of command sent the horses bolting down the street. They had sense enough to know to run away from gunfire when told to do so. Another shot hit approximately where we'd been standing before we moved, and I threw up a hasty glamour, hoping to hide us from the marksman's sight.

But the magic I'd felt might well mean that they were Fae and able to see through my defenses. Rhian yanked open a door—gods only knew to what—and we dived through and slammed it shut. We hit the floor in unison and crawled rapidly toward the door at the far side of the room. I flung up a ward behind me, hoping to make the door resistant to any attempts to open it and follow us.

Three more shots rang out rapidly, one shattering the window behind us. They were followed by four more that thudded into the floor just a few feet from my boots.

"Two of them." I swore. One pistol couldn't shoot that many shots so fast.

"Are you hurt, boss?" Rhian said beside me, adding a few curses of her own as she looked around.

The broken window had sprayed glass across the room and a chunk of it had sliced my hand, but I was otherwise unharmed. It was bleeding but not enough to be a problem.

"I'll live." I hesitated for a moment, gauging the distance to the door and the angle of it relative to the window. Unfortunately the sunlight streaming in from the broken glass highlighted the door clearly, which meant that, if our snipers had the correct vantage point, they could probably see the door from where they were. Which meant going through the door was risky. Though maybe not as risky as staying in this room.

They knew we were here now and might just have other weapons with them. I could think of several options that could turn this room into a death trap.

"How about you?" I asked as I calculated odds rapidly in my head and evaluated our options. We were in some sort of small store, shelves holding dry goods and cans lining the walls. It had evidently been closed or else the owner had had the good sense to flee at the first sounds of gunfire, because I couldn't sense anyone else in the building.

"Bastards ruined my ink," she snarled.

I snapped my head round to her. "You're hit?"

"Grazed my upper arm. I'll be fine." She sounded enraged, which was good. Adrenaline and anger would carry her through the pain of the wound until we could get to safety.

"Did you call for help?"

She touched the charm on her collar and nodded. "Raised the alarm. There will be a patrol on the way."

"Good." I sucked in a breath, then flinched as another series of shots rang out and more bullets thumped into the room.

There was no return fire from the street, just the noises of shouts and screams as the humans made for shelter. Gods. I hoped nobody was hurt out there.

"Do you know what's behind this building?" I asked.

She nodded. "There's an alley that runs back out to the street a block or so down."

Which would mean a block or two closer to the barracks but would also mean emerging back onto the street where the snipers were. If they were sensible they would have picked a vantage point that would give them a good range of fire, and the shallowly sloped roofs of the cheaply built buildings would be easy enough to run along and follow us.

"And across the alley?"

"More shops, a few little houses, and then another block of warehouses that hold ... mostly cloth, I think." She frowned, and closed her eyes for a moment, as though calling up a mental map of our surroundings. Her breathing was quick and light and I could hear the beat of her heart, seemingly strong, but I could also smell blood and that made me think that her wound was slightly more than a graze.

From my current position, I couldn't see her arm, though, so I was going to have to take her word for it for now and worry about it once we were somewhere safer.

"All right," I said. "We go through that door and make for the alley. If it's clear we'll keep going across to the next street and head to the barracks from there. I don't think we should wait for help here. This place will come down around our ears at the first hint of an explosion."

She looked at me and nodded. "On three, then?"

We were both up and sprinting for the door before I'd even finished saying, "Three."

"Right," Rhian yelled, and I went where she said, agreeing with her sense of direction. We pelted down the narrow corridor and then starting flinging open the doors to the left of us as we came to them, seeking the back entrance to the store. The first door revealed a storeroom of sorts, rows more of shelves with no exits that we could see.

The supplies included an unfortunate number of cans of oils of various kinds. One spark in the wrong spot and the whole place would blow. Not a good place to hide. As though our assailants could read my mind, there was a roar from behind us and something exploded.

The force of it flung us forward, but I managed to keep to my feet and dragged Rhian with me.

I opened another door and—thank the Lady—spotted another door beyond it. We raced through the door and stumbled across the floor, the sound of flames and the all-too-familiar smell of smoke trailing us.

I sent a blast of power toward the fire and felt it die down a little, but I was too busy running to pay it full attention. The door sprang open to my desperate twist of the handle and we found ourselves in a small courtyard.

"Gate, boss." Rhian pointed with her good arm. The rear yard was thankfully small and it took only ten strides or so to reach the gate. It was locked, so I boosted her over and then clambered over myself. There was another roaring whoosh from behind us and the middle of the store burst into flames.

"Keep going," I ordered Rhian, and shoved her forward toward an almost identical gate across the alleyway. If luck was with us, our attackers would assume that we were still in the store behind us, but I didn't want to wait to find out if they would come investigating. This second gate was open and we pushed our way into the small building beyond it. A storehouse full of shelves stacked floor to ceiling with sacks of grain.

"Don't these people sell anything nonflammable?" I muttered.

Rhian shot me a quick desperate grin but saved her breath as we made our way rapidly through the warehouse. But when we came to the end of the building, there wasn't a door.

"Fuck."

"Make a hole, boss," Rhian suggested.

"The whole place might go up," I protested. The stocks of grain were valuable in a time of war. Who knew? They might end up feeding our horses in the end.

"Better that it does so with us outside. Do it." She grimaced, her right hand clamped over the upper part of her left arm.

I cursed again and sent a blast of power at the wall. It was brick but old brick and fortunately it yielded, a neat section crumpling outward. I pulled Rhian through and then spent a minute making sure any sparks of heat from the force I'd exerted had died down. We were standing in another alley, and from the far end I heard the sound of running feet. In front of us was a massive brick wall forming part of yet another warehouse.

I drew my sword, hoping like hell that it was some of our men doing a sweep of the area rather than friends of whoever the hell had just tried to kill me. The other end of the alley would lead us back toward the attackers, and I was loath to blast my way into another warehouse without knowing what it contained and who might be in range of the explosion. We had little choice—toward the unseen runners it was.

"Keep moving," I said to Rhian, who now had her pistol in her good hand.

Good idea. I drew mine as well. I'd practiced long and hard to be able to shoot equally well with both hands, and right now the more weapons the better.

We didn't get very far before the sound of the feet grew very loud and a group of my men hurtled around a corner.

"Captain Pellar," the patrol leader exclaimed. "Thank God. We thought you'd gone up with that store back there."

"No such luck," I managed, fighting to rein my heaving breath back. "We're fine. Rhian needs a medic. Is the way back to the barracks clear?"

He nodded. "Yes, sir. There's a back way. And there're two other squads in the main street now."

"Did they get the snipers?"

He made an apologetic face. "Not sure, sir. We were sent this way."

I muttered under my breath. Sometimes I sorely wished for a better form of communication. Our charms were basic. They could alert people to danger or action, but they couldn't yet convey a voice across distances. Which meant I would have to wait to find out if the snipers had been captured.

I didn't like waiting.

I was fairly certain that the snipers would be gone by the time the squads made their way up to the roof. There'd been that flash of magic before the first shot, so they—if they weren't Fae—had some glamour or something at least. Which meant they would, if they were smart, be able to avoid detection. They only had to melt a block or two back from where they'd been and they'd be back across the Night World border anyway.

"Send someone to tell the men that no one crosses the border," I ordered. This could be a feint, meant to draw us somewhere that it was smarter not to go. I squinted up at the sky, where the sun could just be seen over the two tall buildings that formed both sides of the small space. "It's getting late and we don't want another ambush. They can search the immediate area, but they're to report back before nightfall."

"Yes, sir." The patrol leader turned and jerked his head at two of the men, who nodded and took off at a run back the way they'd come. Another of the men came up to Rhian, pulling a bandage and one of the cleansing potions we used out of a pouch at his waist. He cut the remains of her sleeve away with a knife, causing Rhian to say some choice things as she saw the ragged gash across her arm, poured the potion over her wound, and then wrapped the padded bandage in place with quick movements. Rhian thanked him by swearing at him again as he pulled the bandage tight.

I clucked at her. "Be nice to the medic. How does it feel?"

"I'm fine, boss," she said, still scowling at the medic. "Wasn't me they were trying to kill, after all."

"You sure about that?"

"Yep. I'm too pretty for them to want to take me out."

"Well, then, I guess we'd better go find out who I've pissed off today."

Chapter Sixteen

BRYONY

Ash looked up as we entered the room, and my heart bumped a little. *Safe,* a silly voice said in my head. *He's safe.* That voice was closely followed by the more sensible part of me declaring the voice to be an idiot.

I couldn't disagree.

But that didn't stop me drinking in the sight of Ash—somewhat soot-smeared and rumpled—sitting on a table with all limbs intact and still breathing.

He met my gaze steadily as I completed my inspection, then shrugged the tiniest of shrugs, as though saying, "I'm fine. Don't worry," and then jerked his head toward Rhian, who was sitting on a stool about five feet away from him. One sleeve of her shirt was missing and one of Ash's men was bent over her, inspecting her arm.

I nodded and pushed my way through the crowd of soldiers, ignoring the selfish urge to check Ash first.

"Out of the way please," I ordered, and the medic looked up from his work with an annoyed expression that froze when he saw me. He stepped back with a half bow.

Behind me, I heard Guy say something to Ash and Ash murmur a low response.

I wanted to know what they were saying, but I had a job to do. I turned my attention to my patient. A nasty wound scored across her upper arm, half an inch wide and angry looking. Not deep but painful enough.

"What happened?" I asked, more to distract Rhian than anything. I knew a bullet wound when I saw one.

"Someone tried to kill the boss," she said.

My eyes jerked up from her arm to her face. "Pardon?"

Brown eyes studied me. Her free hand reached up to push an errant braid out of her face. "Got your attention, did I?"

"You always had my attention," I replied, feeling the ice creep into my voice. There was no time for games. "All my patients do." Besides which, I'd come rushing here across the City like a lunatic with Guy, who had turned up at St. Giles with a jumbled story of gunshots and buildings on fire and Ash's patrol that had made my stomach plummet like a stone dropped off a cliff. "What do you mean someone tried to kill Captain Pellar?"

"Shot at him. At us," she amended. "But they were gunning for him."

"How do you know?"

"No one in this City knows me well enough yet to want to kill me," she said with a grin. "And the first bullet hit near him. They wanted him."

For what exactly? Damn.

"Did you see anyone?" I focused back on the wound on her arm. Healing would give me a chance to calm the racing pulse that had galloped into life when she said that someone had tried to kill Ash.

"They were up on the roof but out of sight."

Or glamoured. "They?"

"Too many bullets for just one."

"I see." I resisted the urge to turn around and go and give Ash a piece of my mind. I didn't know what earthly good that could do, but it might make me feel better. But first I had to heal Rhian's arm.

I pressed the flesh above the wound gently and she hissed a little. "How sore?"

She grimaced. "I've had worse. Olson—that's our medic—put the yarrow potion he uses on it, but that stuff burns. I think it's half alcohol."

"I see." I knew the potion she meant. The Templars carried the same thing. It was basic but it did a good job at getting the worst dirt out of a wound in the field.

"Well, let's take care of the pain while I figure out the best way to deal with the rest." I took a breath and then let my power sink into her skin, setting a block around the raw flesh.

Rhian smiled suddenly and blew out a breath. "Not bad." She squinted down at her arm. "Can you fix the ink?"

I blinked. "Excuse me?"

She gestured at her arm and the tattoos that decorated the skin that surrounded the wound. I'd registered them before but hadn't been paying much attention other than to notice black swirls across her skin. The bullet had scored at a neat forty-five-degree angle across the dip where her triceps muscle curved, leaving the half-inch-wide strip of raw flesh. Which would heal into a neat scar. And spoil the design.

I frowned. "Can you tattoo scar tissue?"

She winced. "Hurts like a son of a bitch. And it doesn't always take the ink the same. Can't you put the skin back the way it was?"

I'd never actually tried. Once, Guy had come to me, wanting me to do something to hide the Templar crosses on his hands, and I'd refused, not wanting to do anything that would damage his skin. But his inks were old and deep in his flesh.

"How long have you had the tattoo?" I asked.

Rhian tilted her head, thinking. "That one? Ten years or so, I think."

She didn't look old enough to have been getting sigiling done ten years ago, but that wasn't my problem.

"Let me think. Are you hurt anywhere else?"

Braids bounced as she shook her head. "A few bumps and bruises. Nothing that needs a healer."

Well, that was one less thing to worry about. I extended my power again and closed my eyes, following the path into Rhian's flesh, focusing closer and closer into the damage. I could feel the difference between the unmarked skin and the tattoos, feel the taint of the ink in the cells. Could I heal the skin and make it change to match—extending the ink? I didn't know. But I could try.

I opened my eyes. "All right," I said. "I'm going to try something. If it doesn't work, I'll just see how close I can get the skin to normal and your sigiler will have to do the repair job on their own."

"Fair enough."

"Hold on," I said. "This may feel . . . odd."

I extended my power again, narrowing its scope and focus. Normally knitting skin and flesh back together for such a shallow wound would be relatively simple, but the added tangle of attempting to convince it to change color in the process was far more complex. I coaxed it across, practically cell by cell, not entirely sure it was going to work until I opened my eyes and saw the clean expanse of tattoo across her arm.

Rhian looked pale but impressed. "Huh," she said, looking down at her arm. She took a few deep breaths. "Not sure that's going to catch on instead of sigiling, though."

"Did it hurt?"

"Not exactly. The sigiling hurts, but that felt . . . very weird," she said. "Give me a needle any day." She shook her head and lifted her arm gingerly, easing it through a slow range of motion. "Thank you, Lady Bryony," she said, her voice sincere. "I can see why the boss likes you." Her eyes twinkled at me. "You'd better go check him out too."

"Is he hurt?"

"Not shot, not that I saw. But who knows what else might have happened to him?"

"Who indeed," I muttered. The girl was obviously enjoying herself and trying to do something nice for Ash. Which meant that people close to him had noticed how he felt about me.

"Rest that arm for a few hours," I said as I glanced over

my shoulder toward Ash and Guy, wondering if Guy had gotten a more detailed account of what exactly had happened than me.

Probably.

ASH

Guy broke off his grilling as Bryony joined us.

"Is Rhian healed?" I asked before Bryony could start her own series of questions. Curiosity and frustration burned clear in her eyes. Better to head her off at the pass so to speak.

"Of course. The wound wasn't serious."

"She was more worried about her tattoo," I said with a smile.

"I fixed that too," Bryony said, which made Guy turn his head to stare at her.

She rolled her eyes at him. "Don't look at me like that. It was nothing like the queen changing yours."

Guy made a humphing noise, but he didn't ask any further questions, more's the pity. It sounded like an interesting story.

Bryony's dark eyes made a quick inventory of me. "Anything you should be telling me about?"

I didn't think she was just asking me whether I was hurt. But I chose to take it that way for now. "No. I'm fine."

"There's blood on your hand."

"A piece of glass sliced me. Just a scratch. It's already healing. As I said, I'm fine."

"Used to people trying to kill you, are you?" she snapped.

"I've had a little experience," I shot back, then regretted it when a glimmer of remembered pain swam across those eyes. "I'm a soldier, after all," I added to soften the words.

"I know," she said. "But that doesn't mean you have to be a foo—"

"Captain Pellar, sir?"

Sergeant Brooks, one of the patrol leaders, interrupted, appearing next to Guy as though by magic. In reality I just hadn't noticed him. Which meant that I was more tired than I ought to be. Inattentive soldiers turn into dead soldiers.

"Yes, Sergeant?" I asked, trying to keep the fatigue out of my voice. I just wanted five or six hours of sleep. Then I'd be as good as new and ready to worry about who had tried to shoot me. I bit down against the yawn that tugged at my jawbone, eyes creasing with the effort.

"Sir, there're some people at the barracks gate. They're asking for you."

"People?" I queried, not liking the way he'd said the word a little too carefully.

"Fae, sir."

"Veil's eyes, not this again," I muttered. I looked at Bryony. "Don't these people give up?"

"You have been away too long if you think that's likely," she replied. She straightened her shoulders a little and did something that made her dress look suddenly like new. She motioned to the sergeant with a gesture that made her Family ring very apparent on her hand.

"Did they give any names, Sergeant?"

He swallowed. "No, ma'am. Just asked for the captain."

"How many of them are there?" Guy asked.

"About fifteen. Three wearing normal clothes and the rest in some sort of uniform." The sergeant shook his head. "Sorry. I don't know Fae customs well enough to identify them."

Fuck. Someone had brought some muscle along.

I sighed. "Well, I guess I'd better go see who they are," I said, easing myself up off the table. I was starting to ache in a few places—my knee and my back and down the length of one leg. Places where I'd hit the ground in the explosion, I guessed. I should've taking the opportunity to let Bryony give me the once-over after all.

I held out an arm to Bryony. "Will you accompany, my lady?" I asked formally. Having Bryony there couldn't hurt. If worse came to worst, then she was a witness that the Veiled Court would have to listen to. And if things stayed more civilized—which I had my doubts about if someone had brought guards along—then she was a valuable ally.

I thought it safe to assume that she would take my side. For now.

"I'm coming too," Guy said.

I nodded agreement. Muscle of my own couldn't hurt. And I had several hundred men in the barracks, which, in theory, was more than enough to subdue fifteen Fae. As long as those Fae were playing by civilized rules and not willing to just level the place to get to me.

"Excellent."

The sergeant looked at me with a troubled expression, awaiting orders.

"We can find our own way to the front gate, Sergeant," I said. "But why don't you go grab your patrol and a few others and join us there?"

"Yes, sir." He saluted, turned on his heel, and headed for the door, barking orders.

It was Tomar waiting for me. Tomar and someone else who I hadn't expected to see. My father.

I came to an abrupt stop, shocked into stillness. Bryony was paying attention and managed not to cannon into me.

"Your father," she said, low voiced.

"So I see," I said, just as quietly. I gathered my wits with an effort and stepped forward so that the barracks gate was the only thing standing between me and my relatives. Despite wanting to go to my father and actually speak to him, wariness kept me behind the metal of the gate. I contented myself with bowing deeply. "Father."

"Asharic," he replied gravely.

The hairs on the back of my neck prickled. It was hardly an effusive greeting to one's long-lost son. True, he had seen me in Summerdale just a few days previously, but we hadn't had any time to speak privately then.

So. Was he merely being formal because we were in public, was he displeased with me, or was there a third reason for him not making any move toward me?

Behind me, I felt Bryony move closer and there were

faint *clanks* and jingles as the Templars and my men formed ranks behind us as well. My father's gaze moved past me to them. I resisted turning around to see if the men would pass inspection.

Compared to the polished-to-gleaming gray-and-white clad Fae warriors mounted in two neat ranks behind my father, my men—and even the Templars—would look positively shabby.

I studied those warriors carefully. Gray and white were the colors of the court—would have been the colors of the Veiled Queen, but their clothing was carefully bare of the crown that would show they served the queen. That didn't mean they weren't fanatically loyal to her memory and trained to do what the court instructed with little questioning.

There were twelve of them, on horses that shaded from white to dark gray, as well.

The sight of them wasn't promising.

"Is there something I can do for you?" I asked my father, phrasing the question carefully. The more polite version would be to ask what I could do for him, but I wasn't going to commit myself to a promise without knowing what I was promising.

My father's lips thinned, and his pale blue eyes seemed cooler than usual. His hands tightened on the reins, sending a scatter of red and brown light dancing from his Family ring. "I bear a message for you, Asharic."

Still Asharic, not son. My father was keeping his options open. "Oh?" Every muscle along my spine tightened, bracing for action. I made an effort to relax. The Fae were still on the other side of the gate and they couldn't actually reach across and drag me away kicking and screaming—not without having to fight their way through my men and the Templars behind me.

Or using magic to make me do what they wanted.

It was rude to use a ward against a binding in public, but I carefully formed one around Bryony and me regardless. She sucked in a small breath and my father's brows drew together.

"There has been a challenge to you issued in the court,"

Father said, and my stomach did a slow loop before dropping somewhere toward the vicinity of my toes. Fuck and double fuck. This was exactly what I'd been trying to avoid.

I didn't want to be drawn into the chasms and abysses and posturing of Fae politics.

But it seemed that it wanted to get involved with me.

I took a minute to consider my response, biting down the instinctive "tell whoever it is to go fuck themselves," while I marshaled my thoughts. Because refusing a challenge was not really an option. Our laws were clear on that. Refusing a challenge was tantamount to an admission of guilt—not that I knew what I was supposed to be guilty of. It meant I accepted that I had caused whatever offense the challenger was seeking to redress. Even with no one sitting on the throne, the court could vote to reinstate my exile—or worse—on that basis. A steady stream of curses ran through my head.

"Who has issued the challenge?" I managed eventually.

My father flicked his eyes past Tomar to the third man sitting beside him. He wore black, which made it hard to identify him, but now, as he followed the conversation, he shifted a little on his horse and I caught a glimpse of his Family ring. Sa'Oriel.

Triple fuck.

This was Salvia's doing.

My father gave me time to take in this information. The man on the horse just stared down at me as though I were a particularly nasty species of bug who needed to be squished as promptly as possible.

"Invar sa'Oriel has issued challenge," my father said after a minute had passed. "His uncle is here to witness on his behalf."

Invar's uncle. Which, if my memory served, meant the man in black was Felip sa'Oriel. Stellan's uncle as well.

"What kind of challenge?" Bryony asked.

Good question. One I possibly should have asked first. It could be a duel or a test of my strength. The former was bad news. The latter only slightly less so.

"A challenge of strength," my father said.

I tried to remember what I knew of Invar. He was older

than Bryony and I by a good fifty years or so. I hadn't known
him well. Not as well as I'd known Stellan before I killed him.
I had no memory of Invar being particularly powerful.

But I'd had little need to take note of what he could do,
so he could be skilled beyond my knowledge. Or he could,
like me, have grown into, and strengthened, his magic in the
intervening years of my exile. I nodded. "When?" I asked.

"As soon as possible. The court would be pleased to have
this matter settled," my father said, and I understood why
they'd sent him instead of Tomar on his own. I wasn't going
to refuse my father a direct request, as far as they knew.

Not without shaming him more than I had done previously, which I had no desire to do. It hadn't been my parents'
fault that I had come to grief. They had warned me to be
circumspect when dealing with certain houses, but I hadn't
listened—being young and full of myself as I had been.

I had missed my Family while I was away. I loved them.
I didn't want to make life difficult for my father. He stood
high in the court, yes, but he didn't have the nasty ambitious
streak that Salvia and Bryony's father harbored.

If the court turned against him and my mother, it could
get ugly and quickly.

But despite all of that, I wasn't about to present myself
at court without some chance to rest and prepare myself.

"I would be pleased to present myself to the court tomorrow," I said.

That would be a reasonable compromise. It would give
me time to prepare and the court time to summon whoever
needed to be summoned to witness such an event.

My father nodded, and even ventured a tight smile.
"That is acceptable."

I let out a breath that I hadn't realized that I'd been
holding. I looked over at Felip, who was looking vaguely
disappointed. Had he perhaps been hoping that I would try
to get out of it and give him an excuse to try to drag me off
in chains to face my challenge? Pity. Knowing that he was
annoyed made my acquiescence slightly easier to bear.

"Wait," Bryony said. "Have rules been set for the challenge?"

"It is a standard challenge of strength," Felip said shortly. "They will test each other's strength before the court until one of them defeats the other."

"Define defeat," Bryony said.

"Until one does something that the other cannot undo," my father said firmly. "No permanent harm is allowed."

Not overly comforting. All that meant was that we weren't going to be fighting with weapons. There were plenty of ways to kill someone with magic gone "accidentally" wrong, if you chose. It would be frowned upon, of course, but with no queen in the court, there was no one to be the ultimate decider what the punishment should be. In a fight for power, it was expected that there would be some casualties.

If you weren't strong enough to defend yourself, then you shouldn't be participating, was the theory, but that didn't take into account people like me who got drawn in from the sidelines against their will.

If I refused the challenge, then I was basically announcing I was weak. And that would mean that anyone who bore me a grudge could come after me with little fear of reprisal.

For my Family's sake—and my own—I had to defend myself.

But I didn't have to be happy about it. Anger was already burning in my stomach, which meant that I had to tamp it down to keep control of my powers. There was no point tipping my hand and giving my opponent any advantage.

"I will come to Summerdale tomorrow, then," I said. My father nodded. Felip looked as though he wanted to protest, but I was the one being challenged and I had the right to set a time and place for the response if I chose, as long as that time wasn't more than a few days.

Tomar just looked relieved, which made me hope that he, at least, might be on my side. Beside me, Bryony's power pulsed slowly, making the air tingle, which made me think that she was as annoyed as me by the whole thing.

Good. Maybe I should step back and let her smite a few people. She kept her true strength well hidden and I knew she had little interest in the court, but anyone who didn't respect her power was foolish indeed.

My father turned and nodded at the guards, who obediently set their horses into motion and headed back the way they had come. Heartening. It meant that my father was the one that the court had put in charge of that particular troop and that I wasn't going to be spirited away against my will.

Felip sent me a last poisonous glare over his shoulder as he took up the rear behind them.

It was a little too convenient, I thought, him showing up here so soon after the attack on me. Perhaps I should look to that Family to find those who were trying to bring me down.

"Well," Bryony said, when the last of the Fae had vanished from view. "It's quite a day you're having."

"You do seem to be popular," Guy rumbled agreement beside her. "What's this all about?"

"Fae politics," I said. I wondered exactly how much to tell Guy. I didn't know enough about Invar's current place in the court to interpret the challenge more precisely, but I didn't think that telling my employer that I could be dragged into the power struggle for the Fae throne when I was meant to be helping him win a war was going to make the situation any better. "The man in black was Felip sa'Oriel, and he's Invar's uncle. The sa'Oriels are the Family behind the events that led to my exile." I looked at Guy, hoping he'd accept the explanation. I was willing to tell him more in private, but I didn't want all my men knowing what was going on.

Rhian and Charles emerged from the crowd of men behind us and joined Guy. Rhian scowled at the Fae as they rode off. "What's this all about, boss?" she asked.

"It's nothing for you to worry about," I said. That was true enough for now. There was nothing that Rhian could do about the situation, so there was no point in her worrying. The one who had to worry was me.

"I need to go back to the hospital," Bryony said suddenly. Her tone had a snap of anger and there was an answering bite in the roil of her magic. Better to let her go and calm down before I sought her counsel. I wasn't entirely sure what she was angry about. Or if she knew either.

Chapter Seventeen

ASH

Sleep didn't come easily. I curled up on the hard bed in the tiny visitor's room I'd been assigned in the Brother House, trying to will my body into surrendering consciousness—I would have to patrol later—but it fought back, jittery with too much adrenaline. The unforgiving mattress didn't help. I made a mental note to get Rhian or someone to fetch mine from wherever it had been stowed. I could sleep on hard ground when I needed to but preferred something softer when I didn't. The Templars apparently stuffed their mattresses with rocks.

Or my inability to get comfortable was just another way my overstretched nerves were taunting me. My mind joined in the fun by playing a looping tableau of my father and Felip and then, just to really twist the knife, flickering images from the night I'd shared with Bryony.

Her bed was plenty soft.

But I was here, not there. The bed and a small table and chair, plus a skinny cupboard for clothes, were the only furnishings the Templars provided. I was used to spartan at times on the road, but my command tent was more comfortably fitted out than this. I stared at the lack of furnishings, hoping sheer boredom would induce sleep. Eventually it did.

I managed not to dream, or not to remember if I did. Maybe it was the shock of being jolted awake by someone pounding on my door. Years of training had me out of bed and reaching for my weapons before I remembered where I was. Brother House. Templars. Unlikely to be under attack right here in my room.

I scraped a hand over my eyes, trying to drag my brain back from high alert. "Who is it?"

"Guy," came the curt answer.

Now what? I pulled my shirt back on—I hadn't removed my breeches—and staggered over to the door, drawing back the bolt. "What?" I asked, somewhat blearily.

Guy stared back at me, his expression unmoved. Had he slept? He was human; he needed sleep more than me. I tried to remember what patrol he'd been on and then gave up the thought as a yawn fought its way over my face.

"Bryony sent me to bring you to the hospital."

I blinked. "Did something happen?"

"No. This is about the tunnels." The cold set of his face and the displeasure in his voice acted almost as well as a vat of coffee.

"I see." Then, "Give me a minute to get dressed."

Guy led the way down into the bowels of the Brother House and eventually to the gate of a very well-guarded tunnel. It was straight for the first few hundred feet, but then things began to get complicated when we reached the intersection with a second tunnel. And then a third. Our route became a series of branching turns that I kept track of by habit.

"Just exactly how far do these things go?" I asked when we made yet another abrupt turn.

"Far enough," Guy said. "There's a connection to most of the hospital buildings. Maybe all. I've not used them all, but the founders of the hospital wanted there to be ways not to have to go aboveground at night."

"Good thinking."

"Yes." Guy stopped as we reached an intersection with yet another tunnel. We'd been walking for at least a quarter of an hour.

Guy looked behind us, as if checking for any sign of pursuit. Though who exactly would be following us from the Brother House escaped me.

I stopped and listened too but couldn't hear or sense anyone. "The coast is clear."

"Good," Guy said. Then he fished in his pocket and pulled out two small charms made of leather and glass beads. They gleamed with an unusual spark of restrained power, unlike any I had felt before.

I took the one he passed to me and held it up to examine it. "Who made this?" I asked.

"Holly," he said.

"It's strong," I said. "Is this how she makes her living?"

"No," he said with a half smile. "She was a spy."

Was? "A spy?" I hadn't heard that part of Holly's story. I studied the charm again, trying to follow the threads of power bound into it, waiting to be woken. I thought I knew what it was for even though I wasn't sure why we needed such a thing here in what was meant to be the safe heart of the hospital.

"And a thief, sometimes. But mostly a spy. Her charms work best on herself, but they're good for short periods for other people."

That made sense. Holly was *hai-salai* like Fen, and the powers of the half-breeds were unpredictable. Other than the wraiths, of course. They could all walk the shadow. But then, they didn't usually have the skills of glamour and working charms of the others. I guess those are somewhat unnecessary when you can turn invisible and walk through walls.

"If you'd told me, I could've made my own."

"No time," Guy said.

I nodded and peered at the charm again. I could see how it worked now, so I shoved it in my pocket, sending a tiny surge of magic into the leather to activate it. Sure enough, my entire body suddenly vanished from sight. I'd been expecting it, but it was still disconcerting. I'd never liked invisibility charms.

"Show-off," Guy muttered, then activated his own charm—I assumed it was primed to respond to something he did to it, given that, as far as I knew, he had no magic. Seeing such a big man disappear was somehow even odder than vanishing myself.

"Can you hear well enough to follow me?" Guy asked. His disembodied voice made me jump.

"Of course," I said. The big Templar was light on his feet but not as silent as a Fae. Plus, he smelled of leather and, faintly, of horse. Easy enough to keep track of even without the iron song that rose from the weapons he carried.

"Good. Let's go."

I let him get a little ahead of me, then started after him. At the next turn of the tunnel, I stopped abruptly as the sudden bite of iron stung the air. Much more than the annoying buzz from Guy's sword. The sensation surrounded me, making my magic shy away and weaken. Unpleasant. But not nearly so unpleasant as the sudden burning ache in my bones.

Iron. More than I'd ever felt in one place before. I'd been right—there was definitely something important down here. "Wait," I called.

I heard Guy stop. "What's wrong?"

"Just give me a minute." I breathed deeply, trying to adjust. I was used to iron but not so much of it so close. It was relentless, like a fog closing around me and thinning the air, making it hard to think and breathe. I reached for my magic and it was as if there were a wall of ice between it and me.

My skin crawled. I couldn't push through the barrier; my magic was choked off to nearly nothing. My breath went shallow, panicky as I reached again and felt just the merest thread of magic. I wrestled the panic away, took another deep breath. Bryony knew this was here. She must come down here. Which meant I could bear it too. I made myself step forward again. "I'm all right."

Guy took off again and I walked, more cautiously now,

as the iron sensation built and swelled and pressed and made me want to turn and flee back the way we had come. How did every Fae in the City not know this was here? Or maybe they did.

But along with the iron there was an ever-increasing buzz of warding magic. Layers of "keep away" and "go back" adding to the desire to turn around and leave. Maybe it was enough to keep everyone away. It should certainly work on anyone human who came this way.

It didn't, however, seem to bother Guy. Maybe his charm shielded him. The soft pad of his booted feet on the marble-tiled floor of the tunnel stayed steady. We turned one last corner and I came face-to-face with the iron warping my senses. A massive door was set into the stone wall, dull gray and ominous. Wards shimmered around it, sparking like fireworks, but they weren't enough to distract me from the weight of metal around me.

Guy suddenly materialized, looking no happier than he had when we started this journey. I took that as a sign that I could deactivate my charm too and hoped, as I did so, that my face didn't look as green as I felt.

Bryony was stronger than I'd imagined if she came down here regularly. Maybe she'd built up her tolerance over time, the way I had with the weapons my men carried. Though how she'd been able to do so, I couldn't imagine. This close, the iron felt as if it were warping my bones, making my head ache unbearably. My stomach churned in protest.

Guy took another charm from his pocket and pressed it to the door. The wards flared, then died away. He grasped the massive bolts, slid them back, and then swung the door open. He gestured me through with a wave of his hand and I managed to make myself do as requested.

As I stepped over the threshold, the pain in my head intensified with a jolt that felt like an axe blow and I nearly stumbled. Luckily I didn't. I didn't want to find out what it would feel like to make actual contact with the iron when just standing near it was so painful. Exactly how much iron was here? A queen's ransom and more. And all hidden away and kept secret.

Which made me worry more about what was yet to come. What warranted this much protection?

Guy closed the door behind us and I tried not to shudder as the iron bit around me again.

"Are you all right?" he asked, coming over and peering into my face.

"It's not the most . . . pleasant sensation," I admitted.

He nodded. "So I understand. Bryony says it's better inside."

I hoped she was telling the truth.

We traveled a short distance down another tunnel only to be confronted by yet another iron door. I stood and breathed whilst Guy opened it.

I moved more carefully through the second door and found myself in a room lit only by a single old-fashioned oil lamp burning in a bracket near a more ordinary wooden door on the far side of the room.

Gaslight so far below the earth would be risky, I supposed. The rest of the smallish room held only a few tables littered with various kinds of medical apparatus and glassware and a plain wooden desk near the door that had an equally plain chair drawn up to it and a stack of leatherbound books piled neatly in the right-hand corner.

Guy finished locking the door behind us. He came up beside me. "Last chance to change your mind," he said. "Once you go through that door, then you'll know something that very few people know. And that knowledge is not without its risks."

"People are already trying to kill me," I said, trying to sound more cheerful than I felt. "It can't get much worse than that."

He didn't smile at my feeble attempt at humor. "Trust me. It can."

"Will knowing this help me win this war?" I asked.

"It will help you understand part of the reason we fight," he said. "As to the other, well, maybe in time."

"Then lead on," I said.

Whatever it was that was hidden behind that very simple last door, it at least offered the comfort of no longer being quite so close to the iron behind me. At this point, I was willing to do almost anything to get some distance from that.

"Very well," Guy said, but before he moved, the wooden door swung open and Bryony appeared, still looking as though her temper was less than even. The chain at her neck glimmered orange and red, confirming my impression.

"What took you so long?" she said to Guy, without acknowledging me.

"Wonder Boy here was sleeping."

Bryony looked at me then, her gaze unreadable. Unfair, when she was the one who'd told me to rest. I stared back at her, and her gaze sharpened suddenly. "Are you feeling all right?" she asked.

"As good as I ever feel with a ton or more of iron nearby," I said. Making my voice sound close to normal took an effort.

"I have something that will ease it a little."

Ease, not fix. Damn. Still, I'd take any relief offered.

"How do you stand it?" I asked curiously.

"I'm used to it now," she said. "And I limit my time down here. Come through. It's better on this side."

I didn't need a second invitation.

Though I did wonder if I might have made a massive error in judgment in taking this contract in the first place when I saw what lay before me in the room beyond.

A hospital ward. Full of people who either lay too still for true sleep or—for maybe a third of them—seemed to be awake but moved too slowly for my liking. I studied one of the beds. I knew that stillness. Had seen it before.

"Veil's eyes," I swore softly. "They're blood-locked."

"Some of them, yes," Bryony said. "Some are getting better."

"There's no cure for blood-locking," I said automatically. That was a simple fact of life in Half-Light. Any humans who were stupid enough to sample the delights that the Night World dangled before them like hunters baiting a trap and came under the spell of the addictive pleasures of drinking vampire blood were doomed. Maybe not if they were found out the very first time and kept away forevermore, but that rarely happened. And few who had a first taste turned away voluntarily.

From across the room, a figure straightened beside one of the beds. "Not yet," he said in a low voice. "But we're getting closer."

His voice was polite, but as he straightened, I saw the white hair caught back in a tail behind his head.

"He's Blood," I blurted, then felt somewhat foolish. Obviously this was not news to Guy or Bryony.

"Yes," Bryony agreed with a hint of amusement in her eyes. "But he's not going to bite you. Atherton, would you come over here please and say hello to Captain Pellar?"

The vampire nodded, then flowed across the room, moving too quickly. The sight didn't ease my nerves. Only when he stopped beside Bryony did I get a good look at his face—or what was left of it. Scar tissue twisted and formed red whorls where his eyes should have been and marred half of the length of his face as well.

"Shal e'tan mei," I swore again, though I kept the words under my breath. Or I thought I did.

The vampire's mouth twisted wryly. "I agree," he said. "The Blood Court's handiwork has a way of taking you that way."

Bryony touched his arm. "Atherton, this is Asharic sa'Uriel'pellar. Captain of the mercenaries working for the Templars. Asharic, this is Atherton Carstairs. He works with Simon."

And how in all the possible hells had that little alliance come about? I fought for some semblance of manners. "Hello," I said, and started to bow but then stopped myself when I realized that the gesture was fairly futile. Atherton wouldn't be able to see it after all.

"Captain Pellar," he returned affably. "Bryony has told me so little about you." There was a hint of reproach mingled with curiosity in his voice.

"There's not much to tell," I said. "Sword for hire."

His head tilted. "That seems like an oversimplification. For one so . . ." He trailed off and I stared at him. Could he sense Fae powers?

The Blood had their own strange magic—not the least of

which was how they transformed humans into their own kind—but it was nothing akin to the magic we used.

"And what exactly is that you and Simon are doing down here?" I asked Atherton, determined to change the subject away from me. I was fairly sure I knew the answer to that one. There was only one likely answer as to what a vampire and a healer might be doing in such a secret location with a roomful of blood-locked humans.

"We're working on a cure," Simon's voice said from behind me.

I started. Damned iron. Normally I would've been able to sense a sunmage moving behind me as easily as breathing. But the iron made me feel half-blind and dumb. Which made my hands itch for the pistol at my hip as my instincts blared false alarms of imminent danger.

Unless Bryony and the DuCaines were the ones who'd tried to kill me earlier—and I'd bet my entire fortune and that of my Family against that, no matter how annoyed Bryony currently was with me—it seemed unlikely that they'd brought me down here to reveal their biggest secret and then kill me. Though I had little illusion about what might happen to me if I turned around and shared this particular secret with anybody else without their approval.

"Working on?" I looked at some of the patients ... the mobile ones. The only blood-locked humans I'd ever seen didn't move unless instructed. And the worst of them didn't even do that. They just lay where they were until they died.

"We've had a little success."

"How?"

"Firstly something we stumbled upon," Simon said, and his tone suggested that I shouldn't ask too many questions about what that might be just yet. "And then with some assistance from my sister and Lady Adeline."

My eyebrows shot up. "Lady Adeline and her friends know about this?"

"Yes. They're assisting us."

"And how long will that last?"

"Well, it's not like they can take what they've shared back," Simon said. "Even if things do go wrong."

"They could kill all of you."

"Unlikely," Simon said.

"Extremely," Lily agreed, coalescing out of the air beside him. "They might get one of us, but it's difficult to pin all of us down."

I looked at the four of them. Bryony, who was from the highest of Fae Families, Simon, the strongest sunmage in the City, from what I'd been told, a wraith, and a Templar who was legendary several realms away. I had to agree with Lily. Short of blowing up the entire hospital at a time when all four of them were in it, I wouldn't want to try to take them out.

I frowned while I considered the implications of Simon's matter-of-fact statement. If the humans had a cure for blood-locking, then it changed the balance of power between the races considerably. The humans had conceded that the Blood had the right to any blood-locked humans and agreed that those who chose to go to the Night World and drink what was on offer ceded their rights to protection as part of the original treaty.

At the time, they'd probably never imagined that quite so many people would continue to willingly—or stupidly— give themselves into the Blood's power. But they had. There were always those curious or reckless or idiotic enough to think that they would be the exception. That they could drink just once and not be ensnared.

True, there were some humans who managed to stay on the fringes of the Night World and never actually taste vampire blood, but there were far more who fell. And died.

The Blood also fed from their Trusted, of course. Their human servants traded service for the chance of one day being turned and becoming near immortal. The Trusted too ceded their rights, but the Blood didn't lock them. The vampires needed them functioning until—if they did—they earned that final reward. But the Trusted were few in number and of course, for every one of them who turned, there was another Blood to be fed.

The Blood needed the humans. They could drink Fae or Beast blood, but neither of those races was easy prey when unwilling and not many were willing.

No, most of their food came from the humans and most of that from the blood-locked.

If the humans could cure the blood-locked, then they would not be so willing to declare them lost.

And then what would the Blood do?

"So," I said to Simon, casually, "anyone tried to kill you lately?"

He shrugged. And then, oddly, grinned at Lily. "A time or two. No one's managed it yet, though."

"So someone in the Blood knows what you're doing?"

"We think that Lord Lucius suspected," Lily said. "I don't know for sure. Nor do I know what Ignatius or any other Blood lord may know or might have known. Lucius wasn't one for sharing secrets very often, but he may have told somebody."

"If Ignatius knew, why didn't he use this to break the treaty?"

"For the answer to that, you'd have to ask him," Guy said.

Simon sent him a look I couldn't decipher. Guy's grim mood didn't seem to have improved now that the secret was revealed and he'd done his duty in bringing me here. I wondered if he was not as happy with Simon's work as the others were.

"For Ignatius to do that, he would have needed proof. He didn't have proof," Simon said.

"He could have broached the issue," I said. "Forced the queen to deal with it."

"Apparently he thought other methods would be more effective," Simon said. "Perhaps he feared the queen would be sympathetic to our cause."

"And was she?"

"I don't know. I never spoke to her," Simon replied with a shrug. That was evasion. I was good at spotting evasion. I sent a questioning glance at Bryony.

"I don't know either," she said. "She never asked me about it if she did."

"Hmmm." That lack of explanation was apparently as good as I was going to get. "So Ignatius may be trying to kill you or find out what's down here?" That explained the exercise the other night, at least. Testing the defenses.

Which was a concern. What did Ignatius have up his sleeve that he felt confident to try to launch an attack on one of the human strongholds? It was one thing to send a few Beasts—fast moving and excellent night fighters—to pull off a raid, but it was another thing entirely to try something on the scale that would be required to win their way through the hospital's defenses and down here to the tunnels.

Not to mention that they then had to get through the wards. Which would require Fae help, I thought. The wards obviously couldn't be broken with iron. They'd need to be undone magically. And vampire magic wasn't the same as Fae.

"Exactly how many people know about this place?" I asked.

"Everyone in this room," Simon said. "Plus, Holly, Fen, and Saskia. Father Cho. And Lady Adeline and a few of the Blood who came with her."

"No spies, if that's what you're thinking," Guy said firmly. "Especially not now with the border so closely watched."

"There are ways around any perimeter guard." I could think of several forms of communication—magically aided— that could be used for a start. And that was before you got to simple codes. "It's naive to think that there are no sympathizers on this side of the border."

"That's why the wards have all been increased. Here and for the rest of the hospital and the grounds," Bryony said.

"We need earlier warning than that," I said. "Wards closer to the border . . . you have those. We need to sensitize them." I frowned, thinking. Charles would be the best person to use. He had a devious mind and had come up with traps and defenses that had saved our necks from sticky situations more times than I could count. Then the Fae— whether from my men or Bryony's healers—could execute whatever ideas he came up with.

"We can do that," Guy said. "Anything else?"

I shrugged. "I'd suggest you work on nailing down your cure."

"Brilliant," Simon said, deadpan. "Why hadn't we thought of that?"

"What's the sticking point?" I asked.

"Do you know much about healing?" Simon asked.

"A little," I said. "I'm not trained like Bryony, but I was taught the basics and I've picked up a thing or two along the way."

"He healed Bryony's arm in Summerdale," Guy offered.

"Not exactly the most subtle of achievements," Bryony murmured.

"That doesn't mean I didn't understand the theory," I protested. "I just need more practice."

"Let us hope that it doesn't get to that point," Bryony replied, flexing her hand. "Because if we get so low on healers that we need your help, then we're all in trouble." But she smiled as she said it and I risked an answering grin.

"I believe Captain Pellar was asking Simon to explain his theories," Lily said, steering us back from the conversational byway we had strayed down.

Simon touched her hand and then nodded at me. "All right," he said. "It goes something like this. When a human drinks vampire blood, his blood changes."

"Changes how?"

"That's the part that's hard to explain without healing abilities. You understand how we see when we use our power?"

I nodded. Yes. I didn't have the fine control that a healer had, but I knew what it was to sense what was going on inside a body and see the structures in my mind and how they were damaged.

Simon looked relieved. "Good. Then you know that it's something that's sensed more than felt. Anyway, the more vampire blood a human drinks, the more their blood changes. We can sense a difference in the blood between a normal human and one who's blood-locked. We think the changes mean that it doesn't do all the things that blood is supposed to do anymore."

"So you need a way to change the blood back to how it was?"

Simon nodded. "Yes. But it's not that easy. There's also magic involved. The blood-locked are tied somehow to the vampire's bloodline."

"I don't understand."

"If I was blood-locked," Guy said, "and you killed the vampire who locked me, it wouldn't be enough to free me."

"It never has been, has it?" I asked.

"It's not been tried very often," Lily said. "But as Guy was saying, it's not enough to kill the vampire who addicted the person. But if you kill the eldest vampire in that bloodline, then it has an effect. We found out by accident when Lord Lucius died. Some of the blood-locked Simon was treating, they woke up a little when that happened."

Woke up? I looked at Guy for confirmation. He nodded. But he still looked grim. Which was surprising. I would have thought a Templar would be in favor of anything that might save humans from the Blood. "All right. So killing Lucius roused some of the blood-locked. Why?" It seemed the obvious question.

"We assumed that it must have been either because Lord Lucius was the one who locked them or because he was the oldest vampire in the City. More likely the latter. Lucius rarely left anyone he locked alive. But he was definitely the oldest vampire in the City, and for many of the court, he was the oldest of their bloodline," Lily said.

"Not an easy hypothesis to test."

"No," Simon agreed. "So we've been looking for other ways. We'd already been using Atherton's blood to keep the patients we had here alive. His blood kept the patients from getting worse, but they didn't improve either. Then Saskia noticed the difference in their blood."

"Saskia? Isn't she a metalmage?" Metalmages were not healers.

"Her affinity is for iron," Bryony said. "In her case a very strong affinity. She can sense blood and she can tell the difference between the blood of someone who is locked and someone who is not."

"Can you do that too?"

Bryony nodded. "I learned from Saskia."

"You merged?" Merging was one way the Fae used to teach healing techniques. It meant piggybacking onto another's magic and senses so you could follow along whilst the other healed. I hadn't heard of a Fae merging with a human before, but then again, I didn't know much about how human healers were trained.

Another nod. "It was the quickest way. I can tell the difference, but I don't yet know what makes them different."

My curiosity was growing. Bryony was one of the most highly skilled healers the Fae had. And here was a problem she couldn't solve.

"Do you mind if I try?" I didn't expect to be able to solve what Simon and Bryony couldn't, but I'd learned over the years that sometimes a different perspective is more valuable than any other.

Simon turned to Atherton. "Do you have a recent sample?"

"I can take one," the vampire said. "I was going to collect a new batch this afternoon anyway." He turned and made his way through the room to a small cupboard that rested against the far wall. Watching him navigate the room without vision was eerie.

While we waited for Atherton to take blood from one of the patients, Lily asked me about the previous night's patrols. It wasn't a long conversation; there wasn't much to tell. I recounted the details of the attack earlier in the day.

"You didn't catch anyone?" she asked.

I shook my head. "No. By the time the patrol got back to where we'd been, the snipers had vanished."

Atherton came back to us with a vial of blood, thick and dark red.

I extended my senses, trying to think back to the basic healing I did know. I knew how to make blood clot but had never paid much attention to the blood itself beyond that. The liquid in the vial didn't seem unusual in any way that I could tell. I said as much.

"You need something to compare it to," Bryony said. "Simon, let Atherton take some from you."

Simon rolled up his sleeve and Atherton repeated the

procedure, filling a second vial. And then, before Bryony could say anything else, he extended his own arm so that Bryony could take blood from him as well. They held out the vials, Simon's human blood, Atherton's vampire blood, Bryony with the blood-locked's. I studied them and reached out again.

Atherton's blood felt . . . fainter. Much like the vampire himself. It carried that same sense of disconnection from the earth that I associated with vampires. But apart from that it seemed the same to me. Cooler than Simon's, but that was understandable. The Blood are cool to the touch.

Temperature . . . I studied the vials again. And this time reached out with a different sense. The one I used to talk to fire. And this time I saw it. Atherton's blood was cool. Simon's was warm. And the blood-locked was somewhere in between. Much cooler than Simon's even though it had only been out of the patient a few minutes more.

"The temperature?" I said. "Is that the difference?"

Bryony looked startled. "Temperature?"

I pointed at the vials. "Atherton's blood is coldest. Then the blood-locked, then Simon's."

Bryony reached out and touched Simon's vial. Her finger rested on the glass for a few seconds while she looked first at the vial Simon was holding and then the one in her hand. "These two feel the same to me."

I shook my head. "No. That one's colder. I swear it. Look with your magic."

"I'm not as good with fire as you are."

"Try anyway."

She frowned and closed her eyes. After a moment, she blinked. "You may be right."

"What would make blood colder?" I asked.

Simon studied the vial in his hands. "I have no idea. But it's another path to explore. Thank you, Captain."

Chapter Eighteen

BRYONY

I found Ash on the roof of the Brother House later that night. We'd parted ways after we left the hidden ward. He had questions, but I had no more answers to offer and had sent him back to finish his day and then, if he was sensible, to rest before what was to come tomorrow.

I had returned to St. Giles, to complete my work as well, but when I left my office, I was well aware that Ash wasn't sleeping. The pulse of his power sang clearly from the Brother House, not calm as it would be if he was asleep but instead, restless and burning.

Idiot man.

He would go to Summerdale with no sleep and then where would he be?

I argued with myself for a moment or two, trying to tell myself that Asharic wasn't my concern, but I had passed that point when I let him into my bed again and then when I'd stood by him earlier. Not to mention that he now carried one of the most dangerous secrets that the City had.

He was indeed my concern, if not my problem entirely.

And as much as part of me wanted to deny it, I couldn't actually leave him to sit through the night alone.

It was cool up on the roof, the autumn air starting to carry with it the first hints of winter rather than the dying breath of the summer heat. But I was warm enough, and able to do something about it if I wasn't. I carried charms for all sorts of eventualities and besides, if he truly wanted to, Ash could call fire from the stone and make it dance to warm us.

He was standing by the parapets, looking out toward the Night World. I joined him, staring down at the darkened City and the line of lights that bisected it, marking the boundary between day and night.

Beyond that line, more lights flared out across the Night World, but from what I could see of the roads and streets, they were quiet as usual.

"You should be resting," I said.

"I couldn't sleep," he replied. His expression was distant as he gazed out at the flickering lights.

They looked pretty from this distance. Like stars strewn across the ground. Deceptive. The Night World wasn't pretty. It was deadly. I wondered what Ash was seeing or if he was somewhere far away in his head.

"Coming up here isn't going to help that." I gestured at the lights below. "It seems quiet down there. Nothing for you to do."

"There's always something to do," he said absently, but he stepped back from the parapet, turned his attention back to me. "What are you doing here?"

"I could feel you pacing from halfway across St. Giles. It was distracting."

He smiled. "You're worried about me." His smile widened with delight. "Actually *worried*."

"I'm annoyed," I said. "I wanted to get some sleep myself. It's a bit hard with you over here acting like a beacon fire. Are you trying to make yourself into a target?"

"I don't think anyone in the Night World has a gun that can hit me from here," he said.

"No, but they might have magic that can find yours. And besides, I'm not sure the Night World is what you should be concerned about just now."

"What should I be concerned with?"

"Whatever Salvia has in mind for you tomorrow."

His expression grew rueful. "She'll have to find someone better than Invar, if she wants to stop me."

"You think you can beat him?"

"I think I'm stronger than him and I've spent the last thirty years perfecting dirty tricks he won't know about."

"You know tricks of warfare. Not Fae magic."

"Want to bet?" His smile returned. "I'll make it worth your while."

He always did love gambling and egging me on to do stupid things. "You mean you'll bet me that you'll leave me alone if you lose? That seems safe enough. If you lose you won't be in any condition to cause me any trouble for a while anyway."

"It's not a duel to the death."

"I hope not," I said. "But there're a lot of things that can be done to you short of death."

"What do I get if I win?" He wriggled his eyebrows at me, grinning.

"Most likely a whole lot of trouble," I said bluntly.

The grin died and I almost kicked myself. He'd been relaxing and I'd gone and blurted out the blatant truth and brought all his worries front and center again.

"That much I agree with," he said eventually. "It's never a good idea to show your hand."

"Exactly. Remember that tomorrow. Don't get flashy if you don't need to." I paused. "Unless you want to draw the attention of the rest of the court and not just Salvia."

"Trust me, Fae politics is the last thing I'm interested in."

I believed that much. I wished I believed that he wouldn't be dragged into it despite his lack of interest if he won the duel tomorrow. Winning would take power. And power was very much of interest to a Fae Court with an empty throne. A gust of wind blew over the parapet, and the cool air made me shiver. "Then you need to be sensible tomorrow. Keep your wits about you."

"I'll do my best."

"Which is why you should get some rest," I said. "So you can remember to do just that."

"I'm not sure I can sleep."

"Well, maybe I can help with that."

His smile flashed again.

"No. Not like that."

"Why not? If I'm to have one last night of normality, isn't it traditional to send me off with proof of your favor?"

"I haven't yet turned you into a toad," I said. "That's all the proof you're getting tonight. Anything else is just a waste of your energy."

"Not from where I'm standing."

"You're an idiot. That's why I'm in charge."

"Since when?"

"Since always."

He laughed. "I guess that's true. I always was yours to command."

"Good," I said. Then lowered myself onto the flagstones with my back against the wall, cushioning myself with my cloak and a small dose of power. I patted my lap. "Come lie down."

He did so, wriggling into position and settling his head against my legs. "We haven't done this for a long time." He looked suddenly nostalgic.

"Don't go getting any ideas." I had my own memories. Memories of exactly the kinds of things that used to happen once Asharic lay down with me. "Close your eyes."

He did for a few seconds and then one dark eye popped open. "Are you sure we can't do the other thing?"

"Yes," I said firmly. I placed my hand over his eyes. "Now, do you trust me?"

"Always."

"Then relax. Just breathe." I left my hand where it was and stroked a finger along his cheek with the other and then waited, slowing my own breaths deliberately until I felt the tension ease in him and his own breathing settle into the rhythm I'd set.

I took a minute to just savor it. The familiarity of him.

The simple sensation of rightness that came from being near him. And then, before I could be too foolish or he could get bored and decide to rebel, I wound a thread of power through his defenses, sent him into sleep, and settled in for a night of keeping watch.

"You don't have to come with me," Asharic said.

"Shut up," I said, for at least the tenth time that morning. Ever since he'd woken from his sleep, annoyingly good humored and energetic, he'd been trying to convince me he could go to Summerdale alone. "If I let you go without me, you'll wind up as a statue for sure."

He grinned then, swaying with the motion of the carriage. "Your father won't like you coming with me."

"My father doesn't like a lot of things I do. One more won't hurt. And besides, if I'm with you, then he'll protect you."

"You hope. He doesn't like me very much."

"Oh, he hates you. However, he likes me. So he's not going to let someone get to you while I'm nearby."

"That didn't work so well last time we were in Summerdale."

"But he's on alert now. Besides, the court has summoned you. If they're following protocol, then they should be protecting you."

"Until the duel starts. And last time I fought a duel, there was not a lot of protocol enforced."

I wrinkled my nose at him. "Poor little sa'Uriel. No one treating you like a proper Fae Lord? Not indulging your every whim?"

His smile turned a little wild. "No, but I can think of a few whims I'd like to have indulged. You could set a good example."

"I don't need to set a good example. I am a good example. A virtual paragon of Fae virtues."

"Apart from that pesky insistence on living in the City and healing humans."

I nodded. "Everyone needs a flaw or two. Keeps things interesting."

"I agree. I've worked hard at cultivating mine."

"Which are?"

He slid a little closer. "An inability to take no for an answer."

"You had that one from the beginning. No cultivation required."

"An inability to stop thinking of all the interesting things we could do in this carriage to while away the long and boring hours until we reach Summerdale."

My smile faltered, the humor drowned by a searing flare of heat.

Damn him. I'd been resisting him successfully, but once again it seemed that proximity and Ash and I were not a good combination when it came to my self-control. I shifted on the seat, feeling the pulse at my neck speed and an answering pulse spring to life between my legs. I needed to answer him. Needed to keep the banter going and direct it back toward safer ground. But my tongue was thick in my mouth, words stolen by the sudden awareness of him. I had spent the night with my hands on him, his body against mine as he slept. A night of watching and fighting the feelings that being with him sent.

But now I was starting to lose that fight. The carriage was too full of him. His scent. His voice. His body.

"Ah," he said softly. "Have I found a flaw that holds your attention?"

I looked up, met his eyes. "Damn you."

"That's not a no."

"No."

Heat stole around me as though he'd set his power loose. Though I didn't think magic had anything to do with this. It was just Ash himself that made my heart shudder and my skin warm.

His eyes were deep and dark, his expression half-eager, half-wary. "A smart man might think that you were doing this out of pity. A last taste before the end."

"Are you planning on dying?" I tried to keep my tone light. It wasn't a duel to the death, but I didn't trust Salvia one inch.

"No."

"Then a smart man would stop talking before he gave me time to think this through and change my mind." My gaze strayed down his body to where he was hard against the fabric of the leather breeches he wore.

His expression eased into a grin. "In that case, shall we pursue the subject?"

He slid off the seat, dropped to his knees on the floor before me, set his hands on the sides of my thighs.

The smile he directed at me spoke of all the things I wanted him to do to me. I settled back on the seat. All the things I wasn't going to stop him from doing now. While we still had a chance. "What did you have in mind?"

His hands moved onto my thighs, rubbing gently as though memorizing the feel of the silk of my dress. Despite the dress and several layers of petticoats, the sensation was as though he'd laid them on bare skin.

He pulled me forward so that my hips were on the edge of the seat. The carriage bounced a little and I braced myself with one hand against the frame of the window.

"Damn you," I repeated, and Ash laughed then.

"Not for long," he promised. "Open your legs for me, Bryony." He pushed my skirts upward, and I lifted my hips so that he could bunch them out of the way. And if my legs fell open at the same time, well, that was just coincidence, wasn't it?

Ash ran a hand up my calf. "I like it when you do as I say."

"Don't get used to it," I shot back, but the words came out breathless as he pressed a kiss to the inside of my left knee, his tongue wetting the spot before his lips found it with the softness of a butterfly settling on my skin, sunwarmed and weightless. The delight of it shivered up my legs and pooled in my stomach.

"I'll never get used to it," he said softly; then his lips moved higher.

It must be the magic, I told myself, a last desperate lie. Magic that made me rouse beneath his touch as I did for no other man and magic that made me want to hold him and help him and have him even though I knew—knew in the darkest walled-up places of my heart—that it couldn't end well. That he would leave me torn and broken again.

Leave me alone. Leave me without any of it.

And yet still I couldn't stop.

Because it was magic. Magic that shivered through me and around, magic that brought pleasure in a rush and delight like Fae wine as his lips and tongue touched and kissed and tormented.

Magic as his fingers slid to join in the game and drove me further still until I broke against him, calling his name and magic that meant that, even after that, I still needed more and pulled him down to the carriage floor to finish what we'd started. To ride the wild magic, frenzied and hungry and dangerous, that drew us together so fiercely.

Magic that might just be the death of me. Or of him.

And as we finally climbed back onto the seats, the rising height of the Gate visible in the distance, I knew that it was something far more dangerous than magic. Something that I wasn't yet ready to name or face.

The Seneschal must have been expecting us. We'd barely reached the Gate when the door opened and she stepped outside.

She bowed toward Asharic, then to me in turn, and I hoped that the glamours I'd cast after our interlude in the carriage had restored my appearance to respectability.

Ash returned the gesture and moved past before I had time to think about anything like asking him to change his mind. To come back to the City with me and pretend he'd never been challenged. Foreboding made my pulse hammer in my ears as I walked after him.

Ash was waiting by the far door. No hesitation on his part, then. I smoothed a hand down my skirt, took a deep breath, and joined him.

"Let's get this over with," he said. He smiled as though he didn't have a care in the world. The offhand beauty of the expression made my heart beat harder still. He was just going to walk on through as if nothing even slightly dangerous waited for him beyond the threshold.

I grabbed his arm as he stepped toward the door. "Wait."

"What?"

I looked back at the Seneschal, who stood a few polite feet away from us, her face wearing its usual serene expression. "I need to speak to Asharic alone."

"I cannot leave this room until all travelers have passed through the door," she said.

"But—"

"It is the law."

And apparently there would be no arguing with the law. Even though, technically, with no ruler on the throne, there was no one who could actually enforce it. But then again, the Seneschal was tasked with protecting the main entrance to our realm. Not a duty you entrusted to someone who played fast and loose with the rules.

"As you wish. Then you'll have to excuse me for a moment."

I made a quick gesture and threw up an aural ward. The Seneschal's mouth made a small O of surprise, but she didn't make a move to stop me, nor did I feel anything testing the ward, so I assumed she was going to let it be for now.

Ash looked impatient. "What is it? We don't have time to waste."

"My father, when we were here before. He said that people felt you when you stepped into the Veiled World. Said you needed to shield. Do you know how to do that?"

"Of course." He looked somewhat exasperated.

"Then do it."

"I don't see why it's necessary."

I resisted the urge to knock some sense into his head, summoning a patient tone with considerable effort. As much as yelling at him would relieve my nerves, I couldn't help him once we were inside if he was ignoring or avoiding me because he was angry. "Someone tried to kill you here once before. And someone tried to kill you in the City yesterday. I'd rather not be taken out when they try again, so why don't you try not advertising your exact location?"

"You could always stay here." He looked at the door and then back to me, the movement impatient.

"We've already discussed this. Besides, you said Fen saw me with you. Do you want to risk your luck by going against what he saw?"

"He didn't say whether he thought that was a good thing or a bad thing," Ash objected.

I was starting to wonder if he was more nervous than he was admitting to, to be standing here arguing with me. "Let's assume it's good. It's less confusing that way. He's very powerful. Even the queen recognized that much."

"And if you're wrong?"

"Then we'll both probably be dead and we won't have to worry about it. Now, please. Shield yourself."

He touched the sword at his hip. "It seems wrong to go into a confrontation pretending to be weaker than I am. The Fae respect power."

"We want you to survive to get to the confrontation. *I* want to survive to get to the confrontation. You can be as all-powerful as you want once you get there and we'll deal with the consequences. But first we have to make it to the court."

I had assumed that my father would send some of his guards to escort us to the court, but even that gave no guarantee of safety. Not least because I had no way to be sure that my father wasn't one of the ones who wanted Ash dead. I was, however, fairly certain that he didn't want me dead, so if he had sent guards, they should be of some help if we were attacked. If I stuck close to Ash they would have to protect him to protect me.

Once we were in the court, there was more protocol to protect us, but protocol could be a trap as well. And Lady only knew what happened if Ash won the challenge. I wasn't ready to think about that possibility just yet. What I wanted was for my father to be wrong about his strength, for him to lose without being hurt, and for us to return to the City, no longer having to worry about every Fae with ambitions seeing him as a threat.

Then we'd just have Ignatius to defeat and everything would be fine.

Simple.

Ash still looked indecisive, so I decided to cheat a little. I put my hand on his chest, feeling the hard bump of his Family ring where it hung against his chest. Leaning in, I kissed him quickly. "Do it for me?" I asked. I hid a smile when I felt him obey.

I dropped the ward and the Seneschal looked as though she wanted to say something, but before she could, Ash took my hand and tugged me after him through the door.

Chapter Nineteen

ASH

Stepping onto the marble that marked the boundary of the Veiled Court was something that I had done hundreds of times. But rarely had it felt so much like stepping onto a battlefield.

The Veiled Court was never the safest of places to be — not once a Fae becomes an adult at least — and I had been schooled from birth to be wary of that danger and keep my wits about me when I was there, but this felt different.

The last duel I'd fought, the one that was the reason that I was here yet again today, had been fought outside the court. Salvia had engineered it and she had made sure that it had taken place somewhere where the queen wouldn't interfere to stop us. Where she wouldn't find out what we were doing until it was too late. Which was exactly what had happened. It had been too late and the queen had no choice but to exile me.

I had wondered sometimes if Salvia had foreseen that. If she had thought about the fact that if Stellan had succeeded in killing me instead of the reverse, the queen would have been forced to exile *him*. If she had, would she have still risked her precious son to indulge her dislike of me and get rid of whatever threat she thought I represented?

But today, there was no queen to intervene; there was only the mercy of the court—should anyone powerful enough to intervene decide to do so. I had little way of knowing who supported Salvia and the sa'Oriels and who might support me.

Despite Bryony's presence by my side, I had no idea if Lord sa'Eleniel would help me either. Yes, if Bryony was in danger, but otherwise . . .

Well. I'm sure he wouldn't mourn if I were removed from his daughter's life again. I had no intention of putting Bryony in any danger, so I wasn't counting on requiring his assistance.

I also hadn't counted on my father being there to meet me as I descended from the carriage earlier.

The sight of him nearly stopped me in my tracks, but gravity being what it is, it is somewhat difficult to stop in the middle of descending a step, and I managed to keep moving and not show my surprise.

Once I was safely on the ground, I nodded a greeting to him but turned to help Bryony down from the carriage, needing a moment to gather my wits.

I had seen him twice now since my return. But both times had been brief. And not in circumstances facilitating a father-son discussion. Too many others present, for a start. Now he was here alone and obviously waiting to speak to me. Which I assumed meant he had come to some sort of decision about how he would deal with my return.

I wasn't ready for that conversation.

Wasn't ready for the way my hand felt suddenly naked, the weight of the Family ring hanging around my neck heavy beyond belief.

I hadn't felt that way since the earliest days of my exile when the pain of grief and homesickness and recrimination was at its worst as I'd ridden farther and farther away from the City, headed Veil knew where. At the time my destination hadn't mattered. I just needed to get beyond the borders of the queen's territory.

"My father is here," I murmured to Bryony.

Her fingers tightened around mine. "Did you expect him to be somewhere else?" she said gently.

"Quite frankly, yes," I said.

She rolled her eyes at me and let go of my hand, stepping away to give her father room to exit the carriage as well. "Perhaps your father is less of an idiot than his son."

I nodded. "That would have him joining a long list of people, according to you."

That earned me a smile.

"True. And that list will keep growing if you don't do something sensible like go and talk to him." She made a little shooing gesture with her hands. "You owe him that much."

That was true, at least. There was no point to delaying any longer. I had to face my father and hear what he had to say. It would be well within his rights for him to disown me, to refuse to recognize me as his son now that I was back. I'd brought disgrace to the Family by killing Stellan. They didn't have to welcome me home or acknowledge me. True, he'd brought me news of the challenge, but that was a matter of protocol. I'd tried not to read more into it than that. If I allowed myself to hope for reconciliation, it would only make rejection worse. Though I'd brought all of this on myself. However Maxim chose to greet me, I probably deserved it.

I straightened my shoulders and walked over to him.

"Father," I said cautiously.

"Asharic," he answered gravely as he studied my face. I held my breath a moment and then he smiled. "It is good to see you." The smile faded a fraction. "Though your mother and I would have preferred that more favorable circumstances returned you to Summerdale."

"I didn't start this," I said.

"No. Let us hope that today might bring an end to Salvia's nonsense." His mouth went flat and I wondered whether Salvia was coming close to pushing my famously good-natured father to a point of no return. Which was a point that, in my small experience of it, was not a good place to be.

"We shall see," I said. I hadn't made up my mind what outcome of the challenge was the best for me. Losing was problematic and—if the sa'Oriels decided to cheat—potentially fatal. But winning . . . winning might start a whole other chain of problems. But I wasn't about to discuss that with my father. He wouldn't understand why I would want to do anything other than win. "Did Mother accompany you to court?" Change of subject—that was safest. Plus, I had to admit, now that I was here, speaking to my father, the desire to see my mother as well was hard to ignore.

He shook his head. "We decided it was best to keep things simple for now. Head of the line only." He cocked his head at me. "Did you lose your ring in your . . . time away from us?" His hand gestured toward my naked one, his own ring—twice as intricate as mine—blazing like a rebuke.

I had known this moment was coming. I shook my head. "No. But I did not know if you would still care for me to wear it."

He winced. "If that had been the case, I would have taken it from you when you left. But no. The queen exiled you from Summerdale. But she could not force me to disown you. Nor did we want to." He stepped forward and laid a hand on my shoulder. "You are my son. Nothing can change that."

My chest tightened at his words, something long knotted inside me coiling up, then releasing with a bittersweet ache.

For the first time in a very long time I reached for the chain around my neck, pulled it over my head, and undid the clasp. The ring slithered free of the silver links as I held it. It felt heavier in my hand than around my neck, unfamiliar somehow. I stared down at it, watching the colors spark in the sunlight, turning the silver metal around the gems to gold and brown and red. Then I slid it onto my finger.

I didn't know if it would help in the challenge to come, but if not, at least I would lose knowing I still had a family. Bryony came up beside me as I flexed my fingers, feeling the metal warm against my skin.

"It looks good there," she said as she dipped her head toward my father in greeting.

"Yes, it does." And with that, we walked into court.

*   *   *

A lot of protocol surrounds the calling of a challenge in the Veiled World. It seemed that, even without the queen there to enforce the law, we were going to do things the formal way. I knew the forms by heart, so I let them wash over me, replying automatically when required as I studied the assembled court.

Invar stood opposite me, his face impassive as he too listened to Lord sa'Eleniel speaking. He didn't have the fiery red hair of his dead cousin, but he was taller and more broadly built than Stellan had been. And he had the same deep brown eyes as Stellan, the same shape and set to them, which was somewhat unnerving, my mind for a moment imposing Stellan's face over Invar's. As though the dead had returned to judge me.

I shook my head to clear the image. Stellan was long gone. It was Invar I had to worry about now. Like me, he had forsaken full Court robes. Apparently he shared my view that freedom of movement was more important than wearing the correct attire. Even if, unlike me, he actually possessed the correct attire in the first place.

Across from him stood Salvia and Isak with various members of other Families arrayed behind them, giving me a fair idea of whose allegiance lay where. There were far fewer Fae standing with me and my father and Bryony, but there were some at least. And, even better, the largest faction of all lined the fourth side of the square along both sides of the empty throne, proclaiming their neutrality in the matter.

I could take neutral. I figured most of those standing there were making a statement against Salvia rather than favoring me—me being both a known troublemaker and somewhat of a wild card, given my long absence—but anything that wasn't out-and-out support of the sa'Oriels and sa'Namiels was good for me.

If I was more familiar with the court, I could have read the exact relationships in the positions everyone had taken. No doubt my father and Bryony could do just that, but there was no way for them to give me an interpretation while Lord sa'Eleniel was speaking. And once he finished, there would be no time for talking either. As soon as the challenge was called, we would start our fight. Until one of us yielded.

Having gleaned what I could for now, I turned my attention from the Fae to my surroundings. I was still shielding my power, but despite that, I could feel the song of the court and the Veiled World itself. Feel the slow, ancient pulse of the magic that ran beneath it. All that lazy power there to be used, ready to leap to my call.

It stood the hairs on the back of my neck on end and I was very glad that this was the second time I'd been to Summerdale rather than the first since my exile. This time, it wasn't quite so seductive and I didn't feel quite so drunk with it.

There was still a certain amount of temptation to let it run through me and wreak some old-fashioned havoc, but that would only lead to more trouble. The aim today was to stay alive. And to not kill Invar in the process of doing so.

When Lord sa'Eleniel finally stopped speaking, the silence seemed to hang in the air while Invar and I stared at each other. Behind me, and in front and to either side, wards shimmered to life. Meant to protect the onlookers from any stray effects of our fight. And meant to protect us from any interference from others.

I trusted the ones behind me—those set by my father and by Bryony—but I wasn't going to take the others for granted.

My eyes stayed fixed on Invar as I watched him, trying to guess what he might do. He was probably wondering the same thing, but I wasn't going to be the one to start this. He had called the challenge; he could make the opening gambit.

I still held the shields around my power. No point giving myself away and besides, I was hoping to get through this without giving the court any hint of my true strength. This challenge was bad enough. I didn't want to get caught up in any further idiocy while they sorted out who would take the crown.

I counted heartbeats while I waited, a trick I had taught myself on the battlefield. The act of counting calmed me, slowing my heart as I stretched the time between numbers, evoking a form of trance where my focus narrowed and all distractions faded away.

I'd nearly reached fifty before Invar thrust his hand forward and a circle of flame rose around me, the heat of it uncomfortably close.

"Really?" I said to him. As gambits went, it was fairly traditional. But also a strange choice when my affinity had always been for fire. I watched Invar warily, wondering if a second attack lay behind this seemingly innocuous move.

The fires leapt higher suddenly, the flames deepening in color, the heat scorching my cheeks.

I had no doubt he would keep building the intensity if I didn't act. I had a high tolerance to heat, but I could burn like anyone else.

I loosened my hold on my power a fraction and reached for the flame. It died down almost immediately. So this was just a test. A feint to draw me out. Nowhere near the depths of Invar's strength.

Stellan had been strong too. Strong but arrogant. And not the smartest of men. I was hoping Invar shared that with his cousin as well.

Arrogance and pride could be turned to useful weapons in such a fight. Goading a man into making a mistake was sometimes the easiest way to defeat him. The toughest opponents were always the calm and cool ones, and the sa'Oriels weren't known for their even tempers.

I gathered dying remnants of Invar's flames around me, curled them into a ball around my hand, and flung it back toward Invar in a streak of light and heat. Again, a lazy, obvious move, but let him think that we were doing this the traditional way for now.

The point of the challenge was to throw power at each other until one of us did something that the other couldn't undo. At that point, the stuck one would yield and it would be all over.

It was childish in a way, as almost all power struggles are.

But I had yet to come across a single place in all my soldiering where it was done any differently. There were always men and women who strove for power and held on to it with clenched fists, most of them heedless as dogs snarling over a bone as to who they might hurt in the process.

Invar caught the ball, and the flames vanished in his hands.

There was a small murmur of appreciation from the assembled court that this at least wasn't going to be one of the challenges that ended at the first exchange, but I didn't shift my focus to see who might be commenting.

No, I went back to waiting.

It wasn't a long wait. Invar made a complicated sweeping gesture and suddenly vines snaked up through the marble to wrap around my legs and arms, pulling them apart with enough force that it hurt.

There was no time to stall in reacting this time. I sent my magic skimming over my body and outward, snapping the vines and stepping free of the remnants. Some of them wriggled toward me, seemingly intent on recapturing their prey. I set them alight with another quick spell. They burned with a nasty acrid stink.

"Want to try something else?" I said to Invar.

He didn't look worried. Not even the slightest bit uneasy. Which told me that either he was a very good cardplayer or he was holding back just as much as I was.

To push the issue a little I sent a line of fire snaking toward him. He stepped out of its path and then, with a gesture, summoned an icy wind that snuffed the flames.

It was a neat trick. I filed it away for future reference.

After that, the attacks grew more serious. Invar conjured strange creature after strange creature. Birds with razor-sharp glass beaks, hissing metal snakes dripping acid, a cloud of darkness that made the air steam as it approached me. Each time, I managed to turn it back, to counter. Heaps of smoking small corpses—could you call twisted, melted metal a corpse?—began to pile up on the tiles, blood and guts and acid making the tiles deadly slick in places.

We circled the square, stalking each other warily as the

intensity of the attacks grew with each round. I no longer
heard the sounds of the court, straining instead for any
small hint that something might be coming from behind or
from the sides, trying to drown out the sound of my breathing and focus only on what was happening around me.

Invar was serious; that much was becoming clear. The
things he conjured would hurt me if I let them.

But as I was contemplating how to bring this to an end
without too much of a show of strength, Invar flung out a
hand and the marble in front of him cracked and split, revealed a deep fissure. And rising from it came creatures unlike anything I had seen before. Skeletons. Or near enough.
Creatures of wood and stone and something gleaming
darkly like metal made of night, with no flesh and no faces,
just long limbs and hands with too many fingers. Clawed
fingers, ending in gleams of razor-sharp metal. They carried
swords as dark as themselves.

I wasn't entirely sure if the blades weren't actually part
of the long arms, but there was no time to figure that out. As
they stalked toward me across the expanse of marble, moving too fast for my comfort, one thing was clear. I needed a
weapon.

Which was a problem. I hadn't been allowed to bring my
sword with me. And members of the assembled court were
meant to be unarmed as well. Probably some of them had
broken that rule, but any weapons they carried would be
very carefully glamoured.

In fact, the only sword that I knew for sure was in any
sort of reach was the one embedded in the marble at the
foot of the empty throne. It had been inlaid there four centuries ago, when the Veiled Queen had forged the treaty, a
symbol of the strength she held and her intention for there
to be peace—and no need for swords—in the City.

It had lain there for so long, protected by layers of spells
and wards set by the queen herself, that I imagined no one
even noticed it very often. It might as well have been part
of the marble it lay in. But I had knelt by that sword when
the queen pronounced me exiled, my eyes focused on the
gold and silver length of it and the glittering jewels embed-

ded in its hilt so that I wouldn't look up and show my fury at her sentence.

Every inch of it was indelibly etched in my memory.

Though, right now, it didn't matter how well I could picture it. It might as well have been a mile away. The throne was behind the Fae who were watching us, behind the wards that they had raised to keep us in, not to mention that the sword itself was bound behind the magic the queen had used to set it there.

The first of the creatures had almost reached me and I readied myself to twist and blast it, but instead of attacking me, it continued past me, swinging the sword it carried back before whipping its arm forward and flinging the razor-sharp blade into the crowd behind me. Where Bryony stood.

Bryony. I stopped thinking. Without quite knowing what I was doing, I stretched out a hand and dropped all the shields I had been holding, sending my power deep down into the land beneath my feet. I felt a shudder as though the ground had moved under me and then a strange sensation as though the air had warped and arrowed through me with a sharp, sudden pain that made me gasp. But then I was holding the queen's sword and I swept around and sliced the creature in two before turning and carving my way through the other three.

I ended up panting, facing Invar. Who had tried to hurt Bryony. Rage coursed through me. I snapped my hand open, holding nothing back, and Invar froze, bound by the threads of marble that had shot up from the stone to wrap him, binding arms and legs.

I left his head free and his face contorted in fury as he shouted, then struggled, but the marble stayed firmly in place. With another shove of my power, I closed up the gap that he had opened in the marble, neatly carving a second wave of the skeleton creatures in half where they were emerging, and then sent a wave of fire across the marble, searing it clear of the remnants of the other beasts that had died in our fight, leaving it pristine white and gleaming in the sunlight.

Holding the sword ready, I waited one long minute, then another, but it was clear that Invar couldn't undo the bonds I had set.

From beyond the wards, there was nothing but frozen silence.

I turned to where Salvia stood, her face ashen but her eyes full of rage, and bowed in her direction.

"Don't bother me again unless you find someone who can beat me," I snarled, and as the wards started to dissolve on all sides, I left the marble, pausing only to pass the sword to Lord sa'Eleniel. "I have a war to win."

Chapter Twenty

ASH

The journey home was very different. The driver spurred the horses on, keen to beat the sunset and get us all safely back in the human boroughs before dark. Wise man. For my part, I watched Bryony watching me. Waited for her to say something, to ask me how I'd done what I did.

The truth was, I didn't know. Nor, I had to admit, did I know what it meant that I could do it. The only certainty was that I had put myself squarely in the line of fire and, no doubt, made myself some new and powerful enemies. All the more reason to put some miles between me and Summerdale before the court had a chance to rally. I'd half expected that someone would try to stop us from leaving but no one had.

"You have an interesting idea of not showing your hand," Bryony said eventually. I wasn't sure if it was anger or concern underlying her words. Perhaps a little of both.

"He attacked you." The words tumbled from my mouth before I could stop them. The truth might not endear me to Bryony. Nor, if I thought about it, was it a truth that lay easy with me. I'd been in control of myself, had been smart about how I'd dealt with Invar—until he threatened Bryony. Apparently that was enough to snap my control. And now the entire Fae Court had had a demonstration of exactly what power I wielded. And besides that, a demonstration of my feelings for Bryony. Feelings that might just have put her in the line of fire as well.

"I'm capable of defending myself," Bryony said, but her expression softened a little.

"Maybe so. But I'm a soldier. I'm built to defend what's mine."

Her eyebrows arched even as a spark of gold ran the length of her necklace. "Who says I'm yours?"

"Are you saying you're not?"

"You have bigger problems than that to deal with right now."

"You're not a problem." Almost everything else was. The Blood. The Fae. The City. My Family. But not Bryony. Not unless she turned me away.

My fingers twisted the ring on my right hand, trying to find a place for it that didn't feel strange. Family. Roots. A strange concept after my time away. I would have liked the chance to stay awhile and speak to my father, to even see my mother, but that would have to wait. I knew now that they still thought of me as belonging, that I was still welcome to wear the ring. That would have to be enough to keep me content.

That and the fact that Bryony hadn't been able to say she wasn't mine.

BRYONY

I left Ash at the Brother House and made my way back to St. Giles. There was more to be said between us, but now wasn't the time. Slender black shadows were overtaking the last rays of sun across the City, and Ash needed to focus on the night ahead, on his patrols and his men.

I, however, was free to worry. As much as I tried to bring my thoughts back to the City and the hospital full of patients who waited for me, I couldn't shake the image of the queen's sword rising to meet Ash's hand.

Idiot man. Why had he done that?

I pushed open the door to my office, trying to wrestle my thoughts back to the here and now. There was little point to begging trouble from the future before I had to. Besides, I was fairly certain that trouble would come looking without my help.

"What did he do?"

I started, biting back the cry that half rose in my throat. Fen leaned propped against my desk, his long legs stretched before him, clad in leather.

"How did you get in here?" I snapped, trying to recover my composure.

"I told the orderly that you'd asked me to come," he said. Amusement flashed across his face. I wondered if the orderly he'd spoken to had been male or female. Even though it was common enough knowledge that Fen only had eyes for Saskia, that didn't stop women from losing their heads when he pointed his pretty green eyes in their direction and chose to exercise his charm.

Beasts were notoriously charming, and Fen had that blood in his veins, along with Fae and human. However, I didn't find anyone breaking into my office charming and I stalked around the desk, making a mental note to give instructions to the staff about privacy.

"I'll thank you not to suborn my staff," I said as Fen rose and turned so he was still facing me.

"Suborn? Hardly that. A little white lie."

"I'll thank you not to lie to them either."

"Only because you're jealous that you can't." He grinned and then shook his head. "But none of this is answering my question. What exactly did your Captain Pellar do while you were in Summerdale?"

"What makes you think he did anything?" I said, stalling.

"Well, for one thing, something made the magic toll like a bell a few hours ago. Loud enough that even I could feel it. And then there's this vision that's been stalking me all day. Something about a bloody great sword flying through the air. A bloody great sword that looked somewhat familiar."

"There are many swords in this city right now."

"Agreed. But there aren't that many that I know by sight." He spread his hands as though he wished he could sweep the thought he was having away as his mouth tightened. "This one is fairly unmistakable. So what does the Veiled Queen's sword have to do with Asharic?"

I sighed. There was little point in trying to turn Fen away from his inquiries. He was a seer. A seer trained by the queen, if only for a short period of time. He would know the truth of it soon enough. And if I was honest with myself, I could use a little insight right now.

"He called the queen's sword to his hand during the challenge," I said.

"Shal e'tan mei."

"Precisely," I agreed, "Though I think we may have moved beyond that point."

"The sword answered to his power?"

"Yes."

"And how did the court take that?" he asked, somewhat warily.

"That remains to be seen. We left somewhat abruptly after Asharic brought the fight to an end."

"Talk about setting a cat amongst the pigeons. Does he know what this means?"

"I don't think he's thought it through to the logical conclusion," I said. I felt suddenly exhausted, the sleepless night and the tension of the day descending upon me like the weight of one of the giant bells in the cathedral.

"Which is?"

I straightened in my seat with an effort, trying to drive away the fatigue and think. "You're the seer. You tell me."

"You know more about the court than I do," Fen countered. "You were brought up there."

"I wasn't alive the last time the throne was empty. I don't know exactly what happens to fill it again," I pointed out.

"So you have just as much experience with this as I do." I rubbed my temples, seeing the sword spinning through the air again. Flying to Ash as though it recognized its true master. "And honestly, I don't think anyone had thought of trying to call the sword before. Maybe with the queen gone it would answer to any of us."

"You don't really believe that," Fen said.

"Maybe I'm trying a little crazy DuCaine optimism."

"I'm not sure even DuCaine craziness can do much good here." Fen sat down in one of the chairs that faced my desk, his hand rubbing his wrist where the scar from the iron he used to wear to control his powers still showed faintly silver.

"Why? Have you seen something? Do you know what's going to happen?"

"No. Like I said, all I've seen all day is that sword."

"Will you look now?" Ash might be in denial about what he'd done, but I, for one, had a fairly good idea what might be about to happen. It would be easier if I knew if I was right. It would give me time to prepare myself.

"Do you really want to know?" Fen said.

His expression was sympathetic. It didn't make me feel any better.

"Yes," I said with more conviction than I felt. The last time Ash upturned my life, I'd had little warning, nor had I had any when he returned so abruptly. If he was going to capsize me once more, then I wanted time to prepare for the impact.

Fen leaned back in his chair. His expression turned distant, his eyes darkening. His power didn't feel like Fae power. It was different somehow . . . the shimmer of it reverberating through the air, bouncing and echoing and fracturing in all directions before forming a whole once more.

Part of me wanted to tell him to stop, to change my mind, to keep the lie in my mind a little while longer, but before I could, Fen gasped and swore, focus returning to his expression like a whip cracking.

"What is it?" I asked, steeling myself for the reply.

"Torches," he snarled. "They're coming."

Before I could ask who, the cathedral bells started to toll
a warning and the question was no longer necessary.

Ash

The bells tolling wildly from halfway across the City drew
our patrol up to a sudden halt. I turned toward the sound,
swearing under my breath. We were nearly at the eastern
edge of the city, and until now, things had seemed quiet.

But the bells. The bells meant an attack. I couldn't hear
anything that sounded like fighting in the surrounding
streets. Which meant we were in the wrong place.

Fuck.

As if to confirm my assessment, a flare suddenly arced
bright across the night sky, coming from—if my judgment
was correct—somewhere west of the Brother House. Not
only that. It seemed to come from within the human boroughs. Which meant this wasn't merely a skirmish. This was
serious. A second flare followed the first, a dimmer red
against the smoke trail left by the first. Two meant exactly
what I thought. A serious attack.

And that meant we had to get there fast. I turned in my
saddle and started giving orders.

We'd planned for this. Established protocols. Even so, I
didn't like what I had to do. But my men didn't hesitate.

They divided themselves into two forces. The first formed
up behind me and the second stayed with Rhian. They
would remain here.

It didn't matter how big the attack was; it would be foolish to leave the rest of the border unprotected. That would
just give the Blood a free pass into human territory.

Rhian knew her job and she nodded at me across the
stretch of road and then jerked her head in the direction I
needed to go.

I twisted back in the saddle and sent Aric into action. We
weren't quite at the border where the streets were wide and

clear, so we couldn't move at full speed, but our horses were surefooted and well trained and we made good time as we worked our way toward a wider street where we could gallop.

As we traveled I noticed shutters being flung open in the houses we passed, dark silhouettes peering down at us and the odd worried face lit by a lantern or candle.

I had no breath to tell them to bar their windows again and stay inside. They needed to use their heads and follow the instructions that had been communicated throughout the human boroughs. There were evacuation plans in place, of course, but in areas where there was no active fighting the safest place for humans to be was indoors.

Our pace quickened when we finally reached the main road. There was a distant roar and a gout of flame shot into the air, its source unclear. A tall building for the fire to be seen so clearly from so far away. There were a few of those in the City. My gut twisted; I hoped it wasn't St. Giles.

Bryony.

The flares had come from farther away, I reminded myself as I bent closer to Aric's neck and urged him on. St. Giles was as protected as it could be. And Bryony could take care of herself. She'd told me so just a few hours earlier.

I couldn't let fear distract me from what was happening around me. What was most important in this moment and only this moment. Letting myself think much beyond that was a good way to end up dead.

I judged we were about halfway across the city when the pack of Beast Kind came tumbling out of a cross street to meet us. I tried to count them, but in the darkness, with some of them in wolf form and some in the huge and too-fast hybrid forms, it was too hard to keep track of them all. More of us than them. That was about all I needed to know.

I drew my sword. Their numbers didn't matter. Likely this was a skirmish. A diversion to keep us from getting to where we needed to be. So we would cut our way through and keep going. Beast Kind are fast but not as fast as galloping horses over anything more than a short distance. I moved my sword to give the signal that we were to keep moving and heard the rasp of steel around me as the men drew closer in behind me.

The Beast Kind howled at us and started to close and I decided that I could speed up our task. I sent a line of fire arcing toward them across the cobblestones and then a second. The fire sprang up in two walls, obedient to my will, burning fiercely, hotter than normal fire. It must have caught a Beast or two in its path, because some of the howls changed in tone to pain and outrage rather than challenge. I heard the slithering swish of arrows from behind me and smiled grimly as I leaned forward. I trusted the aim of my archers but didn't need to make myself any more of a target than I had to.

Between the twin walls of fire, there was a path for us to travel two abreast without singeing the horses. I gave another signal and reined Aric back so that he slowed. I needed to hold the fire and be ready with a second attack if necessary. Which meant I needed to be able to see what was going on. The men started to flow past me, swords slashing at the Beasts brave enough to leap at them through the flames.

My men cut them down with ruthless efficiency, though I saw one man—I couldn't tell who in the weird orange and yellow light—dragged down from his saddle. Rage flared within me.

I was a soldier, yes, a general of a sort even, but I didn't like losing even a single man.

I sent more power into the fire, flaring it hotter and higher, then turned my attention to sending some of the sparks leaping from its depths and coaxing them to brighten and flare into fireballs to rain down on the Beasts.

More howls sounded and I nodded in satisfaction. Ahead, the men had reached the end of the fire's path and I could see the first of them urging their horses to more speed. Which meant it was time for those of us bringing up the rear to do just that.

"Forward," I bellowed to the men still with me, and Aric took off as though I'd lit a fireball under his tail.

He ran as though both Beast Kind and flames were chasing him, ran faster than I had ever known him to run. Maybe he could feel the urgency pounding through my veins or maybe he was truly scared, but I urged him on, careless of the fact that I had overtaken most of the patrol again.

We were closer now, so close I could hear the sounds of fighting ahead and cries and screams that told me there were people other than soldiers caught up in the attack. The hot, harsh breath of smoke started to fill the air and I sent my power ahead of me, trying to feel for the source of the fire to see whether or not I could quell it.

Maybe that was why I didn't see the net until Aric suddenly reared, squealing a protest, and I, caught off guard, tumbled from his back and hit the cobbles with a bone-jolting thud that stole half the breath from my body. I rolled into a ball, all too aware that there was a full squad of men thundering toward me and not wanting to become so much flattened meat on the road.

But before I had time to worry about that, I was surrounded, tall, white-haired forms coalescing out of the shadows, swords and guns in their hands.

Blood.

What in the seven hells?

It was only then that I noticed how dark it was.

No sunlamps.

Fuck.

It was just about the only thought in my mind.

Fuck and how stupid I had been to let myself get caught up in battle fever like a rank novice. The feeling only intensified as another net was tossed on top of me and I felt the burn of iron.

I rose to my knees, struggling to throw off the net. It tightened against me as I fought it, apparently glamoured to bind me. The iron sapped my strength so that I couldn't blast the spell into splinters. As I thrashed, one of the Blood let off a shot that sparked the cobbles in front of me. A chip of stone gashed my cheek, slicing through skin like the sharpest of Fae blades. Blood began to drip down my face. I froze, not wanting a second bullet to hit me.

Double fuck.

That was all I needed. Fresh blood scenting the air when I was surrounded by vampires and bound with iron.

Though in this situation I doubted they would stop to drink from me. No, they were more likely to just kill me and be on their way.

It occurred to me that they could have done just that already. I didn't dare turn to see where the rest of the patrol was. I could hear the clash of swords and hooves dancing on cobblestones and men shouting behind me. So there were other enemies out there in the darkness. Beasts or Blood, fighting my men.

The sounds of combat grew louder. No one was coming to my rescue just yet. That much was clear.

But I was still alive.

I could rescue myself if I started to use my head. Figure out how to break the binding on the net.

I took a breath. Slowed it. Breathed it out. Drew another in. Felt the calm start to rise within me despite the pain from the iron. My magic was a mere spark now. Not enough to do anything useful like set the Blood surrounding me on fire but maybe enough to free me of the net eventually. I set one part of my brain to trying to study the magic spelling the net through the fog of the iron. By some small mercy of the Lady, none of the net was actually touching bare flesh, which was probably why I was able to do even that much.

Then I looked up at the Blood who'd fired the gun. "What do you want?"

The man—he was shorter than some of the others, but apart from that and the odd red-brown shade of his eyes—he looked much like any other vampire. White skin, white hair held out of his eyes with a dark metal band. Gleaming fangs visible in his mouth where he smiled nastily down at me. "Who says I want anything, Captain Pellar?"

He knew who I was. That was worrying. Had this trap been set for me in particular or was he just lucky that I had stumbled into it? I studied him as I tried to think of the right response. He hadn't deferred my question to anyone else. So I assumed he was in charge, at least of this particular attack. "If you didn't want anything, I'd be dead." I allowed myself a shrug. "I'm still here."

I let my gaze stray a little from the ringleader, trying to count the Blood surrounding me. Eight that I could see. There could be more in the darkness, of course, beyond my immediate range of vision, drawing the shadows around themselves to hide from view. I had no way to tell. So, even if I got free, I would be alone and on foot with Lady knew how many Blood and Beasts lurking in the darkness. So I needed to use my head. Do this the smart way.

Easier if my head wasn't throbbing like a bastard from the iron wrapped around me.

"Presumptuous," the Blood said after a long moment.

I shrugged again. In my experience, angry enemies are often foolish ones. Anger was what had let Stellan down in the end, after all, and he wasn't the only one who had fallen to that particular weakness. "Just stating facts."

He stared down at me. "You have no idea of the facts of this situation."

"No? Care to enlighten me?" I wondered who he was. He seemed perfectly calm even though, if he knew who I was—and I wondered exactly how he did so—he presumably also knew what my powers were and that I could set him on fire where he stood.

So he was used to danger and facing enemies and staying cool while doing so. Well, that could describe any member of the Blood Court—the Blood played politics for even more deadly stakes than the Fae did and didn't turn a hair at murder, assassination, torture, or other gruesome means of achieving their ends. But still, something about him made me think that he was used to command.

Perhaps not completely seasoned like Guy or Father Cho or me, but he held himself in a way that was familiar. Confident of being obeyed.

One of Ignatius Grey's lieutenants?

It seemed likely.

I should've asked whether the Templars had thought to have drawings made of any of the Blood. Holly and Fen and Lily had all spent time in the Blood Assemblies where the

Blood had mixed with the human Nightseekers—Lily in the
very warrens themselves—and surely they could've provided descriptions for someone to base a likeness on. Then
again, I should've done a lot of things. Like not gotten
caught in the first place. I took another long breath, steeling
my mind to ignore the pain of the iron once more.

"Well?" I asked again when he didn't answer me.

One of the other Blood made a snarling noise, aiming his
gun at my head. The vampire before me turned his head,
eyes narrowed, and the one with the gun shrank back, ducking his head.

Fearful.

Which told me that this was maybe more than a lieu-
tenant. Maybe this was Ignatius Grey himself. And now I
had an even stronger regret that I hadn't seen a picture of
him.

I hadn't been expecting a face-to-face confrontation quite
so soon, of course.

And I'd been hoping that the balance of power when we
did finally meet would be different than it was right now.

Should I take him out if I got the chance? I could if I got
free of this bloody net. I could use fire and burn all eight of
them where they stood. But again, without knowing how
many more were out there, doing so meant being willing to
sacrifice my own life.

Once I was dead, the fire would go out. And a vampire
can heal burns, so it was possible he might survive.

And I didn't know if this was Ignatius Grey and therefore a target worth sacrificing myself for.

So I stared up at maybe-Ignatius and waited for him to
speak, wondering how the hell I was going to get out of this.

I didn't know what had happened to the few soldiers
who had been with me, could only hope futilely that they
had gotten away. The ones who had already passed through
the flames would be heading toward the main action. And
the ones Rhian had led would be no help. Rhian was too
well trained to let them turn back if they thought there was
trouble behind. They had orders to carry out, and she would
see that they did so.

Too well trained by me.

Right now I regretted that decision more than a little.

Ignatius—I was going to call him that for now—still studied me as if he could see into my soul. Maybe he could. Or maybe he could read the future around me like a seer—not that I'd ever heard of a Blood seer. Or maybe he was just trying to intimidate me.

Well, if that was his game I wasn't going to let him see that he had even the slightest impact on me.

"These cobblestones are hard," I said, using my best bored-beyond-tears voice that I used on recalcitrant clients. "Is there a point to this encounter?" If this was indeed Ignatius, then one thing he was used to was bowing and scraping. Maybe I could annoy him into making a mistake.

"They said you were arrogant," Ignatius said.

They? Who were they?

"Indeed?" I maintained my bored tone.

"Yes." He tapped a hand against the sword hilt at his hip, and a chill of fear sank through my stomach.

I ignored it, tightening my focus on the vampire. "And that's a bad thing, I assume?"

"Arrogance is acceptable in its place," Ignatius said. His fingers curled around the sword hilt, and the blade was suddenly glinting in the flames, its point a few inches in front of my throat.

Fast. Damn fast.

Fuck.

"Bound by iron and kneeling in the dirt before your superior is not that place, however." The point came a little closer. I kept my eyes on his face.

"You may have a point," I said. "But that doesn't change the fact that my knees are sore." There was no part of me that didn't hurt, but I wasn't going to let him know that.

"Do you think I care about you?" he hissed. The sword jerked, the point sliding across my cheek, on the other side of the cut from the stone.

The cut stung like acid, and drops of blood pattered down onto the cobblestones. I ignored the pain—it was hardly the worst wound I'd ever suffered—and stared up at the man who'd inflicted it. "This is a lot of trouble to catch me if you don't."

"There are those who are interested in you. In your continued existence or lack thereof. You have a certain value."

I was starting to get an idea of exactly who Ignatius might have been talking to.

If there was anyone in the world who wanted me dead, it was Salvia and her faction in the court. Particularly after today.

Though she must have spoken to Ignatius before today, as there was no way she had gotten a message back to the City ahead of me. There had been no other traffic on the road from Summerdale. Coming or going. Unless, of course, they'd worked out some other means of communication.

"Interesting. So I'm your hostage?"

"No. You're a way of getting something I want."

The chill in my stomach deepened. What had Salvia promised Ignatius? I was growing more certain that this was him. If it was indeed Salvia making devil's pacts with the Blood, and not some other group of enemies that I didn't even know existed, then I was fairly certain this wasn't going to end well. She didn't want me buried in a dungeon somewhere—she wanted me out of the picture. Permanently. The question was whether Ignatius would play along with her plan or he had his own ideas of how he could use me.

I braced myself, reaching harder for my magic. The iron made the effort something akin to pouring acid into my brain, but I kept up the attempt even when I felt myself start to sweat.

"Whoever they are, how do you know they can give you anything? If you kill me, then my Family will come after you."

"The sa'Uriels are not high in the court anymore."

"No one is high in the court. Not while there is no queen to hold favor with."

"Still, they have few friends."

"It doesn't take many Fae to burn down a city and raze your little underground kingdom with fire," I said.

"Not if they are brave enough to come to the City. But your kind has mostly lost their stomach for conflict, it would seem. So I think I'll be safe enough."

"Don't count on it," I snarled even as I filed away the fact that he hadn't denied it was his kingdom.

He flicked the sword again, but this time I saw the movement as it started and threw myself back in time. Resulting in the net biting closer still, pain flaring higher. Fuck.

Ignatius laughed. "Impressive. Perhaps this will be more fun than I thought."

"Perhaps it won't," a cool female voice said out of nowhere, and suddenly there was a blade at Ignatius' throat and a gun at his side. And I was looking up at a pair of determined gray eyes in pale skin.

Lily.

"Get up, Asharic," she said.

I scrambled upward, almost stumbling. The net tightened more.

The Blood around me stayed frozen in place. Apparently none of them were willing to risk their precious leader to stop me.

"One of you pull that net off him," Lily snarled. To my surprise one of them did, tugging it free with too-fast vampire movements. Then he fled into the night. Wise man. I put a few hasty steps between me and the net, trying not to fall over as the pain started to recede. Out of the corner of my eye, I saw my sword lying on the cobbles a few feet away. Just out of reach. I wasn't yet sure enough of my ability to move fast to make a move toward it.

"Going to kill me, wraith?" Ignatius said, his voice rough with frustration. To his credit he didn't sound scared.

"Probably," Lily said. "It's about time someone did. I should have done it before I left the warrens." She pressed the knife a little closer. "You always were a blight on the court, Grey."

"If you do, you'll never know," he said.

She had looked perfectly calm until Ignatius spoke. Then she frowned.

"Know what?" she said.

"I think you have a fair idea," he said. "But there are orders, if I die. There are those who will pay the price immediately."

Lily's frown deepened. "You're bluffing." Her voice was tight beneath the seemingly calm lilt of her words and her knuckles whitened where they held the dagger.

I wanted her to kill him, but if she did, then two of us didn't have much more of a chance of fighting our way out of here against the others than I did alone.

"Lily," I said.

"Asharic, go." Her voice cracked like a whip. She'd make an excellent soldier, I suspected. I also suspected that, if what I'd heard about her was true, there was no way she'd take up that profession. Not once this war was over anyway.

"Lily . . . ," I repeated.

"I'm perfectly safe." She jerked her chin toward the direction my men had headed in. "You're needed."

I hesitated, then cursed under my breath. She knew her abilities better than I did and she was a wraith. Ignatius couldn't hurt her. But if she was forced into the shadow, then there was nothing to stop them coming after me again.

I nodded at Lily and then turned and ran, snatching my sword up as I went.

Chapter Twenty-one

ASH

We beat them back before the dawn, chasing the last of the Beast Kind back across the border.

Between the Templars and my men, we patrolled the border and started sifting through the damage the Night World forces had done.

They had attacked the heart of Greenglass, one of the wealthiest of the human boroughs, razing shops and a bank and the chambers of the human council and leaving a trail of burning buildings to mark their path to those targets.

Making a point, I thought. That they could get deep within our defenses. We still didn't know how they'd overcome the sunlamps on the border, or what had happened to the squad who'd been patrolling that particular stretch of road. I doubted we'd find them alive.

They'd been my men, though, and we would search for them until we found the bodies if we could. So I could send word to their families, those that had them.

I didn't leave men behind if I could help it, but I had, over the years, accepted the fact that men died in war.

Still, I held each of the names of those men in my mind,
adding to the list of offenses that Ignatius was accumulating.

I had taken a Beast claw to the leg and sundry other cuts
and bruises during the night's work, and it was only adrenaline that had carried me this far. Its effects were fading
now and my injuries and the aftereffects of the iron net
made me weak and shaky. After I'd reported in to the
Brother House with Rhian and the others, Guy had sent me
with the other wounded to St. Giles.

To Bryony.

I wanted to see her. If I hadn't been injured I would have
gone anyway. I wanted to see for myself that she was unharmed even though the Templars assured me that St. Giles
hadn't been attacked this time.

If Salvia had it in for me, then she wouldn't hesitate to
use my vulnerabilities against me. And Bryony had stood
with me in court. And I'd called the sword to stay the attack
against her. I'd made my feelings plain, even if Bryony
hadn't yet accepted that she had too.

But in doing so, I'd put her in danger.

So I needed to see that she had come through the night
unscathed.

What she might say about the fact that I hadn't done so
remained to be seen.

BRYONY

It was an hour past dawn before I saw Asharic seated
amongst a group of wounded men, his face smeared with
smoke and blood, his eyes closed as he rested against a wall.
A bandage circled his right thigh, the fabric grimy but the
red blood staining it clear enough despite the dirt.

Hurt.

I stepped forward before I could stop myself and almost
stumbled as the room suddenly whirled around me.

Across the room I felt Ash's power flare and I latched onto that, seeking strength as I steadied my breath.

Graham, one of the orderlies, caught my arm. "Lady Bryony? Are you all right?"

I nodded grimly. "Yes. I just need to eat something." I took a shaky breath, the room stable again now, the sick feeling in the pit of my stomach easing a little.

"Fetch Lady Bryony tea," Ash ordered. "And whatever food is available. Something sweet."

I looked sideways at him. How had he reached my side so quickly? He looked about as shaky as I felt. "You should be sitting down."

"So should you," he said. He shot a look at Graham, who nodded quickly and scurried off. Ash's arm locked through mine and he guided me to a nearby bench. "You've exhausted yourself."

I sat because there wasn't much option not to. After a few seconds, Ash sank down beside me, grimacing as his leg bent. "I think I'm not the only one," I said. I reached toward the bandage, but his hand caught mine.

"Just rest a minute," he said. "My leg isn't going anywhere. Besides which, there are others worse off than me." He twisted, looking back at the group of soldiers he'd been sitting with. Several of the healers, Simon directing them, were assessing them with practiced swiftness.

"They'll be seen to," I said, trying to sound reassuring. I'd dealt with Templars long enough to know that I would get little sense out of him until he was happy the men in his charge were being taken care of. And he definitely wouldn't let me treat him until they were seen to. Not unless he was far more gravely hurt than this.

I sent a tiny thread of power toward him, trying to see what I could feel of the wound beneath the bandage and to judge whether I agreed with his assessment. The wound felt hot and—

"Stop that," he snapped.

"I—"

"Do you want to faint here in front of everybody?" he continued. "Rest. No more healing until you've eaten something. I'm sure I can't convince you to sleep, but you need to eat."

I straightened. "You don't get to order me around in my own hospital."

"Maybe not. But if you don't act sensibly, then I'll be forced to do something more drastic."

"Such as?"

"Maybe I'll turn *you* into a frog," he said with a smile. "That way you'll stay out of trouble."

"You couldn't turn a toad into a frog, let alone me," I retorted, but I subsided. I might be safe from him changing me into anything other than a woman foolish enough to fall for him, but he could, given that he had some healing knowledge, do something like put me to sleep if I pushed him.

Besides, he was right. I needed food. I was no sunmage to recharge my power with sunlight alone, and the night had been long and busy and I hadn't slept at all for two nights now.

I settled back against the bench. Asharic grunted approval, leaned back, and closed his eyes again. From which I gleaned that his leg was hurting him more than he cared to admit.

"What happened to your face?" I asked. Underneath the grime his left cheek had a crusted-over slash that was too straight to be caused by anything other than a blade.

"Ignatius Grey," he said absently.

"What?" I sat upright again. "Wait. Did you kill him?" That was the more important question than how exactly he had encountered Ignatius.

"No such luck," Ash said. He opened his eyes again. "Have you seen Lily?" he asked.

That was a change of topic I wasn't expecting. "Lily? What does she have to do with anything?"

"Well, for one thing, she's the reason Grey didn't kill me," he said.

I started to rise and his hand curled around my arm with gentle insistence. "Sit."

"You can't just say something like that and then expect

me to sit here like nothing happened." I twitched my arm free of his grip, irritated that he was acting as if an encounter with Ignatius Grey wasn't noteworthy.

"Nothing did happen, really," he said, sounding far too reasonable for a man with bits of him held together with linen bandages and willpower. "But back to my question. Have you seen Lily?"

"Yes." I bit back the torrent of questions flooding my brain. "Yes, she was here most of the night, helping."

He blew out a breath. "Good. That's good."

"You are going to tell me what happened," I said.

"Yes," he agreed. "But not until you've eaten and my men are seen to. It's daylight now. I don't think the Beast Kind will try anything more without the Blood to back them up. They have their own wounded to tend to."

I didn't point out to him that the Blood and the Beast Kind weren't the only ones that he had to worry about. Instead I sat beside him until Graham returned with tea and a plate piled high with rapidly cooling toast that was slathered with jam and butter almost thicker than the bread itself.

Cold toast wasn't my breakfast of choice, but it was good, quick fuel. I made Asharic eat some too and drink the tea—human, not Fae—but I couldn't blame Graham for that. There was no time for brewing Fae tea, though I could have used some. Human tea provided a rapid hit of energy, but it didn't have the restorative powers of one of my own brews.

By the time Ash had watched me drink several cups and finish the toast, all of his men had been taken off to wards or treatment rooms.

The flow of incoming patients had slowed enough that there was no one else waiting for my attention—or anybody else's—and more orderlies appeared with trays of toast and tea, handing them out to healers and patients well enough to eat and those who'd accompanied the wounded with speed and efficiency.

"It looks like everything is momentarily under control," I said. "Which means, Captain Pellar, that you will let me look at that leg now."

He put down his teacup and nodded. "All right. But no interrogating me about Ignatius while you do. I'd like to get some sleep today, and it will be faster if I tell everybody at once."

I pressed my lips together, but I couldn't fault his logic—it would be quicker to tell his story just once—so there was no point arguing with him. "No questions," I agreed.

ASH

The color had returned to Bryony's face by the time she had me settled in one of the small treatment rooms. But as she gathered a variety of potions and cleaning materials and bandages and lined them up precisely on a tray with movements that were a little too tightly controlled, I was beginning to wonder if it was tea or temper that had restored her.

Obviously she didn't take kindly to waiting to hear my explanation, but that couldn't be helped. There were a few people who needed to hear my report and I didn't feel like giving it multiple times or answering the same questions over and over again.

Neither was I in the mood for being scolded by Bryony. My leg felt as if it were on fire. Lady only knew what muck the Beast had had on his claws, but the gash he'd carved in my thigh stung and throbbed like the very depths of hell.

The rest of me ached in sympathy. Or from the echoes of the iron, the night's exertion, and gods knew how many blows and bruises and strains I'd gathered over the course of the hours.

I hissed a little as Bryony doused the bandage around my leg with pale yellow liquid. It was cool but only increased the burning.

"It will hurt more if I pull it free without loosening the dried blood," she said curtly.

"I'm not complaining," I pointed out.

"Good." She studied the bandage for a second, then pursed her lips together and soaked another swab of cotton in the liquid. The scent of it was fresh and clean as she pressed it against the cut on my face.

I clenched my jaw against the fiery sting, which only made the cut ache more, and made sure I didn't make a noise.

Bryony's hands were gentle, which was more than I could say for the expression she wore.

"Do you have any other cuts?" she asked when she was done with the ones on my face.

"I don't think so," I said. "Just bruises."

"Take your shirt off," she said.

I felt my eyebrows lift. "Here?"

"Don't flatter yourself," she snapped. "I need to see what other damage you've done to yourself." She picked up the dish of dirty swabs from beside me and then put it down again with enough force to make the table the tray sat on shudder.

I reached out and caught her wrist. "I'm all right," I said.

"You don't even know the meaning of all right. In one day you bring half the Veiled Court down on your head and let Ignatius Grey cut you, and to follow it all up you let a Beast gnaw on your leg." Her words tumbled out with a passion, her tone rising with each word.

"Technically he clawed me, not chewed on me," I said gently.

"As if that makes a difference," she said. "Idiot man." Her voice wobbled a little on the last syllable. Wobbled. As though she might cry. Bryony, who never cried.

"Well, it's less painful," I said, and tugged her closer. When she was close enough I eased off the bed so I could stand. Fire arced up and down my leg again, but that didn't matter right here and now. What mattered was making Bryony feel better. I pulled her against me. "I'm all right, love. Truly. Good as new once you fix me. Maybe even better."

She resisted my embrace, standing stiff in my arms. "Don't call me that."

"Love? Can't help it. It's the truth."

She tilted her head back, the dark blue of her eyes deeper than I'd ever seen it. "I—"

"You don't have to say it back," I said. "Not until you're ready."

She ducked her head at that and curled herself against me, burying her face in my neck. I held her while she took several shuddering breaths, feeling peace spread through me at the feel of her body against mine. The night had been full of darkness and death, but this—this was light and life and it was what I was fighting for. To make a safe place for her.

Veil take money and glory and whatever other victories war might bring. I would be happy if I could keep Bryony happy and safe. For as long as she let me do so.

I brushed a kiss over her hair and she turned her head, her hand curling to the back of my head, her lips seeking mine.

There was urgency in her kiss. Urgency and confusion and relief, I thought while I could still think about anything more than the feel and taste of her. Everything else, all the pains and aches and fatigue, evaporated momentarily and a different kind of fire rushed through me. My arms tightened around her and pulled her closer. But as I shifted my weight onto my injured leg, the wound protested and I winced.

Bryony must have felt the movement, because she pulled away. "I need to look at that," she said.

"I can think of other body parts that would prefer your attention," I grumbled, but I let her go. She sounded normal again, and in truth, unless I was going to lie back and let her do all the work—which was not without a certain appeal— our business could wait until after I was healed.

"I'm sure you can," she said. "But if I need to be patient, so do you." But a smile curved her lips, and the midnight blue eyes were heated now, not stricken.

"You don't play fair," I said as she started to unwind the bandage from my leg.

"Neither do you," she pointed out. Then her smile turned wicked as she eased the bloodstained length of fabric away from my trousers. "Now take your pants off."

Bryony

In the end, we gathered at the Brother House. Ash and I had met Simon and Lily en route to my office after I'd finished patching him up. Simon's eyes had the icy glint they got when he was truly angry, an expression that made him look far more like Guy despite the difference in their coloring.

Apparently Lily had told him whatever part of the story about her and Ash and Ignatius that was hers to tell. Judging by his face, it wasn't a good story.

Beside him, Lily was quiet as usual. And, as usual, impossible to read. She'd been raised by a Blood lord even more dangerous than Ignatius Grey and had learned impeccable control at a very young age. But she stayed close to Simon, as though hoping to calm him before they got wherever they were going.

Which was to find me, apparently. Before Simon could speak, Ash held up his hand and said, "I've already told Bryony that I'm going over this once and once only. So let's find Guy and it will go a lot faster for everybody."

Simon nodded and he and Lily fell into step with us. I passed the time—and tried to distract Simon—by asking him about his patients and getting him to brief Ash about the status of the men he'd come to St. Giles with. Ash had demanded a report after I finished with him and I'd had one of the healers fill him in, but I figured hearing it again from Simon couldn't hurt. It might mean that Ash would actually rest after we had met with Guy.

I'd felt the fatigue dogging him when I healed him, but there wasn't a lot I could do to ease it. I'd had just enough strength to heal his wounds. . . . I couldn't lend him more to push back his weariness. The easy stride with which he hurried us toward the Templar stronghold reassured me that his leg was no longer paining him though it would need a little more time to heal fully.

Ash wasn't the only one that needed rest. Right now I could lie down on the marble tiles and sleep for days. Sleep and not have to worry about what was coming and not deal with unending streams of pain and injury and death. I'd been a healer for a long time, but sometimes it was a heavy burden.

Now was one of those times. Because I couldn't save all of them. There would be people out there dead who never even had a chance of being healed.

All because of Ignatius Grey and his stupid ambition. Why hadn't Ash killed him? Wouldn't that have been an end to it?

My hands curled at my sides and I made myself relax. If Ash could have killed Ignatius he would have. To think otherwise was a measure of how much I needed to sleep. If I wasn't so tired, I would be able to regain my balance, be able to see reason.

If I wasn't so tired, I wouldn't be wishing so hard that I could still be in Ash's arms. My heart wouldn't ache quite so hard at the thought of spending another night like the last one when I hadn't been able to shut down the thought that Ash was out there in danger, that he could be killed.

Could leave me again.

Time and again that thought had flared, and on its heels came terror and panic that I'd had to fight down and lock away, only to have it return. I'd done my best to ignore it, but it had been there through every moment of that endless night. And it was there still because I knew, even if he didn't, that there were more than one set of enemies arrayed against him.

Wanting him dead.

Wanting to take what was mine from me.

What was mine even if I couldn't speak the words. Because telling him the truth would only make it harder.

Only make the loss worse when it came.

Guy met us at the door of the Brother House. He had Fen and Holly with him. And Saskia. I hadn't expected her. Her face was half-grimed with smoke and sweat, as were her hands, and there were char marks on the sleeves of the thick woolen shirt she wore with leather pants and boots. Perhaps she'd been helping the Templar armorers keep up with demand.

She looked as tired as the rest of us as she stood, half leaning against Fen, and smiled a greeting to Lily and Simon. Holly, standing on the other side of Fen, looked tired too. Tired and irritable. She had helped at the hospital half the night and I'd sent her with a group of healers to treat some of the less seriously injured Templars here at the Brother House a few hours before dawn when the crowds at the hospital had threatened to become unmanageable. I knew she would rather have done something more active, spent time prowling the streets like Lily, but unlike Lily, she wasn't a wraith and she had promised Guy that she wouldn't risk herself that way.

She had agreed, but she didn't like it, and it showed.

"Looks like everybody is here," Ash said.

I gave him credit for not asking whether Saskia and Holly needed to be here. Maybe he had the measure of the DuCaine stubbornness already. If Saskia was here, then she intended to stay and she'd been through enough of the journey with us that none of the others would tell her to leave, as much as her brothers might wish to. Holly was just as stubborn as her future sister-in-law and she could, on top of that, probably just find a way to listen in on us using one of her charms, if not outright break into the room, if we tried to exclude her.

"Yes. We can use one of the meeting rooms," Guy said.

"Will Father Cho be joining us?" I asked.

"He is tending to other matters just now. I'll give him my report after this."

He led us up to a room on the second floor, which was more secluded than the other meeting rooms I was familiar with, and waited for us to take our seats. When everyone was settled I felt Ash throw a ward around the room and a second later, felt the cool green of Simon's power working to reinforce what he had done. No one would be listening in on what we spoke of here.

That done, Ash began to talk, telling the tale of his night's adventures. Of Ignatius Grey and of how Lily had intervened. Simon's scowl returned at that part, but he kept silent. Fen's expression was carefully blank like Lily's, and Saskia and Holly both looked worried.

Guy, on the other hand, looked almost happy with the news that Ignatius had shown himself.

As Ash came to the end of his story, Guy began to ask questions, going over the details from a number of different angles. When he eventually subsided, Ash looked relieved. He stretched his arms out against the table, rolling his shoulders.

"Any other questions?" he asked.

"Not for you," I said. Though I would have questions for him soon enough. Like why he hadn't told me he'd been bound by iron for a time when I healed him. That explained some of the bone-deep exhaustion I'd sensed in him. I could have done something about it during my healing, if I'd known it was caused by iron. But that was a conversation for later. When I could yell. "But I'd like to hear from Lily what happened after you left."

Ash nodded. "Come to that, so would I." He turned to where Lily sat next to Simon. "Care to tell us that part?"

She smoothed her hand over her head, as though checking that all her braids were in place. They were, though I didn't like to see them there. In the days after Lucius had first died . . . before Holly and Guy had met, she had worn her long hair loose. Seeing it tied back again only reminded me each time I saw it that she was a warrior.

A warrior on the hunt.

"There isn't much to tell. I kept Ignatius occupied for long enough for Captain Pellar to get away and then I shadowed and got away myself."

"You could have killed him," Guy said. "Why didn't you?"

"Because of what he told me," Lily said. "He said that I'd never know if I killed him."

"Know what?" Holly asked.

"Know what happened to the Fae women he's been taking," I said, feeling cold fury in my stomach. I'd been focused on Asharic's part of the story as he told it and hadn't fully thought through the implications of what Ignatius had said to Lily.

"Women?" Holly said. "Like Violet?" Her eyes went dark as she spoke the name. Regina had been taken because she'd been with Violet, doing a dress fitting for her, when the Beasts came for her. She'd died because of Violet.

"Yes," Lily said, eyes on Holly, face sad for an instant. "Like Violet. I've spent some time searching but not as much as I would like." She looked at me and I remembered the conversation I'd had back down beneath St. Giles with Adeline. And the ones I had with Lily since. About what Ignatius might do with a Fae woman.

"What does Ignatius Grey want with Fae women?" Ash said, looking confused.

I looked at Lily. She nodded, the movement almost imperceptible.

Chapter Twenty-two

BRYONY

"It's possible that Ignatius is trying to breed himself a wraith," I said.

Ash's eyes went wide. Everybody else looked as one toward Lily and Simon.

"Lily, what do you think?" Holly asked.

"Ignatius saw what I did for Lucius," Lily said. Her voice had the edge of ice in it that it always held when she was determined not to give anything away. "A wraith is a valuable weapon." She turned her gaze on me. "It's why the Fae dislike us so much."

Fen frowned. "But it would be years before a wraith would be able to do for Lucius what you did."

"You don't have to be that old to carry a gun," Lily said. "Lucius waited until I was older, yes, but Ignatius may not have his patience. And who knows? Maybe Lucius had already begun this experiment."

"No," Guy said. "No, he wouldn't have been so eager to get you back if he had a replacement waiting in the wings. Fen's right; a wraith would have to be a long-term plan."

"I don't care about that," Lily said. "I care about the

women that he may be using. And I care about any child that may or may not exist. A child like me. Who will not become like me—be reared by a monster as I was—if I have anything to say about it." Her tone was flat and final. All of us had learned what that tone meant.

"So we defeat Ignatius and we rescue these women," Ash said. "Simple."

"Not so simple. Ignatius told me that he had contingency plans in place. If anything happens to him, then the women will be dead as soon as the news reaches the warrens. If he's telling the truth and they are still alive, of course. He's not going to let us win that easily. And that's assuming we win."

"Of course we're going to win," Guy said.

Lily shook her head. "How many died last night?"

Guy's fist clenched. "We lost about thirty soldiers. Almost that again in civilian casualties."

"And that was just a skirmish," Lily said. "Nowhere near their true forces and they kill sixty of us in a night. Even with Asharic's forces, we are outnumbered." Her gaze came to me again. "We need the Fae."

"We don't have them," Ash said bluntly. "Unless they have a change of heart, we're in this on our own."

"Which is why I'm going to search the warrens and find these women and then we will get them out."

"How, exactly?" Guy objected. "You want us to launch an assault on Blood territory to rescue just a few? We have a city to save."

"Don't give me one of your speeches about the greater good, Guy DuCaine," Lily said calmly. "I am going to find these women. Then, if you won't help me, I'll find a way to free them myself."

"Of course he'll help," Simon said. He put a hand on Lily's arm. "Don't do anything foolish."

She scowled at him a moment, then subsided.

I let out a breath. Good. No one could stop Lily searching for the Fae women—which she'd been doing on and off for months anyway, so I wasn't sure why she thought she could find them now—but we didn't need arguments amongst ourselves as to the right path to take.

Ash leaned back in his chair. "So now you know. Ignatius has emerged from the shadows. I think we can expect attacks every night from now on. We need to prepare." He stretched again and then yawned enormously. "But first I need some sleep. Why don't we meet again in a few hours? We could all use some rest."

He pushed back his chair, but before he could stand, Fen held up a hand. "I think we're ignoring another important part of this story," he said.

Damn, I had hoped that we weren't going to discuss that part. That I might have a few more days. But I couldn't bring myself to stop Fen from speaking.

"What part?" Guy asked, yawning himself. He covered his mouth with his hand, the Templar cross bloodred in the morning light.

"The part where Ignatius wanted to take Ash specifically," Fen said.

"He thinks he can weaken Ash's forces if he takes out their commander," Guy said. "A reasonable thought. Though wrongheaded of him." He nodded at Ash. "Your men are well trained and Charles seems capable enough. No offense, Asharic. I don't wish ill for you."

"A reasonable thought if the problem Ash represents to Ignatius and those who support him is as leader of his army," Fen said. "But that isn't the only thing he is."

Cold sweat broke out on my back. *Don't say it. Don't say it. Don't say it.*

I saw a horror equal to my own break out on Ash's face.

"Fen—" he started.

"The Fae don't need a change of heart," Fen said, his tone filled with the vibrations that told me he was speaking of something he had foreseen. "They need a king. Someone strong enough to command them to rejoin the war. Someone powerful. Powerful enough to call the queen's sword to his hand perhaps."

All eyes turned to Ash.

His eyes had turned to storm clouds, denial and anger warring on his face. "I'm no king," he said. Then he stood and strode from the room.

Ash

I didn't get very far from the meeting room before I heard footsteps following me. Bryony. I knew without looking, could feel the turmoil in the depths of her power. But I couldn't make myself stop and wait for her. I wasn't ready to discuss the monumentally stupid thing that Fen had just said. Me as king?

No.

A thousand times no.

Locked up in Summerdale, with nothing but Fae politics to fill my days?

A fate worse than death.

A life sentence, in fact. A lifetime far longer than any human could imagine.

I hurried my pace, walking so fast I was almost running. But the sight of me fleeing the halls of the Brother House would hardly inspire confidence in either the Templars or my men, so I schooled myself to keep to a walk.

Still, I was almost gasping when I passed through the massive entrance doors—ignoring the Templar who offered me a salute as he held the door open for me with his other hand—and stepped into the sunlight. Gasping with rage and with a foreboding that I wasn't going to be able to get out of this so easily.

I walked a few more feet, almost blind in the bright daylight. But then my foreboding was confirmed as my vision cleared and I recognized the faces of the men on the tall horses gathered in a neat line outside the main gate.

Fae faces.

Fae here in the City. Fae waiting to see me.

My father and mother amongst them.

I stopped dead where I stood, the urge to run flaring again. I could do it. Head for the stables and get on Aric's back and ride until we had left this bloody City in the dust.

Only that would mean leaving Bryony as well.

Again.

Shal e'tan mei. Fucking the fucking Veil six ways to hell. And the queen. Why had she had to die? And why couldn't my fucking fellow Fae find themselves a ruler and leave me the hell out of their games?

My frozen state gave Bryony the chance to catch up with me. She moved beyond me a step or two, watching the Fae as I was. Then she turned back to me.

"I think your father wants to speak with you," she said. "And he's not the only one."

"Bryony, if you have any love for me, then go over there and send them away."

Her eyes went wide and the chain at her neck sparked a dazzle of light like fireworks. "I'm sorry," she said. "But you have to do this."

Then she stepped back and there was nothing to do but walk forward to greet my parents.

Which led me back to another of the cursed Templar meeting rooms. This being my parents, one of my uncles, and a delegation of other Fae who, according to them, bore me no ill will, I could hardly leave them standing in the street. Besides which, if they were here to discuss what I thought they were going to discuss, it wasn't something I wanted every Templar and his dog—not to mention my own men—hearing.

Bryony came with us, shooting me a look that told me that if I tried to turn her away, then she might finally fulfill one of her threats to turn me into a frog—or worse. Of course, if she could, half my problems would be solved, but knowing her, she'd then organize for me to be the first frog king of the Fae and I wasn't going to give Salvia the satisfaction of being able to stomp on me and kill me that way.

My father cleared his throat as if he was expecting me to say something. I stayed silent.

"Lord sa'Uriel," Bryony said eventually. "What brings you to the City?"

She might as well have been discussing the weather or making arrangements for some inane social ritual like tea drinking, her voice was so carefully polite and carefree.

"We came to discuss what happened at court yesterday," Father said. "You both left too quickly for us to talk to you."

"We're fighting a war here," I said pointedly. "I won't apologize for not taking the time for social niceties."

My father pinned me with a look that made me feel suddenly about fifteen years old. "I approve of your retreat yesterday. It was a wise move. Salvia did not behave well after you left."

"Please tell me one of you had to stab her," I said.

"Not quite. But she threw quite a tantrum."

"A tantrum for which there was quite a noticeable lack of enthusiasm," added my uncle, Erik, with a certain degree of satisfaction.

"Yes," my father said. "Salvia played her hand and lost, it seemed."

"She'll bounce back," I said. "I'm not going to hold my breath waiting for her to stop hating me."

My mother waved a hand at me, the light making her two Family rings glitter like a miniature rainbow. The colors of her original Family—sa'Liniel—were blue and green and purple and they sparkled prettily on her left hand. They also neatly rounded out the orange, brown, and red sa'Uriel colors of the even larger ring on the fourth finger of her right.

"Salvia wasn't the only one who played her hand," she said gravely. "You called the queen's sword and it came to you. Asharic, that means something."

"It means I'm an idiot," I said through gritted teeth. "Nothing more."

My father sighed. "No, my son. It means more than that. Do you think you're the first one to try such a thing since the Veil fell? There have been quite a few contests of power. And the Veiled World hasn't answered to a single request."

"What makes you think that it answered mine?" I said.

"The land holds the court's power," my mother said. "You know that. The queen put that sword there and charged the land to hold it safe. Which it has done for centuries. Until yesterday. When it gave it to you."

My stomach roiled. "No. Don't even think about it."

"Asharic," my father said. He gestured at the others who accompanied him. "We didn't come here to see how you were doing. We came here to offer you the crown."

"No," I repeated. "I don't want it."

"It doesn't matter if you want it," Bryony said. Her voice sounded odd. Distant. "It matters that it wants you."

She might as well have picked up a dagger and stabbed me with it. "I said *no*."

Another dazzle of light sparked from Bryony's necklace as her power flared, making the air shimmer. "Lord sa'Uriel. Ladies. Gentlemen. May I speak to Asharic alone?"

My father nodded, then stood. He bowed to Bryony, shot an unreadable look in my direction, and then led the party out of the room.

Which left Bryony and me staring at each other across the table. It felt more like a wall the size and height of the Templar battlements.

"Have you lost your mind?" I asked. "I can't be king."

"You already are. The land answered you. It answered you the second you stepped over the threshold when we went to see the court. This is inevitable."

Not to me it wasn't. "Let me make this clear. I do not want to be king."

"And I don't want to watch this City die," Bryony said. "Which is exactly what will happen without the Fae to help us. Don't you see? Fen was right. If you're king, you can make them come back. You can save us."

"Who's going to save me?" I shot back. "I — " I stopped, my throat closing. "You can't think I want that, Bryony. Walled away in Summerdale. Apart from everything. From everyone." I searched her face but her expression was implacable. "I don't want it. Do you?"

"Me?" She recoiled suddenly. "My life is here. My life is the hospital."

"Exactly," I said. "So how can you expect me to live away from you? Unless…" I hesitated. This was precisely the wrong time to say it and never how I'd imagined it in the endless nights I'd spent dreaming that perhaps one day I would get to see Bryony again, that the Lady might smile on me and my fate change so that I could be forgiven and get to go home.

But it seemed the Lady still found me her favorite source of entertainment and she wasn't done fucking with me yet. But still I had to say it. "Unless you come with me. Marry me. The queen chose to be alone, but it's not against our laws for the king or queen to marry."

She went very still, frozen in place as the color drained from her face. Even her chain was quiet, icy silver against her snow-white skin.

"Bryony." I moved around the table. Took her hands. "It wouldn't be so bad. Not if we're together."

She shook her head, shivering suddenly. "I can't go back there. That place . . . it's wrong to live like that. Not caring about what goes on outside Summerdale. Thinking that only the Fae matter. That we're better than all the other races."

"But that's what you're asking me to do," I said. My voice shook. "To freeze myself. To give up everything I want. Don't you love me at all?"

Bryony stared at me and tears brimmed in her eyes. "I do love you," she said. "But you have to be king. You have to end this war. I couldn't live with myself if I asked you not to do that to be with me. But I'm sorry, Ash. I can't do it with you." She looked down for a moment and when she looked up the tears were falling. "And if you say no, then you're not the man I love anymore."

Damned if I did and damned if I didn't. It was a feeling I was all too familiar with. A feeling that I seemed cursed to experience far too often.

Bryony loved me. I'd thought that was all I'd ever wanted to hear. If she'd told me that just a few hours ago, I would have been the happiest man alive. But now she told me and, in the same breath, told me that that love wasn't enough to make her share my fate. I couldn't even blame her for that.

In her place I wouldn't want to tie my fate to me either. To doom herself to a life of politics and scheming and wondering if the court was plotting against you and your Family as they had plotted against the queen.

"I understand," I said, and reached out to touch her face. Bent to kiss her one last time. Her lips were cool against mine, the touch so soft and fleeting because I couldn't bear for it to go any longer. "Good-bye, love."

I heard the first sob escape her lips as I walked from the room.

As I expected, my father wanted me to come back to Summerdale and claim the crown there and then. I was too tired to fight him, still shocked by what was happening and by the fact that Bryony had rejected me. So I did what he wanted, figuring that at least, being in Summerdale and soaking in the power of the land for a few hours might make me feel semialive.

The only thing I put my foot down about was when my father wanted to send for Bryony to accompany us.

"Lady sa'Eleniel has patients to attend here," I said. "There was fighting here last night and there are many wounded. I will not trouble her with this nonsense." There must have been enough anger behind my words that my father didn't argue the point. He and my mother both eyed me a little oddly as I climbed onto Aric's back, but they stayed silent as we rode away from the City.

We set a punishing pace back to Summerdale. It was easier on the horses the others rode, Fae bred as they were. But I knew what Aric was capable of, and more than that, what the Fae healers could do to restore him on the other end. He would no more take harm from this than he would if he'd rested for the day in his stall in the Templar stables, and the run would do him good besides. Sunlight and no fighting or Beast Kind bursting out to attack us would restore his faith in the world perhaps. Even if it couldn't restore mine.

With every beat of his hooves carrying me closer, curses rolled through my mind. Curses on the Lady, on Ignatius Grey, on Salvia sa'Ambriel, and on most of the court who were supposedly waiting for me at our destination.

By the time we actually reached the Gate, I'd worked up a fine head of steam.

The Seneschal bowed low at my approach, which spoiled any last lingering hope I had that this might all be some horrible nightmare.

I bowed in return, because she at least had done nothing but her duty her entire life and the last thing I needed was to start my reign—and that was a phrase that still made me want to laugh wildly—with the gatekeeper of my realm angry at me no matter my own mood.

Within the gate there were carriages waiting for us, and servants with robes—it seemed I wasn't going to escape Court dress this time—and still others to take our horses.

I made sure Aric was taken care of and then climbed into a carriage with my parents. They sat opposite me, their expressions bland.

"I'm guessing you never expected to be taking this particular journey," I offered. This was the first time I'd been alone with both my parents in thirty years. I had to make some attempt at conversation, despite the anger burning in my stomach. After all, they were still willing to speak to me and I'd caused them little but pain since I was exiled. Though maybe I was covering myself in enough glory to make up for that now.

"Oh, I don't know, Asharic," my mother said with a small smile. "I always knew you had power. And potential."

"Thanks for the warning," I said.

"There was nothing to warn you about while the queen lived," she replied. "And even then, I didn't know exactly how powerful you were. I'm not a seer, after all."

"Thank the Lady for that," I said. If I'd had any inkling that this might be my fate, then I'd have asked for a lot more gold from the Templars to agree to even come near the City. Though that was a lie. It was Bryony who'd drawn me back once I was free to return. Bryony whose hold I couldn't break.

Not that that had done me any good either. Now I had a few more memories of her and worse, would have to live with actually seeing her from time to time—after all, she would be one of my subjects—and not being able to touch her. I wondered if the queen had had a lover before she'd taken the throne. And if she'd had to leave him or her behind as well.

I'd never know.

My parents and I exchanged small talk—them asking concerned questions about the fighting last night and whether I was hurt—as we traveled toward the court. I half hoped that someone might be stupid enough to attack us as they had Lord sa'Eleniel's carriages. I could do with a few people to kill painfully right now. It might make me feel better.

But it seemed that no one was bold enough to challenge me today.

All too soon we reached the court.

There was a squad of the Queen's Guard—the King's Guard I guess they were about to become—waiting for us. The captain held the queen's sword out to me, the blade of it—its curious metal gleaming in the sun blazing down on us—flat across his palms.

I glanced at the sun. Wasn't the land supposed to shape itself to my mood, if I were king? I was in no mood for sunlight. Give me a few thunderbolts instead. Freezing sleet and a tornado even. But the sky stayed blue. Perhaps the land was free to ignore me when it chose. Or maybe I actually had to be proclaimed king to hold it to my will.

I had no idea exactly how that happened. The queen had been crowned hundreds of years before I was born.

"What happens now?" I said to my father.

"We go to the court and you state your claim. If no one challenges you, then you're king."

I stared at him. "That's it?"

"There will be a coronation at some point, but that's just pageantry," he said. "You're king if the land accepts you and the court offers no challenge."

"In that case, let's get this over with," I said. "I have business elsewhere."

I saw several of the Fae who'd traveled with us arch their eyebrows at this and smiled grimly to myself. They wanted me to be king, so apparently I was going to be king. But once I was king, I was going to do things my way.

After all, if I couldn't do that much, what was the point?

The sound of my bootheels striking stone seemed louder than it should when I stepped onto the marble that marked the boundaries of the court.

There was little space that was free, other than the avenue—maybe eight feet across—that had been left clear. A path that led straight to the throne, I noted. The rest of the marble was crowded with more Fae than I had ever seen in one place before. I suspected that every member of any Family with the slightest link to a High Family was here. And maybe quite a few that hadn't.

I stared down at the throne. My destination.

And I began to walk.

The silence was deafening. There was no breeze and it seemed everyone was frozen in place, only the faintest rustling of clothing as they turned to watch me pass breaking the eerie stillness. In contrast, the earthsong of the Veiled World thundered in my head, louder than it ever had, the sound of it curiously triumphant.

I wondered what would happen if I told it to shut up but didn't want to risk the experiment. I walked on, the skin between my shoulder blades crawling as I braced myself for the attack I half expected. But none came and I reached the throne still alive.

Sick at heart and half-delirious perhaps but still alive.

I turned to face the assembled Fae, wondering what the hells I was meant to say as the Guard took up position behind me and to each side. My parents melted into the crowd and the other Fae took their places in the front row of the crowd to my right. I ignored them as I studied the faces in the crowd, willing my heartbeat to slow. As luck would have it, the first face I truly recognized belonged to Lord sa'Eleniel. Who nodded once, then looked past me, obviously seeking his daughter. When he didn't see her, he frowned. Then turned that frown at me. I made myself look elsewhere. And found Salvia's face in the crowd. She looked as though she wanted to strangle me.

Good. Let her try.

I straightened my shoulders and let the point of the

sword drop forward so it rang against the marble. I had no
fear that I might blunt the blade. I doubted little short of
being dropped into a volcano could blunt that blade.

"I am Asharic sa'Uriel'pellar," I said, trusting that they
would all be able to hear me. I'd never struggled to hear the
queen anytime I attended court. "Today I was offered the
crown of the Veiled Court. Does anyone care to challenge
my right to claim it?"

Silence.

I waited. It wasn't going to be straightforward. I knew
that Salvia couldn't let it go quite so easily. Sure enough,
another sa'Oriel redhead—one I didn't recognize—stepped
forward.

"And you are?" I said.

"Kilvian sa'Oriel," he said. He looked vaguely green
though resolute.

Fucking Salvia.

I nodded at Kilvian. "Very well." I hefted my sword and
the crowd drew a collective breath. Then I pointed the
blade at Kilvian and flung a binding spell at him, drawing
on the power flowing beneath my feet. He froze in place,
mouth half open. His chest rose and fell, the breaths growing quicker as he fought against my spell. I waited. A minute passed. Then another. It was painfully clear that Kilvian
couldn't best me.

I heard stifled laughter somewhere in the crowd.

Bloody Fae. There was nothing funny about this situation.

I lowered my sword. "Anybody else?" I said. I fastened
my gaze on Salvia. "How about you, Lady sa'Ambriel? Anyone else you care to throw at me?"

A flush crept up her throat, hate flaring in her eyes. But
she stayed where she was. Which pretty much told me all I
needed to know about her. She was a spider, that one, good
at pulling strings but, at the face of it, only as strong as the
web she wielded. She didn't have the power to challenge me
herself.

"No," she said when I waited long enough to make it
clear that I expected an answer.

"Good." I looked out over the crowd. Found my father and mother again. My father smiled at me. No escape, then.

"I am Asharic sa'Uriel'pellar," I said again. "Your king." The marble shook then, a long, low ripple, as the sword I held sparked silver fire.

The court sank to its knees, Salvia sa'Ambriel taking a few seconds longer than the rest to give the obeisance.

I looked out over them and wanted to smack sense into all of them. But it was done now. I was king.

Which meant starting, as I meant to go on.

"Captain," I said. "You will escort Lady sa'Ambriel to the—" I'd almost said queen's palace. "To the palace. You will keep her there until I return to speak to her. She is to see no one."

"By what right—" Salvia started to rise, the words sputtering from her mouth.

"I am king," I said. "I can do as I please. But as it happens, I believe you to be guilty of treason to the crown and the court, Lady sa'Ambriel. And I will not let you poison my court as you tried to poison the queen's." I stared at her, not caring about the fury on her face. "And I will thank you not to speak again until I speak to you." I laid a binding on her with a gesture, taking care to let the power I used echo so that everyone was aware of what I had done.

Salvia's eyes widened and her mouth moved, but no sound came out as four of the guards surrounded her and drew her away.

"Let me be clear about one thing," I said to the rest of the court—to everybody who had come to listen. "I am not the Veiled Queen. But I am your king. And I share her desire for peace. I will re-form the treaty between the races and I will be starting that process as soon as possible. So ready yourselves. Because there will be no more hiding here in Summerdale. Not until the treaty is restored and there is peace. We will fight the Blood and the Beast Kind. We will not leave the humans to stand on their own. No matter what the cost."

Chapter Twenty-three

BRYONY

Ash was king. King of the Veiled Court. He hadn't, from what I had heard, adopted the veils that had been the queen's conceit, so I wasn't going to call him the Veiled King. I was hoping not to call him anything at all. I hadn't seen him since he returned from Summerdale two days earlier, but there was no mistaking the sense of him that pulsed through the City. There was no longer an empty place at the center in the Fae lines of power. Once more they had a beating heart.

A heart gained while mine had been shattered again. And if I was ever to mend it, I needed not to see Ash. I'd used the very full hospital as my excuse and remained at St. Giles, getting my updates on the Templars' plans via Simon and Fen and Lily.

They told me about Ash's plans as well. I could avoid the man, but I couldn't avoid news of the new king, it seemed. I heard about how he had issued an ultimatum to Ignatius, giving him until the end of the week to rejoin negotiations for peace. About how he had sworn to bring Ignatius to heel if that ultimatum wasn't met.

More than I wanted to hear even if it was information I needed to know.

Ash hadn't come looking for me. I didn't know whether I was thankful for that or if it only made things worse. If I could feel any worse. Ash was king. Lost to me again.

But unlike before, this time he was lost but still close by. Still within reach. There was no pretending he didn't exist. That fact was undeniable. As was the fact that he didn't have to be out of reach.

If I was willing to give up everything I'd worked for and become a pretty ornament in the Fae Court.

It would make my father happy. It would make Ash happy, but the thought made me want to crawl out of my skin. No matter how much I missed Ash and how many times I found myself wishing for something to ease the searing ache in my chest.

So I did what any sensible person would do. I denied the pain and poured my energy into the hospital while we waited out the days until Ash's offer of negotiation expired. Day by oh so long day until only one more day remained.

Hiding, some might call it.

And if so, who could blame me for that? Hiding brought some small respite at least. This morning, I had retreated even farther, seeking sanctuary within the four walls of my office and giving orders for no one to bother me.

For half an hour there was blessed silence and I managed to actually reduce some of the tottering piles of paperwork that had taken root on my desk to mere stacks. Even on the brink of war, there was no end to the myriad details that had to be dealt with to keep St. Giles operational.

The details that had been in danger of going untended and unresolved in the chaos of the last few days. Perhaps some would call me callous for shutting myself away to deal with things so seemingly trivial, but surely it was more callous to let the hospital grind to a halt by neglecting something so basic.

If there was one thing the City needed right now, it was hospitals that operated well. St. Giles was the biggest hospital we had and the one that absolutely could not fail, given what lay beneath it.

I had just finished writing a response to an aggrieved note from my paymaster when Lily stepped into my office.

Literally stepped in. She appeared out of nowhere, coalescing like smoke in a way that still made the hairs on the back of my neck stand on end despite the fact that I'd seen her do so before. She was usually careful not to be too blatant with her abilities around the Fae—including me—out of respect for our beliefs or else out of something that only she could explain.

But this time she took no time for courtesies. And she held a baby in her arms.

I stared at her. At the baby. Then found my tongue.

"That's a baby." Not my most brilliant comment, but I truly couldn't think of anything else to say.

Lily gave me a look that suggested her assessment of my remark coincided with my own and shifted her grip on the squirming bundle. The bundle squawked in protest.

I stood instinctively. "Where did you get a baby?"

She looked grim. "I found Violet and two other Fae women."

"Violet? In the warrens?" I knew the answer to that already, but part of me had to hope that it wasn't true, that Lily had found her elsewhere.

But Lily nodded and my heart clutched, new pain added to the ache already there. Alive. After all these months. Months at the mercy of Ignatius Grey. Not a fate I'd wish on anybody.

"But how? The warrens are vast."

She nodded. "Yes. And I've been searching for weeks. I thought I knew them well, but there are sections that I'd never seen before. They go on for miles and miles. I've been trying to make a map. I thought it would be useful when we have to go into the warrens for real."

Lily the pragmatist. Apparently, unlike some of us, she didn't expect this to end in any way other than direct conflict with the Blood. I had to face the fact that I agreed with her assessment. I didn't think Ignatius would back down and come crawling back to Ash's negotiation table. "And yet you found Violet?"

"Holly made a charm to find Fae blood. Saskia helped her," Lily said. She stared down at the baby. "And Captain Pell—I mean—the king, he did something to give it more power. It helped. They were very deep."

Locked beneath the earth. No sun. No air. No living things around them. Practically buried alive. I shivered and tried not to let the horrifying image in my head linger. "Go on."

"The charm took me deep. To a part of the warrens that I didn't know. At first I thought that the charm had gone wrong and that it was abandoned. Or empty at least. But I was shadowed and I could hear a baby crying."

"But you can hear things in the shadow usually, can't you?"

She nodded. "Yes. But this was different. It sounded like the baby was right beside me. But distant at the same time. I can't explain it exactly. I followed the sound and found a suite of locked rooms. Violet was there and two other Fae women. And the baby. She was crying."

Her voice sounded odd and she glanced down at the child again.

"Is she hurt?" I asked. I extended my healing sense toward the baby and then froze when I couldn't feel her.

"Lily," I said slowly as I finally realized what it was I had missed about Lily's story and the implications of the baby being here in her arms. "I didn't think you could bring other people through the shadow."

Her head came up slowly. Her gray eyes glowed with emotion. I couldn't tell if it was anger or wonder or a mixture of both.

"I can't," she said. "She's a wraith."

The room spun around me for a moment. Another wraith. Ignatius was breeding wraiths. Just as we had feared. "I think we need Simon and Guy," I said faintly.

Simon arrived before Guy did. He took one look at Lily holding the baby and shot a confused look at me before he went to Lily and repeated the same query that I had made about the baby's health.

"She's all right," Lily said quietly. She gazed down at the baby, looking equal parts fascinated and apprehensive.

Simon extended his hand toward the baby, holding it there for a moment, but apparently he was satisfied with whatever he sensed. He turned back to me, eyes questioning.

"She found Violet," I said in response to the unspoken query. "And the . . . child." I tried to quell the instinctive antipathy I felt at the thought of a wraith child. Lily had taught me that wraiths could show loyalty and love, but the prejudices I'd been raised with ran deep despite my best efforts to ignore them. "In the warrens. With two other Fae women."

"Their names were Alder and Heather," Lily said absently. Her attention was on the baby. Watching her with a degree of wariness. As though she might explode.

Maybe she would. A wraith child was an explosive discovery. "Did they give you Family names?" I didn't recall an Alder amongst the Fae living in the City. There was a Heather, from one of the sa'Keriel lines, though, on the short list of names of the missing Fae women we'd managed to compile.

Lily shook her head. "One of them was sleeping. The other one, Alder, didn't talk. Violet said that Alder was the baby's mother. She asked me to take the baby." She looked up at me. "Violet didn't look well. None of them did."

I shuddered and Simon's head whipped back to Lily. "Wait. Are you saying this baby was born in the warrens?" He looked down at the child again. "Lily, is this baby a wraith?"

Lily nodded. "Yes."

Simon said something low and foul below his breath. "Ignatius *is* trying to breed wraiths."

"It seems he has succeeded," I pointed out.

"Or Lucius did and he's just carrying on what was started," Lily said.

"I still don't understand why," I sighed. "I understand the appeal of a pet wraith as a weapon, but it was a major breach to take Fae women. Enough to bring the queen down on their heads if she'd had proof." And enough to send Ash into a fury too, I thought. But that could be dealt with. It might not even be a bad thing at this point.

Lily and Simon exchanged another long look. "She doesn't know?" Lily asked. "You never told her?"

Simon shook his head. "There was never any need."

"Need for what?" I asked just as Guy knocked on the door and opened it. He halted at the sight of the baby in Lily's arms.

"I get the feeling I missed something," he said.

"Lily brought the child out of the warrens," I said.

"She's a wraith too," Lily added, cutting off the need for further explanations. She rocked the child a little, her movements uncertain. I doubted Lily had spent much time around babies. They weren't commonplace in the Blood Court or the warrens. Trusted didn't have children.

I watched the child for a moment, wondering if I should take her. Or Simon. I could heal a wraith—I had healed Lily before—and if the baby's mother was unwell, the baby was likely to be malnourished.

But she looked peaceful enough in Lily's arms and I didn't know what I would do if the baby shadowed. I didn't even know if wraith babies could shadow so young. Lily had brought her out of the warrens, but had the baby shadowed or was it the fact that she was a wraith that allowed Lily to move her through the shadow? I wished I knew more about how it worked. The Fae cast wraiths out as soon as their abilities were detected and they were generally discovered soon after birth. By their absence from the earthsong, not by shadowing. Looking at the baby's face, rounded and soft like any child's, I wondered why we did so. How a mother could give up her child. Then remembered what we'd been discussing before Guy arrived.

"There was something you were going to tell me," I said to Lily and Simon.

"It's Lily's to tell," Simon said. "If she wishes."

Lily was silent as she looked at him a long moment. Then she shrugged. "If I tell you this, you need to keep it secret . . ." She hesitated. "Unless it becomes necessary to tell. But it will be safer for everyone if it doesn't. Safer for us, at least."

Something about the way she spoke made me think "us" in this context meant her and the baby, not her and Simon as it usually did. "All right," I agreed. "I won't tell if I don't need to. Guy?"

Guy nodded slowly. "Yes. I will keep your secret. Unless it needs to be known."

Lily sighed. "All right. There's something I learned about wraiths from Lucius. When I went back to him after you and Simon took me, he drank my blood. And when he did, he was able to shadow."

I gaped at her. I had never heard of such a thing. Never even thought it might be possible.

"Hell's balls," Guy said. "That's—"

"Deadly knowledge," Simon interrupted him. "If it became known, then Lily would be in terrible danger."

"And the baby," Lily said. "Any of my kind. If there are others."

There had been other wraiths, in the past. I didn't know if there were any now. If there were, they had the sense to live far from the City and the Fae.

Something I was suddenly wishing I had the sense to do as well. Because there was someone else who needed to know this secret. "It is dangerous," I agreed. "But we need to tell the king."

"Why?" Simon said.

"Because Ignatius may know this as well. And if he does, then he doesn't need a grown wraith as a weapon—he just needs children to feed from. He just needs their blood. An army of vampires who can walk through the shadow? That would be the end of the City. So the king needs to know. He intends to make peace with Ignatius if he can. I think we need to change his mind. If there's any chance that Ignatius knows about this, then we cannot let him become Lord of the Blood. He needs to die."

Ash

The baby in my arms felt solid enough. She was warm and wriggly and surprisingly heavy, just like every other baby I'd ever held. Not that there had been that many. But unlike every other baby I'd held, this one, if I closed my eyes and looked for her with my magic, was invisible. Didn't seem to exist.

A wraith.

Ignatius had bred a wraith. Could have bred more. And if what Lily and Simon had just finished telling me was true, that was a whole new pile of trouble landing on my head.

The source of the trouble blinked up with me with her blurry baby gaze and hiccupped.

I handed her back to Lily, anger beginning to burn through me. Ignatius had stolen Fae women. Had presumably caused them to be raped. To breed wraiths to be his slaves and make him near invincible. That was what lust for power did to people. Made them close enough to insane. "So Ignatius wants to be able to walk through walls."

"Maybe. We're not sure that he knows about this. He may just want a wraith because Lucius had one," Simon said. "But still, if he does know . . . he can't be let go."

My stomach was cold despite the fury heating my veins. But I knew what I had to say. I knew what I wanted to do too and it was something completely different. But I was king now and I had to do what was best for the City. "I offered a peace. I can't turn around and withdraw that offer with no more proof than this baby."

"He's kidnapped Fae women," Bryony said sharply. "Your subjects."

"He's done worse than that over the last few months, I'm sure," I said, hating myself as I said the words. "But a peace will stop any more deaths. Will restore order. And give me laws to work with if he oversteps the bounds."

"A peace with Ignatius Grey will not last," Lily snapped.

"I'm sure they said that about the peace the queen

forged," I said. I was trying to be rational. Sensible. Kingly. My head ached as though I wore an iron crown.

"You can't mean to let this go unpunished?" Bryony looked appalled. But then she'd been avoiding me since I returned to the City, and the fact that she disliked my plan couldn't sway me. She didn't want to stand at my side, so her words could carry no more weight with me than anybody else's.

"It will be a matter discussed during the negotiations." If the negotiations took place. "If Ignatius does not choose to make peace, then I will deal with him differently."

None of the group before me looked happy with my decision. Lily, least of all.

"I'm going back to the warrens," she said. "I can't just leave those women there. Once Ignatius discovers the baby is gone, he'll move them. Or worse."

"You can't bring them out through the shadow like you did the baby," I said.

"No. But I can hide them, maybe. I can take charms and weapons and maybe even an unlit sunlamp through the shadow with me." She looked at Simon, a question in her eyes. "Maybe Holly can figure a charm to make the sunlamp work after I leave it with them. Ignatius will have plenty to occupy his mind tonight. If I can move them, stay with them, they have a chance."

Simon's face turned grim. "Lily, it's too dangerous."

She shook her head. "No." The word was blunt.

I hadn't often seen her disagree with Simon, and her expression was a little pleading. But her shoulders were square and her chin raised. I didn't think any of us would be able to change her mind.

"I grew up without a mother. This baby needs a chance to know hers."

"Alder may not want her," Bryony said gently.

"Maybe." Lily's expression was set. "But I'll give them a chance. If Alder doesn't want her, then I'll take her."

Simon's face turned startled, but then he smiled and nodded at Lily, blue eyes accepting that much, at least.

It wasn't easy to see the two of them. United. The love

they shared was stronger than their differences. Happy together. Everything I wanted. Everything I was denied by the crown I had been forced to claim.

"What you choose to do is not my affair," I said. "I can't help you directly—that would be breaking the terms of the peace offer—but I won't stop you. Just don't tell me when you go."

Lily nodded. "If you'll excuse me, then, Your Majesty. I have things to do."

"Go," I said.

Simon followed her out. Which left me with Bryony and Guy. Bryony was glaring at me. Guy looked from her to me, rolled his eyes, and then followed his brother. He'd known Bryony a long time. Apparently he knew better than to chance her temper. I didn't think I was going to have that luxury.

"If you're going to yell at me, can you do it quickly?" I said, gesturing to the desk in front of me that was stacked high with papers and maps and dusty many-inch-thick law books. The Templars had given me a room to use as an office here in the City. The Fae wanted me to use one of the chambers in the building that had been used by the queen's Speaker for the Veil, her liaison with the humans, but the Speaker was dead, another victim of Ignatius' plotting. I didn't have time to appoint a new Speaker or to establish a new bureaucracy. I hadn't even worked out whether I wanted a Speaker. So working here was easier for now. Besides which, it meant no splitting of our forces to set up a separate guard for me there. "I have work to do."

"You need to stop Ignatius. You could stop Ignatius. Right now," Bryony said. She wore purple today, a dark shade that made her look even more like a thunderstorm, the color of the darkest hearts of the sapphires in her Family ring. Her hair was bound up with silver that matched the chain at her neck. A storm she might be, but just like a storm, she was glorious.

And I was a fool to think so.

I got up from my chair and moved around the table to join her. "You think I should just set the whole City on fire to get to Ignatius?"

"You have power. You should use it."

I sighed. "Bryony. I can't."

"Why not? What's the point of being king if you can't do that much? Why are you wasting your time here, filling in paperwork?" She swept a hand toward the desk and the papers, sounding furious.

My own temper snapped a little in response. "This was exactly why I didn't want to be king. It isn't about doing what you like. What did the Veiled Queen spend most of her time doing?"

Bryony shrugged at me, looking irritated.

"Nothing," I said. "Not acting. She ruled. She enforced the laws but she also kept to them herself. She didn't look for trouble or start fights if she didn't have to. She was a good queen. And I mean to be a good king if I have to be one at all. Trust me, I've fought enough battles and wars to know that it's easy to be a bad ruler. To let greed and power warp you and to act out of self-interest or fear rather than have the guts to do what has to be done. I'm not going to do that. I want peace. I don't want more death. And I don't want to turn into someone like Ignatius Grey."

"You would have peace if you made Lady Adeline the ruler of the Blood Court."

"The Blood have to work that part out for themselves. Lady Adeline seems reasonable and trustworthy for one of her kind, but I'm not going to interfere with that process unless I have to. If Ignatius will negotiate, then I have to give him a chance to."

"Ignatius killed the last person who wanted to negotiate with him."

"Well, if he kills me, that will make this whole mess someone else's problem," I quipped. She didn't smile. "You wanted me to do this. You told me to be king. And I am. But that means that you have to abide by my decisions, just like everybody else." I stared at her. "Unless you've had a change of heart?"

I tried to keep the note of hope out of my voice. Bryony didn't say anything. "We could stand together, Bryony."

"I—"

Frustration boiled in me. "You what? What's so hard about this? You love me. Tell me you don't."

Silence.

Infuriating woman. "You can't deny it. Because it's true. So I don't understand why you won't just be with me. Don't you want that? It doesn't have to be how it was under the queen's rule. We don't have to be hidden and frozen and so bound up in the Veiled World. I can make changes. I have to make changes or we'll all just end up right back where we were. Can't you trust me that it will be all right? Haven't you missed me?" I reached for her then, took her hand. Felt the pulse of her power as it met mine. And the roar in my pulse that told me that she was mine. "Don't you feel that too?"

"I—"

I bit down, gave her space to speak. Held back the thousand arguments tumbling through my head. All the talking in the world couldn't change her mind if she didn't love me.

"I don't know," she said. "I'm a healer, Ash. I work with the humans. I have to be in the City. You have to be in Summerdale."

"Not every second of every day."

"You don't know that. You don't even know what will happen tomorrow."

"I'm not Fen, no. But not knowing the future doesn't mean that you have to be scared to hope, does it? To try? Do you want to be apart again? Because I don't."

"I can't answer you," she said. "I need time to think. And there are more important things to worry about."

"More urgent things," I said. "Things I have to worry about, things I have to prioritize, but they don't have to be more important to me than you. Not if you don't want them to. I can be a good king and a good man. If you'll trust me."

She turned for the door. "I can't answer now, Ash. I'm asking you for time. Please."

"We may not have that much time," I said.

"Then that will be my regret to live with," she said. "But I need it."

Chapter Twenty-four

BRYONY

The hours until sunset crawled by no matter how much work I tried to hide behind. Every glance out the window to judge the angle of the light, every chime of the cathedral bells marking the passing hours mocked me.

I'd spent the few hours' sleep I'd snatched alone, but Ash walked my dreams. Looking haunted as he had looked yesterday. Asking me to come with him and then melting away before I could give him an answer. Bearing the weight of the choice we'd forced on him.

Alone.

I hated thinking of him that way. He'd always been one to surround himself with friends and crowds of people when we were younger. I'd watched the Veiled Queen and she hadn't had many friends. Definitely no husband to stand at her side. Which was her choice, but I understood why she'd made it. How could she tell who truly loved her and who just wanted the queen's favor? She didn't need an heir, because that wasn't how our court worked. Maybe she'd wanted a child, but she'd given that up to rule us. And now it was Ash giving up everything he'd wanted.

Including me.

I'd forced that choice on him too. So what did that make me? Foolish? Wise?

Regretful, and living with an ache that felt as though someone had severed a vital part of my body.

I'd risen too early and sought out Simon, who was also trying to keep himself busy. Lily had left for the warrens before dusk the previous night and she had yet to reappear.

Simon was near frantic with worry, though he hid it reasonably well. But I knew him. Knew how he thought. Knew her absence was eating away at him.

Eventually I sent a note to Fen asking him to meet us in the hidden ward.

When he appeared, I pointed him toward Simon. "Can you tell him if Lily is still alive?"

Fen closed his eyes a minute. "I still see her," he said. He looked down at Simon's hand. "And I still see that band around your finger."

Simon's shoulders sagged and he closed his eyes for a moment. "Thank you," he said. "But I'll feel better about all of this when she's safely back here."

"We all will," I said sympathetically.

"I'll feel better when someone cuts Grey's head off," Fen said with feeling.

I shot him a look.

"Oh, don't pretend that I'm the only one hoping that Ignatius doesn't show tonight," he said. "We'll all be better off once he's six feet under. Let Asharic forge his peace with Lady Adeline and then it might last."

"Have you seen anything about tonight?" I asked curiously. Sunset was only a few hours away now. Surely that was near enough for Fen to be able to see clearly.

Fen tugged at the gem dangling from his ear. "No. It's still too crowded, too many possibilities, I guess. Or some of the key players haven't made up their minds."

"Wonderful," I muttered. "I really hate this."

"We know," Simon said.

"You might feel better if you were with Asharic," Fen

said with a grin. "Why aren't you with him, by the way?
Both of you are horribly bad-tempered when you're apart."

"None of your business," I said. Then I paused. "Have
you seen something about Ash? Do I need to be with him?"

"The Lady smiles on love. Isn't that what they say?" Fen
said cryptically.

"They also say she smiles on drunkards and gamblers," I
said acerbically.

"Well, Ash is gambling with this play," Fen said. "Though,
to be fair, whichever way he stepped, he'd be gambling at
this point. So maybe the Lady will smile on him for that
too." He shuddered suddenly and grimaced. "I wouldn't
want to be in his place. In fact, in his place, I would've
jumped on the nearest horse and fled the City as soon as
they asked me to be king."

Simon snorted. "You didn't run when you had the chance,
Fen."

"Your sister is very convincing," Fen said. "Besides
which, no one was asking me to rule the Fae. That's a thank-
less task if ever there was one. And a lonely one."

I ducked away from his pointed look. Message received.
Fen was on Asharic's side. Which made me wonder again
why I couldn't be.

Ash had chosen to wait for Ignatius outside the ruins of the
Treaty Hall. The wreckage of it hadn't been touched, no one
having had either any time to spare or the will to start re-
building. It was symbolism, I supposed. A sign that he intended things to return to how they had been.

I only hoped it wouldn't become a symbol of something
else. Another Fae defeat.

Ash stood before the steps leading to the gaping hole
where the doors to the hall should have been. The Fae were
arrayed to the west of the square, taking up their traditional
position.

The humans took the south with the Templars forming
ranks between the spaces the Beast Kind would take and
the rest of the humans. It was a clear message that no one

would be allowed to incite violence here. The Fae had already combed every inch of the square, searching for enchantments, the mages assisting them. There were to be no surprises this time. Not if Asharic had anything to do with it.

His face was set, grim even. Someone had found armor for him that was far more elaborate than the leather and simple mail he usually wore.

It was silver and gold chased with the colors of his house so that he looked almost as if he wore flames.

I wondered how it had been made so quickly but then remembered it would have been Fae smiths, not metalmages, who would have wrought it. The biggest question was who had convinced him to wear it. I suspected his father.

His head was bare, though, the edges of his dark hair lifting slightly in the breeze while he waited. He wore no crown. The Veiled Queen had worn veils, not a crown. I didn't know whether Ash was making a statement or whether he simply didn't feel that he should wear one until he had actually been crowned.

Either away he didn't need it. No one would mistake who was in charge at that moment. The sense of his power filled the square like smoke. Even the humans with no magic seemed to feel it. They might not know what they were feeling, but they showed their respect.

But to me, he wasn't the mysterious Fae king. He was the man who I once thought would be mine. The one I could no longer have. Not unless I wanted to turn myself into a living symbol as he was.

I took my place beside Holly and Fen. I should have joined the Fae, but right now I didn't feel part of them. So I stood with my friends. Friends who, like me, didn't truly belong to one world or the other. Friends who had chosen a side out of love and loyalty, not obligation.

And even with friends as close as these, I felt the lack of Ash by my side like a burn.

I bore it as we waited for the sun to lower those last few inches. For darkness to fall.

To see what the night would bring.

There was tension in the air. Tension and outright fear as the skies darkened.

The humans had become used to locking themselves away for the night over the last few months. Now they were standing here waiting for the enemy to appear.

Except they didn't.

Not one.

"Well, that's clear enough," said a voice at my ear, and I turned to see Lily. Holly and Fen turned too and Holly flung herself forward to embrace her.

Lily looked tired and dirty but no worse for wear.

"Did you get them out?" I asked softly.

"Not out. But hidden. They're safe for now, I hope." She pulled a sheaf of papers from inside the leather vest she wore. "And I have more maps for Asharic." She cocked her head at me suddenly. "Why aren't you with him?"

"Long story," I murmured.

"She's being an idiot," Holly said at the same time. She narrowed her eyes at me. "And don't bother trying to glare me into submission, Bryony sa'Eleniel. That man loves you. Any fool can see that. And he needs you."

"Would you give up your life for a man?" I asked.

Lily snorted. "She already did. So did I, for that matter. And it wasn't giving something up—it was choosing something different. Something better. Holly's right. Don't be an idiot." She nodded toward Ash. "You should go to him."

But it was too late. Because Ash stepped forward and gestured for silence when the crowd started to mutter and chatter as he did so.

"The Blood and the Beast Kind have forfeited their rights under the treaty," he said. "But hear this. I will reforge a peace."

His voice echoed strangely and I wondered just how far it was carrying. All the way into the Night World, most likely.

"And I will accept anyone who wants to lay down arms and come to the negotiation table, but until then we are at war," Ash finished.

There was cheering at that. Cheering that made me think

I would never truly understand people. There was nothing worth celebrating in the act of war. But maybe it was just a conclusion, one way or the other, that they wanted. I couldn't blame them for that. It was what I wanted too.

ASH

"You're going tonight, then."

I looked up from the maps I was studying for what felt like the thousandth time whilst we debated where best to deploy our forces. Bryony stood at the door of my office. No one else seemed to have heard her.

There were at least twenty men in the room and none of them had the good sense to notice a beautiful woman.

Soldiers.

Idiots. I should know. I was one.

My father arched a dark eyebrow at me before he turned his attention back to the maps, making me revise my opinion. My father had heard her. And he was wondering what I was going to do about it.

"Gentleman, I'd like to speak to Lady sa'Eleniel alone," I said. I didn't need to raise my voice. Some of them looked surprised, but all of them hurried out of the room, my father stopping to nod to Bryony and then turn and wink at me.

I didn't know what he had to be so amused about.

Bryony was clutching a sheaf of papers in her hands, a dark blue cloak covering whatever she was wearing.

"Come in," I said.

"I don't want to keep you," she said, but she walked forward to join me by the desk.

"You're not," I said. "We're nearly done here." I hoped I was telling the truth. I was used to commanding two thousand men. Now, with the Fae swelling my forces, I could call many times that if I needed to. It made everything more complicated. My mercenaries were still recovering from the news that their commander was now the Fae King. I needed not to rattle them further by getting my first command decisions wrong.

I only wished someone could make me feel better about it all. But the king, it seemed, stood alone. Not even the woman before me was willing to change that. But I still couldn't turn her away. Wasn't going to deny myself a few minutes of the sight and scent and sound of her. I waited, wondering what she had come to say.

"Are you going tonight?"

"Either we take the fight to him or he brings it to us. I, for one, am sick of waiting." I wanted it over and done with, one way or another.

Her lips pressed together as she looked at the uppermost map, one of the ones that Lily had drawn of the warrens. "Isn't it risky to go into the Night World?"

"Yes. But I'm hoping that there will be less damage to the humans that way. I'm leaving a force protecting the border in case Ignatius tries to mount some sort of sneak attack, but I want to keep the fighting out of the human boroughs as far as possible."

"It's a long way from the hospitals." She bit her lip, one hand straying to her chain. It shimmered the same color as her cloak for a moment.

"There are enough of us with some healing skills to make do." I didn't say that fighting against desperate Beast and Blood there were likely to be more corpses than injuries. She understood that.

"I could—"

I cut off her words with a sharp gesture. I would fight because I had to. But there was no way in seven hells I would let her go anywhere near the Night World. "No. You couldn't. You're staying here, where I know you're safe. Where you can do what you're best at. There will be patients enough, I imagine."

"I can't just wait around," she said.

"And I can't do what I have to do if I'm worrying about you every second."

"Yet you want me to sit here and worry about you."

My heart sped up. "Will you be worried about me?" I asked.

Her eyes were endlessly deep. But this time she didn't evade me. "Yes."

I smiled as hope flared. "Well, then, that makes it easier."

"Makes what easier?" She sounded confused. And starting to be irritated. Which was good. I preferred her on her feet and fighting to pale and scared.

"It's always easier to fight when you have something to fight for," I said. I tugged the Family ring off my hand. Laid it in my palm. "I'm not really supposed to wear this anymore." The king was supposed to have no allegiance to a Family. All the Fae were his responsibility. I needed rings of all colors now. I studied the ring for a moment. I'd only had it back on my finger for a short time and everything had changed again. Still, there was somewhere else I wanted it to be. I held out my hand to Bryony. "Will you take it? Keep it safe?"

Bryony froze. An offer of a Family ring was an offer of marriage. I didn't know if I was mad to ask again, but she'd come here to see me. So I had to try one last time. If only to know what I really was fighting for—the Fae and the City or something far more precious. A future with Bryony standing beside me. "Bryony?" I prompted. "Will you take it?"

She sucked in a breath. And took the ring from my hand. Closed her fingers around it. Then she moved closer and kissed me. One fierce, brilliant kiss. Enough to carry me through the darkness and bring me safely home again. Or so I hoped.

"Come back safely," she said. Then she shoved the sheaf of papers at me. "Lily made you more maps. She said she marked where she hid the Fae women on these." Her words were coming too fast, as though she wasn't entirely in control of her voice.

"Bryony, we need to—"

"Later. After." She took another gulping breath. "When you come back to me." She pulled the hand holding the ring close to her chest. "We'll talk then." She was gone from the room before I could come up with a protest, leaving me with the taste of her on my mouth, a bare hand, and a fistful of maps.

Another hour or so passed before we were ready. I stood beside Guy and listened as he relayed the orders we'd decided on to my—our—assembled army. An army the likes of which probably hadn't been seen since the Veiled Queen took on the Blood all those centuries ago and bent them to her will. I hoped I could pull off the feat a second time.

I let Guy's words wash over me, let my thoughts drift slightly as he spoke of the plans and the orders to spare anyone who surrendered. To try to spare as many as possible of the Trusted and Nightseekers that we encountered.

To show mercy.

I hoped we could, though I knew that some would lose their heads in the heat of battle and that there would be deaths aplenty on both sides before I was done. I would have to bear the weight of those deaths. I had done it before. Perhaps not on this scale but I would find a way. But first, I wanted a last breath of peace, so I thought of Bryony. Of the midnight colors of her and the brightness and fire that she tried to hide beneath the cool front she presented to the world. The fire she showed to me.

I wanted to feel that fire again. And for that reason, and no other, I would fight my way clear tonight and I would bring Ignatius Grey to his knees and bring peace back to this gods-damned Half-Light City. Cause it to change its name and come out of the darkness that threatened to engulf it.

Or I would die trying.

Bryony.

I thought her name one last time and then I led the way into the Night World.

Flames.

Flames and darkness and the sounds of metal clashing. The night blurred together into a whirl of those three things as we made our way toward our goal. Fought our way deeper and deeper into the Night World with blood and steel, meeting Beast and Blood and humans who stood against us.

Guy and Simon and I fought together. I hadn't expected Simon, but he wielded his sword with as much deadly grace as his brother and several times called sunlight to clear our path of looming Blood. I was aware of Rhian fighting near me several times, carving her path with her usual ruthless efficiency. She too had a Templar beside her. A one-handed Templar whose sword flamed with sunlight.

Liam.

Well, I wasn't going to argue about his right to be here even if a one-armed knight was more vulnerable than the rest of us.

It took several hours to reach the mansion that was the point of entry to the warrens that Lily had marked. Other squadrons would be trying different paths down into the depths. I thought I heard the cathedral bell tolling midnight far behind us, but that might have been just my imagination. The night was clouded and dark, so there was no way to mark time by the passage of the moon above us. It would be darker still where we were about to go, so the time didn't really matter.

There was a brief respite when we reached the mansion, a few minutes taken to let the men join up again. Those who could.

I squared aching shoulders and nodded at Guy. He shouted more orders, and I boosted his voice so that it would be heard by all.

I wished I could boost everything else as easily. Make the men fresh and unharmed. But I couldn't do that much. I was tired and so was everyone else who fought with me.

And the worst was yet to come.

I decided that perhaps a little demonstration might at least lift their spirits, so I stole Liam's idea and called a flame to dance around my blade as we headed down into the warrens.

Fighting our way through tunnels and darkness was just as bad as I expected it to be. The Blood had extinguished all

the lanterns—they and the Beasts could see just fine in the
dark after all—and left traps and dead ends for us to throw
ourselves against as they came floating out of the darkness
to attack us.

We had lanterns and the sunmages used sunlamps to aid
us, but we had to be careful not to tire them out. There was
no way for them to recharge their powers down here.

Worst of all were the forces of Trusted who charged out
to meet us. It was hard to show mercy when someone was
trying to take your head off. The casualties piled up, each
crumpled corpse dressed in red-stained white making me
sick to the pit of my stomach.

But still we fought on, searching for Ignatius Grey, until
we'd come so far and so deep that even I couldn't tell exactly where we were. The earthsong came from all around
me, though it was strangely muted, as though the Blood had
done something to twist the sound of it. Still, it was power
to draw upon and I used it to light torches as we paused,
panting, when we reached a large open area where tunnels
branched in all directions.

There was still no sign of Ignatius.

"How long do we keep going?" I muttered to Guy. "We
could go round in circles forever down here."

Guy grinned at me. "Not losing your nerve, are you, Your
Majesty?"

Beside him, Simon laughed. There was a cut on his forehead that had dripped blood over half his face. The effect of
crusted blood and soot smeared across his skin made his
smile more disturbing than funny.

"No," I said. "But I'll be bloody glad to get out of these
Veil-damned tunnels."

"You and me both," Guy said. He wiped his forehead
with the back of his hand, which only smudged the dirt on
his face farther across it.

I wondered if I looked as bad as they did. I had ditched
the armor I'd worn before the Treaty Hall. It was pretty; I
would give my smiths credit where it was due. But it wasn't
what I was used to and I didn't want to be hampered by
strange armor. So I was wearing my old mail and leathers

and carrying my own sword, not the queen's. I reached for the canteen hanging at my hip and swigged water as I considered our options, recalling Lily's maps to mind. I had a copy of them stuffed beneath my mail, but this wasn't really the time to take a long enough break to study them in detail. We had to keep moving. I corked the canteen and wiped my mouth, tasting blood and sweat on my skin.

"Which way, Your Majesty?" Simon asked.

Where was Ignatius? Where would I go if I was him? Up or down? If he'd been a wraith, I'd have picked down. Down where he could hide in the earth and laugh at us as we searched for him. But he wasn't and I had to hope like hell that he didn't have another handy wraith baby to give him wraithlike powers to walk the shadow.

So for him, up had to be safer. Offered more chance of escape.

But maybe that was what he wanted me to think.

I spat a curse as I tried to choose, seeking the Lady's guidance on this insane throw of the dice we were attempting.

Before I could give the order to move onward, Lily stepped out of the tunnel to my right.

"I found Ignatius," she said. "He's this way."

I could've kissed her. Simon did kiss her, looking as though he didn't know whether he wanted to do that or kill her. Guy just grinned, a quick, savage gleam of white in his soot-smeared face.

I knew how he felt. If there was one thing I was going to do if I lived through this, it would be to see what I could do to change the attitudes of the Fae to Lily's kind. I knew what the dislike was born of; I knew how wraiths were made. The violent joining of near-turned Trusted and Fae women. Some humans went into a kind of frenzy in the hours before they died and rose again during the process the Blood used to create more of their kind. And it was men in this state who sired wraiths.

She was born to darkness, yet Lily strove for the light. And she might just have saved us all. I was going to make sure that there weren't more wraiths born against the will

of the women who bore them, but I was going to make sure
we would honor this one and any of her kind who chose to
make themselves known. And Alder's baby would be
taught to be proud of who she was.

I didn't yet know if I could save her mother, but I could
offer her that much.

I gave Simon a minute more to satisfy himself that Lily
was all in one piece and not hurt and then I told her to take
us to Ignatius.

Our progress went more swiftly. I didn't know if Lily had
already cleared the tunnels we traveled through, or if the
Blood were falling back, but we only encountered a few
parties of them standing in our way. Between Simon's sunlight and my fire, we made short work of them. I didn't want
to risk any more of the men with us until we reached our
destination. I took care to damp down the flames behind us,
having no desire to go up in flames if the warrens caught
alight, but we moved swiftly, following Lily's unwavering
directions.

We ended up several levels above where we'd started,
close to the surface, I thought, maybe only two or three
levels below the earth. Lily paused at a massive metal door.
"He's in there," she said. And then she faded out of sight.

I blinked at her disappearance and then pulled my focus
back to the door. The last barrier between me and my
quarry. It was barred with iron. Perhaps Ignatius thought
that would stop me, but he'd misjudged me and the company I fought with. If I could stand to be in the ward hidden
beneath St. Giles, then this small amount of iron here
wouldn't stop me.

I summoned my will and reached for the muted power
around me and blew the door inward.

I ducked through the shattered doorway. Ignatius stood in
the middle of the room, pointing a pistol at me. Alone. I
skidded to a halt and lifted my own gun. Was it coming
down to this? At who was faster to pull the trigger? I almost
laughed. The last time I'd fought a duel with weapons, it had
been Stellan and swords. The Fae didn't fight with guns.

They were a human invention. One I'd learned to embrace in my years away from the City but battles weren't duels.

"So you made it this far, Your Majesty," Ignatius said. "Well done."

I tilted my head at him. "Ignatius Grey, I bind you to stand trial for crimes against the City and the treaty."

He laughed then. A weirdly rough sound. But I didn't pay much attention to it. I watched his hand where it held the gun. And I saw the tiny movement as his fingers started to squeeze inward. I flung a binding spell at him, but I wasn't quite as quick as Lily, who appeared behind him and casually knocked him out with the hilt of her dagger. She smiled as she peered down at him where he lay unconscious on the expensive carpet. "That was for Reggie, Alder, and the others, you prick," she said. Then she turned her smile on me.

"I believe this room might be booby-trapped, Your Majesty. I suggest you take this"—she pushed Ignatius over with her foot—"and get out of here."

"Excellent suggestion, my lady," I said with a bow. Guy hoisted Ignatius over his shoulder and then we ran like hell.

Chapter Twenty-five

BRYONY

The cathedral bells started to ring wildly, jolting me from a half doze. I'd sat down for a minute with the tea Father Cho had insisted I drink and closed my eyes just for a moment....

But the sound of the bells brought me to my feet. I barely knew where I was, but I let my feet carry me out of the room and grabbed the nearest Templar.

"What do the bells mean?" I asked him.

He laughed and pointed. "Come see for yourself, my lady." I followed the line of his finger and got my bearings at last. I was near the entryway to the Brother House, and the doors were open. I ran for them, nearly cannoning into Father Cho.

"I was just coming to fetch you," he said, steadying me with his hands. He grinned up at me. I couldn't remember the last time I'd seen the Abbott General smiling. It was infectious, that grin, and the dancing light in the tired dark eyes.

Father Cho stepped out of my path and ushered me forward. It was still dark, but I walked out onto the steps in time to see Asharic and Guy ride into the courtyard and come to a halt under the row of hanging lamps lighting the courtyard, Simon and Lily close on their heels. Guy was carrying someone in front of him. Someone tied hand and foot, I noticed. Someone that Guy deposited none too gently onto the cobblestones once he dismounted.

The man's long hair was white against the dark gray stones. So was his skin.

"Ignatius Grey, I presume," I said half under my breath.

"Indeed," Father Cho said. "God is good."

"*Eluria e'tan mei,*" I agreed. Bless the Veil. And bless the woman who had borne that title. We were about to avenge her. And the king who replaced her seemed to be—at least to my frantically seeking eyes—whole and unharmed.

"*Eluria e'tan mei,*" I repeated, and watched Ash give orders for Ignatius to be locked up below the Brother House.

I followed him down to the cells, added my power to his as we bound the cell in ward upon ward, adding to the binding that Ash had cast on Ignatius and the silver shackles that held him spread-eagled on the low wooden bed they'd laid him on. He wasn't going to move or escape or take the easy way out, if either of us could help it.

"What are you going to do with him?" I asked after Ash had sent the guards away.

Ash stared through the grille in the door. "Put him on trial."

"Do you think he'll confess to killing the queen?"

He drew down the cover that closed off the grille with a snap and turned away from the cell. "That one? I doubt it. But there will be others eager enough to save their skins and make peace." His voice was tired. "But that's a problem for tomorrow. We have to finish the job tonight. Round up the alphas and as many Blood and Beasts as we can."

"Let the others do that." I laid my hand on his cheek. "You're exhausted."

"I'm the king," he said. "It's my fight to end."

"You've already ended it. You've got Ignatius. Spread word of that and the rest of them will give up."

"I'm not sure how many are left," Ash said. "Not Blood,

at least. There was fire in the warrens by the time we got out."

"Yours?"

He jerked his head toward the cell. "His. He booby-trapped half the goddamned place. I decided not to interfere."

"Adeline won't be pleased."

"Adeline can build her own damned warrens," Ash said. He closed his hand around mine, then stopped. "You're not wearing my ring."

"It's a little big." I pulled my chain free of my dress, showed him the ring safely hanging there. "I didn't want to lose it."

He went very still, his eyes seeking mine. "What does that mean?"

Time for the truth. Because there was no denying it. My life would have to change some, but I would take that over a life without Ash. "It means that you're not doing this alone," I said. "Lady help us both."

He smiled then and my heart seemed bigger than my chest suddenly. "Don't think I'm going to sit and embroider in Summerdale. The court and all its stupid rules bore me senseless."

"I'm the king," he said. "I get to make the rules. And one of them is whatever my lady wants."

And then he kissed me and the night fell away.

ASH

In the end, the trial took more time to organize than it did to hold. As I'd predicted, Ignatius' former allies were all too eager to confess his crimes for him in exchange for amnesty. Some of them I granted it to. Most of the Beast Kind packs had had a swift and deadly change of alphas, and the new alphas were all keen to sign a new treaty. I would keep a careful eye on them but hoped that Ignatius would be enough of an example to keep them in line for some time to come.

Even Salvia had found her tongue in the end and confessed that she had worked with Ignatius, helping him with the attacks on the Treaty Hall and the queen. I hadn't threatened her, but she had told me anyway, perhaps assuming that I was as vindictive as she was and that I would harm her Family to wring the truth out of her.

Her testimony alone, witnessed by my father and Lord sa'Eleniel and the other heads of the Families, was enough to condemn Ignatius.

I hadn't made up my mind what I was going to do with Salvia herself when I returned to the City. I didn't want to execute her, but exile was not a fitting punishment for treason. She had named others who were also now waiting on my judgment, but none of them were highly ranked. Some would have been coerced and some just following orders. I doubted many had known just how far Salvia's plot went, but I would deal appropriately with those who had.

On the morning of Ignatius' trial, they brought me word that Salvia had been found dead in her chamber in the palace. I didn't know if her husband had brought her poison or she had found some other way. I didn't ask, just ordered that her body be returned to her Family. Maybe that was cowardly of me, but it was justice of a kind and I had enough death on my hands already.

With more to come. One more in particular, today.

"Are you sure you want to do this?" Bryony asked me one last time as we waited outside the humans' council chamber where the trial was to be held.

"Yes. It's time to end this. Time for peace."

I bent and kissed her hand where my ring covered half of one finger, the colors like fire tamed to solid form. "Go take your seat."

I watched her go. Waited for my name to be called. Then I walked into the courtroom to sentence Ignatius Grey to death.

The outcome was a foregone conclusion. We had the evidence we needed and there could be no mercy in this case.

The Veiled Queen had established her peace with a display of power and law as well.

It seemed that I was to follow in her footsteps a little longer.

Not surprisingly, Ignatius stayed silent throughout the short trial. He listened to the list of charges. Assassination of the queen, engineering the breaking of the treaty, the explosion at Treaty Hall. The attacks on St. Giles and other targets. Destruction and death and treachery to spare. Buried close to the end of the list was the kidnap of Fae citizens. Compared to the other offenses, it must have seemed minor to those listening and I hoped that it would stay that way. Better not to have the truth of what he'd been doing down there in the depths of his warrens known too widely. We didn't want others amongst the Blood to begin to wonder why a wraith was such a prize.

Ignatius had refused to confess anything to me and I'd refused to allow the Templars or anybody else to attempt to extract the information from him. I might be executioner, but I wouldn't be a torturer if I didn't have to be. And I didn't have to be, given the number of witnesses ready to speak against him. I spared the Fae women that part too. No one needed to know the details of what they had been through, unless they chose to share them. They were safely back in Summerdale under the care of the healers.

So I spoke the words I had to speak and watched them lead Ignatius back to his cell.

And at sunset I waited for him in front of the ruins of Treaty Hall, sword in hand.

There'd been arguments aplenty about that in the time since we'd captured him. Guy and Simon and even Lily had argued for the right·to wield the sword. But I'd refused them. Simon would regret it, if I read the man right, no matter how much he might think he wouldn't. Lily would do it with no regret, but I didn't want her to have more blood on her hands. She deserved all the grace the Veil could grant her from this point onward. Without her, Ignatius might well have been the one wielding the sword.

She had brought the Fae women out of the warrens on

the night we defeated Ignatius and somehow shepherded
them through the fighting back to St. Giles besides. I still
didn't know how she'd managed it. It was going to take the
women a long time to recover. I had gone to see them and
Violet had told me just a little of what Ignatius had done to
them. And that there had been others before them, who
hadn't survived his attempts. But now, thanks to Lily, they
had a chance.

Alder, as Bryony had predicted, was so far refusing to
see her baby. She gave her a name, though. Thea. And she
asked Lily to take care of her. Lily had agreed, but she sent
word to Alder every day of Thea's progress. And beyond
giving her daughter a name, she had given me something
more. Her story. Of how Salvia had kidnapped her from her
Family—a minor branch of the sa'Ambriels—and given her
to Ignatius. Which was something Salvia had managed to
leave out of her confession. Alder didn't know why they had
done it, but her testimony was enough to have sealed Salvia's fate. Which left me somewhat grateful that Salvia had
taken the matter out of my hands. Two executions in one
day would be hard to stomach.

But hopefully Salvia's and Ignatius' deaths would ease
some of Alder's wounds and those of all the others damaged in this war. Maybe enough to bring us all some peace
in the light.

Thea meant "light," so Saskia informed me. It seemed an
odd name for a wraith, but I trusted Lily to give her the
strength to live up to it. Simon would give her humanity as
well. And, unless I misjudged things, Lily wouldn't give up
until Alder had some involvement in her daughter's life too.

But that was the future. A good future. The future that I
strove for. A City made whole again.

I looked out at the square while I waited. This time the
Blood—those who'd survived—answered my summons as
true dark fell. At their head stood Lady Adeline, who'd
taken the reins of power into her black velvet gloves and
didn't show any intention of letting go anytime soon. I
hadn't asked her exactly how she'd consolidated her power.
She was willing to sign the treaty and that was enough for

now. I trusted that she had learned enough from what had gone before not to try to overstep her bounds.

The Beasts and the humans waited. And my Fae. Bryony stood closest to me, wearing a somber blue dress. But my ring gleamed still on her hand and that was enough for me.

There was a hum of noise through the crowd as Guy and a squad of Templars led Ignatius toward me.

My stomach clenched in protest, but I set my teeth. My rule. My justice. My hand.

Guy looked at me, something that might have been sympathy flashing in the ice-blue eyes, before he bowed and stepped back, leaving me alone with Ignatius.

I wondered if he would try anything. I hoped he wasn't that stupid.

"Ignatius Grey, for the crime of treason against the treaty and the murder of the Veiled Queen, you have been sentenced to death. Do you understand?"

He nodded.

"Do you wish to say anything?" It was tradition to offer last words.

A head shake, long white hair blowing in the cool night wind.

"Very well." I stared at him wishing I felt something more noble. Wasn't I supposed to feel triumphant? Kingly? Victorious? Mostly I just felt tired and angry. "Fire or steel?"

He smiled then. "Makes no difference to me, Your Majesty. Do your worst."

I gritted my teeth. I was tempted to blast him to ash where he stood, but that felt too easy somehow. My justice. My hand. If I was to hold this peace, then every last person had to know what breaking my laws would bring. I drew the queen's sword. Took a breath. And took his head off with a single blow.

Aftermath

BRYONY

"This is a strange way to celebrate after a wedding," I said as Ash led me down into the tunnels beneath St. Giles.

He paused on the next step, twisting back to look at me. "Well, you have to admit, it was an unusual wedding. I'd go so far as to guess that there has never been a wedding quite like it before."

"You may be right at that," I said, pausing to catch my breath. I fought the urge to laugh, a symptom of too much champagne. "A wraith marrying a sunmage in a garden with the Templar Abbott General officiating. And the Fae king in the wedding party. That's one for the history books." I did laugh then, remembering. It had been a strange and long three months. Full of change. The treaty was in place once more and the peace seemed to be holding.

The Fae Court wasn't finding Ash to be quite the ruler they'd expected. He'd declared that there had been enough veils and mystery and that the Fae couldn't spend all their time hidden in Summerdale. It was to be an uphill battle but he seemed to be winning so far. If only because he was leading by example and spent a lot of time in the City. He

even spent nights here, in the house he'd acquired for us—
telling me that it was undignified for the Fae King to sneak
around St. Giles to spend the night in my bed.

I didn't argue that much. After all, we had plenty of fun
sneaking around his palace in Summerdale, finding new and
interesting places to be alone and take the moments of freedom we both needed.

Still, change was hard and tiring no matter how good it
was, and today had felt like a gift. The early-spring day had
blazed with sunshine, and Lily and Simon had blazed in
turn with enough joy to warm anybody's heart.

"I can think of better ways to celebrate," I said as we
turned the last corner to the hidden ward and killed the
charms.

Ash grinned, looking ridiculously handsome in his wedding clothes. "There's plenty of time for that," he said. "Besides, I know you. You don't relax totally until you know
everything in the hospital is running smoothly. Simon made
me promise that you'd check down here."

"At least he has his priorities straight," I said as I worked
the wards to open the door. I barely noticed the iron for once.

"So I understand." Ash grinned again and ushered me
forward. I wondered exactly how much champagne he had
drunk—maybe he'd followed Fen's lead and switched to
brandy after the dancing had started. Though everybody
wanted to dance with the king, and Ash had spent a large
percentage of his time guiding all the women present
around the dance floor, so I didn't see how he'd had time to
drink too much.

We made our way through to the outer ward. As usual,
there was only a low lamp burning. Atherton was nowhere
to be seen. Lady Adeline had invited him back to the Blood
Court, but he had so far refused the offer.

But maybe the change would sweep him up too in time.
As long as it didn't sweep him away completely. We needed
his skills here at St. Giles.

I opened the door to the inner ward and stepped through.
Only to stop dead. Because it wasn't Atherton who waited
for me or rather, not only Atherton.

Everyone was there. Guy and Holly and Fen and Saskia—still wearing the spectacular silver gown she had worn to the wedding. Holly was still dressed up too, though Guy had shed his formal clothes and was back in Templar gray and white. Atherton wore his usual black, being the only one who hadn't been able to attend the wedding. And standing in front of them all were Lily and Simon. The white flowers in Lily's hair were starting to wilt, but they both looked gloriously happy. And . . . expectant, was that the word? . . . as they smiled at me.

My heart began to beat faster. "What in the name of the Lady are you doing here?" I asked. "Don't you have a wedding night to get to?"

I didn't think it was possible for Simon to smile wider than he had been doing all day, but he managed it. "We'll get to that," he said. "But first there's something I wanted to show you."

I felt Ash's hand at my back pushing me forward gently as the seven of them moved apart, to reveal one of the beds. Sitting on the edge of it was a thin girl with pale brown hair. One of our patients. One of the blood-locked. I knew her face and her body well. Had spent hours tending her—and the others—with Simon and Atherton.

But I'd never seen her smile. We'd brought some of the blood-locked back a little way. Enough that they ate and walked again but they moved like sleepwalkers and showed no emotion.

But this girl—I struggled to remember her name as elation started to surge through me—was smiling. Smiling at me now as she climbed to her feet.

"Hello," she said. "I'm Florence. Who are you?"

I smiled back at her, unable to stop myself. Simon had done it. He'd found the cure. A cure for blood-locking. "My name is Bryony," I said to her. "Welcome home."

ABOUT THE AUTHOR

M. J. Scott is an unrepentant bookworm. Luckily she grew up in a family that fed her a properly varied diet of books and these days is surrounded by people who are understanding of her story addiction. When not wrestling one of her own stories to the ground, she can generally be found reading someone else's. Her other distractions include yarn, cat butlering, dark chocolate, and fabric. She lives in Melbourne, Australia.

CONNECT ONLINE

mjscott.net
facebook.com/authormjscott
twitter.com/melscott

ALSO AVAILABLE
from

M. J. Scott

IRON KIN
A Novel of the Half-Light City

Saskia is a metal mage. She hopes that forthcoming
treaty negotiations will forge a lasting peace between
humans and the other denizens of the half-light city.
To ensure it, she forges an alliance with a dangerous
Fae named Fen. His visions may hold the key to
peace…but he may also be Saskia's undoing.

Praise for the series:

"Doesn't miss its mark—I loved it."
—#1 *New York Times* bestselling author Patricia Briggs

Also in the series:
Blood Kin
Shadow Kin

Available wherever books are sold or at
penguin.com

facebook.com/acerocbooks

R0139